Hollywood, 1940.

It's the Golden Age of the Feelies.

All one-time actor and unlicensed matrimonial private eye Clark Gable has to do is impersonate a wealthy scriptwriter for a few hours, and sign the contract for the biopic of the inventor of a device which has changed the world of entertainment forever. What could go wrong? Already, he's seeing ghosts—but that's nothing unusual. Europe is devastated by war and America is sleep-walking into Fascism—but what's that got to do with him?

Always thrilling, but by turns witty, eerie and romantic, multi-award winning writer Ian R MacLeod's latest novel is a dazzling collision of fantasy and history. Like the Feelies themselves, *Wake Up and Dream* is film noir with Technicolor wraiths.

WAKE UP AND DREAM

WAKE UP AND DREAM

**IT'S THE GOLDEN AGE OF THE FEELIES.
WHAT COULD GO WRONG?**

Written and Directed by
Ian R. MacLeod

2011

Wake Up And Dream Copyright © 2011 Ian R. MacLeod

Cover Copyright © 2011 Ben Baldwin

The right of Ian MacLeod to be identified as Author of this Work has been asserted by him in accordance with the Copyright, Designs and Patents Act 1988.

Published in September 2011 by **PS Publishing Ltd.** by arrangement with the author. All rights reserved by the author.

FIRST EDITION

ISBN
978-1-848631-95-3 Signed edition
978-1-848631-94-6

This book is a work of fiction. Names, characters, places and incidents either are products of the author's imagination or are used fictitiously. Any resemblance to actual events or locales or persons, living or dead, is entirely coincidental.

Design and layout by Alligator Tree Graphics.
Printed in England by the MPG Biddles Group.

PS Publishing Ltd / Grosvenor House / 1 New Road / Hornsea, HU18 1PG / England

editor@pspublishing.co.uk • http://www.pspublishing.co.uk

Wake Up And Dream

In memory of Peg Entwistle

And for Jim Goddard

ONE

A perfect morning in late June. The last of the mist had burned away and the smog had yet to settle as he took the offramp from the new Olympic Parkway and rattled north through Hollywood in his battered '36 Ford. Stargazy queues were already lengthening outside the feelie houses for today's first shows. *Backstabber Wife*, starring Trudy Rester—whoever the hell she was—was on at the Aladdin, and *The Wonderful Prairie* and *Midnight's Dust* were in continuous double bill at the Classic, both featuring Saffron Knowles and James H. Pack, and he hadn't heard of them, either. Not for the first time, he told himself that he should pay more attention to the industry on which this city thrived.

Today was his chance. Up along Franklin beside the high fences of the new Paramount-Shindo studios. On past the stores offering sightseeing tours and the boys selling maps of the stars and girls selling themselves and the plateglass boutiques and the bars which were already open for the morning, or hadn't yet closed from the night before. And up. Into the hills.

There were pines. White clouds. Air so clean it tasted like God's aftershave. The Ford's engine made an ominous coughing sound as it climbed the hairpins. It wasn't used to this kind of world. Neither was he.

He took the grade above Stone Canyon. The road here kicked and turned, with fine views all the way to the Pacific. He was struggling with his street guide as it flapped on the passenger seat when a siren blooped behind him. Cursing, he pulled away from the drop and into the farside verge as the other car swung around in front just before a large private estate sign that announced Woodsville.

Not a police car, although you'd have to look twice to be sure. The same black Mercury sedan the LAPD used. It even had the siren, and the blue toplight, although a badge on the side announced Gladmont Securities. Upscale areas like this used these kinds of companies to keep out sightseers and ne'er-do-wells.

Just to show willing, he uncricked himself from his Ford and put on his best *aw shucks* grin as the security guard—who was lean and tall, and carrying a gun in a pop-down leather holster on his belt—approached. The sunlight was turning the waters of the reservoir beneath them to glittering gold. The sun was doing a pretty good job up here all round.

"You got business in this area?" The security guard was wearing aviator sunglasses and the sort of uniform you saw in pictures of those German parades, right down to the peaked cap. The armband might as well have had a swastika, but it was just another Gladmont Securities shield.

"Wouldn't be here otherwise."

The security guard's reflected gaze traveled up and down more slowly. Absorbed in greater detail the suit, which was faded yellow at the hem and edges from too much dry cleaning, the frayed necktie which had worked loose from his shirt collar, which was loose and frayed as well, and finally the shoes, which lacked the intense shine of the trouser knees. The gaze then traveled back to the dusty, two door, black Ford Tudor which had seen considerably better years, let alone days.

"Maybe this'll help . . . " He reached into the outside pocket of his suit coat and removed a letter. It drooped from the dampness of his fingers as he held it out.

The security guard's thin lips pursed as he studied it. "So you're the addressee? Clark Gable?"

Nice, that: *addressee*. "Yeah. That's right."

"And you're here to see a Mrs April Lamotte up in Woodsville?"

"She wrote the letter. Said that was what she wanted. As you can see, I'm supposed to be there at ten o-clock."

"You realize it's quarter gone already?"

"The longer we stand here, the more I'm late."

"Do you have any other proof of identity?"

Making sure he got the letter back first, Clark reached into his top pocket and produced one of his business cards. Watching as the security guard studied it, he decided he really needed to splash out on a fresh print run without the telephone number changed and then crossed out.

"So you're a private eye?" The security guard folded over the card's corner and pocketed it.

"That's what it says. My permit's in the car."

The security guard didn't exactly raise his eyebrows; at least not as far as Clark could tell behind those sunglasses. It was more subtle than that. "You're carrying a gun?"

"Never could bother with the things." He opened his arms to show willing. "Pat me down if you like."

What Clark could see of the tan, long face remained resolutely deadpan. This guy wasn't much like any security guard he'd ever encountered. Far too young and too slim to be an ex-cop, and most of the rest were paid bullies. Then there was his light voice and cultured manner, which didn't fit either—more like the guy was playing a role—although he reckoned the explanation was most likely the usual one you found when you came across someone doing seemingly odd work in this city. With those nice cheekbones, that regular complexion and thin, expressive mouth, he was probably just another actor between roles.

The security guard gave an eloquent smile, then he turned from Clark and with a rasp of his steel-tipped heels strode over to the far side of the road. He began to whistle tunelessly as he regarded the view. "Some fine morning, isn't it, Mr Gable?" he said eventually.

"I was just thinking the same myself." The whistling began again. The birds sang. The guard remained standing gazing at the view across the reservoir. Clark got the impression that this was one of those moments which could go on and on.

"By the way," he asked, "you don't happen to know the exact way I should be going to get to my client, do you?"

"The *exact* way?" Something close to amusement played across the guard's face as he turned and wrapped his long fingers around his gleaming belt. "Don't think I do. All I can honestly recommend, Mr Gable, is that you keep on going in the direction you're already on . . ."

TWO

Woodsville. An exclusive development of the kind you saw advertised in the back of shiny magazines, but never for real. He passed a clumpy-looking guy pushing a wheelbarrow beside the lush hedges. A place like this, even roadsides were planted with brilliant borders and kept trim and neat.

There were no gates. No dogs, either. Or only the sort that sat on their matrons' laps and licked the cream from their coffee. No sign of any of the security guard's colleagues, either, and Clark was just starting to wish he'd stopped to ask the wheelbarrow guy for directions when he saw a big slab of polished stone carved with the word *Erewhon* on a slope beneath a fuchsia hedge. He braked and turned up the steep drive.

The overheating Ford made it across the last of the gravel before it stalled. There were big bushes of bright flowers. There was cool dampness in the air which felt good on his face as he climbed out and unpicked his suit from off his back and around his crotch. The house was a Chinese puzzle in glass and brick, when he'd been calculating on mock Gothic or farmhouse French. But that was probably next door, and the one which looked like a Greek or a Roman temple would be the one beyond that.

Two cars were parked by the steps. One was a dark red Cadillac Series 90, the latest model with the V16 engine, and the other a rare and beautiful cream-colored French sports coupé—a Delahaye. His Ford Tudor, which was wheezing and ticking like an unsprung clock as it cooled, didn't look like a machine which had been designed to serve anything remotely like the same purpose as these. The Delahaye was particularly superb. Its top was down. There were so many buttons and switches it looked like the console of an airplane.

Erewhon's front door was smoked glass. The sides around it were angled, and of glass as well. Several dozen different versions of Clark Gable swam up to him as he climbed to the last stretch of marble and searched for a doorbell, or a knocker, or anything resembling a handle. Then came a small, electric hum, and the doors opened neither in nor out, but sideways into hidden recesses.

Stepping inside, he called hello. Seemingly with a will entirely of their own, the sides of the door hummed shut behind him. The huge, polished hallway shimmered with dark reflections like silent birds. Should have done what he often did when he first saw a client and wandered around back on the pretense of not being able to find the right entrance—which would have made perfect sense here. Or talked to the neighbors. Or the servants or the houseboys. Or that gardener, maybe. Anything, really, other than just charge straight in like he had. He'd got distracted by the beautiful roadster, and the way the sun had flashed and sparkled on that reservoir, and the security guard, and the eau de cologne-scented air.

The hallway opened into a kind of atrium. His voice echoed and was lost as he called hello again. There was glass above him. Clouds fractured where the edges of the panes met as if they'd been put together like some huge, moving jigsaw. He caught glimpses of antique sofas and rugs in empty rooms. Flowers everywhere. Some of them were real. Some were in paintings. With some he couldn't tell.

He reached a corridor. It was long and wide and tall, set to the left with dozens of windows open to the gardens beyond. White curtains drifted, bringing in the scent of cut grass. Midway along it, something else seemed to be moving, although he took it at first to be the curtains' shifting reflections caught in mirror glass.

Close to, he realized that this was something else. He felt a cool pre-thunderstorm prickle across the hairs on his hands and forearms and down his neck which even he, who rarely went to the feelies, recognized as coming from a Bechmeir field. But this wasn't like the dusty grids which fizzed behind the projector screen in thousands of theaters in every town and city across the country. This field coiled like gusting snow—or a dust devil—in the space between a black plinth and the swan-neck which curved six or seven feet above it. Held between the two charged plates which this structure, elegant in itself, supported, the feelie wraith gave off a faint crackling as it shimmered and danced. The plinth looked to be made of solid marble, although he guessed that it wasn't; you had to put all the electronics somewhere, and he presumed that it was in there. A brass plaque—or solid gold, for all he knew—was inset into the plinth. Finely engraved on it was the single word *Muse*.

This, he supposed, was what you got. What you got, that was, when you'd already got the house, and the Cadillac and the Delahaye and all those gardens and the walk-in closet you could get seriously lost in.

He felt a thickening in his throat and the imminent pressure of sound within his ears as he looked up at it. It really had been years since he'd been to a feelie theater, and he'd forgotten just how powerful the sensation was when you stood before the plasm of a Bechmeir field. And how unsettlingly weird. No use telling yourself that some tiny nub in your brain was simply picking up the amplified waves of a clever recording. No use thinking of wires and transformers. And here, unaccompanied by the usual moving images and soundtrack, the feeling seemed to be strengthened rather than weakened.

Instead of a shapeless blur, the swirl, the presence, of the wraith seemed to form itself into a misty amalgam. Translucent mouths smiled down at him. Limbs stretched out in chill embrace. He caught flashes of vanished laughter, dark whispers of lost lives. He blinked hard. He knew how easy it was to get drawn in by a Bechmeir field's tawdry allure. But it didn't feel tawdry. Not at the time. That was the damndest thing.

"You're like everyone else who comes here, Mr Gable..."

He turned. Something was coming towards him from the far end of the corridor. It seemed for a moment to be dark and indefinite, and he felt a sense of dread. But then he saw that the figure was human, and that it was female, and plainly composed of flesh and blood.

"...that damn thing stops almost everyone in their tracks. I'm April Lamotte. You obviously got my letter." She held out a hand. She smelled expensive and she'd recently put on some kind of hand cream, but the grip was hard and purposeful. As was the way that she was looking at him. "Have to say you're not quite what I was hoping for, Mr Gable. No, not at all, really. But I guess you'll have to do."

"Mrs Lamotte . . . " He cleared his throat as she finally let go of him. "You have a very nice place here."

She glanced around as if the thought had never struck her. "You don't think it over-ostentatious?"

"I'm hardly equipped to judge."

"But you wouldn't want to live here?"

"Not sure I'd know how."

"There probably is a knack to it." She gave a sharp laugh. Standing as close to the wraith as they still were, he tried not to shiver. "One I'm still attempting to learn . . . " She turned and headed back along the corridor towards the room from which she had emerged, glancing back as he followed in a way which he might normally have thought of as almost flirtatious. Here, he wasn't sure. This really was a different world.

THREE

"Please sit down."

April Lamotte looked gracefully young in the measured way that only rich, mature women ever did. She was wearing a pale green silk pants suit and seemingly little else. She was slim, almost thin—not his type, really—and her feet were bare. She had lustrous center-parted, red hair. He already had her down as a sharp and determined piece of work as she gestured for him to sit on a long couch.

His ass sank and his legs bobbed high, but she remained standing, her fingers turning her gold wedding ring in quick circles, and he was glad to see that small sign of nervousness.

"You did as I asked? You brought the letter? No one else knows or is at all aware that you're coming here?"

He nodded. Clients were often over-obsessed with secrecy, and that security guard who'd stopped his car really didn't seem worth mentioning. "Discretion's a given in the sort of work I do, Mrs Lamotte."

"As you can see, I've given leave to all my servants. *None* of this must come out. Absolutely *nothing*. Ever. You understand? I'd like that letter now. May I have it please? And the envelope...?"

He watched her flick a large silver lighter, turn the papers under its flame and lay the burning, blackening remains in a big crystal ashtray. The process made him wonder again how the letter, and the enticing fifty-C note which had come with it, had arrived at his delivery locker back in Venice with no stamp or postmark.

"Maybe," he said, "you could tell me a little more of what all this is about. Perhaps we could begin with some basic details—"

"I'm more than aware of the sort of work you do, Mr Gable. Before you start asking questions which aren't appropriate, I should tell you that I don't want a divorce. Neither is my husband having any kind of affair. In a way, perhaps, that might have helped."

"You say you know what I do, Mrs Lamotte," he said. "But I think you should know what I don't do as well. There's no violence or coercion. I don't carry a gun. Beyond parking fines, for which I bill as normal, I try to avoid breaking any kind of law. I may help evidence along but I don't manufacture it. In fact, most of what I do is simply to find out about what people are already doing, and then make sure it's witnessed and photographed as cleanly and clearly as such things ever can be. My hourly rate's three dollars."

April Lamotte made a small gesture of dismissal; even the tripling of his normal fee didn't faze her. It was hard to tell the exact color of her eyes, although he'd have guessed at green. There was a slight pinch at the tip of her nose which, in its own way, wasn't unattractive. The light was strange in here, dim after the brightness of those corridors, lit from a semi-circular bay of half-closed drapes which covered a wider sweep of window, but caught within the gloss of so many shining objects, this silk-clad woman included, that it sort of had a quality and substance of its own. Like fresh paint, the shine of that Delahaye's dials, or that feelie ghost.

"You'll have a drink?" She slung ice from a silver bucket into a cut glass jug.

Clark, who had sunk down so far by now into the couch that he was in a sort of embryonic hunch, attempted the gesture of someone who wouldn't normally think of drinking this early in the day but was prepared to be sociable.

She poured with quick ease. He strained over his knees to take the glass, which was heavy and cold and deeply cut. The fluid inside was flecked with stuff which could have been mint, but the taste was so cold and sharp it was impossible to tell. Just the way he always did with any client, he watched the way April Lamotte drank. A short sip, and that was all. She was no lush.

"Mind if I smoke?" He tapped a roll-up against its case. She nodded and took one of her own from a lacquered Japanese cigarette box. Her cigarette was baby blue. They shared the flame of the lighter. She blew a plume of smoke. Outside, the soft sounds of morning filled this opulent valley. Birds and bees and distant lawnmowers were chirruping and buzzing and droning. Something about the way April Lamotte was standing there, sheathed in the glisten of silk, reminded him again of that feelie ghost along the corridor. He pushed the idea away.

"What I want from you, Mr Gable," she said, "what I'll pay you for, and pay you royally by your standards—is for you to play my husband. I want you to become Daniel Lamotte."

FOUR

If there was one thing which he'd learned in his job, it was when to make an exit. He could swig back the rest of this drink, make some stupid non-apology, climb out of this couch. Keep the fifty, of course. And go.

"I'm sorry, Mrs Lamotte. I could take your suggestion one of several ways—and I don't say that some of those ways don't leave me flattered—but not one of them is the kind of work I do. If you're looking for a chaperone, I guess I have a few friends who do that sort of thing when they're between acting jobs. And if you're looking for... Well, if you're looking for *more* than a chaperone, there are some guys I know who—"

"I'm not looking for any of those things, Mr Gable. Or anything else you might imagine."

"Well..." He gazed up at her, wondering why the hell he was still sitting here. "That's okay too. I'm really not here to judge. But I'm not here to waste your time either."

"You're going to tell me next you're a busy man, I suppose."

The tone, the swagger, was new. April Lamotte was some piece, no doubt about it. She was unlike pretty much every other client he'd ever encountered. And he was almost certain by now that she was wearing nothing underneath her silky green trouser suit.

"I'm asking you not to leave, Mr Gable. *More* than asking. If you do, there will be consequences. Your State license, for example. That document you always say you have in the car, or at the office, or in the pocket of your other suit. As if you *had* another suit." She gave a nasty chuckle. "Or a proper office. Or pay road tax on that rusty old car. Believe it or not Mr Gable, I've had you looked into—discreetly, I might add—and I *do* need the help of someone like you. You fit the bill in most ways, even if you're not perhaps as good a match as I'd been hoping for . . ."

April Lamotte strode over to a dresser. She came back with a framed photograph. "Here."

The frame was heavy and gilt-edged. He had to squint and tilt it before he could get a proper look at the photograph inside, which was of a guy standing before a low wall in that kind of hunch that tall men often affect. He was thickly bearded and wore heavy tortoiseshell glasses, along with suede loafers, pleated slacks and a white button-up tee shirt. His dark hair was messily slicked back so it stuck out around his noticeably protuberant ears. He wasn't smiling and he had his hands stuffed in his pockets. He didn't really look the sort of person who liked having their photograph taken.

"You can't tell from the photo, but Dan's got buck teeth much like yours. Never would have them fixed. Says they're part of what he is. And he's pretty much your exact height and build—*and* he's got those jug ears as well. " She gave another of those sharp laughs. "So maybe I shouldn't have been quite so disappointed when I first saw you. I mean, how close can two men get? There's Dan's beard of course. False ones always look false. But all you need to do is say that you've shaved it off. You know how different men look after they've done that. Then you can add in the way you'll look with something like Dan's glasses on as well."

She was getting way ahead of him. "So . . . " The photo made a dull clang as he laid it on the glass-top table. " . . . what is it that you want me to do?"

"As I say, I want you to become my husband. But only for a few hours. The risks are so small that they're barely worth mentioning. And the rewards—well, what would you say to a thousand dollars?"

"I'd say that nobody gets paid that sort of money unless they've earned it. Or the person who's paying is desperate."

"Desperate." She considered him and the word, her head tilted. "I wouldn't say that exactly. But I do need your help. And I can make it *extremely* difficult for you if you walk out."

"Where's your husband now?"

"I'll come to that."

"And you want me to—"

"I'll come to that as well. But first, let me tell you something about me and Dan... I won't bore you with my life story, Mr Gable, but you should know that I grew up in mid-state nowhere and was always ambitious. I knew I wasn't bad-looking, but I realized young that getting runner-up place in the local beauty pageant wouldn't wash for much. My sister and I used to talk about it—make plans nights as we lay in bed. I decided to train as a nurse. I reckoned that that was the best chance I had of getting rich, and that LA was the best place to try. You know—changing the sheets and wiping the ass of some rich old guy in a big mansion who doesn't see his family from one year to the next. A whirlwind romance, maybe a few blissful months of marriage, and then..."

"That's a neat plan."

"Is, isn't it? Only trouble was, I wasn't the first. You wouldn't believe it, Mr Gable, but even the nursing agencies in the city of Los Angeles have a casting couch."

He had to smile. "I believe I can."

"I still had a plan, I still had hopes, but this was the start of the Great Depression and the only work I could get with my diploma was at the Metropolitan State Hospital—you know, the Met?"

He nodded. Of course he knew about the city lunatic asylum out in Norwalk. Kids on the streets taunted each other with its name.

"So there I was. Pretty much penniless and emptying bedpans and tightening the straps on straightjackets on sixteen hour shifts so I could afford to eat. I don't know if you can imagine what working at the Met's like."

"To be honest Mrs Lamotte, I'm not terribly keen on those kinds of places."

She paused to give him a look. "Who on this earth would be? Some of the patients—and a fair few of the people who work there—are enough to make you wonder what it means to be human. I'd come off shift and take the train back into the city so tired I was past sleeping, and I'd stop by late evenings at this rundown diner up on Bunker Hill called Edna's Eats. It was there that I first saw Dan. He was just this quiet guy sitting nursing a coffee. But there was something about him. We ending up talking, and he admitted eventually that he was a writer. He wasn't that proud of anything he'd written, but I was curious . . ."

She walked over to a cabinet on the room's far side. Its doors revealed a bookshelf of shabby yellowish spines. She took some out. "You see."

Dime novels. He turned them over. They had that rough yellow paper feel and smell of cheap glue. *Vixens in the Dark. It Came From Beyond. Midnight Lust. War on the Alien Horror. Beautiful Corpse.* The covers were deliciously lurid. Knives and guns. Taut bosoms and slack lipstick mouths. Futuristic cities and strange pulsating machines.

"He'd already written all of those," she said as he studied the authors' names. Sid Tulla. Frank F. Freeman. He particularly liked Luella Stand. "His real name was Daniel Hogg, and he said they were trash, but I bought a few and I read them on the train back from the Met. Those books, of their kind, were stunningly good, and I told Dan so, and I don't think I've ever seen anyone more pleased."

"So you decided this guy was your ticket to the high life?"

"We fell in love, Mr Gable. I know this probably sounds ridiculous to you—and it certainly hadn't been part of what I'd planned on getting out of this city—but there you are. We fell in love and we moved in together in this rathole apartment, and I soon realized that Daniel Hogg was wasting his talent."

"His name wasn't Lamotte?"

"Can you imagine anyone ever making it in this town with a name like Hogg? So, that was one of the first things we decided to change. I liked the Daniel bit, and my name, Lamotte, was just about the only thing about my past life I was proud of. So he became Daniel Lamotte even before we married and I got him to start writing screenplays which, even back then before the feelies, was obviously where the real money was. That, and I also got him to fire his agent."

"Sounds like you were already doing that particular job for him, Mrs Lamotte."

Those eyes, which he decided really were green, flashed. "I haven't brought you here to justify myself. You can take this story any way you like . . ."

A story, he thought, which would have made a decent enough script itself. In fact, it probably was one, circulating somewhere from studio to studio in twentieth draft. Nurse (you'd probably need to make her an aspiring actress as well; no one would ever believe a good-looking broad in this city wanting to be anything else) meets pulp writer at some midnight diner. Maybe he's scribbling on a notepad. Maybe she's read one of his books. Or maybe she just spills coffee in his lap . . .

"I know this sounds over-fancy, but Dan lived to write. He'd never written any kind of script before, but the stuff just flowed out of him, and it was good. Between us, with him doing the writing and me quitting nursing and doing whatever was necessary—and I do mean *whatever*—to get his scripts noticed, we finally started to get some work. He was especially good at twists and endings—events which seem inevitable once you've seen them, but which you'd never have been able to predict before. Have you seen *Freedom City*? That was one of Dan's very earliest. And then along came the feelies—"

"I don't go much for the feelies, Mrs Lamotte."

"But I guess you've heard of *The Virgin Queen*?"

He nodded. Not that he'd actually seen that one, but even he'd heard of it. A ruffs and codpieces epic, it had come out in around 1933 or 4 and, as much as anything, had been responsible for convincing the world that the Bechmeir field was the future of the entertainment industry.

"Funny, isn't it? One of the most famous of all the feelies, yet no one remembers the name of the guy who wrote it. Even those idiots at the Academy passed it over. But it brought us the kind of life I'd dreamed about when I came to this city. Dan's work sold, and it did well, and for a few years we were happy. We both were . . . "

He let his gaze travel slowly in the shafts of sunlight which were playing in narrower and brighter patches across the parquet as the light outside strengthened towards noon, and then he looked back to Mrs Lamotte. Even with her strange request, and although Daniel Lamotte was supposed to be the sort of writer who was above such things, he was still expecting some standard plot-twist to emerge at the end of this story. The new blonde secretary with legs up to here. That bitch in the house opposite who always sunbathes in the nude. The pool boy. He was used to most kinds of tale as to why lives and marriages went wrong.

He risked raising a questioning eyebrow. "Everyone gets happy for a while, Mrs Lamotte. It's an unwritten law of the universe. And then they get less so. That's another law. And that's normally where I come in."

"I suppose you're right." April Lamotte sighed. She did such a good job of the sigh that he wondered if she really hadn't put in time as an actress as well as a nurse. Then she and her barefoot reflection resumed pacing the shining floor. "And after the success of *The Virgin Queen*, Dan could write the scripts he wanted and know they'd sell. But maybe that was part of the problem. He'd always written under pressure. But now he had time, opportunity, freedom. We'd bought Erewhon and had a pine lodge up above Sierra Madre. We were doing well and there were some real successes—*Sometime Never, Prospector, Friday Means Tonight*... but each new idea was harder than the last. By about 1938, Dan hadn't produced a script in a whole year."

"He'd stopped writing?"

A new cigarette. A fresh plume of smoke. "You disappoint me, Mr Gable. If I didn't know you'd lived in this city all these years, I'd wonder where you'd been. You're like me—you came here to find riches and fame. Almost got there as well, didn't you? Toured as an actor, got a contract with one of the old talkie studios. You were well on the way to somewhere, even if that somewhere ended up as where you now are."

"Well—thanks."

"So you of all people should know enough to understand that writers never stop writing, or at least trying to write. He tried everything. Doing without sleep or not getting out of bed for days. Holing up in our pine lodge. Then he started going off on these jags. I found him once out by the Third Street tunnel under Bunker Hill. He was huddled up and howling like a baby."

She shook her head. "It slowly tore him apart. I mean, he was always shy and nervy—he always left dealing with the outside world to me. But now it was something else. He just froze. Wouldn't speak, would barely move, for hours, days. Lying in bed or the same chair. Sometimes, he'd just stand in one place like time had stopped inside him. It was scary. Or he went manic. It was like this terrible fear. Something at the back of everything that was always haunting him. But I guess part of me had always known that this side of Dan was there. Even when we were first staying in the top floor of a cheap rowhouse, I sometimes had to... Well..." She flicked ash. "I had to nurse him. Calm him down, or get him up and back to coping with things. Of course, I knew where to get the necessary stuff. But now, Dan was boozing as well. I've used private clinics to dry him out, had witch-doctor psychiatrists try to work out what the problem is. All to no avail. And then he bought that wraith, that fucking *ghost* in the hallway that he said—can you believe this?—was a birthday present for me. Got some twobit studio to mix the auras of all his favorite performers into this one recording, and then put it on a loop. Cost us a fortune which by then we couldn't afford. And he'd just stand there gazing at that thing as if it really was his muse, even though we both knew it was taunting him. God knows why I turned it on today. Maybe I'm taunting myself as well. But with Dan it was still all about writing. And I still did everything I could to help him. Believe me. I did *everything*. I wanted him back. I wanted my Dan, my Daniel. And I knew that the only way to get him was to have him writing feelie scripts again.

"This spring, though, things started to improve. He was off the booze and I'd cut down on the tablets and he was watching lots of feelies in our viewing room and talking about writing something in a way I hadn't heard in ages. Not like it was some demon that was haunting him, but just a simple task that needed doing again. But he said Erewhon gave him the jeebies and he needed to get back to what he called the best of times, by which he meant when we didn't have a dime to rub together.

"So he got this rental, a cheap place Downtown. Called it reconnecting. He went there, and he took his typewriter with him. That, and a few reams of paper and some old clothes. And I let him go, Mr Gable. I let him go not because I'd given up on hope, or had given up loving him. I let him go *because* I hoped. *Because* I loved..." She gave a soft, sad smile, and he was way beyond telling whether to be moved or impressed. "I wasn't abandoning him. We'd meet up sometimes at the same diner where we'd first met. It was almost like old times. And he seemed happy. 'Course, he wouldn't say much about what he was writing. When things are going well, writers never will. Just said he was really on to something. Said the whole thing was alive around him in this city. And then, finally, when he did show me, I knew he was right. I wept the first time I read the treatment for *Wake Up and Dream* through, Mr Gable. I really did."

He nodded. He could imagine that April Lamotte was capable of many things, but weeping over a feelie treatment somehow didn't seem like one of them.

"But Dan was already fading. I knew the signs. He was starting to worry the way writers always worry, and he was getting back into the pills and the booze in ways that were beyond my control. From being the greatest thing since the Bible, the whole project became a heap of mule shit. Perhaps you can imagine. Perhaps you can't. Basically, and once again, Dan just started to crack up . . . "

"So he's back again now in some clinic?"

"About a week ago. A place up in the hills. I had no choice."

"And you've got a feelie script you want to peddle, and a husband who isn't up to doing a pitch?"

"That's almost the size of it." She ground out her latest cigarette. "But not quite. Dan's a respected writer. *The Virgin Queen* was a huge hit, and the studios still scent money when they hear Dan's name. He sent the script off on spec without even checking with me, but I was able to broker a deal—Senserama Studios, no less. We're almost there, Mr Gable. The contract's approved and written, and it's waiting at their lawyers to be signed and witnessed. But Dan has to sign it."

"Couldn't you stall? You're obviously acting as his agent, can't you sign on his behalf?"

"The studio won't hear any of that. They know Dan's a recluse, but there are limits. It's *got* to be Dan. And you know what producers are like. If we let this go, it could be gone forever."

He nodded. He knew that the attention span of an average studio executive was shorter than a toddler stacking wooden blocks.

"And—and I won't beat about the bush, Mr Gable—Dan and I need the money. This whole lifestyle—this house, the cars you saw outside, the gardens, not to mention the clinics . . . All of this," she gestured, "doesn't come cheap."

"How about you simply dust your husband down and spruce him up for a few hours? After all, you said he just needs to sign something."

"Dan's in a bad way, Mr Gable. He's been to some very dark places. He's under restraint even now. And I can't disguise what the Senserama contract's worth—you'll be seeing it anyway if you agree to help me get it signed. It's five thousand dollars upfront on twenty five when the final script's approved, and I'm offering you a straight one thousand. I can make the appointment for tomorrow and you can have the check cashed by the next day."

"You really think I'm that much like him? I mean, for all the charming things you said about my looks . . ."

"That's not important. Dan's publicity shy, and the lawyers will never have met him before. The beard's easy. You've just shaved it off, and you know how different a man looks without one. Dan wears his hair differently, but it's nothing that some Brylcreem won't fix. I've got some theatrical glasses—you know, the sort with plain lenses—which are pretty much exactly like Dan's pair, and they'll make a big difference as well. Who's going to argue if you look like Dan, and you're wearing Dan's clothes, and you're with me?"

"I'd need to practice his signature—know something about his voice and manner."

"That's obvious. And I'm guessing that this won't be the first signature you've ever forged."

"I'll need to take a look at that feelie script, if I'm really supposed to have written it . . ."

But he was treading water. Truth was, now the whole thing was laid out before him, he felt oddly relieved. After the dark threats and her strange tale and Erewhon's peculiar atmosphere, the idea of impersonating a scriptwriter for a few hours, even if it did involve forgery, fraud, criminal misrepresentation, embezzlement and maybe even theft, felt like no big deal. Then there was the money, and the challenge of doing something that briefly took him back toward his lost career. And, last but by no means least, there was April Lamotte.

FIVE

```
THE VIRG N QWEEN
STRRING PE ENTWISTLE
```

P ure chance, he supposed.

He'd been driving aimlessly around the city, trying to settle his thoughts, when he noticed the letters hanging askew above the columns of some grubby little theater at the edge of Watts. Ignoring the blare of horns and the *hey buddy* curses, he cut in at the nearest space.

"Stalls or balcony?"

He bought his ticket in the dank foyer out of the fifty from his cash advance, and found a seat high, at the back, away from the stink of the restrooms. The lights, which had been pretty dim in the first place, dimmed some more. Then a projector began to clatter, shooting a bright finger through the fug of cigarette smoke toward the curtains, which twitched like something alive, then jerked apart.

That silver screen. The pure anticipation of its emptiness. Yeah, he remembered—the sacred possibility that those wavering shadows would draw you in and wring you out and leave you feeling things you'd forgotten how to feel.

But newsreels first—just plain old sound and picture like in the old days, the Bechmeir field not yet on. Joe DiMaggio's seemingly endless streak, and the Red Sox and the Dodgers, and Hitler surveying Paris from the top of the Eiffel Tower, and German Foreign Minister Ribbentrop arriving at Lakehurst Fields in the *Hindenburg* to give a series of speeches on the theme of *Peace Between Two Continents* despite

Roosevelt's attempts to ban him. All this to a breezy soundtrack and Harry von Zell's cheery voiceover.

The adverts were something else. Now, with a fizzing humming and their characteristic sea-salt smell of charged plasm, the powered-up generators began to pour their energies across the fine metal grid behind the screen. Even before the field itself was actually visible, the tired air within the theater began to change, and there was an extra glow, an indefinable *presence,* to Jo-Ann Corkish as she rode toward you from across the plains of her prairie ranch. Not that Clark had ever really liked this sensation, or felt comfortable with it, but by the time she'd dismounted, taken out her pack of Luckies from her straining denim breast, lit one up and inhaled, something cool and deep and profound seemed to enter your lungs. When she smiled, you felt a warmth as if the summer sun had suddenly fallen upon your face.

With the feelies, you didn't just see, or hear. You *felt*—and by the time the last Wrigley's Doublemint advert had filled Clark's mouth with useless saliva, he was ready to take the Matson Line to Hawaii wearing Arrow Shirts, drinking Ron Marito rum and smoking several different brands of cigarette. He really *could* do with a new Chevy. And, he thought, as the first swell of the soundtrack of *The Virgin Queen* washed over him, he might even be able to afford one with the money April Lamotte was paying.

The late afternoon daylight felt thin and pale when he re-emerged from the theater.

April Lamotte had been right. *The Virgin Queen* was some feelie. Even the creeps and itches hadn't been as bad as he'd expected. It was almost enough to convince him that the whole medium wasn't some twobit trick. Not that Clark—for all he knew about English history, which he could have written on the back of a very small postage stamp—was convinced that the real Queen Elizabeth would have been quite so flirtatious in those scenes with the Spanish monarch, or that a European monarch would ever have gotten as involved in fighting back the Armada as she had on the deck of her ship. But none of that mattered—

not even watching some old and scratchy print with a muffled soundtrack and blurry feelie reel which caused washes of out-of-phase plasm to jitter at the edges of the dirty curtains like emerald flames.

Everything had seemed so *real*. The way the color-changing aura of Elizabeth's joy danced in the gray beam of the projector above as she played in the gardens of the palace in those early scenes. Her rank fear as she crouched in that grimy cell. The sly arrogance that oozed from Hank Gunn's aura in his brilliant performance as her wily spymaster Walsingham. The execution of Mary Queen of Scots was a masterstroke. The way the music quietened and all the braying voices faded, until all you were left with was the crowd's horrible need running on the feelie track like some sickness burning in the back of your throat, and the sound of Mary's footsteps as she climbed the steps toward the block, and the cold squeeze around your heart of her uncomprehending dread... Then the cut to Elizabeth in tears. Clark was crying as well—of course he was; he couldn't help it. So was the whole audience. It was a brilliant sequence, and he wondered whether it had been written that way in Daniel Lamotte's script. If it had been, the guy was a genius. If it hadn't, he was still pretty good.

Then there was Peg Entwistle. To see her face once again, but looming out from a huge screen, bigger and more distant than the moon yet close enough to touch, and equally lovely. Those big gray eyes. The tilt of her head. The curve of her lips. You couldn't doubt for one moment that this was exactly what the real living, breathing, Elizabeth would have been like. And to think that people used to say that all Peg could play was best-friend supporting roles and kooky comedy. With her classy British accent, with her pale good looks and that hint of sadness and steel, she'd been born to play Elizabeth.

Yes, he'd done a good job of forgetting what it was like to watch a feelie, just as he'd forgotten many things, and the colors of the everyday world seemed pale as he pulled out into the thickening evening traffic and drove west toward Venice, occasionally checking the rearview to see if he was being followed.

SIX

Venice wasn't LA. Venice didn't even feel like California. It was one of the many things he liked about the place.

Albert Kinney's dream—the canals, the palaces, the concrete gondolas—had become a reality back in the 1920s, even if the fancy new center for the arts he'd imagined he was creating had soon become a raucous fairground under the pressures of economic necessity. Most of the more ambitious attractions had long since gone. The canals had silted up. The water rides had run dry. The fake volcano which had once erupted twice nightly in flares of fireworks now lay collapsed behind a rotting fence. Nodding pumpjacks and flaming leftoffs soured the air with the rotten-eggs stink of hydrogen sulfide since the discovery of oil just to the south. Still, you got used to it—Clark had worked as a wildcatter—and if all this meant that Venice was a cheaper place to live than it might have been otherwise, well that, too, was fine as far as he was concerned.

The frontage of the Doge's Apartments still bore a slight resemblance to the Italian original when he'd last consciously looked up at it. Some of the pinkish patterned tiles clung doggedly to the brickwork, and several of the lower windows were shaped into approximately Gothic points. But he had other things on his mind as he pushed through the swing door carrying a cheap cardboard suitcase containing Daniel Lamotte's things.

He'd checked his mail in the locker—nothing but the same brown bill envelopes he'd tossed back in there yesterday—and was heading for the stairs when a voice called behind him.

"Hey, Mr Gable—I got a message for you..."

Glory Guzman was easing herself out from her cubbyhole. Glory was one of those large people who gave the impression of having reached some final and apotheotic state of fatness. He waited patiently as she mopped her big Aztec face with a handkerchief. As well as supposedly cleaning the apartments—a service noticeable mainly for its absence—Glory kept an ear out for the communal phone in the downstairs hallway and occasionally took messages. But it didn't do to hurry her.

"... This lady, she asking for you. She say she worry 'bout her husband, how he a good man and professional. She want talk you but no give her name..."

"You got a number?"

"She no even says that to me. She just keep say she worry and she somehows find you name."

The message wasn't untypical of a new client. It wasn't that easy to come right out and admit that you wanted someone to check up on who or what your beloved was screwing. Some of them even remembered his name from back in the day. Talked like they were his biggest fan for half an hour as if all that old filmstock hadn't long rotted before they got around to saying what they wanted. Some of them—and this was briefly the way he'd thought April Lamotte had been headed—really did just want to put some half-remembered schoolgirl dream to rest and simply fuck him.

"Well, thanks, Glory. If she calls again—or anyone else for that matter—can you stall her? Say I've got a case on at the moment, should only take a day or so to sort out. If she turns up or somesuch, try to get a deposit out of her. A ten if she looks up to it. Cash, not check. You know how it works..."

Glory nodded the sort of nod which said she might consider doing something like that, but that he shouldn't count on it. Glory did grudging and grumpy like few people he'd ever encountered, but he still liked her. She was doing what most people who ended up in Venice were doing, which was trying to escape whatever it was that had driven them out of LA. In her case, it was the fear that her son Julio would end up like his father: dead on some street corner in a zoot suit and cheap French shoes.

From the little that Clark had seen of Julio recently, the signs didn't look good. With the new State laws about registration and repatriation, things were getting difficult for all Hispanics.

He was about to turn. Then he stopped. "Say—that letter I asked you about. The one that didn't come with the post. You don't remember anything more about it, do you? How, who, when it came?"

Glory gave a slow shake of her head.

"And, er . . . You haven't noticed anything else, have you Glory? People asking after me, or simply just hanging around?"

Glory shook her head even more slowly.

Up in his apartment, he re-heated that morning's coffee and fixed some stale bread and corned beef and spread it with what was left in a jar of mustard. He then fixed a roll-up from his wallet of Bull Durham and put his legs up on the bed, occasionally glancing at the unopened suitcase which he'd left by its foot as he smoked.

His own john, his own gas ring, his own shower with his own cockroaches. One comfortable chair, and his very own dirty plates stacked in the tiny sink with its fine view through the window of the flames and the nodding-bird pumps of the oilfield spreading into the distance. All of it suited him just as well as did the whole of Venice.

He liked his work, too. Or much of it. Maids' affidavits, grainy photos, soiled sheets, used Trojans in the wastebasket, hotel records, stray bits of underclothing, the wrong color pubic hair . . . Sure, it wasn't acting, but by his lifetime standards, what with two divorces and God alone knew how many broads and jobs, his venture into unlicensed private matrimonial work had been a model of persistence.

How many years was it now? Six? Seven? No, goddamit, it was near-on ten. Sure, it was messy. Sure, it was unpredictable. But he guessed that those were the things he most liked about it. You never quite knew what was around the corner, and in that sense, and in quite a few others, it wasn't so different from acting. Even used some of the same contacts. Girls still looking for that big break who were happy to sidle up to some guy in a bar and rub at his resistance and maybe decamp to a nearby hotel room for that all-important photo-opportunity if the money was right. He'd done his own version of that kind of stuff himself when he was working for guys who no longer trusted their wives, despite his ritual show of squeamishness in front of April Lamotte.

But *acting*; that whole stupid business of pretending to be someone you weren't—the way Peg had done so brilliantly in that feelie—was like some kind of drug that you could kick for ages, yet never really be completely rid of and clean. He sighed, clicked on the bare-bulb light and picked up the case. Flipping it open, he breathed in the faint, gingery smell of another man's sweat.

A crumpled pale beige summer suit, labeled Janvier—an expensive tailor's on Washington Boulevard. Keys, a billfold and a grotted linen handkerchief bulked the pockets... These must have been the clothes the guy had been wearing before she had him carted off to the funny farm, which wasn't a happy thought. The billfold contained a ten and a deuce, which he took as additions to his advance. A driver's license and a State identity card—*Nordic Caucasian; Disabilities, none*—in the name of Daniel Harold Lamotte. Wingtip burgundy shoes. A white soft collar shirt. A gold Parker pen. Those glasses, which looked and felt to be made out of real tortoiseshell. He checked himself in the mirror with them on. He didn't look just different; he looked somehow blurred. After holding them up to the light to check that the lenses really were clear, he wound the expensive Longines wristwatch and set it to the right time and put it on his wrist; the strap even fitted at the same notch. What the hell was Lamotte wearing now—a straightjacket? At least there were no underclothes, worn or clean or otherwise, which would have been taking things too far. But the whole case gave off an intimate feeling—part scent, part presence. Almost an aura in itself.

April Lamotte seemed to have thought of everything. Here was another copy of the guy's signature torn from the bottom of an old contract, in case the one on the driver's license wasn't enough. The bulging manila envelope at the bottom of the case contained a copy of the treatment of *Wake Up and Dream*, just like he'd asked.

SEVEN

Scripts usually went through a variety of differently colored versions before they were finally printed out for shooting—often, the variations continued even then. This particular badly typed and butterfly-clipped carbon which April Lamotte had given him was white; by the usual protocols, the next draft would be blue. The address it gave on the front sheet wasn't Erewhon, but a flat at a place called Blixden Avenue, which he assumed was the Downtown bolthole April Lamotte had mentioned. He flicked over the castlist to get to the opening shot.

```
WAKE UP AND DREAM-A BIOPIC OF LARS BECHMEIR
SCREENPLAY BY DANIEL LAMOTTE

   No credits. The first thing the audience see as
they settle in the theater are lines of faces,
young and old, pretty and ugly, just like their
own, but right up there on the screen. Some are
yawning, some expectant. Some are pretty, some
ugly. It's a typical scene. The CAMERA pans over
more and more faces. The FIELD gives out nothing
at first but a general sense of anticipation.
It's like the audience on the screen and those in
the feelie theater are the same. Then, as an
underlay, with the DANIEL LAMOTTE THEME riding
with it on the SOUNDTRACK, comes a mixture of awe
and unease. CAMERA fixes on a young boy's face.
He's pale, scruffily dressed. His mouth and eyes
```

```
are wide. Then, a drumroll. Applause. The flare
of a nearby spotlight glints in his wide open
eyes. And we switch CAMERA POV to the kid. Roll
CREDITS.

The show begins.
```

Rags to riches. Poverty to fame. Europe to America. East to west. The story contained so many of the ingredients for a successful feelie that it was a wonder it hadn't been made years before. Especially when you considered who it was about.

Lars Bechmeir had been born in Germany at the turn of the century to a family of traveling circus players. Alongside the strong men and bearded ladies and lion tamers, Bechmeir's parents had performed a mind-reading act, and it was something they were surprisingly good at. So good that their only son was puzzled by how they often managed to make accurate guesses even when their usual system of signs and signals failed. Lars was a bright lad, and curious about the world. Perhaps he might even have shaken off his lowly upbringing and gotten to university, had the Great War not intervened.

Like all young and able German men, Lars Bechmeir was conscripted. Like most, he ended up in the version of hell that was the Western Front. The only uncommon thing about Lars Bechmeir's war was that he survived. That, and that his terrible experiences made him think even more deeply about how people reacted to each other; how atmospheres of fear, aggression and occasional joy were so easily and quickly transmitted. How bouts of savagery, or mercy, or bravery, or fear, seemed to pass from soldier to soldier like some contagious disease.

What, Bechmeir wondered, if people communicated with each other not just through their commonly understood senses, but also by some other means? Of course, he knew the idea wasn't original. He even knew how the many experiments which had attempted to prove communication between minds always failed. But Bechmeir wasn't thinking about people sat behind screens and looking at cards in some bright laboratory.

What he had experienced and witnessed in the trenches, above all what he *felt*, led him to believe that this hidden sense was a primitive thing, dealing not in higher-brain abstractions like words or images or thoughts, but in the raw stuff of basic emotion.

We are, he decided, minutely touched by the cloaking aura of every person we meet. It explained the mass actions of mobs. It explained sudden feelings of attraction, repulsion or fear. It even explained the feeling of peacefulness so often found inside churches, and the homeliness of a happy house, and the sense of dread which clings to places where something terrible has happened. It might even explain why people imagined they saw ghosts.

Lars Bechmeir fled war-ravaged Europe and headed for America with the vision of a means by which people shared each other's feelings. If we could reach into each other's minds, he reasoned—if we could really feel what another person felt and understand their joy and suffering—there would surely never be war again. He lived a few years in Chicago, sweeping the floors at the university and occasionally having use of the library. Then, like millions of others, he went west. He labored, he begged, but he still worked obsessively on his idea, which by now was a wad of calculations and speculations stuffed into the back pocket of his only pair of dungarees. It was on this journey that he met his wife Betty, whose sharecropper parents had been thrown off their land.

In a barn in Minnesota, which Clark believed was now open daily for public tours, Bechmeir was finally able to capture on specially treated photographic paper those first famous images of his wife's aura. Only a thumbprint smudge, a blur as if of faint gray wings flapping around a silhouetted body, but it bore out all that he had long theorized, even down to the essential weakness and changeability of the human aura. Now, at last, he had his proof. And, he reasoned, if this aura was essentially nothing more than a weak electromagnetic field which he called plasm, not only could this plasm be captured as an image, but, most likely, it could be recorded—and if it could be recorded, these recordings could be re-transmitted, and they could then be amplified, and edited. In one leap, Bechmeir had moved from the theory of a mild but little-credited extra sense to an idea which would revolutionize the world.

Lars and Betty Bechmeir continued west. Inevitably, they reached LA. In a series of run-down rooming houses and abandoned garages, he worked on generating this newly discovered field artificially. At least in LA, there was a ready supply of electronic equipment which the rapid progress of recording technology had discarded, and he made much use of cannibalized parts and the borrowed know-how of technicians he met in bars. He could see many uses for his discovery, but he soon realized that the most rapid progress could be made in what was then called the movie industry.

But who would listen? Not the major players—not to a crank clutching a carpetbag with some weird idea about thought-waves. Which was what finally brought Lars Bechmeir to the top floor of the Taft Building for an appointment to see Howard Hughes. Hughes was a wealthy man and a movie producer, for sure, but he was already more famous for his eccentricities and his forays into aviation. For all his successes, Hughes was regarded as a loose cannon, but if you were looking for someone who would be fascinated by the idea of a device which could record the emanations of the mind, it would have been hard to find anyone better.

Even before the vacuum tubes of the frail and rudimentary device had been warmed up and wired together across his desk by the small, nervous guy with a German accent who'd shuffled into his office on worn out shoes, Hughes had been persuaded. When, after much further coaxing, a shimmering field of plasm stuttered from between two spikes of metal, and the everyday sounds of city traffic wafting in through the windows were briefly eclipsed by a strange but palpable sense of dread, he was fully convinced.

Bechmeir had already filed patents for his discovery, and, even then, he was determined that his device should be made available to the world as a whole. Still, he took Hughes' backing to push on with developing a commercial prototype in the old schoolhouse down in Willowbrook where he was by then working, and which subsequently become a museum and home to the Bechmeir Trust. Rumors were soon rife about this strange new form of entertainment the Hughes Corporation was said to be developing, and then of the talkie—no, it would be called a feelie-movie—in which it would be premiered.

Reactions to the first showings of *Broken Looking Glass* at Grauman's Chinese Theater were mixed. There were teething troubles. Reels broke. Valves overheated. There was a small fire. Many claimed to have been made nauseous by the strange, crackling aurora which spluttered before the screen. Others said they felt nothing at all. The Actors' Guild and the other studios were hostile. A Catholic bishop condemned the whole enterprise for tampering with the very stuff of the human soul. Then, and in the tradition of most of Hughes' movies, the story itself was no good.

But the press loved the whole thing. They loved Howard Hughes and they loved wacky ideas and they loved premieres. Above all, they loved Lars Bechmeir with his trim beard, owlish glasses, double-breasted safari jacket, trademark meerschaum pipe and soft German accent, and they loved his marvelous recordings played through a clever wire machine, conjuring up wraiths which puttered and danced like flames of marsh gas, reaching out their ghostly arms to touch minds with the raw stuff of human emotion. They loved handsome and prematurely-grayed Betty Bechmeir as well. The pair made a good couple—were photogenic in a down-home sort of way—and the press soon came to portray their life story as the best and latest version of the rags-to-riches American Dream. From that day forward, nothing was ever the same. Lars Bechmeir was soon up there with Thomas Edison. In most people's eyes, in fact, he was above him, seeing as Edison kept all his money, whilst Bechmeir promised to channel the proceeds of his patents into a charitable trust.

By the mid 1930s, all the movie theaters in the country were re-equipping themselves with Bechmeir field generators, and the idea of the plain old talkies, which had seemed so revolutionary five years before, was old hat. After all, who would want to merely watch and listen to something played up on a screen when you could actually feel it as well? And if the other advances which Bechmeir had promised—in education, in the sciences, in the understanding of the deeper workings of the mind, and in improving mental health—had failed, or been slower in arriving, and even if poor old Howard Hughes himself had gone mad, people barely noticed, and they cared even less. They were too busy going to the feelies, or counting the blessings of this burgeoning new industry which had helped drag America out of the Great Depression.

Which was how, Clark reckoned, this story should have ended if it had been fiction. Lars and Betty Bechmeir might have given most of their money away to charity, but they were nevertheless seriously successful and authentically rich. And they lived in a fine house in LA; what else could anyone possibly want? Few major openings in and around the city—libraries, dams, new power stations, even first nights of the rapidly declining live theater, and, of course, premieres of feelies themselves—were complete without the Bechmeirs' attendance.

But then, Betty Bechmeir's body was found one morning in May 1936 dangling by a rope from the Colorado Street Bridge out in Pasadena. Despite an exhaustive inquest, the true reason for her death was never explained. Soon after, Lars Bechmeir, previously a man in vigorous middle age, suffered what the papers first reported as a fall, then as a major stroke. The next time he was seen in public, his voice was slurred and he was in a wheelchair. It was no surprise when their palatial house in Beverly Hills was put up for sale and Lars Bechmeir vanished from the public eye. Sightings of him in the years since had become as common as sightings of Bigfoot in the press. Lars Bechmeir in some backwoods log cabin in Maine, or dining out in Paris. That, or reports that he was fully recovered and working on some magical new device, or had remarried, or had become a hopeless vegetable, or was dead.

Bechmeir's tragedy and subsequent disappearance had elevated him from all-American hero to bona-fide myth. The problem, though, from the point of view of producing a feelie about his life—and presumably the reason why it had never yet been done—was how to deal with an event as shattering as Betty Bechmeir's apparent suicide, and her husband's subsequent illness and reclusiveness, yet still retain that all-important happy ending.

And that, for all the neat tricks and fine writing in the script he was reading, was to Clark's mind the cleverest thing about what Daniel Lamotte had achieved. Betty Bechmeir might have been seen as an all-year-round version of Mother Christmas, but the woman he portrays is far more complex and serious. She's seen suffering, death and poverty in her life just as Lars Bechmeir has. And she feels things at least as deeply. That's the very reason she buys into her husband's vision so easily, and stands by him through thick and thin. It all fits with the success of those crude early experiments on recording auras which he conducted on her and then—and here was the really elegant part—with Betty's unease, which even their triumphant success cannot remove. She's *too* in tune with other people's feelings. She cares too much, and has seen too much, for any kind of success to wash those feelings away.

So, when she drives off into the thunderstorm on that climactic night, it doesn't feel like a cop-out or a let-down. You fully understand that, just as Christ submitted to crucifixion, Betty Bechmeir loves us all too much to carry on living. As he finished the treatment, Clark was blinking back tears. At least for the time he was reading it, he really did believe that Betty Bechmeir was actually *taking away* some of the world's pain as she drove toward the Colorado Street Bridge.

EIGHT

Needing some air, he pulled on a sportcoat and took the dim-lit stairs down through the Doge's Apartments past all the usual nightly sounds of arguments and murmuring radios, and headed north toward Albert Kinney Pier.

Quiet tonight. The dancehall closed. The Ferris wheel, stilled and its lights dead, was a huge black spiderweb cast across the starlessly hazy night. Wrappers fluttered about his feet. The sigh of the Pacific came and went through the gaps in the pier's boarding.

He leaned on the railing. As he rolled himself a cigarette and blew plumes of smoke into the darkness, he ran through possible explanations for the strange role which April Lamotte was asking him to perform. The one in which she'd killed Daniel Lamotte and he was helping to provide her with some kind of alibi bothered him the most. But, for all that April Lamotte was plainly a woman who was capable of many things, he just couldn't believe that she'd murdered her husband. If his intuition, long-honed in dealing with worried spouses, told him anything at all about April Lamotte, it was that she was genuinely trying to sort her and her husband's lives out. But was she telling him everything? His intuition also told him that most definitely she was not.

A cold prickle—the sort of thing you paid for when you went to the feelies, or got for free when someone walked over your grave—passed across him. He looked back along the pier. There was no one about. But, for an odd moment, *something* did seem to be moving towards him from amid the dark and empty attractions. Not quite a figure—its shape wouldn't stay that clear. He had it down as simply some kind of dust devil, although he'd never seen such a thing before out here in Venice.

Nothing but a stir of warmed air and darkness, it picked up swirls of beachsand and scraps of litter as it moved toward him with an odd quality of purpose. Certainly not a figure. Or if it was a figure, it was a ragged blur of scraps and shadows, the shape not of one figure but of many, and it was running towards him as if from out of the end of some incredibly long tunnel, and it was bringing with it an odd and breathy hissing.

He blinked, and the whole sensation faded. The wind stirred, and then there was nothing back down the pier but sea air and darkness. He put it down to the sound of the tide, and the breeze, and the loose fry wrappers blowing around him, and his tiredness, and seeing that wraith, and then Peg Entwistle in that feelie . . .

The light was off in Glory's cubbyhole when he got back to the Doge's Apartments. Most of the radios were off as well. Where the furniture creaked, where people cried out, it was to other rhythms.

He let himself in, undressed, climbed into bed. He lay there for a long while, staring up at the ceiling.

NINE

He parked his Ford in a lot beside the Equitable Building at just gone three next day, June 27. Checking the polished glass of the shop windows as he walked south, he saw a lanky man with big ears and slicked back brown hair, casually well-dressed, wearing heavy brown glasses and carrying a small cardboard suitcase. These were expensive clothes—Daniel Lamotte had a sort of crumpled style—and they were a good fit. Even the shoes.

He'd arranged to meet April Lamotte opposite the Taft Building on Hollywood and Vine at half past the hour. Historically appropriate, he reckoned, seeing as that was where Howard Hughes had maintained his offices until he'd been carted off to the funny farm. The lawyer's office was a couple of miles on along Sunset toward Downtown, but it made sense that she pick him up someplace else. He saw that he'd arrived ten minutes early when he checked Daniel Lamotte's Longines watch.

The glasses were starting to slide with the sweat off his nose. He felt around in his pockets for a handkerchief—it was fresh, and monogrammed D L—but his fingers felt a gritty residue. Particles of sand glittered on his fingertips. He brushed them off, told himself to focus, wiped the lenses, put his glasses back on. He was an actor once again, and this was simply another role. It was just a question of imagining that the whole of Los Angeles was a giant stage. He bought coffee in a paper cup from a doughnut-shaped stand using a dollar from Daniel Lamotte's billfold. Mussolini had just declared war on the British and the Russians had invaded some place called Latvia according to the newsstand. More interestingly, stockings made out of something called "nylon" were about to go on sale. He'd just finished the coffee when he saw the Delahaye heading east, top down. Even amid the expensive machines that teemed across this particular intersection—the Cadillacs, Buicks and Bentleys of all the feelie industry players who worked around here—it stood out.

April Lamotte pulled in at the curb and gave him a smile far warmer than anything he'd seen the day before as she leaned across the bench leather seat and gestured him in. She was wearing something burgundy with padded shoulders and big lapels and puff sleeves. The outfit was belted at the waist and fitted snug around her hips and down to her beige-stockinged thighs. She was also wearing a diamond-studded wedding ring and matching gold and emerald necklace and bracelet. Clark heard the thrum of the Delahaye's exhaust, felt the expensive heft and swing of the door, as he sat beside her and slung the suitcase on the back seat.

"Bang on time."

"You must have been early." She was still smiling. Then she let go of the wheel and leaned over and slid the glasses neatly off his ears and laid them on the dash and put her arms right around him. Her lips sought his mouth with smooth ease. He felt the hard push of her tongue. She was still wearing Chanel *Cuir de Russie* and she was fuller-bodied than he'd thought. Her hand trailed down across the top of his thigh as she finally drew away. He saw the guys around the doughnut stand watching open-mouthed as she pulled off. If she was looking for witnesses, she'd certainly got them.

"That was some greeting."

She laughed. "You *are* my husband. But don't forget to put those glasses back on. Dan always wears them."

He did as she said. "'Cept when you're kissing him?"

"Yeah. Except for then."

She drove the way Clark would have expected her to drive: well, but with a pushy unconcern for other traffic. And this car really was something else. Even with the top down, you could feel and smell the straight eight engine's growl over the scents of leather, burr walnut, Kidderminster carpet and April Lamotte's Chanel.

She felt in her purse for one of her cigarettes, then pressed in a button in the Delahaye's central console which, after a few moments, popped back out again. The coil which now glowed inside enabled her to light it.

"That's neat."

"Is, isn't it? I got a pack of Luckies if you want a smoke." She gestured a green-lacquered fingernail toward the glovebox. "Forgot to tell you yesterday they're the brand Dan prefers."

He opened the dashboard and found the pack. He tapped one out as she swerved to accelerate past a line of trucks.

"Just press the lighter in. You should use a book of matches otherwise. Dan doesn't like pocket lighters, says they leak too easily, although I've bought him a few over the years. Monogrammed *All My Love* and forgotten in a drawer somewhere. You've been married, haven't you? You know the sort of thing."

The sensation of smoking a real Lucky Strike was nothing like as good as the feeling he'd got as Jo-Ann Corkish lit one up yesterday in the feelies. But it wasn't bad. "Anything else?"

"Anything what?"

"That you haven't told me."

"You've practiced the signature?"

"Uh-huh. A whole hour this morning."

"You've read the script?"

"You weren't shitting me when you said it was good. As long as you don't expect me to say too much about it."

"Don't worry. The whole contract's already fixed. All you need do is sign . . . " He watched her teeth go over her bottom lip. The lipstick was burgundy as well. "Then, when we're finished I thought we could maybe go for a meal. I've booked a table at Chateau Bansar."

"Thanks." He guessed he should probably be impressed, and grateful. "And then that's it? We're done? No call-backs or encores?"

"Exactly. You haven't kept anything? The clothes, the script, Dan's signatures?"

"I'm either wearing it, or it's in this suitcase."

She smiled. "You know, you really *do* look like Dan. Driving like this, it's weird. It feels like I'm sitting right by him."

"How is he, anyway?"

"He's getting better."

"When did you last see him?"

"A couple of days back." The Delahaye's speed fell a few mph as her foot dropped off the gas. "Seeing as you ask."

"Does he know anything about what's happening today?"

"Imagine what it would do to someone in his frail state if I started trying to tell him that I've hired this guy to impersonate him."

"He'll have to know eventually."

"I guess he will. Meantime, you're Daniel Lamotte. Do you really think you can do it, Mr Gable?"

"Sure. But maybe we should cut the Mr Gable act. Seeing as we've got no chance for a dress rehearsal."

"Yes." She touched at her coiffure, which the wind was doing nothing to disturb. "You're right."

"Dan?"

"Yeah. Dan."

"And you're just April? Not bunnikins or sweet-tits or flot-not?"

"You have an odd sense of humor, Mis . . . " She smiled and tossed her cigarette into the slipstream. " . . . *Dan*."

They were slowed to a halt by a parade beside the twin radio masts of the Angelus Temple. A brass band of American Legionaries led a procession of capped and uniformed types, the largest and most prominent of whom were wearing Liberty League sashes in blue and red. All ages. All sizes. Women and men. All of them white. The cops were smiling, too, as they held everyone back. He saw that they were also wearing Liberty League badges on their lapels. A few years ago, any display of political allegiance by a city employee would have been illegal, but Herbert Kisberg's term as governor had put paid to all that.

April Lamotte traced the leather rim of the steering wheel and glanced at her watch as the parade dragged on. Some of the other enforced spectators were getting restless, but the cops were grinning in that way which suggested that you'd better grin along. After all, this was California. You just had to smile.

Clark smiled, too, in a neutral way he'd once practiced for the role of this guy—schmuck, really—he'd played in a fleapit off Broadway, who'd thought the entire world was a swell place until some Prohibition gangsters kidnapped him. Even then, he couldn't stop smiling, and thinking the world was essentially a kind and decent place. That was why the gangsters had finally shot him, and by the final scene you ended up feeling that it was nothing more than the stupid bastard deserved.

It was all kids now. Scout Cubs. Camp Fire Youths. Pocahontases and Hiawathas. Pioneers. Many of them were carrying banners. NEUTRAL AMERICA. NO FDR THIRD TERM. GIVE IT UP WINSTON. END THE DRAFT. SUPPORT NEW EUROPE. LIBERTY LEAGUERS AGAINST WAR.

He watched it all trail by.

TEN

The offices of York and Bunce were in a smart new concrete and glass mid-rise a block down on Main from City Hall. April Lamotte was able to park almost directly out front.

"Hey, wait," she said as he moved to open the Delahaye's door on to the sidewalk. "Let's have a proper look at you first."

She laid a hand on each shoulder, drawing him close. Her eyes traveled over him. Close up, they were as green as he'd imagined. Even greener. Her white teeth bit down over her burgundy lower lip.

She straightened his glasses as if they weren't straight already, then gently stroked the hair back around his ears. "That's better." Her hands traced down his arms. He felt his cock start to thicken as they settled on his thighs. "You look just fine. Ready?"

He swallowed. Nodded. "Yeah."

She slid herself around.

"If you're leaving the top down..." He gestured to the cardboard briefcase on the backseat. "You'd better put that in the trunk."

She hesitated for a moment, then nodded. He watched her as she walked around to the back of the car and leaned down into the trunk, which was carpet-lined, and empty apart from a thick length of hose. She smoothed down her skirt.

"Let's get this done."

This was nothing like the lawyers' offices he was used to. No battered files and worn-out linoleum. No note about trying the bar opposite if there was no one around. This was all new wood and old paintings, although the air had that frosty, sterile feel which characterized all air conditioned spaces. So did the receptionist.

She consulted her list with a red-taloned finger. "You're here to see Mr Amdahl."

"Yes, that's correct," April Lamotte said before he could get in a word. "If you'll..."

But already the receptionist was dialing her phone. Which, allowing for the length of those nails, was some feat. Her talons tapped a little dance on the desktop as the handset purred into her ear. She was actually rather beautiful, Clark decided, studying the honeyed fall of her hair. Women who worked prestige front-office desk jobs in this city generally were. That, and young. He'd often puzzled about what happened to these specimens after they passed from their twenties. Studying the slight sag of her jawline, he wondered if she didn't have similar thoughts.

A voice crackled from the phone. There was a conversation, mostly of yeses and nos.

"He'll be down to see you presently," the receptionist said as she laid the handset down. "If you'll just take a seat..." She gestured. But, before Clark and April could get their bearings amid the leather couches, a door swung open.

"Mr and Mrs Lamotte! You're here about the contract?" Amdahl had an outdoor tan and a fake gray pelt of hair.

"Pleased to see you," Clark muttered in a timbre which April Lamotte had suggested he make slightly quicker and lighter.

"Yes. Absolutely." Amdahl nodded. He didn't look the sort to give anyone much attention just as long as they paid their bill.

They followed him down a corridor set with big sepia blow-ups of some of the lost stars of the silent and talkie eras. Mary Astor. Herbert Marshall. Rudolph Valentino. It was as if York and Bunce were trying to tell their clients something about the industry in which they worked.

Amdahl's office lay up the first wide flight of stairs, and looked exactly how you'd expect a successful media lawyer's office to look. Wide windows gave a fine view across Echo Park toward Edendale through the afternoon's softening haze. He produced a fat folder and proceeded to lay out papers from it across his desk.

"These are the finished versions. Five copies. It's all been checked. Mrs Lamotte was sent a copy of the drafts last week. But, of course, you're the signatory, Mr Lamotte. It's your hard work we're selling here. I'm happy to explain it all as much as you like."

"I think I'm okay." He unclipped the gold Parker pen from his inside pocket. "I mean, if I can't trust April here, who can I trust?"

They all laughed.

Even allowing for the five copies, a surprising number of signatures was required. Endless *heretofores*, *hereinafters* and *notwithstandings* on cream sheets of legal vellum. As far as Clark was concerned, it might as well have been in Greek, although he was just glad to see that his hand had decided not to shake.

"And we'll need a Bible to swear the actual affidavit on . . . " Amdahl's smile soured to a momentary look of alarm. "Not *Jewish* are you?"

"Uh . . . " Clark glanced towards April, who gave a small negative blink. "No."

"Stupid of me to ask." Amdahl's smile had returned. "Of course, the California regulations *do* allow registered Yids to make contracts, but it's really getting to be more bother than it's worth. Oh, and you did tell us that neither of you have any children who we need to call witness on—is that correct, Mrs Lamotte?"

Faust, Clark decided, as April Lamotte assented to their childlessness, would have been required to sign less documentation than this.

Eventually, it was done.

"Congratulations." Amdahl gave their hands a muscular shake. "I'll send the copies back by courier. First thing tomorrow, it'll be on Senserama's desks for their signature. A week at the very outside and we should all be done. This has been a real privilege. I'm a big fan of your work, Mr Lamotte. Let's hope this thing runs and runs."

"So do I."

"We all do," April Lamotte added as she slipped her arm around Clark's. "Dan's had his ups and downs lately—some very difficult times, to be honest, haven't you darling?—but we're hoping we can put the past behind us and move on."

Clark nodded, gave her ass a squeeze, and said *sure*, although he was puzzled as to why she was raking up his problematic mental history at this of all moments.

"That's . . . terrific." Amdahl cleared his throat. "And maybe, seeing as we're close to the cocktail hour . . . ?" He gestured towards a glass-fronted cabinet.

"Well, I—" Clark began.

"That's real nice of you." April Lamotte gave a burgundy smile. "But Dan and I are planning a small celebration. We've booked a table at Chateau Bansar."

"Chateau Ban*sar* . . . ?" Amdahl looked impressed.

ELEVEN

No challenges. No ambushes. And no sudden surprises—unless you counted the brief issue of his possible Jewishness. He felt a sense of anticlimax as they stepped out from the cool offices of York and Bunce, back into the city's noise and heat. As roles went, dressing in someone else's clothes and mimicking their signature was hardly up there with playing Shakespeare. But who needed all the hassle and rejection when you could get paid a thousand bucks for doing this instead?

"So—where's this Chateau place?" he asked as April Lamotte did something complicated with the Delahaye's keys to get the engine throbbing.

"Up past Silver Lake." She looked at him and smiled before pulling swiftly out into the rush-hour traffic. "Well done, by the way. I think we did it, didn't we?"

"I think we did."

Traffic was slow at first as she drove back along Sunset and then Hollywood. It always was at this time of day. Beyond the hanging veils of smog, the Santa Monica Mountains seemed scarcely there. So, as they shimmered in the heat pouring off the blacktop and the lanes of queuing cars, did the people on the sidewalks and the nearby buildings.

He lit himself a Lucky Strike using that clever lighter, and lit April one of her pastel cigarettes. She touched his hand with her burgundy-nailed fingertips for longer than seemed entirely necessary as he passed it to her. In pauses in the traffic, she demonstrated a few of the Delahaye's other tricks. A top of the range Motorola. Windows which powered themselves up and down from the press of an electric button. Electric locks, too. Adjustable vents that blew out what passed in this city for fresh air.

Traffic began to clear as they passed Barnsdall Park and turned north on Cahuenga. The Delahaye's motor began to roar.

Chateau Bansar was up a drive which wasn't even signposted, and which wound on for so long, and through gardens so spectacular, that Clark found himself wondering when their designer's invention would run out.

There were lakes and Chinese pagodas. There were Grecian temples and a huge and genuine-looking waterfall cascading over genuine-looking rocks. A stag deer regarded them from an outcrop. He'd just decided that it was a thing of painted plaster when it raised its head and bolted off.

The chateau itself was all fairyland turrets and balconies, floating in a haze of spotlights against the setting sun. A car valet liveried like a medieval page took the Delahaye and drove it off down an underground ramp so as not to spoil the scene. They wandered beneath arbors and around fountains. Peacocks were preening and cawing. There were swans on a moat.

"Is this what you and Dan do regularly?"

"No." They were arm in arm.

"So there's no chance of anyone recognizing us?"

"Absolutely nil. Why do you think I chose it? But don't forget, you are still Dan tonight." He felt her shrug. "I just felt we both deserved a treat."

Wrought-iron candelabra, real fires and sweeping wooden floors. Minstrels playing something minstrel-like from a minstrel gallery. A green-lit carp-filled pool. The woman who checked their reservation and led them around the mosaic pillars to their table was wearing a wimple.

The other diners were dim figures—each alcove was shrouded in ivy and lit by genuine flames—but if you peered hard enough you could make them out. This was a gossip columnist's paradise, and Clark didn't doubt that all these handsome faces murmuring to each other over expensive wine belonged to people he should have heard of. Trudy Rester and Saffron Knowles and James H. Pack, maybe, and all those other billboard names he'd given up noticing these last few years. But that would *have* to be Monumenta Loolie. No one else in the world had breasts like hers, and even he knew about those.

He wondered about the old names—those briefly immortal faces he'd glimpsed along the corridors of York and Bunce. Mary Pickford. William Desmond Taylor. Colleen Moore. A few still lived in this city, or so he'd heard. They'd enough money to keep hold of some fragment of the dream even if no one now remembered or cared about who they'd been. Then there were those other names. People who were just starting to get used to the limousines and the easy fucks and the swish hotels before it all disappeared. People like himself.

The menus were huge and handwritten and had no prices. He was vaguely worried that April Lamotte might decide to deduct his half of the bill off the thousand bucks she was paying him, but for one night he was happy to play along. After all, they had pulled off something pretty impressive together, hadn't they?

The Champagne was poured. They clinked glasses.

"Cheers."

"Cheers." He took a slug of the Champagne, then slid the bottle out of the ice bucket and poured them both some more. "When do you think Dan . . . uh . . . *I'll* be back in good enough order to get back to work?"

Her gaze hardened fractionally. "I don't know."

He considered the bubbles in his Champagne. Someone as sharp as she was, he was surprised she wasn't ahead of him. "What I mean is, April, the contract's just step number one. The studio will want all the usual stuff once the project goes into development. You know—meetings, revisions. More meetings, more revisions. Table top readings and re-writes for some star who thinks they know about how to make a script work. All the crap that writers have to go through."

"I guess so." She was twisting her wedding ring, although she stopped as soon as she noticed him watching.

"And if Dan's not . . . If *I'm* not—Hell, April, no one here's listening . . .

What I'm trying to say is that I could help you and Dan some more. *I* could go to the meetings, do the pitches, suck up to the executives. Whatever. And not just for this feelie. Not if the stuff's as good as *Wake Up and Dream* is. The Dan who does the writing could keep himself as far out of the way as he wanted from all the shit that rains down in this town. And, if they ever *did* find out that there were two Dans, the studios wouldn't care anyway. Not, and pardon my French, the tiniest fuck. Not if the writing's successful. I mean, who the hell's losing out? More likely, they'd want to make a new feelie out of the whole scam."

"You're not quite the hard-bitten cynic you like to think you are. You're worse. You're just an outright romantic, aren't you?"

"You got me there." He grinned back at her and raised his glass. "So? What do you think?"

"I think we should order. You're hungry, aren't you? I sure am."

Clark, who liked his food plain even at a joint like this, settled for steak and fries with a brandy sauce. She ordered some kind of fish that still had its head on when it arrived. Once the waiter had gone away, he tried probing some more.

"You know what I still don't understand? How you found me. Sure, I advertise, but it's mostly word of mouth. The normal business I do, anyway. Then you said something about hiring some kind of private dick to find me. I know a lot of those guys. And the way that letter arrived, and all the stuff you somehow found out about me. It requires certain skills. So I was wondering..."

"You're right. I did hire someone. But the whole deal was that they're discreet."

"You're not going to say?"

"Would you want me to go around talking to everyone about what *you've* been up to?"

"No, but—"

"Exactly. But I did find out some things about you, as you say. Cuttings, mainly. Nothing but a name, and a face. But still, I'm curious. I mean, I don't remember any of the silents and talkies you were in, and doubt if many people do. But you really were close, weren't you? You nearly made it. So—what was it? What happened? You can't just tell me it was just those teeth and the ears. If they bothered you that much, you'd have had them fixed."

Now *she* was probing, and in directions he didn't want to go—especially not after seeing Peg in that feelie and all the memories that had been raked up since. So he ordered some more Champagne and told April Lamotte instead about what had got him into acting in the first place, and about what it was like to grow up in a down-at-heel boomtown like Hopedale, Pennsylvania (might as well put hope in the name, the locals said, because you wouldn't find it anywhere else). Times when he was plain old Billy Gable, and the best he could have hoped for out of life was to follow his dad into the oil wildcatting trade or pull the molds off tires for the Firestone Rubber Company over in Akron. But he'd always felt there was something else out there, even though he didn't know what it was or how the hell he was supposed to get to it. The closest he'd come as a kid was when his stepmom Jenny read him *Great Classics of the World* with that fine voice she had before the TB took hold. Most important of all, though, was seeing *Bird of Paradise* performed by the Akron Players at the music hall on Exchange Street. What hit Clark most was the way the stage made a doorway into a different world. For all that you could tell the princess wasn't really Hawaiian and the stage boards creaked and the volcano in the background didn't look much like a volcano, he was there with them. This was magic.

He went to see the same play the next night, and again the night after. Then he waited outside in the back alley for the actors to emerge. Luana the Hawaiian princess now looked more like the sort of woman you'd find behind the counter of the local grocery store, but he already knew that there was something these people had that he wanted. When, sitting drinking with them around the corner in a bar, he asked if there might be any kind of work going, and they agreed that he might be of some help shifting scenes, he was already hooked.

By now the main dishes had come and gone. So had the second bottle of Champagne, and April Lamotte had ordered a third before he could wonder whether it was a good idea. She seemed to have mellowed as she leaned across the table, working her hands around her neck and then up into the roots of her hair, even though she'd been filling up his glass more often than hers.

"*Everyone* in this city is hooked. The people here..." She gestured, and leaned forward some more. "Or the bus station whores. Me. I mean, I wouldn't be here, would I—not one of us would—if it wasn't for the dream. Or nightmare. I sometimes wonder. I mean, even today... What the hell's it all for?"

He watched her blink away the glitter that had formed at the edges of her eyes. *What the hell's it all for?* In this business, in this city, nothing ever changed. By this time in the evening, the same question would be asked at many of Chateau Bansar's other lit tables, and in thousands of cheap lodging houses, and down at the bus station by the whores.

"Not that Dan can help the way he is. He's sweet. He's brilliant. But, God, he's *hard work*. No one knows what it's like to live with a writer—I mean, it never gets into the stuff they write, does it? Or even the biographies... What about Mrs Shakespeare, eh? What about Mrs fucking Dickens? They sat at home, they took the shit, they peeled the potatoes and made the bed and put the meals on the table and told the kids playing out front to shut up because their genius husband's writing. Or trying to write. Or quite possibly not writing at all..."

The glitter came again. It spilled from her eye and soaked into the powder on her cheek. She rubbed it away. "This was supposed to be a celebration. I'm sorry."

He took her hand. "No. It's okay." She gave a louder sob. Her elbow knocked her glass, and Champagne glittered across the table.

Looking up, he saw that a waiter was already hovering at the edge of their alcove, looking dumbly concerned. Taking April a little closer in his arms, he told him to get them some fresh napkins, and the bill.

TWELVE

It was fully night now, and the waiting Delahaye's engine was already running, and the inky blue sky shone in rivulets along its long cream flanks. Clark took off the tortoiseshell glasses and gave them a wipe with his DL monogrammed handkerchief as if to get rid of some kind of blurriness. But what he felt was clear-headed. Anyone would, having glimpsed the size of that bill.

"Why don't you drive?" Less tearful now, April Lamotte let go of his arm. "Like I said, Dan, it's your car."

The pull of the engine. The way the suspension rode. He was doing fifty just on the curving driveway out of Chateau Bansar.

"Which way?"

"No hurry. Your car's down by Los Felice isn't it, so why not try Mulholland? We can drive up through the mountains and cut down through Ventura." She laid her hand over his on the gearstick as they waited at the turn. "It's the kind of night for a drive."

The smog had blown away in a light wind from off the ocean. The city spilled below them like a box of glittering jewels.

He'd forgotten. He really had. He'd been living and working in this city—at least, the fringes of it—for all these years, and he'd been like someone asleep. Fairyland didn't stop with those last views in the rearview of Chateau Bansar's turrets. Up here, driving a car like this above Hollywood, you felt you were traveling pretty much as high and as far as it was possible to get in this world.

He re-found Cahuenga and lost most of the traffic by turning east along the wide detour of Mulholland Drive. The dials twitched. His hands turned easy on the wheel. The Delahaye took the switchtails like a salmon taking the rapids on its way to spawn.

Glimpses east across Cahuenga Ravine toward Griffith Park. That big sign. HOLLYWOODLAND. Grey in the darkness. There'd been talk all these last ten years of getting it demolished but it was still there. He eased the big car on. Nothing but darkness ahead of them now. Nothing but stars above. A couple of times, he caught headlights in the rear-view. He braked slightly, curious as to what kind of automobile it was that was managing to keep up. But the lights hung back.

"You like the Delahaye?"

"Yeah. Who wouldn't? Mind if I take these things off now?" Without waiting for a response, he tucked the glasses into his top jacket pocket.

"You sure as hell don't drive like Dan."

"How does he drive?"

"Like a writer. The only risks he takes are in his head."

He took another bend. The mountains were dark, the city a glittering sprawl.

"Let's stop somewhere." She'd slid closer to him. Her hand was on his thigh. "There's an overlook. You see that turn ahead?"

He took it fast in a spew of dust. The tires rumbled to a halt just before the thin wooden fence that guarded the precipice.

"That's better isn't it?" She reached over him and turned off the engine and the lights. Silence fell. The city lay spread below them. He could smell summer thyme and Chanel *Cuir de Russie* and hot rubber. She didn't pull back when he reached his arm around her shoulder and touched her hair.

The overlook was empty. Just them and the Delahaye and this night-lit city. Although, as his eyes grew more accustomed to the darkness, there looked to be the shape of some other car parked right off in a corner against the dusty edge of the land. But there were no lights, no movement. The only sound came from their breathing, and the cicadas, and the murmur of Los Angeles which rose up from the mountain-cupped bowl.

"I brought this." Briefly, she pulled away from him to rummage in her purse. Something metallic glinted. He caught the tang of bourbon as she unscrewed the cap.

He chuckled. "I'd never had you down as the type."

She chuckled as well.

The bourbon was sweet and hard. He wiped his lips, swallowed back the oddly metallic after-tang, handed the flask back to her. She touched it to her lips, then gave it back. The cold metal still held the warm print of her hand.

"So," Clark murmured as bourbon fizzed with Champagne in his blood. "What happens next?"

"Tonight? Or with me and Dan?"

He let the question slide. His fingers had been toying with April Lamotte's hair. Now, they touched the jeweled lobe of her ear. Part of him was still doing its best to keep some detachment. She was, after all, a client, and he still hadn't gotten that main check.

"This city isn't good for any of us," she said. "It sucks us in. Look what it's done to Dan." She shifted slightly and laid her head across his shoulder. He breathed the scent of her hair. The flask was nearly empty and still in his hand. For its closeness, her body felt coiled and tense. "People, when they first came here from back east to make movies, they said it was because of the quality of the light. But what they didn't talk about was the quality of the darkness. I mean whatever's lurking underneath..."

He blinked. His eyes stung. He thought again of that sign they'd passed, and of all the things he'd done, and hadn't done. April Lamotte was right about LA. He felt it as something huge and black and ravenous, pouring up toward him in a hissing roar.

She was still talking. "... so I reckoned that if we can get this new feelie finished, maybe it'll be time for Dan and I to leave. I mean, he's always said he just wants to write. And there are other, better, places you can write than LA. In fact, I can't think of any worse...

"We could escape, we could cut our losses and shed the ghosts and live someplace else. And better, and cleaner, and more cheaply. Dan and I used to talk about re-locating to England. About writing real books there—proper novels that said something true. Of course, that'll only work when the Germans have taken over, and Dan doesn't like the Nazis much. So maybe we could try Argentina. It's like this country was a hundred years ago when everything was new and fresh. We could sell Erewhon and get a ranch. He could write and I could... You okay?"

He nodded, swallowed. He'd heard people talk about escaping this city too many times before. It was as big a dream as the one which brought them here in the first place. Bigger, if anything, because it never came true. The dry roaring in his ears wouldn't go away. "Think so."

"Maybe I shouldn't have given you that flask." She pried it from his hand. "I can drive back. There's no hurry, is there?"

The dim outlines of the car's interior—the dials, the wood, the chrome, the switches, her stockinged legs, the leather bench—all seemed to blur. Then she reached forward across him toward the dashboard. Keys tinkled, the starter whirred, and the engine—a choir of pistons, a stroked tiger—resumed its easy purr. Then she fiddled with something else and a leather top slowly buzzed over them like a black wing, shutting out the stars.

"A little privacy," she murmured in the humming warmth after the hood had completed its journey with a series of sharp clicks. "And it *was* getting cold." He felt her fingers trace the buttons of his shirt. "For all the many things Dan's been for me, he's never been much of a husband in the physical sense..." The interior of the car was far darker now, but the closure of the top and the engine's throb hadn't shut off the hissing in his ears. He blinked again as her fingers found a space between the buttons. "You don't wear an undershirt?" Her breath had quickened.

"Never have."

Her burgundy suit was black now, and he saw the paleness of her flesh widen as she worked the top of it down from her shoulders and her arms. It was tailored in such a way that, underneath, she didn't need to wear a bra.

She leaned around him. Almost straddling him now as she removed his glasses. Her scent came to him in a dizzy wave. "You *sure* you're okay?"

Her breasts were full, and he longed to touch them, but the way she was sitting over him, and the dark weight of whatever else now seemed to be oppressing him, made it hard for him to move his arms. Her hands were on him, stroking the inner and outer sides of his suit jacket and down into his pants' pockets, but with a purpose that didn't feel entirely sexual. When her fingers went to his throat and touched him there as if to feel his pulse, he was reminded that she had once been a nurse.

"How are you feeling?"

He was vaguely aware that April Lamotte was sliding away from him and re-buttoning herself up. Of shifts and rattles as she collected things.

"You okay? Clark? Dan? Mr Gable? Can you hear me?"

He opened his mouth. His throat was filled with something dry and sandy that wouldn't cough up. Her fingers touched his eyes. He tried to blink, bat her away, but his limbs seemed lost. He felt the rock of the springs, heard the door slam. Heard another door opening, closing. Decided that it was probably the trunk. The Delahaye's vee eight engine was a warm, dull pulse like the pounding of his heart, which changed slightly as a dark oval, some kind of hose, was wedged into the corner of the window beside him.

There was movement. Footsteps. The indistinct sound of another car starting, a flash of headlights. Then, as he tried to claw himself toward consciousness and scrabbled for a key which wouldn't budge, then window and door buttons which did nothing, he was only aware that he was inside a car, and that its motor was running, and that he was entirely alone.

THIRTEEN

The darkness stayed with him for what seemed like a long time. Then, vaguely, as he slumped down and forward, he was aware that the car radio had come on. Glowing dials through the choking haze, and the soothing strings of the Fred Waring Orchestra and the down-home southern drawl of Wallis Beekins on NBC with *stories, interviews and good old gossip live and living from the Land of the Stars . . .* The words and the city spread below him vanished through spasms of pain into a black, stinking tunnel.

Funny, really, to have come so far, and yet to have got nowhere. The same empty nowhere that everyone ended up, he supposed. He was floating further out from the blackness now, and the intense burning in his lungs and throat was lessening. Just a guy in a car on some midnight overlook slowly dying from lack of oxygen. He could see himself with a curious detachment. Could see the pumping black hosepipe jammed hard through the window which his paralyzed limbs were too feeble to remove. He was a slumped body, starting to judder now, the lips graying, the eyes rolling in some final spasm, that someone would find in the morning when all life was gone, and briefly wonder about why and how. But not that much . . .

The weirdest thing was, he knew he wasn't alone. Something else was there with him inside the car. It squirmed up and out of the foul black air like a swimmer surfacing, and formed changing arms, and a face that wouldn't stay still. With terrible eyes flecked with engine fire, with clouds of the exhaust roaring from its oily mouth, it leaned forward to regard him. The thing seemed to be made entirely of smoke. His tongue thickened in his throat, rooting for empty air as he tried to cry out, but it was useless, hopeless...

The thing, the shape, the presence, wouldn't leave him. Perhaps it was death itself. And he knew it was close now. So close that he could feel it touching him. He saw his own hands lying lost and remote far down through the darkness, and felt stronger hands which burned and throbbed enclosing them. Their grip was remorselessly strong, and outflowing arms followed, drawing him into an ever-deepening embrace. And through it all there was a terrible pressure, an endless roaring.

He was past struggling. He was beyond help. But the thing of fumes really was holding him, lifting him, jerking his limbs like a puppet. He felt his head crack the steering wheel, felt his teeth snap sharp against his tongue. He saw his own hand twist out in front of him, saw it ablaze with rags of dark. Then his arm was wrenched sideways, and a sharp pain, bizarre in its ordinariness, slammed through him from his elbow. The pain flared again when the same movement repeated, but this time was followed by a glittering crash, and an extraordinary rush of air.

He grayed out for a moment. He gasped, gagged, his belly a writhing knot, as the fumes rushed out. But he was breathing. He was *breathing*, and the window beside him was broken and the black pipe which had been belching death had flopped away across the gravel and he was Clark fucking Gable and he was alive and his throat burned and his left elbow hurt like hell.

The engine was still running. He fumbled again at the key, wiggling the damn thing to and fro. Still wouldn't budge. Everything in this car was clever, electric; far too clever for him. He felt down around the ignition slot. Something small and rough had been wedged in there with the key. He picked and fumbled with numb fingers until it finally gave. Half a matchstick. Nothing more. He turned the key again. The Delahaye's vee eight subsided with a small, polite cough. The radio dial glowed. The soothing night sounds of the Fred Waring Orchestra playing *A Cigarette, Music and You* still poured out from the expensive Motorola speakers. He fumbled the door handle through a grit of broken glass. This time, it opened easily.

He stumbled from the car, fell to his knees in a spill of glass. He stayed hunched on all fours for some time, coughing and retching until the effort got too much and he slumped flat. Then, some unknowable time after, he came back to proper consciousness and—slowly, warily—used the Delahaye's open door to drag himself back up. He leaned swayingly against the car and looked around the dark overlook. Some kind of *presence* had been here with him. He was sure of it—as sure as he was that it wasn't some last spasm of his dying body that had broken that door pane. He listened. All he could hear was Wallis Beekins' soft burr from the radio, the chirp of the cicadas and his own thudding heart. He held up his hands, but the faintness and blurring came only from his dried and weary eyes. They were streaked with nothing but dirt and blood.

The night. The cicadas. Murmuring music. A solitary car went by above him on Mulholland Drive. He listened for another, but he guessed it could be a long wait. The city glittered thinly now. It was late, and dark.

Loosening his necktie, hawking and spitting, picking shards of glass and bits of gravel off himself, he clambered his way around the Delahaye's panels, pulled off the hose that had been fixed around one of the twin exhausts and threw the thing far out over the overlook barrier. He checked the trunk. Empty. No cardboard suitcase. Then he limped over toward the corner of the overlook where he'd thought he'd seen a parked car. That, too, had gone.

He slumped back down inside the Delahaye, holding the wheel and breathing hard. His head was pounding and his mouth tasted like a motor workshop floor. He found one of Daniel Lamotte's handkerchiefs and used it to wipe his hands and face, then brushed out some more of the glass. He checked inside the lit glove compartment and stared at the packet of Lucky Strikes which lay there, but the last thing he felt like was a smoke. The radio's backlit dial looked like sunset over some fairy city.

... and that's the last word worth hearing tonight from here in Tinseltown. To America and all her brave allies, this is Wallis Beekins wishing God's blessing and goodnight.

Then there was only hissing. Clicking it off, starting up the Delahaye's engine, he reversed from the overlook and turned back up onto Mulholland Drive.

FOURTEEN

Coming at Stone Canyon from over the mountains instead of up from the city as he'd done yesterday, he had to reorientate himself. When he passed a pull-in and saw the glint of the reservoir under a quarter moon behind him, he realized that he'd gone too far. He swung the Delahaye around to head back uphill, and nearly lost the road as he did so. He rubbed at the blackness in his eyes as the offside front wheel spun over emptiness. Told himself to concentrate and slow down. The car still stank of fumes even with the air streaming in through the broken window, but he didn't want to do a better job of killing himself than April Lamotte had done. Or risk getting stopped by the cops.

It was quiet up here in that way that even the valleys above Hollywood eventually grew quiet. Too early to be called late; too late to be called early. The house parties and the private showings finally finished, the stars and the players grabbing a precious few hours of beauty sleep before the next power breakfast or early make-up call.

Here it was. Woodsville. He drove more slowly from the bend into the estate, looking left and right along landscaped roads which climbed in rivers of silver between darkened drives, until he saw a copse of firs by the left hand verge which he reckoned to lie about two hundred yards from Erewhon's entrance. He pulled in, edged the car back and forth until it was parked mostly in shadow, then stopped the engine.

He sat. Waited. Listened. Only the wind now through the treetops. His elbow ached, he still felt awful, and the stink on his clothes and the taste in his mouth of automobile exhaust seemed worse now that he was breathing fresh canyon air. The car door made a clattering sound as he opened it. A bigger wave of nausea came over him. Hunched across the car, he waited until, in a sour acid flux, whatever was left of that expensive meal at Chateau Bansar emptied itself out of him.

What was he going to do when he got to Erewhon? He had no idea. There was no doubt that April Lamotte had tried to kill him, but why? Just thinking about it set his head spinning. It was a suicide she'd tried to stage, right? But if she wanted to kill Daniel Lamotte, surely she'd have killed *him*, not someone who looked like him . . . ?

He wiped his mouth. The deal had always been too good. Should have thought this through earlier. But at least he was still alive—he had that on April Lamotte. He was alive, when she thought she'd succeeded in killing him. Her guard would be down tonight. She'd be relieved, relaxed, doing whatever she was planning on doing next. He probably even had the keys to Erewhon right here along with the Delahaye's in his pocket. And he knew he didn't have a great amount left to lose. Not when you considered all he'd already lost or thrown away. In that narrow sense, Clark Gable thought of himself as a realist.

The air here was denser, scented with all kinds of night plants. Wet fronds shoved against him as he hunch-ran along the side of the road. Something large and winged fluttered briefly against his face. Then, he saw the entrance to the drive leading to the house. He slowed. How big were the gardens? How long was the drive? Should have paid more attention yesterday, Clarkie baby, although he could hardly have expected to plan on the events of tonight. Still, doing what he was doing right now didn't feel so odd. Creeping through undergrowth toward someone else's home was a regular part of his work. Although he'd normally have brought along a camera loaded with high sensitivity film. He'd have dressed in darker clothes as well, although this suit was a whole lot grayer and more blotched now than it had been a few hours ago.

He ducked across the road to the marble sign beneath a fuchsia hedge. His fingers traced that odd word *Erewhon*. Then, as he worked his way around to look up the drive, he froze. A dark figure was standing in the shadows just up from Erewhon and on the far side of the road. A wave of dread washed over him. That thing in the car . . . But no. The figure was moving, hands in pockets, swaying its legs and working its shoulders in the way that a person might do in order to keep limber and warm. And the figure was slim, and tall, and dressed in some kind of uniform. He even caught the gold glint of a badge. Slowly, as noiselessly as he could, Clark backed off and around the fuchsia hedge. Leaning into the undergrowth, he took in a long breath. He could still hear the figure shuffling, hear the soft tread of boots on dew-damp grass. Could hear him whistling. It was a sound as thin and empty of melody as the wind passing through the nearby trees, but far more chilling. Whatever it was that the Gladmont Securities guy was doing here, it couldn't have much to do with his normal business of keeping Fuller Brush salesmen out of Woodsville.

Clark backed further off, the nausea returning and his breathing more rapid now. He could wait here, he guessed. Or run. Venice? But April Lamotte and whoever else was involved in this knew exactly where he lived. Maybe somewhere further, safer, more anonymous. But where— and safe from what? He didn't trust his judgment tonight. He knew his reactions were dulled and raw. But what the hell *was* this about? What *had* April Lamotte really been trying to do?

So he got this rental, a cheap place Downtown on Bunker Hill. Called it reconnecting. He went there, and he took his typewriter with him. That, and a few reams of paper and some old clothes. And I let him go, Mr Gable. I let him go . . .

FIFTEEN

He took empty Wiltshire, past the Brown Derby and the Ambassador Hotel, then turned north and uphill away from the civic quarter. The streetlamps were fading. The sky in the east was already gray. Feral cats darted from gone-wild gardens as the Delahaye climbed the steep streets of Downtown.

On a series of rises, starting with Bunker Hill and heading north and east towards Pound Cake, the wealthy Angelinos of the previous century had built themselves an enclave of grand houses, given their new streets hopeful names like Spring and Flower and Olive, and settled down to live the kind of life they felt they fully deserved. A hundred years had passed. New Downtown had become Old Downtown and now Santa Monica, Beverly Hills, North Hollywood, Malibu and new valley estates like Woodsville were the places to live.

Pausing briefly to renew his old sense of direction, he took a left up from New High Street. Bladen? Barden? No, it was *Blixden* Avenue. As soon as he saw the street sign, he was sure that this was the address he'd seen on the topsheet of *Wake Up and Dream*. Some apartment—room 4A. And here at the far dead end was a residence that had once, according to the chiseled engraving on the gate pediment, been called Appleton Manor, and now had Blixden Apartments roughly painted on the brickwork beside. Yes, this was the place: a dark old mansion at the dark end of a street which had seen better centuries, let alone years, it was typical of the way these once-proud lodgings had been divided. Odd bits of once-new window and half-assed plumbing warted the brownstone front. On the opposite side of the street was a weed-grown lot where one of the other large houses had finally given out altogether and collapsed like a rotted tooth.

What had April Lamotte called it, *reconnecting*? It sure as hell would have given the guy a change of perspective, Clark thought, as he stepped out into the early morning chill and worked the Delahaye's door quietly shut. A dog was barking somewhere, but otherwise there was no one about. The type of residents you got on Bunker Hill didn't get up much before noon, as he recalled. He flicked quickly through the Delahaye's keys. The others were all new and shiny, but this well-worn Yale would be a good fit for a place like Bunker Hill. He creaked open the front gate and took the weeded path. There were the brass plates of a couple of registered offices beside the door, although they were so tarnished he doubted if the companies still existed. That, and a bellpull which he had no intention of pulling. There was no sign of a lock. He took hold of the big old doorhandle. It gave with a loose *clonk*.

The breath of ages swirled about him.

Floors creaking. People snoring. A man coughing. Taps dripping. The scurry of silverfish and cockroaches across communal kitchen floors. A vegetable stench which probably wasn't vegetables at all. Whatever had made him think the Doge's Apartments was a run-down dump? Old buildings really did retain an atmosphere—years of emotion were absorbed by their surroundings. Then, yet more slowly, it seeped back out.

He blinked and waited as the hallway slowly emerged in the pre-dawn wash of the fanlight above the doorway. A gas chandelier—a huge aggregation of tubular iron and cobwebs—hung from a dangerously cracked rosette. A wide and once impressive stairway curved up to his left. Common sense suggested that 4A wouldn't be the first room he encountered, but he checked the two doors to the right, just to be sure. One had a card offering palm and tarot readings attached by a rusty pin. The other had nothing to indicate what it was. Down at the far end, another door led toward what Clark guessed was the old kitchens or cellars. It was locked.

The stairs' first runner announced his presence with a shuddering creak, but, through years of practice of getting quietly in and out of houses for reasons that weren't always entirely professional, he managed more quietly after that. A balcony curved one way across the second floor, and a corridor went the other. A mossy rooflight gave everything a greenish, underwater glow. The doors up here were numbered, their fine old mahogany roughly painted by what looked like the same less-than-artistic hand which had scrawled Blixden Apartments over the bricks outside. Following the passageway, he finally came to 4A. He listened for a moment, then glanced both ways along the bucking corridor. A woman laughed somewhere. A mattress creaked. A man cried out. The key fitted in the loose sort of way which suggested long use. It snagged, then turned.

He felt quickly for the light as he eased the door shut—expecting, what? Daniel Lamotte's rotting body? April Lamotte waiting with a gun?—but only a tall cream-painted wardrobe and the humped blankets of a slept-in bed, actually no more than a mattress, swam into view from the bare lamp's wan glow. Heaped in most of the other available spaces, including the floor, were piles of typed manuscripts. A blackened sink hung precariously from the wall beneath an equally blackened mirror. A cheap office desk stood close by the window. The air smelled sour and stale.

He picked his way through a detritus of empty Cream of Kentucky Bourbon bottles and cans of Campbell's Tomato Soup. No sprawled bodies. No pools of blood. No bullet holes. No hanging corpses. No chopped-up limbs. The wardrobe contained nothing but clothes.

He pulled off the jacket and drooped it over the back of the chair and slumped down at the desk. A reporter's typewriter sat there amid the overflowing piles of notebooks and cigarette butts: they were all Luckies. He flicked randomly through a few of the many typed pages. They all looked broadly similar to the white version he'd read of the script for *Wake Up and Dream*.

He glanced around again, trying to call his professional mind into order and get a proper impression of the place. This really was the pad of a writer, that much was for sure. He'd have put the occupant down as a troubled and penniless bachelor, but maybe that had been the effect Daniel Lamotte had been trying to recreate in an effort to entice his muse down from that pedestal on which he'd placed it back at Erewhon. The room was in such a mess that it was impossible to tell if anyone else had been here before him, but if they had, it would certainly be difficult to work out what they had taken.

There was no paper in the typewriter. He lifted a fresh sheet of pale blue paper from the sheaf on the left hand corner of the desk and wound it in through the rollers. He hit the m key. Then he searched around for the gizmo which made capital letters. After all tonight's chaos, it was neat—the way the machine's gleaming innards levered up—and the clacking sound it made was oddly reassuring. It filled the room in a way which his own presence alone did not.

```
m My n ame ias dDani eel Lame
```

He stopped. Dim corners of the room seemed to shrink back in scuttles and eddies as he glanced around him. He even felt his face to see if he was still wearing the glasses, which he wasn't. There was also a faint hissing sound. He shook his head. Gas? No, just tiredness. Or draughts. Or maybe ghosts of the times of lost grandeur in this house—some mustachioed patriarch who'd moved here from back east, big with his plans of all the things which he'd build in this new city... And the ladies with their parasols and calling cards... And clocks ticking and maids whispering, and all the many people who must have died here, or been born... Clark could feel the cold breath of all of these memories whispering around him...

Dragging the paper out and balling it, he looked around for a bin to aim for in the manner of all frustrated writers and failed to find one. Close by the desk, though, he noticed a darker shape lying on top of the other detritus. Just a sheet of carbon paper, although the thing felt slick and oily between his fingers when he lifted it up. It only seemed to have been used once; amid the deep gloss of fresh black ink, he could still even make out the marks of the individual letters on the sheet.

He held it up to the blotched mirror above the sink, and squinted hard.

```
Thrasis Thrasis Thrasis Thrasis Thrasis Thrasis
Thrasis Thrasis Thrasis Thrasiss Thrasis Thrasis
Thrasis Thrasis Thrasis Thrasis Thrasis. .
Tthrasis Thrasis Thrasis Thrasis Thrasis Thrasis
Thrasis Thrasis thrasis Tharsis Thrasis Thrasis
Thrasis Thrasis Thrasis Thrasis yThrasis Thrasis
Thrasis Thrasis Thrasis Thrasis Thrasis.
ThrasisThrasis Thrasis Thrasis THrasis Thrasis
Thra
   sis aaa aa Thrasis

   Thrasis

   t THRASIS
   Thrasis

   Thrasis

   Thrasis Thrasis Thrasis Thrasia Thrasis Thrasis
   Thrasis Thrasis TThrasiis Thrasis Thrasis Thrasis
   Thrasis Thrasis Thrasis Thrasis Thrasis Thrasis
   Thrasis Tharsis Thrasis Thrasis Thrasis Thrasis
```

A stronger sense of things shifting washed over him. No, this time it was actual nausea. Dropping the carbon, he twisted on the sink's tap. Distant pipes honked and yammered. Lukewarm water gushed. He splashed his face and drank. Then he jerked off his shirt and necktie and took the dried-up cake of soap and used it to wash himself.

His body ached. His throat felt raw. His left elbow throbbed. But at least he was alive. At least he wasn't dead in that fucking car. After drying himself with a stale towel hung over the sink bracket, he peered once into the blotched mirror. All he could see was a vague blur. He tried rubbing it clear with the towel, but that only made it worse.

The shape of a face was there, but it wouldn't settle. The stuttering movement reminded him of watching an old movie when the film kept slipping on the spool. No, it was more like one of those flip-things he'd made from corners of exercise books at school, with a face with a slightly different expression drawn on each page. And there was still that hissing, murmuring sound.

He blinked and glanced away from the mirror to steady his gaze. A wave of relief passed over him when he looked back and saw the blurring faces had steadied into something resembling his own. But it lasted barely a moment. The face hovering before Clark had something like his eyes, and mouth, and ears. But they weren't the same. The nose was broader, and the cheeks and the jawline were covered by a poorly-trimmed beard. When he reached toward his chin, a hand within the mirror did the same. His fingers touched dense, springy hair.

He didn't know if he cried out. But the hissing grew louder. That, and an undertow of echoing moans. And a terrible sense of pain. And then, like a balloon deflating, like a door slamming, like the wind falling after a thunderstorm, it was gone.

Clark grabbed back hold of the sink. He was staring through the smudged glass at nothing more than his own face. He looked ill and tired, for sure, but that was all. As certainly as some other presence had been in here with him, he was now certain that it was gone. Outside the sash window, another beautiful California sunrise was spreading across the sky. He slumped back to the desk chair and cupped his head in his hands.

SIXTEEN

A muffled voice. A knocking.

He started. A grubby fall of yellow light lay pooled beneath a window. The knocking came again.

"Mr Lamotte..."

Mr La—? Then he remembered. And with memory came a sourness in the back of his throat at the huge rush of near-impossible events. He groaned and eased himself from the cluttered desk across which he'd been lying. Pens and papers fell. His bruised elbow gave a sharp spasm. He'd called out "Yeah?" before he thought about keeping quiet.

"Sorry to bother you..."

He looked at the Longines watch on his wrist. It was already half past eight. He was in this guy's room and he must have dozed off—no, slept. He stumbled up from the chair and across the littered room, hesitated, stumbled back to fumble in his suit jacket for the glasses and hook them around his ears, then stumbled back to the door and worked it open a crack. The female he saw in the gap was young, and fairly attractive.

"I heard you come in last night," the young and fairly attractive female said. She sounded friendly enough, although she was staring at him in an odd way. "I knew that you'd be working this morning like you do. So I decided that I might as well interrupt your muse now rather than make a bigger intrusion later. Like that visitor from Porlock."

"Porlock?"

"You know. Coleridge. Kubla Khan."

"Oh. Yeah." He remembered the poem from a book Jenny had once read to him. He let the door swing open a little more.

The woman—girl almost to his eyes, although he guessed she was past twenty—was of mid-height. She was dressed in the sort of mannish clothes, and had the kind of mannish haircut, which he would have associated with a certain kind of lesbian back in his theatrical days. Brown slacks, low-heeled loafers without socks, a striped blue shirt with the front and tails hanging. She didn't seem to be wearing any make-up.

"You know who I am?"

"D Lamotte. Flat 4A. The D is for Daniel. You used to have a beard—that whole Walt Whitman look. I think I prefer you without." She held out a small bundle of post. "So I guess this must be yours."

He took the bundle from her and tucked it under his arm. "Thanks, ah..."

"You don't remember my name?"

"Sorry."

"It's hardly like we've seen much of each other. I'm Barbara Eshel from 3A next door." She held out her hand through the gap. Unlike most of the women in this city, she didn't paint her nails.

He was conscious of her eyes still busily taking him in. The stained and ruined clothes. The black rings he must have under his eyes. He probably also still stank of puke and gasoline fumes.

"I've, ah, been away."

"Which explains why it's been so quiet in here these last few days..." He saw her wrinkle her nose as she glanced inside at the room.

"That's pretty much the whole story."

"But it's not, though, is it?"

"You got me there," he muttered.

"I mean," the girl continued, "you're a famous screenwriter. *This Point Backwards* was one of my favorite feelies when I was a kid. You should be a whole lot more famous than you are."

"Oh? Right. Thanks."

"And *The Magic of the Past*. Didn't you write that as well?"

He had no idea. He gave a vague grunt and pressed lightly back against the door.

"And *The Virgin Queen*."

"Yeah. Everyone seems to remember that one."

"But, I'll bet ten gets fifty, not who the writer was?"

"It can be tough."

"I know. I mean, being a writer myself. Or at least, someone who produces words... I've listened to you type all these last months. It's been a sort of companionship, having you nearby—like a friendly ghost. Then last week you just stopped." She smiled and shrugged. "And now you have your mail."

"Thanks again." He smiled back at her as he closed the door, then listened for a moment to the creak of her footfalls, wondering as he did so about all the other things he could have asked her. But maybe not. He wasn't so much in uncharted territory here as right off the edge of the whole map.

There were just two letters and not much else. A *One Of Our Operatives Called When You Were Out* card from the water company, although he imagined that kind of stuff was paid for out of the communal rent. A few flyers for weird churches and get-rich-quick schemes and talent scouts. All the usual detritus you found on a typical LA doormat. He used a chewed pencil to slit open the first letter.

METROPOLITAN STATE HOSPITAL

June 21 1940
Dear Mr. Lamot

I am instructed by the Directors and trustees to
t hank you for your fuurther enquiry regarding
an appointment to interview one of our
residents.

Y°ur request has been fully reconsidered, but
infortunately must still be declined. Whilst Mr
H oward Hughes continues to be the subjec of
much public speculation, it remains against both
his and the Metropolitan State Hospital's
interests for him to have external contacts,
both on clinical and humanitarian grounds.

I trust this f ully answers your enquiry.

I remain, etc

J. Kilbracken
J. Kilbracken.
Clinical D¹rctor

Clark tapped the pencil against his teeth as he read the letter again. The Met had had some well-known residents in its time, but Hughes was probably their most famous current guest. It made sense for Daniel Lamotte to try to speak to the guy now, even if he was insane, to tie up any loose knots in *Wake Up and Dream*. He thought for a moment longer, then folded the letter back into its envelope and laid it aside.

The other was in a heavier, creamier envelope. The sort of stationery which he associated with upscale lawyers. He almost broke the pencil ripping it open. It was beautifully typed and the letter heading, with BECHMEIR TRUST heavily embossed, was a classy dark red, with the Willowbrook ex-schoolhouse which was now also a museum as the address.

BECHMEIR MUSEUM
WILLOWBROOK

20 June 1940

Dear Mr Lamotte

WITHOUT PREJUDICE

Thank you for your further query of the 16th inst, which has been passed to me as Charitable Director.

As you know, our Founder has not engaged in public works for several years. However, we note once again your interest in a project involving his life, and at this time wish to express no fundamental objection to it.

We are copying this letter to our Attorney at the address below, whom we suggest you or your Production Company contact at your earliest convenience with regard to arranging an appointment. In any event, an appropriate donation toward the Trust's many good works from any profits arising would be appreciated.

Yours truly,

P. Losovic
p.p.

P Losovic MD (Miss)

Hardly a ringing endorsement, p.p. as well, but at least they were only fishing for money, and they weren't threatening to sue. He knew enough civil law to understand that there was nothing that Bechmeir or his trust could do directly to stop a biopic as long as it wasn't defamatory, which nothing in the script he'd read suggested it was. Still, the Trust's support, whether bought or not, would be incredibly useful. He imagined Lars Bechmeir resurrected back there in spotlight with his avuncular smile and trademark pipe and cane, walking up the red carpet on the night of *Wake Up and Dream's* premiere. What a publicity coup that would be.

Trying the desk drawers, he found a dented pack of Lucky Strikes in the top right, and a book of matches with *Edna's Eats* printed on the front, which rang an odd sort of bell. He noticed that his hand was shaking as he lit one up. He found a wad of other papers in the second drawer down on the right and flicked through them as he smoked. There was a receipt from a firm called RTS Taxis for twelve dollars sixty—a huge amount for any taxi journey—from last Thursday, June 20th. Not the sort of thing anyone would normally keep, or even ask for, although it didn't seem so odd to Clark. After all, he was self-employed, and he knew what the IRS were like. Another receipt, this one from some production facility off Pacific Boulevard called Feel-o-Reel for eighty dollars, dated back on March 27th. Big bucks. He remembered that wraith back at Erewhon. Clark had to admire the guy if he was planning on claiming that so-called Muse against tax. There was also a dog-eared green admission card to the reading rooms at the Los Angeles Central Public Library, which was nothing more than what you'd expect any self-respecting freelance writer to possess.

The rest was letters. Mainly, they went back through May into early June, and were answers to other requests for interviews or information. Most were about as helpful as the two he'd just opened. *Regret* this and *sadly* that. He supposed it wasn't just actors who had to put up with rejection.

He placed the new correspondence on top of the old, then checked the other drawers. Nothing but all the usual desk detritus—rubber bands, paper clips, pencil sharpeners, bits of string, dried-up bottles of ink. The final, bottom left hand drawer seemed to be either locked or jammed. Then it gave and something hard and heavy inside clunked. It was a .38 snubnose Colt.

He lifted the gun out, checked the safety, and swung open the cylinder, which was fully loaded with five rounds. He sniffed the barrel; it smelled of freshly lathed metal. There was also a box of slugs, which looked to be unused as well. The snubnose Colt was a common enough piece—it fitted easily into a shoulder holster or even a coat pocket—but what possible use could it be to a writer like Daniel Lamotte?

He laid the Colt back down on the desk with a small shudder; he had a near-phobic dislike of guns. Why had a guy like Daniel Lamotte gone out and got himself one—and recently by the look of it? Was *this* research, as well? More likely, he'd done so because he feared for his life. Yesterday Clark had dismissed the idea that April Lamotte was capable of killing her husband, but that was before he'd discovered what else she was capable of.

This whole weird business reminded him of trying to put together a jigsaw he'd had as a kid. It was something Jenny had brought home from a bring-and-buy, not that they had much spare to do either, but he'd cherished that old jigsaw of the States of America in its even older biscuit box. Of course, there was no New Mexico then, or Arizona, and Colorado and Arkansas were missing, and Alabama, Mississippi and Texas had lost their printed paper fronts.

Getting the whole thing to fit together had been so frustrating that little Billy Gable had been tempted to get one of his dad's saws from the workshop and hack a few of the most obdurate states up. He and Jenny had eventually worked out that a couple pieces of a different States of America jigsaw had somehow gotten jumbled in with the rest. Sitting at Daniel Lamotte's desk, he felt the same overpowering need to fit the spilled mess of recent events into some recognizable whole.

April Lamotte. The way she'd dressed him up, primed him—bribed, and fed, and then near seduced him, all in the coldest possible blood. And those little touches. Things which were still going off like cold bombs in his head. The way she'd mentioned, oh so casually, that he'd been having a difficult time in the office of that lawyer. And those tears at Chateau Bansar—they fitted in as well. That was, if you wanted to create the impression of a troubled man in a troubled marriage, the kind of character for whom even signing a big new contract might just be the tripwire to gassing himself up on some Mulholland overlook in his fancy French car.

Confront the bitch. That was the only way out. He didn't just owe it to himself. He owed it to Daniel Lamotte.

SEVENTEEN

These clothes really did stink. He checked again in the wardrobe. Both the pale linen suits hanging there were almost equally crumpled. So were the shirts. But at least they were fresh. He stripped down to his undershorts, pulled off the socks. Then, seeing as there were also some fresh undershorts inside the wardrobe, he pulled those off as well.

He took off the glasses and washed in the rickety sink, and risked checking his face again in the mirror, which was now nothing more than a grubby sheet of silvered glass held to the wall by rusty screws in three of its four corners showing a face something like his own. He searched briefly for a razor, then remembered Daniel Lamotte's straggly beard.

He shifted the keys, billfold and identity papers from the old suit coat to the new, hooked the Ray-Bans into the top breast pocket, and pocketed the remaining Lucky Strikes, and matches as well. He stared at the Colt for a long moment. Then he checked the safety, and slid it into his outside suit coat pocket.

He could hear the click of a typewriter coming from one of the other rooms as he headed out through the old house. He thought of that girl Barbara Eshel in room 3A and her talk of friendly ghosts. On the front stoop he checked the Longines watch. Just past ten o-clock. Then he felt in his top pocket for the tortoiseshell glasses, only to discover he'd already put them on.

It wouldn't be true to say that Blixden Avenue had exactly come to life this morning, but it wasn't entirely dead. An ice-vendor's old carthorse nosed its feedbag. A guy had his head buried under the hood of a rusty old car up on bricks. And some kids were around kicking a can. They looked about as feral as the cats he'd seen earlier.

There was a phone booth beneath the shade of some overgrown willows about halfway along the street. He walked down to it, worked the door open. The way the air smelled inside, he left it open. Miracle of miracles, this year's city telephone directory still hung from its chain. He hefted it up, flicked through to the Gs. It was no great surprise to find that there was no listing for a company called Gladmont Securities.

He fumbled in his pockets for change, lifted the receiver, fed the slot, asked to be put through to the Venice exchange, then gave the number for the communal phone at the Doge's Apartments. He waited several rings. Then several more. He pictured Glory scowling in her cubbyhole. Finally, on about the twentieth ring, there was a breathy clatter as the receiver was lifted.

"'Lo?"

"It's Clark here."

"What *you* want?"

"Just to let you know I'm okay."

"'S'if I care."

"Anyone been around? Any visitors? Messages?"

The pause seemed to last almost as long as the ringing tone.

"Come on, Glory."

"That woman. She call again. Say she don't trust her husband."

"Any number?"

"I think maybe."

"Have you got it?"

"I'm no answering service."

"Glory..."

He waited as she tromped off, and had to feed the phone some more nickels before she came back again. He ripped a page out of the directory, scrawled down the number she gave him, balled it into his pocket and promised that, sure, yes, absolutely, he'd call.

"And nothing else? No callers, no one asking questions?"

"Only question I ask is why you think I do this for you."

He thanked Glory and hung up. A can thwanged off the Delahaye's front wing as he headed back up the street.

"Hey, hey!" He shouted. "What the hell d'you think you're doing?"

The kids just eyed him. Then one of them—not the largest, but obviously the leader—swaggered over with the manner of someone who wouldn't normally cross a street for anyone or anything, but was prepared to make a rare exception this morning. Squinting through crusted eyes, the kid gave Clark the up and down. He was in short pants and a holed gray jumper which showed even grayer bits of bare rib beneath. He wore pumps with flapping soles, without socks. He was roughly five feet tall. Clark guessed him to be about twelve years old.

"That's an expensive car, you know."

The kid, making the same kind of effort he had to cross the road, just about managed a shrug. "Pity about that broken window. All it takes is one person to take a piss inside it and all them fancy carpets are ruined."

"You got any idea," Clark asked, "who I am?"

"If you don't know that yourself, pal, you got problems." The kid had a quick, crackly voice. "Alls I know is you're just come out of that termite hotel." The kid gestured. "My da says there's nothing in there but fags and queens."

"You got a name, kid?"

"You got one?"

Clark hesitated only fractionally. "I'm Daniel Lamotte. Used to have a beard before I shaved it off. Maybe you've seen me around . . . ?"

"You mean the guy who goes out late evenings in a grubby ice cream suit, then comes back with a whole load of bottles? Ain't been around for a few days . . . Although you don't *look* much the same."

Clark fingered his jaw. "Like I say, it's the beard. Say, shouldn't you be at school?"

"Shouldn't *you* be at work?"

He had to smile. "You know my name, kid, but I still don't know yours."

"Why should I tell you?"

"Why not?"

The kid considered. His mates were still watching. "Name's Roger

Preston," he eventually drawled. "Next time you have ze questions, you vill know vhere to go." He was putting on one of those crappy German accents Clark had heard in radio trailers for the latest feelies.

"Sounds like a deal. Here, Roger..." Reaching into his jacket, he produced a dime. "Maybe this'll help, now we both know who we are?"

"Won't do any harm." All in one swift motion, the kid had pocketed the coin.

"Oh. One last question."

"Fire away."

"You say I haven't been around for a few days. D'you know exactly what day it was that I left?"

"Like I say, if you can't—"

"Okay, okay. But did you happen to see anything unusual around that time?"

Roger scratched at his belly through a hole in his jumper. "What kind of unusual?"

"Oh, I don't know. Cars. People. Maybe an ambulance. Perhaps the police. Any kind of thing."

"Oh, I get it! You were so soused you can't remember—like my da?"

"Well, maybe."

"Can't say as I did. Like I say, you're around getting boozed in that faggot hole, and then you're not."

"Well thanks, Roger. See you around."

"Not if I see you first."

Working open the Delahaye's door, Clark started up the engine. The kids stood and stared. Even the old carthorse seemed to be watching as he reversed out of the dead end and drove off down the street.

EIGHTEEN

Another blue sky. Another clear, sharp morning, with the smog blown clear to the Pacific's glinting rim. Every angle of every rooftop and the glinting hubcap of every car were so uncannily sharp it was like some special effect in a big-budget feelie. But none of it felt real.

He remembered the lit radio's hissing, and Wallis Beekins' voice. For all that his throat was still raw, his elbow throbbed, glass fragments sparkled in the Delahaye's carpeted footwell and the car still stank of burnt gasoline, whatever had happened yesterday felt like it belonged to some distant age. Those near-last moments on the overlook especially.

Suicide was, he supposed, what men often did, especially in this city. Drive up to some scenic spot and put a hose from the exhaust in through the window. Just let the dark carry you away. Better than a gun; more modern, and far less messy. For women, it was still generally pills, booze, maybe a hot, scented bath and a few deep cuts with a razor. Or you could hook a noose around your neck and jump off a bridge the way Betty Bechmeir had done.

He took Sunset past Barnsdall Park and whatever the builders were putting up in place of the burnt-out lot that had once been Grauman's Chinese Theater—more shops, probably. Life everywhere. Pretty women. Streetcars, cars, horsedrawn carts and buses and streetsweepers and outdoor cafés all bustled in the sunlight. But, as the land rose and he took the valley road north on this clear smogless day and the whole city began to spread below him, it all looked like some complex checkerboard, and the surrounding mountains were purple-headed Gods, hunched in debate over what game they would next play with all those tiny creatures which scurried beneath.

No other automobiles hovered in his rearview as he drove on toward Stone Canyon, but after what he'd seen last night, he had no intention of driving straight up through Woodsville's front entrance to Erewhon. He did instead what he should have done the first time around, not to mention the second, and slowed as he got closer to the estate until he saw a wide but unassuming dirt track heading up and off. Places like this always had another way in for tradesmen and garbage collectors. Passing along a tall metal-posted chainlink fence, he pulled off and stopped the Delahaye in scrub. He waited. The sun was already hot. Dust settled and ticked on the car's panels. Gripping the gun in his pocket, he climbed out, eased the door shut and walked through an open gate into the back of the Woodsville estate.

Nothing more than he'd have expected. Hedges, heaps of grass cuttings and looping power and telephone lines. Then he saw a stooped figure pushing a wheelbarrow down a laurel avenue. Clark barely had to increase his pace to catch up. As he did so, he realized that this was the same guy he'd noticed the first time he'd driven up to Erewhon, pushing what was probably the same wheelbarrow. The way he moved, the whole look of him, was pretty distinctive.

"Hi there."

The man, little more than a huge boy really, stopped and put down his wheelbarrow and turned. He had the egg-shaped face, loose lower lip, and pudding-bowl haircut of the sort of person Jenny would have described as being *blessed by simplicity*.

"Was just coming in the back way. Looking for a place called Erewhon."

"Who are you?" Pudding-bowl didn't exactly look hostile. But it was hard to tell.

"I, ah, live there. Name's Daniel Lamotte. Perhaps you know me? Or April Lamotte?"

His bottom lip pushed itself out. "You mean Mrs Lamotte from Erewhon?"

"That's right. She's my wife. You know her?"

"Sometimes gets me to do stuff," he mumbled as he rooted in his ear, then studied his fingertip.

"You, ah, work on keeping all the grounds of Woodsville nice and tidy, right?"

He nodded.

"Sorry—I guess I don't know your name?"

"Evan."

"Well, Evan, I'm Mrs Lamotte's husband. I guess you haven't seen me much . . . ?"

Evan just gazed back at him with a look which suggested he really just wanted to get on with pushing his wheelbarrow.

"Tell you what, Evan." He pointed up between the hedges. "Is Erewhon this way? I'll just follow you . . ."

They reached a sort of inner crossroads, where all the back pathways through which this estate was serviced intersected. There were trashcans, lawnmowers, shacks, an old flatbed truck, moldering piles of compost, a lazy drone of flies.

"Don't happen to have seen my wife around much lately?"

"Like I say. She sometimes gets me to do stuff."

"You mean in her garden at Erewhon? I guess she gets her own gardeners in usually, though?"

He shrugged.

"Like what kind of thing?"

"Bonfire a couple of days ago. Just help her burn stuff."

"A . . . You mean, *she* was burning things?"

"Just papers." Another shrug. "She came an' asked if I'd got some stuff needed burning to help it along. 'Course, I always have . . ."

"Papers. Right. You, ah, wouldn't happen to know if she or anyone else is around in Erewhon right now?"

"Don't think so. Been quiet lately. Saw her car go out, though."

"You mean—"

"Red Cadillac. Saw it go by out down the road 'bout an hour ago."

"And she was in it? Alone?"

Evan nodded. He glanced longingly toward the waiting manure heap, and then his wheelbarrow. His eyes were starting to glaze.

"Well, thanks, Evan. You've been a big help. Which of these tracks leads to Erewhon by the way? Sorry, but I don't know this way much . . ."

"Right up there." Evan gave Clark a just-must-be-stupid look. "There's a sign right over the top spells it out."

Clark was about to turn. Then he stopped. "Say, Evan. Just one last question. You don't happen to know who does the security around Woodsville—I mean, working here, you must see them about . . . ?"

"That'd be Mr Hugens."

"What's he look like?"

"Mr Hugens? Oh, he's . . . " Evan puffed out his cheeks and made a circling movement around his waist with his arms.

"Sure—big old Mr Hugens. Of course. You ain't seen anybody else around, have you? Guy in a black Mercury sedan with a badge on the side says Gladmont Securities?"

"Only person I seen lately round here 'part from you is the telephone man."

"Sure, the telephone . . . " Once more, Clark was about to turn, but, squinting up in the warm sun, he saw that this was also the place where Woodsville's many phone lines intersected. After bunching against a final, fatter telephone pole, they then traveled down and into a small, concrete-sided shack less agricultural-looking than the others. "So there was some problem or other with the telephones needed fixing?"

Evan nodded. His look had settled to bored.

"He work the wires up on a ladder?"

" . . . No."

"He came and worked on the problem right in there, in that little exchange?"

"I guess."

"What was he like, this telephone guy? Thin? Good looking? Tall?"

Evan just about managed a nod.

Another modern touch in Woodsville's oh-so-modern world: a new automatic exchange. Pick up a phone, dial out a number and hey presto, you were right through without having to speak to another human being. Clark tried peering in through the window of wired glass. The heavy door had a sign with a Ma Bell logo on it, a warning against trespass, and a bolted hasp with a very thick padlock. He felt a surprising amount of give when he gave it a gentle tug. A harder pull, and the thing simply dropped apart in his hands. Glancing back to see that Evan was busy tipping his wheelbarrow over into a steaming pile of compost, he pulled open the door and slipped inside.

The space was narrow, dimly lit, filled with an electric buzz. A sudden flurry of clicking made him reach into his pocket for his gun. But these were just relays—this was how this place worked. Not that Clark knew about anything electrical unless it ran something inside a car, but he'd had a salesman come and see him only a few months back, tried to tell him about this new way forward for private investigators: forget about those grubby hotel sheets and dinner receipts and photos, all the modern dick needed was a wire tap. The Feds had been at it for ages—Clark had a dim recollection that it was how they'd done for Al Capone—but now, thanks in no small part to the burgeoning popularity of the feelies, the technology of wire-recording was available to anyone with the need of it, just as long as they weren't too worried about legalities and could step up a fifteen dollar deposit followed by twelve equal monthly payments of ten.

Another clatter as a call to somewhere went in or out. He could see how the racks of relays were individually labeled with house names. He ran his finger along the dusty housings until he came to the one which, hand-printed on a stuck-on scrap of paper, was labeled E<small>REWHON</small>. He peered more closely at this particular gray-enameled block of clever electrics. Then he checked the ones up and along. There was no doubt. Only the screwheads of Erewhon's telephone relay showed the clean glint of recently exposed metal.

Re-closing the heavy door, he looked more carefully at the loose padlock before hooking back the latch. In a bright circle, the tumbler for the key had been neatly drilled out.

Erewhon's glassy rooftops flashed at him from above waving trees as he squeaked open the gate leading to the back lawns. Still keeping close to the perimeter, he worked his way slowly around the grounds. You'd expect some kind of activity at a place like this, even if the lady of the house was out. Pool boys, gardeners, maids, masseurs, florists, handymen—all the legions of the cheaply paid who kept a place like this functioning even in these newly automated days when cars lit your cigarette and phones dialed themselves. But everything about Erewhon felt empty. No obvious movement at the windows—or cars outside the front, either, when he got to the side which faced the drive.

Then he caught an unmistakable smell. Watching out for poison ivy, he pushed through a recently crushed stretch of thicker undergrowth and reached a wide, clear black circle of burnt ground. It looked like one of those flying saucers people had started seeing had landed here. Taking hold of a burnt stick, he picked over the bonfire's residue. A few crusty leaves of what might have once been sheaves of paper adhered to the earth, but the next rain would get rid of even those. Skirting the edges and about to give up, his eyes caught a flash of blue. Poking through the withered grass, he picked up the corner of a butterfly-clipped sheaf of blue paper. Typed repeatedly on what was left of the end sheets were the beginnings of the words:

```
Wake Up
```

He dropped the scrap into his outer pocket. Then he made his way at a quick stoop between the bushes toward Erewhon. The house shone. Every window was closed, and every room he looked into seemed still and dark. Assuming now the easy posture of someone who had every right to be here, he walked around to the graveled front. This time, the sliding doors didn't move when he climbed the steps, but the bright silver key on his keychain fitted the black marble inset with smooth perfection.

NINETEEN

Absolute quiet. Not a breath of movement. That curving staircase which seemed to hang on nothing but shadows. A gloss on the floors so deep that walking over them felt like crossing a lake. He reached down into his suit coat pocket and felt the Colt's ribbed wooden grip. All the doors along the corridor which had previously been open to the garden were shut. With so much glass, and on a day this warm, the air was overpoweringly hot. There was a sour and musty smell, too; the big flower arrangements which had seemed so impressive before were wilting now as the water in their vases evaporated to sludge.

The wraith wasn't running this time, either. Just an empty plinth, with wires running out the back and a switch he hadn't noticed before on the side, although he certainly had no inclination to try to turn the thing on. The big room where April Lamotte had seen him, with its trophy tapestries and decorations, smelled as stale as the corridor, although it wasn't quite so hot. He'd been expecting—he didn't know what. But *something*. Instead, every which way he turned, all he saw was reflections, illusions, shadows.

The place felt almost overpoweringly empty. Yet everything was neat. Everything was just-so. The sort of neat and just-so, it occurred to him, that comes when someone tries hard to scrub away at their life until all that's left is surface brilliance.

He checked the other downstairs rooms, and down in the kitchens and the quarters for the maids, which were empty as well: the mattresses bare, the wardrobes clear of anything but a few coathangers. He peered inside big refrigerators and freezers; barely anything in them, either. He sniffed at the drains, and at the few drinks left in the drinks cabinet. He looked behind picture frames and inside toilet cisterns. Nothing, zilch, *nada* ...

Then there was a study, a small room far too tidy to be somewhere in which a guy like Daniel Lamotte would ever work. The desk was bare apart from a new black cradle-set bakelite phone, a letter-opener and some geometrically arranged pens. The desk drawers contained nothing but more stationery. He pulled them all the way out and felt around and underneath just to be sure, but found nothing more. The wood double file cabinet beside the desk was unlocked. The two big drawers held too many bills and receipts for him to do more than flick though, although he didn't doubt that any incriminating stuff would have been incinerated in that bonfire. But *what* stuff? And where exactly *was* April Lamotte?

He paid more attention to the bank statements, all of which were recent, and stacked with the kind of figures he wasn't used to seeing in his own communications from the Cali Fed and Gen. There'd been some big payments in, and then out again, recently. Tens of thousands of dollars since the spring. More evidence of someone getting ready to head off somewhere? He riffled back into the lower cabinet where he thought he'd noticed some legal-looking documents, and found secured loans, mortgages, terms of indenture. He remembered April Lamotte standing in the strange gloom of that room down the corridor. *I won't beat about the bush, Mr Gable. Dan and I need the money* ... That wasn't quite the picture he was getting here, but it was certainly the case that she'd used Erewhon's considerable value to get hold of a lot of fresh capital, and then done something with it all which looked to involve transferring large amounts of cash.

Blackmail? Was *that* it? Or maybe she was shunting everything to one side before she tried to declare for bankruptcy? Leaving papers like this which told any kind of story might have seemed odd, but Clark reckoned that everything here was either easy for someone else to check up on or was already on public record, and would have raised even more suspicions by its absence. What was missing here was the rest of the story. Whatever that story actually was.

He slid the two drawers back without taking any of the papers. After all, he had a key, and he was getting a feeling by now that April Lamotte wouldn't be coming back to Erewhon any time soon. Then, on second thoughts, he crouched down and reopened the file cabinets and felt around the inside backs and corners. His fingertips brushed something. He leaned harder and winced at the soreness of his bruised elbow. Then he had it. He lifted it out.

A torn out scrap of newspaper. On one side there was nothing but a bit of newsprint sky. The other showed an advert.

> **NERO INVESTIGATIONS**
> Fully State-Licensed
> Discreet and Professional
> "We Provide Answers Without Any Questions"
> Huntingdon 1799

She'd been coy enough about many things, but she'd admitted using some kind of private dick to find him, and Nero Investigations fitted the bill. Thing was, he knew who ran the set-up. Abe Penn might be a few steps up from him in the PI foodchain—with a valid license and an office with a working phone and maybe even a service secretary—but Clark couldn't believe that Abe would set him up with someone like April Lamotte without warning him. There might be little honor left in his particular trade. But there was some.

He picked up the phone and dialed Abe's number, picturing those relays down in that little exchange as he heard the clicks and buzzes. The line rang. It rang again. On the tenth ring, he put the handset back down in its cradle.

He looked more closely at the one picture on the wall. It was a glossy image in the full garish color of a realtor's brochure of a pine cabin surrounded by trees and the glimpsed peaks of mountains. The gold lettering said, *Larch Lodge, Bark Rise, Sierra Madre*. Not the sort of place which any backwoodsman would ever inhabit, but he remembered how April Lamotte had said something about a place they owned up in the mountains that Dan had gone to in one of his failed attempts to reconnect. He lifted the picture down, worked the photo out from its frame and stuffed it, along with the Nero Securities advert, in an inside pocket.

Upstairs, everything was just as empty, and just as swish. Along with a pool room which looked to have never been used to play pool in and several pristine guest suites, he found a dedicated feelie viewing room. It also functioned as a kind of library, with leather, brass and wooden fittings, although there wasn't a single book. The tall, dustless shelves along the side walls were stacked instead with boxed reels of film-stock and feelie wire. After all, why would a modern writer actually need to *read*? He studied the long rows with their title labels stuck beneath them for a few minutes, but they meant little to him—with his interest in the feelies, it was hardly likely they would. But yeah, now here *was* something just a touch out of place. There were odd gaps. Missing titles that were somehow suddenly as obvious, and as recent, as punched-out teeth. One of the labeled gaps he even recognized. It was *The Virgin Queen*.

He headed back along the thickly carpeted landing to a final set of double doors which, it turned out, led to the main bedroom suite. Midnight blue velvet curtains hung half-open before the shut doors of a Juliet balcony. White sheepskin rugs and low white divans floated amid their reflections like puffy summer clouds. There was a frieze behind the bed: a marquetry of polished woods suggestive of flames or the wings of birds. At least here, though, there was evidence of recent activity. The ash tray on the glass bedside table next to the phone was an over-brimming heap of pastel stubs, and there were several small indentations on the side of the mattress as if someone had repeatedly sat down and got up again from it, although the bed didn't look slept in. Still, he peeled back the blankets and carefully inspected the sheets. Freshly laundered. He detected none of the usual stains or scents.

The bath in the en-suite bathroom looked big enough to swim in. So, almost, did the toilet bowl. There was a steel and enamel cabinet hung on the wall. Bottles, syringes and pipettes filled its shelves. As he checked their labels he got a waft of that medicine cabinet smell. He wasn't much up on medical Latin, but he knew what Luminal was. *I had to nurse him.*

Calm him down, or get him up and back to coping with things. Of course, I knew where to get the necessary stuff . . .

He went back out into the bedroom and checked the walk-in closets. Dan's clothes took up a lot less space than his wife's—but he'd never been inside any marital home where that wasn't the way. He tried to picture April Lamotte in this room. Tried to picture her here last night, sitting on that bed and staring at that phone and getting up again and pacing this room and smoking all those cigarettes as she waited for the call from the police to tell her that her husband had been found dead in his car up on a Mulholland overlook. Tried to picture her here on other nights. Tried to picture her here with Daniel Lamotte.

He slid open bedside drawers. No rubbers, French postcards, German handcuffs or Swiss lubes. Hadn't she said that there wasn't much going on between them sexually, or was that just another ruse? He pocketed the half packet of Lucky Strikes he found on Dan's side. On April's, there was nothing more than you'd have expected a woman to keep where she slept. Odd bits of jewelry. Sanitary stuff. A few loose aspirin. He had another feel around the back of the drawer to check he wasn't missing anything and felt the slide of something papery and took out a small brown rectangular business envelope. There was no stamp but April Lamotte's name and address was neatly typed on the front. It had already been torn open, and looked to be empty. No. Not quite empty. The envelope slid and hissed when he moved it. He widened the top into a vee and tipped it toward his cupped palm. A thin stream of sand whispered and glittered. He wiped his hand, thought about putting the envelope back, then changed his mind and slid that into his pocket. Not that it made any sense. Not that anything here made much sense.

Erewhon was a plateglass brick wall. Best thing he could do would be to drive back to Blixden Avenue, grab as much other evidence as he could, then head off someplace and lie low for a while just to see what happened. Maybe he'd never know what April Lamotte had been up to, or whether her husband was dead or alive. Would that really be so bad?

He studied the long dressing table. Expensive perfumes and creams were lined like a miniature city in glass. He lifted one up, took off the cap, and sniffed. Chanel *Cuir de Russie*. A blunted lipstick in her shade of burgundy lay nearby. He rolled the thing in and out. Then, he heard the sound of tires on gravel.

Drawing out the gun, he stepped quickly back to the side of the half-drawn drapes and parted their edge to look out. A car—a Bentley tourer in British racing green—was heading up Erewhon's drive. It stopped out front. A largish guy got out. Hands on hips, he looked the house up and down. He was wearing what you'd probably term a business suit in this city, although you'd have put it at the gaudy end of weekend wear anywhere else. The plaid was bold but, for all of the colors which had gone into its weave, the bright mustard necktie managed to clash with every one.

The guy walked up to Erewhon's door. Electric gongs shimmered. A pause. The gongs shimmered again. Then he stepped back into sight. Once more, he looked up and around. He was young, and tall, and well-built in the way fit, affluent young men often are before they turn to fat.

"Hi? Is anyone *about*?"

He scanned the lawns.

"Mrs Lamotte? Anyone? *Mr* Lamotte . . . ?" In puzzlement, the guy shook his head. Wings of light brown hair shone like some glossy new man-made fiber as he tucked them back into place.

Clark dropped the edge of the curtains and re-pocketed the gun. He could let this character leave. But hadn't he just spent this morning trying to work out what was going on? He decided to risk it, and with the decision came a strange, pleasurable rush. Pushing the tortoiseshell glasses back up to the bridge of his nose, he turned the key in the balcony doors and stepped out.

The guy beneath looked up at the sound of the doors opening, shading his eyes against the sun.

"Can I help you?" Clark asked in a lighter, quicker voice.

"Yeah, well. I was . . . ." The guy was still squinting, staring. "Are you *really* Daniel Lamotte?"

"Guess I must be."

"Hey. Well, this is brilliant. I've been trying to call. Gee . . . " He flipped back his glossy hair once more. "I can't believe it. You're really *Daniel Lamotte!* This is just so, so . . . I'm your biggest fan. The absolute biggest.

I bored your wife with just how much I admire your work when we spoke. Sorry. Sorry. You probably don't even know who I am..." He spread his arms. "I'm Timmy Townsend, senior production executive at Senserama. It's my job to get *Wake Up and Dream* up on the screen. And what a job that is, eh?" He did a little spin and turn on the gravel, his arms still spread. "What a fucking job!"

TWENTY

"Dan, Dan . . ." Outside on the gravel, Timmy Townsend pumped Clark's hand. A Liberty League badge flashed on his lapel. "It's a real privilege. An absolute honor."

Timmy Townsend oozed happy confidence. His eyes shone. His grin was far more disarmingly boyish than any actual boy's, and he often broke into chuckles as he spoke. It was as if the combination of wealth, looks and charm which he'd almost certainly been born with was continually reoccurring to him.

"Neat little hangout you got here. So, anyway, I just got a call from my secretary telling me the signed contract's arrived. Seeing as I live down the valley and I got your address, I thought I'd look in and say hi. Is April here right now? Haven't you got some place in the city you hang out when you're working?"

Before Clark had a chance to think of a plausible reply, Timmy Townsend was talking again.

"I was just astounded, Daniel—or it's Dan, right, isn't it? Dan, yeah, Dan? somehow, I pictured you with a beard—when your latest script landed on my desk. My secretary, love her to pieces, the woman's a fucking genius, she knew how much I loved that movie about the queen . . ." He shot a finger at Clark and cocked his thumb.

"*The Virgin Queen*."

"Yeah! Absolute work of genius. I'm not shitting you when I say that it's one of the main reasons I'm working here in this city . . . Blew me away when I saw it at the showing room at our weekend place in Nassau County when I was a kid. I mean, we Townsends made our money in oil, but the feelies are the hot new ticket. I've gotta show you the Senserama facility, Dan. I really have."

Facility? Clark realized Timmy Townsend simply meant the studio. "Well, sure. That would be great. Sometime if—"

"Hey! Why not *right now*? I mean, I know you writers are always busy, and I sure don't want to distract you from your work now that the studio's money's riding on it—but, hey Dan . . . " He chuckled and spread his arms and turned, embracing in the gesture not just Erewhon and its grounds, but all of Woodsville, and the whole bowl of the city that Clark could see shimmering beneath them on this fine morning. " . . . why the hell not?"

Clark said he'd follow Timmy Townsend in the Delahaye, and gave him some guff about kids smashing a window and him not wanting April to see the damage as the reason why he'd left the car parked around back of the estate.

He decided he was getting a feel for this automobile as he pressed the right button to bring down the top and picked up the studio executive's green Bentley above the reservoir and followed him down into the city along the switchback bends. He liked the way it handled. The way, as they began to hit traffic, other vehicles gave way and onlookers gawped. The driver's door clattered and tinkled when you opened it, but you barely noticed the rim of shattered glass once it was shut.

It would have been easy to turn off into a side street and lose Timmy Townsend now that they were heading through the wide avenues of Hancock Park. But he stayed on the guy's tail. That buzz he'd felt yesterday when he'd entered the offices of York and Bunce, and even more strongly when he stepped out this morning onto Erewhon's Juliet balcony, was still with him now. And what, the thought returned to him as he glanced back in the rearview mirror and saw a reverse glimpse of the Hollywoodland sign caught between the buildings, did he have left to loose?

Senserama Studios lay on the fringes of the Baldwin Hills. The remains of the old MGM complex wasn't far off, but that was up for sale or redevelopment, and most of the rest of this area of the city was filled with new estates, golf clubs, country clubs and mansions set back far on green lawns. The high chainlink fence outside the studio was overshadowed by a giant billboard for their latest roadhouse production, a Biblical epic called *The Throne of Forever* featuring a typically scantily clad Monumenta Loolie. Then came an equally big billboard featuring Senserama president and current State Governor Herbert Kisberg's face. Brown-skinned, blue-eyed, blonde-haired, white-toothed, and with just the right amount of cosmetic care around the crinkles of his smile, he didn't look far off being a movie star himself.

The security guy at the entrance raised the barrier and saluted as he let them by. Clark followed Timmy's Bentley past the hanger-like soundstages signs toward signs marked PRODUCTION, and had to slow for a herd of longhorn cattle crossing the road. He parked outside a three story office amid a line of other Bentleys, Rolls Royces, Lincolns and Cadillacs. Drawn between the extra-wide white lines marked RESERVED FOR AUTHORIZED STUDIO VISITORS, the Delahaye seemed at last to have found its spiritual home.

"Beauty of a car," Timmy said, leaning in. "Weren't kidding about that door, though. I'd file a police report if I were you." Then he did one of his characteristic spin-and-turns. "So—welcome to the salt mines...!"

The women sashaying past along the corridors of Accounts and Production made the receptionist at York and Bunce look like Lon Chaney with a hangover. The walls were lined with framed posters of Senserama's many successes. Any moment now, Clark thought, someone's going to come up to me and ask who I really am. But it never happened. It was like being onstage. It was like a dream.

He was introduced to vice presidents and deputy managers in charge of this or that. Of course, the way Timmy told it, they were all indispensable—*absolutely vital*—parts of the Senserama team. Senior or junior, male or female, they all had the same muscular handshake and equally muscular smile.

Timmy's own office was spacious, and entirely empty of the usual production company mess of overspilling file cabinets and bookcases stuffed with unread scripts. Apart from a golf putter leaning in the corner, it was hard to see what the man did here all day. But there was plenty of evidence of what he got up to outside of Senserama. The walls were covered with glossy ten by eights. Timmy Townsend convincingly cowboyish on the backs of several expensive horses. Timmy Townsend out in the forest with various kinds of game dead at his feet.

"Why don't I show you were the *real* work gets done?" Timmy suggested after he'd spun for a while like a kid on a ride in his recliner leather chair.

Just as Clark remembered, it was always a long walk from one part of a studio to another. They crossed roads and backlots under the hot sun. A troupe of kids dressed as fairies pranced by. They saw a woman dressed like a medieval princess carrying a live goose.

"I can't say enough about what a fan I am of your work, Dan." Timmy laid his arm across Clark's shoulder. "That scene in that historic pic you wrote—I mean, the way that French-sounding broad, the one who gets her head chopped..."

"Mary Queen of Scots?"

"That's her. The way you did that. Absolutely brilliant. I mean, *absolutely* brilliant. Course, *Wake Up and Dream* is *another* biopic, which I sort of liked straight off..."

Clark, who felt he'd earned an interest in *Wake Up and Dream*, wondered where this was going. He knew that simply "liking" anything in this industry was the equivalent of seeing it as a heap of dogshit. Let alone with addition of a "sort-of".

"Do you know, Dan, how many companies were talking of doing Lars Bechmeir about five years ago before his wife went and killed herself? Fucking *dozens*. But what do you do with *that* for an ending, eh? And, I'll be honest, that was my first reaction when I looked at this treatment as well. I thought, uh-oh, a work of total genius and all of that—with your name on it, it has to be—but where the hell are we going in the final reel . . . ? But what you did with that was brilliant. I can see it playing in Pigswill, Idaho." He gave a squeeze of Clark's shoulder.

"Thanks."

"But the way you make it seem like it's a kind of sacrifice, that she's doing it for us all—like, well, Jesus. Sheer master stroke. There was talk of a Thomas Edison biopic a couple of years ago with some nobody called Tracey in the lead. Didn't get off the ground, which leaves the whole high concept guy-with-an-invention theme entirely free. It's unpissed snow."

Clark had encountered Timmy Townsend's type many times before. For all the bullshit, for all the bad deals and back seat handjobs, Timmy clearly still believed as firmly in the dream on which this whole industry floated as did the latest wannabe actress climbing off the Super Chief at Union Station with nothing but a fresh pair of panties and a new hairdo.

"Difference with Edison, of course, being that he's dead. I mean, he *is* dead, isn't he? That, and he'd sue. Bechmeir being alive is a whole different ballgame. Not that we actually need his *permission*, but imagine what a blast it would be if we could get him to come to the premiere."

"I got a letter from the Trust this morning," Clark said. "Something about them having no fundamental objection to the project. Gave the name of their attorney, though."

"Got that letter with you?"

He shook his head.

"Better make sure our lawyers get it. But I really don't think we need worry. Herbert Kisberg's on the board of the Bechmeir Trust. You won't believe how *up* we all already are for this project at Senserama. It's like the feelie's already made. Things are just falling together . . . "

Calling the soundstage they were walking toward merely a building really didn't do the place justice; it could have housed the *Hindenburg*. No, Clark decided as they stepped in through a tiny gap in the massive sliding doors, the Hindenberg could have flown around in here.

Women in period dress, shackled slaves and Klu Klux Clansmen lounged, chatting, sweating, smoking and fanning themselves with scripts. Scaffolding rang. Transformed hummed. Klieg lights clanged on and off. Frazzled looking technicians clustered in agitated debate. They were shooting, Timmy shouted over the clamor, a drama set in the pre-civil war deep south which was to be called either *White Gables* or *The Cotton House*. Even though *Gone With the Wind* had been such a notorious flop, Senserama still reckoned that there was money in the whole Dixie/Confederate thing.

Clark was introduced to the director, a fat, distracted man with a straggly beard who emanated a stronger version of the tired body funk which pervaded the entire set. The guy seemed vaguely familiar—he was almost sure he'd once done a screen test for him—but there was little chance that anyone here would ever bother to recognize a reclusive screenwriter, let alone a guy who'd last worked as an actor in the ancient days of the talkies. The director turned to bellow through his bullhorn that this was the last take before lunch. Clark knew that meant there would almost certainly be another. Some things might change in this industry. Others didn't.

Two thirds through the shooting script of *White Gables* or *The Cotton House*, our southern belle had escaped from the clutches of the rebel slaves with the help of some brave Klu Klux Clansmen. Now alone and destitute, she had finally made it back to the house of her birth. In this scene, the actress—whose name Timmy had purred with appropriate reverence—was required to stagger along the front path to the door of the spackleboard mansion, her gasping and emoting progress tracked by several cameras, an overhead boom and a feelie iconoscope.

Her face already transformed into the pallid mask which the lighting and the monochrome filmstock would transform into a vision of long-suffering beauty, and wearing a suitably torn and dirtied ballgown, she put aside *Harper's Monthly* and stepped up to the first taped marker on the soundstage floor as the shot was readied. Technicians called their okays. But for the dull electric humming and the subdued whirr of the camera motors, the entire set fell silent, and the director called *action*.

As always, the take itself—the actual business of the actress crawling up the fake path towards the fake steps to throw herself down before the fake front door—seemed anticlimactic. This might be a big scene, but it would need cuts of the door, cuts of our heroine's tear-glinting face, a swelling soundtrack, and probably overdubbing of her gasps and sighs, not to mention some enhancement of the feelie track, before any self-respecting audience would be convinced.

Clark stood behind the iconoscope operator. Then he took a couple of steps back; even before the power had been upped to its full level, he felt a familiar crawl in the pit of this belly. He'd never really liked these things. Bechmeir field receivers were frail and complex devices; trolley-mounted contraptions of precision steel and copper fronted with bulging eyes of silver-treated glass which seemed to peer blindly into the scene which they were recording. Inside were electron guns and magnetic focusing coils and step-up transformers which fed a massive Uher wire recording machine along fat lengths of cable, and also threw a faint representation up on a cathode ray tube for the iconoscope operator to follow what the machine was seeing. All in all, they were pretty much up there on the pinnacle of what the human species could achieve. But he'd always got that crawling, snagged-nail-across-steel feeling when he was close to them, and being back here on a soundstage more than reminded him that it hadn't gone away. He found this faint green image projected onto the operator's viewscreen especially disturbing. As the actress moved, a vaguely human shape, a flame seen through misted glass, shivered and sparked across the screen.

Then the director called and everything was powered down and the actress returned to her magazine as he conferred with the technicians and then, although still seriously dissatisfied in the manner of all directors Clark had ever encountered, called for a print, which meant that the studio would now invest the several hundred dollars required to process and synchronize the film into a viewable rough cut. With all this expensive equipment, the highly trained people paid to do little most of the time but stand around and wait—the sheer, abject *waste*—you could see at close hand on a feelie set where all the money went.

"Smoke?" Townsend offered a gold cigarette case as they stood by a catering truck with some chattering Mexican extras dressed as Eskimos.

Clark shook his head. "I got these." He tapped a Lucky Strike out. "This is *something*, eh?"

"Yeah." He felt almost relaxed. They'd just had coffee and bacon rolls, and it was good to be back out in the cool and quiet of the open air.

"Looking a bit peaky if you don't mind me saying so, ol' Danny boy."

"I was up late."

"Out celebrating the contract? I mean, you and your wife?"

"Matter of fact, we were."

"*Must* get together with you both. There's a party tomorrow night at Herbert Kisberg's place. You both *absolutely* must come. Say, by the way," he added, dabbing a spot of grease from his cheek with a handkerchief which matched his mustard necktie, "what you said a few weeks back in your letter..."

Letter? "Yeah?"

"You know—about sending me that new draft with an entirely different approach to *Wake Up and Dream*."

"Is that how I put it?"

"Pretty much word for word."

"Can I ask you, Timmy—I'm just keeping track—what color is the draft you've got?"

Timmy Townsend thought deeply for a moment. which looked like something he wasn't used to doing. "White, I think. Yeah. I'm certain of it."

"You've never seen this blue draft which I said I'd send next?"

"No. Absolutely not. 'Course, I'd be more than happy to take a fresh look at wherever you're at. I mean, we're bound to need some rewrites..." Timmy Townsend waved a finger. "But I know you writers. Nothing's ever quite the way you want it. But, believe me, Dan what you got already is fucking dynamite. Start dicking around with that and the whole thing might blow up."

He was led across other dusty backlots to Post Production. In these offices the complex patterns of sounds, images and feelings were put together to create the final illusion.

A woman was singing operatically in a sound booth in one of the audio suites. Another was laughing. Sound engineers beyond glass screens turned dials and fed wire reels through the heads of recording machines. On the floor above, the scene wasn't so dissimilar, at least superficially, as feelie engineers pondered cathode ray tubes or consulted frequency charts of the range of human emotions, although once more Clark felt his skin begin to crawl. Here, still as nothing more than a representation of a signal cast against luminous glass, was Bet Doonsday's aura, and here was Slowly Simpson's. To Clark, they looked more like shimmering green butterflies flown out of some unpleasant dream. Of course, a real star needed a strong and consistent aura—that sense of *presence* which you got when certain people entered a room—although it was an open secret in the industry, Timmy confided, that they were given artificial help in this area during the recording process, just the way they were with padded bras, stack heels—and added echo on the voice soundtrack. More and more these days, they were calling in specialists to provide that kick of happiness or terror which made a great feelie seem real.

Clark was shown where these extra tracks were laid down. Here, inside the wire rabbit hutch of a Faraday cage to keep out interference, a woman who could do happiness like no one else was laughing. Who cared if she had a face like the backside of a bus? And here a bearded man who'd spent his childhood being brutalized in a basement was screaming so hard before the cataractic eye of an iconoscope that his face seemed about to rip apart. This was raw emotion, pure and simple, and eminently marketable, which could be mixed into any kind of feelie which needed that extra punch. Many of these recordings, Timmy explained, would be sold on to other studios. Or, increasingly, to a wide range of other outlets. The commercial demand was growing so fast it was hard to keep pace.

"We and Motorola are already talking to Sears. Think how it would work in a food hall—not to mention the lingerie department, eh?" Timmy nudged Clark's ribs. "The use of feelie tracks in retail is going to go *massive*. We've already got nibbles from Howard Johnson's. It'd be like the scent of baking bread at a bakers, only a hundred times better... But I really can't let you go without trying some of our finished product."

The feelie showing room had the usual plush chairs and reek of stale cigarsmoke which Clark associated with all showing rooms, but there were no loudspeakers, no screen, and no projection housing at the rear. All that stood between the open red curtains was a wide frame of thinly woven metal. Without the screen which would normally have been hung in front—and but for the rising buzz of the transformers and the fat wires which terminated around it—you might have thought this Bechmeir field generator to be a giant frying griddle.

The lights were dimmed in the traditional way, then Timmy clicked his finger to signal that someone should feed through the reels. Clark thought of that wraith he'd seen dancing between the two charged plates back at Erewhon, but here the field was spread across the breadth of a theater. Even before that pre-thunder buzz had increased and the black space before him began to glow, something cold and strange brushed past him. If such a sensation exists, this, he was absolutely certain, was how it felt to have someone—or something—walk across your grave.

The equipment here, of course, was all state of the art: new valves, high volts, maximum wattage. Push the field signal much higher, Timmy explained, sat beside Clark in a shuffle of nervous energies so bright you almost expected to see him start glowing as well, and people got nausea and headaches. Higher still, and you'd give them burns until you eventually fried their heads. *The Virgin Queen* was a relatively old feelie, and Clark had seen it in an old theater played on antique equipment. This was cutting edge.

With a faint crackling, the space before him filled into hazy curtain—a thing of no color at all at first, which danced and shifted as if caught in an invisible wind. Then the wind seemed to grow stronger—he could feel the chill of it—and the curtain flashed agitations of color, and those colors reached to something deep within. This, he thought, as spectral landscapes of plasm pulsed and faded before him, was how God must have imagined the universe before it existed. As a thing of pure spirit, as an outpouring of nothing but soul.

What Clark witnessed passed through the entire spectrum of

emotions. Though the greens of happiness and the blues of contentments to the darkest reds of anger and the falling blacks of grief. And it wasn't just humanity. Every living thing was alight in this different existence, this new way of seeing the world. Trees swayed in leafy waterfalls. Animals glowed like coals. But the auras of people were the true glory of creation in their flickering complexity. We aren't simply moths or butterflies, Clark realized. We are all angels.

He saw the lantern blaze of a kid finding his presents on Christmas morning. He saw the dulling flicker of an old woman whose last friend has died. He saw a mother's grief and the jarring fires of hatred. He saw the joy of a funfair, and tumbled from there into glorious coronas of unconditional love. But that fairground bumper-car tang was still sharp on the back of his tongue, and his hair pricked and his skin felt odd and slick within his clothes. With that hissing, with that crackling like distant fireworks, with that sparky, acidic smell and a feeling at the bottom of your belly that you got when the train you were in seemed momentarily to be moving when it wasn't, the colors came and went. Greens and reds and flares of pure white, yes, but also the paler shades of everyday existence—those papery yellows and faded pinks and washed out blues of the workaday world. He saw them tumbling around him in strange snowfalls, and thought again of Daniel Lamotte, this guy whose life he was suddenly living, and the lost story that he was somehow chasing.

But the reels were still playing, and Timmy was still ablaze with enthusiasms. "You see this one here, Dan. Now, this is a real doozie. Our engineers have been working on it for months and it's been a tricky little bastard, but we finally reckon we've got it right. Can you tell what it is? Can you guess? 'Course you can! It's patriotism pure and simple. Just a question of mixing the right amounts of pride and down-home-sentiment, and then a touch of ambition, and then a whole lot more outright anger underneath it all than you'd probably expect. Can you *see* it? Can you *feel* it? Doesn't that get your balls tingling and something coming up right there in the back of your throat like your momma's just given you the biggest hug? Not giving away any secrets, old fella, when I tell you that Herbert Kisberg's going to be announcing himself as a presidential candidate for the Liberty League in the next few days, and we'll be using this recording in the fall rallies for sure. Even had a nibble from our friends across the pond. You know what that lot are like already with the salutes and the uniforms. Imagine how apeshit the crowds would go with this running when Adolph or Benito step up on stage. And imagine how much we could charge ... !"

Then came a final waft of salt air like the stirring of a subterranean ocean, and the field generator faded to static gray. Clark was dazed and blinking like a sleeper awakening from a week long bender when finally Timmy led him back out into the sunlight, but the different world he'd glimpsed floating up there before him wouldn't go away. He could feel the auras of the feelie houses seeping out around him like the smog which was rising up from the freeways to haze this late afternoon. He could taste the sour nickel tang at the back of his throat, and a crawl under his fingernails like he'd been trying to drag himself out from under the earth.

A new world had been forming itself around him, and he'd barely noticed. It was a world where every white American could own the latest Cadillac and streamline fridge—and where all the black, brown and the yellow ones made obliging servants. Armies of these happy Aryans would soon be sitting at home relaxing in the aura of a Buddhist master, or laughing uncontrollably, or fuming with righteous anger, at whatever on their new feelie radiogram was currently spilling out. They would always eat hungrily at their drive-in diners, and shop with a genuine passion for new things, and worship with true reverence, and lounge through midsummer heatwaves in the delicious feel of being cool. Soon, they would be able to spend their entire lives rutting like teenagers in the first flush of love with all worry and pain extinguished until they died smiling, surrounded by their relentlessly adoring family...

"You won't be a stranger now, will you?" Timmy asked as Clark climbed back into the Delahaye in the Production parking lot. "Where's the best place to contact you, Your house up in Woodsville..." A look of *you writer's* puzzlement crossed his broad face. "Or that place on Bunker Hill...?"

TWENTY ONE

Clark's first thought when he pulled into Blixden Avenue and saw the lights of a black sedan blinking blue through the dusk was that the Gladmont Securities guy had tracked him to Downtown. His next, as he saw the LAPD badge on the side, was that Timmy Townsend had reported the damage to the Delahaye's window, under the impression he was doing him a favor. His last was that it was already too late to turn around.

There were two uniformed officers. One had been speaking to the kid Roger. The other stood on the steps of Blixden Apartments amid an assortment of residents. Barbara Eshel was there, along with two thin looking men and a hunched old woman with a gypsy headscarf.

He parked the Delahaye, pulled the keys, climbed out and checked that his glasses were still on his face. The cop who'd been talking to Roger waddled over. For all his lumbering gait, he wore a somber expression of a variety Clark had rarely seen on an LAPD officer's face.

"Are you Mr Daniel Lamotte?"

He pocketed the keys. The cop's gun was still in his holster. Everyone on the street was looking over at them. "That's me. What can I do to help?"

The cop was big and pink. You could hear the bubble of his breathing. The other cop who was coming down the steps to join them was young and fit. They often matched them up that way, although they both seemed oddly nervous. Clark had met cops in a whole variety of situations, but he was still struggling to get a feel for what was going on here.

"I'm Officer Doyle. My colleague over there is Officer Reynolds. We just need to have a word with you, fella. You got a room or somewhere we could talk?"

"Can't we just do this out on the street?"

Instead of asking Clark what the hell sort of game he was playing, Officer Doyle just nodded. Signaling to his pal to stay back, he put a soft arm on Clark's shoulder and led him a short way down Blixden Avenue. They sat down together on a wall beside the street postbox. The cop looked down at the cracked sidewalk and pulled at his earlobe. Finally, he looked up.

"We've been trying to get hold of you now for a few hours. You *are* Mr Daniel Lamotte, right? That place up in the hills—"

"Erewhon? Up above Stone Canyon? I sometimes work down here. I'm a writer—"

"Yeah." The cop's lungs simmered. "So we found out." He licked the sweat from his lips. "It's your wife. I'm sorry, but there's no easy way of telling you this. Fact is, there's been a body found. We got a report from some hikers about a red Cadillac Series 90 Sedan parked on a scenic byway up toward the San Bernardino Mountains. There was a dead woman inside the car, a hose was poked in though the side window from the exhaust and the engine was still running. The plates and the ID match April Lamotte."

TWENTY TWO

Officer Reynolds drove the patrol car down from Bunker Hill. Clark sat in the back with Officer Doyle. Reynolds had a Liberty League badge just like Timmy Townsend's on his uniform lapel, but the fatter, older cop didn't. They had the regular radio on—NBC, even, although it was a shade too early for Wallis Beekins. It murmured in the background through his haze of thoughts. *Three Little Fishes* by Kay Kyser, and they swam and they swam and fell right over that dam, just the way he was falling. Then a newscast about Marshal Petain making up to the Nazis in France, then how the Republicans at their convention in Philadelphia were talking of choosing some dark-horse-nobody called Wilkie, and the big mystery of who the Liberty Leaguers were going to put up—a mystery to which Clark, with an even deeper falling, realized he had the answer.

Was *this* the real trap which April Lamotte had been setting for him—to implicate him in her own death? But that made no sense. Just as likely, the body they were taking him down to City Hall to identify wouldn't be hers. No, *that* was it. And somehow, in some way he hadn't yet figured, she was setting him up for a murder rap ... But that didn't make much sense either. At least these were plain old street cops in uniform and not suits from homicide. They'd gotten hold of this sheet simply because they worked the district which covered Stone Canyon and were after some easy time-and-a-half.

Twilight outside now. The streetcars on Broadway threw sprays of sparks. City Hall loomed, its windows a lit mosaic, the white flecks of a few gulls still floating on the fading thermals above. Janitors and cops drifted in the big marble entrance hall. Many of the specialist departments of the LAPD—drugs, homicide, sedition, vice—worked out of City Hall, and the corridors beyond had the feel of a busy precinct station. The air smelled of Gestetner fluid, Thunderbird wine and vomit. Officers in shirtsleeves and shoulder holsters shepherded whores, smokehounds, political discontents and transvestites into offices and holding cells.

The Coroner's Department and the city morgue lay down some stairs in the basement. No windows here and half the lights were off, leaving spaces of black along the corridors. A typewriter was clicking somewhere. A phone rang unanswered.

"It's this way..."

The air had already dropped a few degrees as Officer Doyle held open a final door.

It wasn't like in the feelies. They didn't lead you into some tiled auditorium and rack out the body from one of those sliding trays set in a wall. What they did was take you into a small room. Posters on the walls about agricultural credits and the dangers of orange blight and the boll weevil. An aproned mortician pushed a sheeted gurney through a rubber flap door.

"Okay, Mr Lamotte." He felt the old cop's hand rest on his shoulder. "You ready?"

He nodded yes.

"I'm just going to pull back the sheet so that you can see the face, right?"

Officer Doyle signaled to his younger colleague, who, looking like he'd much rather be somewhere else, stepped around to the front of the gurney and, using the tips of his fingers, lifted the top of the sheet back and off.

It was April Lamotte. Her lips were blued beneath what was left of that burgundy lipstick and her lively green eyes had been closed and were just starting to sink and her red hair had been flattened and pulled by the way she'd been handled. But it was her. There was a meaty smell which he knew would soon get stronger, and a faint reek of car fumes and vomit which the perfunctory wipe-down which the morticians had given her hadn't quite removed, but stronger still was the odor of Chanel *Cuir de Russie*. It was April Lamotte, and, for a corpse, she looked surprisingly beautiful. No bloating of rot and gas. Only a mild roadkill stench.

Officer Doyle's hand squeezed Clark's shoulder. "For the record, do you recognize this person?"

"Yes. It's April Lamotte."

The cop's hand squeezed again. "Maybe you want to be left alone in here with your wife for a moment?"

"No. It's okay."

He stepped back. The young cop was about to pull the sheet back up to cover the body, but the whole scene still didn't seem real. He reached out to touch the translucent flesh of April Lamotte's shoulder. He was half expecting his fingers to pass right through, but all he felt was cold flesh.

TWENTY THREE

He was sat down in a fish tank with a silvered glass wall. What looked to be that same picture he'd seen of Herbert Kisberg on the Senserama billboard smiled at him from beneath crossed stars and stripes and Liberty League flags. There was also a poster of a woman wearing a few rags and not much else brandishing a sword labeled *Truth and Democracy* at an ape with the words *World Communism* written across its skull. Some handy draftsman had given the ape Negroid features and added a speech bubble. *Sorry, Lady,* the ape was saying, *even us coons caint sometimes get it up.*

He smoked his last Lucky Strike. Officer Doyle sat on the far side of a scarred wooden desk. Officer Reynolds sat with a pencil and a notebook in the room's farthest corner. Both of them were also smoking. If there was a time to come clean about this whole stupid façade, the message trickled through his brain, it was now.

"What I need to do, Mr Lamotte," Officer Doyle said, leaning a roll of uniform-encased belly fat toward him across the desk, "is to prepare a report which I can then pass on to the Coroner's Investigator. There'll need to be an inquest. There'll also have to be an autopsy, I'm sorry to say. We need to establish cause of death, although the facts look pretty clear-cut."

Clark heard the muscles of his neck creak and click as he nodded yes.

"Basically, a report was radioed in from the Forest Rangers' office at Arrowhead around noon yesterday morning. Like I said, some hikers had found this car the way I described and with your wife's body in it. The engine was still running, although it was near out of gas. Working back, we reckon she probably parked there between one to two hours earlier. Say, about ten, or ten thirty. We got the call here in the city because of the deceased's presumed identity." The cop cleared his throat. "And Officer Reynolds and me arrived there about the same time as the tow truck and the Coroner's photographer. It's an overlook up above Running Springs. Pines and that kind of stuff. It's a pretty spot. Any idea why your wife might be driving out that particular way...?"

"I think we've got a lodge up there."

Officer Doyle glanced at his colleague. "Think?"

"No. We have. I'm sorry. I mean—"

"Sure. I know this is difficult. Just take your time. It's okay. Anyway, we got your wife's ID and address straight off, but when we turned up at the, ah, Lamotte residence this afternoon, there was no one around but this gardener guy who sees to the grounds of the surrounding estate."

"Evan."

"Yeah." The cop flicked through his notebook. "Mr Evan Brinton. Weird sort of guy, if you don't mind me saying. He wasn't much help. And your house was all locked up. No residents or employees. We tried the neighbors—discreetly, I might add—but nothing going. We finally got to Blixden Avenue through your tax records, Mr Lamotte, believe it or not. Oh, yeah—and Mr Evan Briton informed us that you'd been talking to him earlier that same morning. Said you'd come the back way where he works. Does that sound right to you?"

"April and I were out last night. I'm a screenwriter, and we've—I've—just signed a new contract for a big feelie. We had a meal as a celebration. It was at a place up above Silver Lake called Chateau Bansar."

"Can you spell that?"

He did. The cop wrote it down.

"Then I dropped her off at Erewhon....I guess it was around midnight. And I drove back Downtown. I just didn't imagine..."

"So you didn't spend last night at home with your wife?"

"No."

"Any particular reason?"

"I spend a lot of my time at my place Downtown. I find it easier to write there."

"And sleep?"

"Yeah. That's how our marriage works."

"I see." The old cop nodded. "I mean, Mrs Doyle and I, we share the same house an' all. But that's hardly any of my business."

Clark closed his eyes and rubbed the bridge of his nose. Saw April Lamotte leaving Chateau Bansar. Saw her in his arms and sobbing tears, with the car valet and waiters as witness. "We'd had an argument at the restaurant."

"About anything in particular?"

He shrugged in a way that he hoped might express the hopelessness of trying to explain any marital argument.

"And then you came back to Erewhon to see her again this morning?"

"Yes.

"So went into the house at—what?"

"Like Even said, it was around ten this morning. And like *I* said, we'd had an argument the night before. And there was this big contract. Things that needed sorting out..." The screwed-down chair wouldn't move when he tried to shift it forward. "I came the back way because kids in downtown had thrown a stone in through the window of my car the night before and I didn't want her to see the damage. Of course, she wasn't there."

"Find anything unusual this morning inside your house?"

"No. Absolutely nothing."

"So, Mr Lamotte, to be exact, the last time you saw your wife was when you dropped her off last night after that meal?"

"Yeah." A muscle at the corner of his eye pulsed. "That's correct."

"And you didn't hear from her after that?"

"No—and before you ask, I was at Senserama studios with the production executive who's bought my feelie script from about noon this morning to the time you saw me arrive at Blixden Avenue. His name's Timmy Townsend. You can check up with him if you like. Or why don't you try asking a woman named Barbara something who lives next door to my apartment, if you haven't already done so? She came by to give me some mail early this morning..." He wiped at his mouth. The shocked indignation was starting to feel genuine. "Look—my wife's down in the morgue and all you're doing is asking a whole lot of questions. Where is this *leading*?"

"I'm sorry, Mr Lamotte." Officer Doyle's face glistened like pink marble. "This is just a part of the job we have to do. Someone's died, and we have to try to find out as much as we can, and as quickly as possible. I ah . . . " He pulled at his ear, then glanced over to Officer Reynolds, who inclined his head in a slow nod. "This is an even more difficult question. Mr Lamotte—was there any reason for you to think, fear or suspect that your wife might kill herself?"

Images of April Lamotte. Red-haired and beautiful in that green pantsuit as she paced Erewhon, and even redder haired and more beautiful when she drove up in the Delahaye along Sunset to pick him up what felt like half a century ago. Her kissing him. The smell of Chanel *Cuir de Russie*. The lipstick taste of her mouth. The wet push of her tongue. The determined and well-organized way she'd set out to kill him.

"No," he said finally. "She was . . . She liked to be in control. She's not the type who'd ever give up. Not unless . . . " But unless what? He saw her again at Erewhon. And then outside that swish restaurant. His eyes prickled as if they were filling with dust. A swishing, windy sound rushed though his ears.

"Right." Once again, as if looking for some signal, the old cop glanced over at the young cop. "Did Mrs Lamotte like hiking, the out of doors?"

"Not especially."

He nodded. "She was just wearing regular low heels and slacks. Apart from a road map and some handmade cigarettes, the car was pretty much empty. But there was this . . . "

Officer Reynolds stood up. He walked over and laid a small reporters' springbound notepad on the table, turned it around so Clark could see it properly. Then he sat down again. The handwriting on the front sheet was the same neat script he'd seen on some of the documents in Erewhon's study.

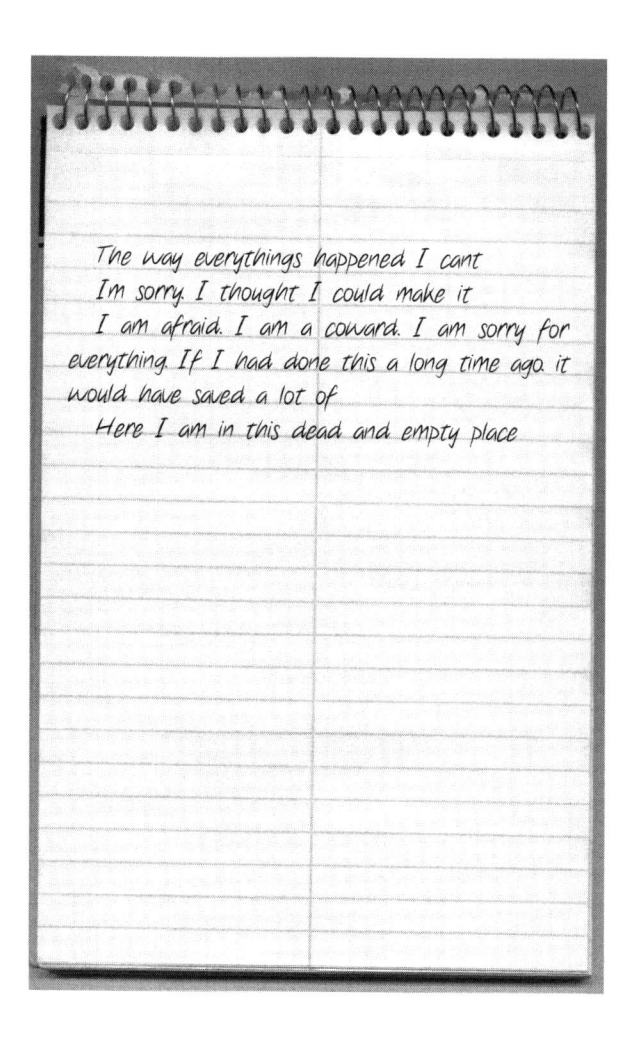

The way everythings happened I cant
Im sorry. I thought I could make it
I am afraid. I am a coward. I am sorry for
everything. If I had done this a long time ago it
would have saved a lot of
Here I am in this dead and empty place

TWENTY FOUR

The two cops led him out of the fish tank and pointed him down the corridor toward the restroom. He felt the swaying bulk of the snub-nose Colt as he rooted in his pockets for enough change to get a fresh pack of Lucky Strikes from a row of vending machines, then a tepid cup of cardboard-flavored coffee, which he knocked back in one. He checked his watch, but the hands had stopped; it had been more than a day before, and a long way back in Venice, when he'd last wound it.

The smell of the restroom flung itself at him as he pushed through the door. The place looked like it had seen some very heavy use, and absolutely no cleaning, for at least the last couple of days. Make that weeks. Cubicle doors hung broken. Several of the toilets and the whole length of the urinal trough had overflowed. The floor was awash with translucent heaps of paper, toilet blocks, cigarette butts, newspapers, and yellow lakes of piss set with heaped islands of turds. Even though this was a mens' restroom, there were even a few sodden and bloodied scraps of what looked like women's sanitary pads. Pissing up against a wall outside would probably be more hygienic, but he picked his way across the drier spots toward the one toilet cubicle which gave an impression, misleading as it turned out, that it might be properly functioning.

He wondered as he pissed into the near-overflowing bowl about all the people who came through a place like City Hall, and the business of life which got done here. Births and deaths. Taxes and cadavers. Crimes and punishments. Threats and beatings up. No wonder this itchy sense of dread and disappointed waiting had seeped into its walls so soon after it was built. Made with sand from California's fifty eight counties and water from its twenty one missions—a lot of Angelinos liked to say the next earthquake would show the folly of ever putting it up. Unthinkingly, he pulled the flush, then jumped back. But he needn't have worried. It didn't work.

There was a single sink on the way out. With the stains which drooled down its sides and the rusted steel mirror hung sideways above it, it made the one in Daniel Lamotte's pad in Blixden Apartments look like the height of luxury, but he felt he had to use something to try to get himself to feel clean. Balling a handkerchief in his hands, he worked open the faucet, and was rewarded by a surprising gush of hot water. No soap, of course, but he gratefully rinsed his hands and took off the glasses to splash his face. This water was about the first good experience he'd ever had in City Hall. It cleared his head—almost shook something out—until he remembered April Lamotte's half-beautiful corpse. Things she'd said came tumbling back to him.

I'm asking you not to leave, Mr Gable. More than asking...

You're not quite the hard-bitten cynic you like to think you are. You're worse. You're just an outright romantic...

I sometimes wonder. I mean, even today... What the hell's it all for?

People, when they first came here from back east to make movies, they said it was because of the quality of the light. What they didn't talk about was the quality of the dark...

He could even hear the cadence of her voice. He spluttered and gasped. A sense of dread passed over him as he put the glasses back on and blinked into the lopsided steel mirror, but the face which peered back at him was still mostly his own. And the City Hall noises which he'd heard earlier—the echoing screams, the doors banging, that odd hissing sound—were louder here. Even in midst of death and all that, life went on... Still, it felt weirdly cold, as if a window had been pushed open, although this restroom was entirely enclosed. And that hissing sound....He tried twisting the faucet off harder to see if that would make it stop. It didn't.

Dark streamers seemed to be flapping behind him when he glanced again into the mirror. It was as if an invisible wind was blowing, but nothing actually seemed to be physically moving. Apart, that was, from the hairs on the back of his neck, and the skin along his spine. He turned, expecting—he wasn't sure what . . . Nothing but filthy cubicles, and one of the striplights in the ceiling flickering on and off. That was what he was hoping for.

The clamor was louder now, bringing the hollow howl of voices, the flap and bang of doors carried through dark spaces. And it wasn't coming from some other part of City Hall. He was certain of that now. His skin chilled. He felt giddy. Something sour and bad and airless was coating his tongue.

Then he saw it again. At first it was just a substanceless blur—like looking at the shimmer of a dust devil across a summer field. Then, and this was somehow more disturbing still, it actually started to *act* like a dust devil, and pluck up scraps of the wet mess over which it hovered and draw them up into a loose but increasingly defined swirl. It grew a shape of sorts, legs at first, and then a torso, and a gathering suggestion of arms. It no longer resembled a dust devil. If it looked like anything at all, flapping as it was with a mess of toilet paper, piss and ordure, it was like some schoolboy mixture of the mummy and the invisible man. But it was horrible—and the horror, as a face finally began to grow, had nothing to do with filth of which it was made. What it emanated was a sense of inexpressible pain. He got an impression of broken limbs, destroyed flesh, of mouths, eyes, faces, all differently distorted, but equally agonized.

"What the hell *are* you?"

He didn't even realize that he'd spoken, but the shifting thing seemed to take heed of his voice. For a moment, there was a sense that the shapes fighting within it tensed, cowered. Then, in a shriek of light, they dissolved. Not so much vanishing as spreading out, slamming into the walls, leaving nothing but a shocked silence and the bathetic *plop* of sodden toilet paper to the floor. Sour ripples washed out to him. Whatever it was that he'd just witnessed, it had been real.

TWENTY FIVE

City Hall smelled once again of nothing but sweat and old coffee as he walked back along the corridor from the restroom toward the solidly unmistakable figure of Officer Doyle standing at its far end.

"You okay, fella?"

For lack of any better response, he nodded.

"May as well get you home. That place up in the hills?"

Erewhon's glass walls. Its endless swallowing reflections. That medicine cabinet. April Lamotte's bed. "I think I'd prefer to go back to Bunker Hill."

"Not a problem."

"What happens next?"

"I think that's about it, Mr Lamotte. This of all times, I can't thank you enough for being so cooperative. Just so as you know, it'll probably be a few days before the Coroner's Department release the body. You'll need to get in touch with a chapel of rest."

"A what?"

"Chapel of rest's what a lot of the undertakers in this city like to call themselves now."

"Right."

"'Fraid we'll have to keep hold of your wife's car and possessions for a while as well until the Coroner delivers his report. The car's in the pound. Still works okay as far as I know, but you might need to show it to your insurers. Her other stuff's all bagged up—her clothes and things. It's evidence until the case is formally closed, although we can let you have the money and keys and so forth. You want that sorted now?"

He hesitated only fractionally before he said yes.

He could tell the old cop was switching off, the way he was left alone with a mailbag stuffed with April Lamotte's belongings. But he'd never felt comfortable about the part of his work which involved going through other people's clothing. Especially if they happened to be dead. But here it all was; the things any woman would probably wear if she went out for a morning drive into the hills, although the labels were more than averagely expensive. Bra and panties. Socks and shoes. Slacks with a good press in them. A linen blouse which still felt laundry-crisp. Everything reeked of carfumes far more strongly than her body had, and he had to draw his hand away when he touched a crust of drying vomit. His vision swayed. He looked around the little room—at a broken chair, at a notice board pinned with dates for the Vice Squad Sea Fisherman's Club which petered out back in '38—daring anything to come, anything to happen. Nothing did.

He made himself feel in April Lamotte's pockets. Found only a handkerchief, keys. He checked them against his own keychain. Apart from the ones which belonged to the Cadillac and Blixden Apartments, they were the same. There was a small purse. He unclipped the clasp. A clip of about thirty dollars, a silver lighter, a spare handkerchief, the same sunglasses she'd worn when she picked him up, and a silver holder for a half dozen of those pastel cigarettes. That, and a pencil. The point was still sharp—used for no more than a few lines. Wherever April Lamotte had been planning on going, she'd sure been traveling light. That pine lodge? But why would she choose to stop and write those things and kill herself on the way?

Heavy footsteps along the corridor; Officer Doyle returning. He closed the purse and felt quickly around the bottom of the mailsack. He got an *aha!* surge when he found what felt like a sheaf of paper, but it turned out to be only a Sunaco fold-out map of Los Angeles and the surrounding district of the sort that gas stations gave out for free if you took a full tank. It looked barely used, but it felt oddly sandy, gritty... For lack of anything else, he stuffed it into his inside suit coat pocket.

Officer Doyle grumbled about life in the manner of all old cops as he drove Clark back through the city.

"Time was, we'd spend our days arresting felons. But now there are these Youth Vigilantes the Governor's got sworn in in those mass rallies. Wander round the streets in those uniforms like they own the place. I mean, if there's some lowlife needs the crap beaten out of him, I'll do it myself..."

"I guess."

"... Spend so much time trying to track down pinkos and fairies and abortionists and every other kind of freak, there's hardly any left for the real villains. And what's this three strikes and you're out crap? I mean, what the fuck has crime got to do with baseball, if you'll pardon my French. And the Comstock Act! Just don't get me started. An' you only have to drive along Vine round about midnight if you *really* wanna see lewd and lascivious, but the pastors and the League of Concerned Housewives an' all the rest don't give a damn about that. Just last week we were supposed to be raiding this socialist bookshop, but when we get there the fire department's beat us to it." He chuckled disappointedly. "Some Liberty Leaguers had already burned the place down. I tell you, live and let live, but good old fashioned police work's gone down to nothing. All that's left for us to do is hold back the crowds..."

A filthy barefoot woman wearing a ratted fur coat and what looked like some kind of tiara was pulling an old luggage trolley laden with her possessions up past Angles Flight. A sign at a taxi rank said NO LOITERING NO NIGGERS. A Rolls Royce swished heedlessly by, its windows a magic lantern filled with hopelessly beautiful faces. A Champagne bottle struck the blacktop in a shower of green sparks as it took the corner. Clark wondered if this city really was changing, or if it wasn't becoming more and more of what it always was.

"We've got this new project. Chief says they're gonna put them receiving Bechmeir things—what do you call them?"

"Iconoscopes."

"That's it. Put them ico-copes in all the interview cells. The DA's got shares in one of the companies that makes them, so you can work out the rest yourself... An' as if we needed some dumb new machine to show us that criminals lie. See, what you really need to do good cop work is brains." He tapped the top of his cap as they took the turn into Blixden Avenue. "That's one thing that's never gonna change."

Officer Doyle pulled the car in at the far end of the street, and stepped around to let Clark out. "By the way, what you said about those kids damaging your vehicle. I'm guessing those were the same little street rats who were out here this evening. I'm sure I can put in a word with the beat officer, make sure they ain't so cocky next time."

"No, no—it's okay."

"You *sure*?" He laid a fat hand on Clark's shoulder and gave it a momentary squeeze. "But just take it easy, will you? You're a good guy. If there is a heaven, I'm sure your wife's up there, smiling down on us poor suckers right now..."

Clark stood and watched the cop's car backlights fade. Then he noticed that an old gum wrapper had been stuck on the Delahaye's windshield. He lifted the wiper to take a look.

```
SORRIE BOUt YOU
WIF MISt＊ LAMEOUt
FOM ROGER
```

Even in the dark, he now knew how to avoid the creak on the first rise of Blixden Apartments' stairs. It was only when he'd closed the door on room 4A and peeled off his shoes and socks that it occurred to him that he could have driven back home to Venice. Or simply found a cheap hotel. But he was back here now, so deep in over his head that he didn't know where the surface was, and he'd never felt so tired in his entire life.

Although nothing had been obviously changed or moved, the room looked in an even bigger mess that it had this morning. The empty tins. The bottles. The cheap scraps of furniture. Those windfall heaps of notebooks and papers. Blundering around it all, he laid the snubnose Colt down on the table amid the scattered drafts by the typewriter, then went to the window and rocked it open to let in some air. Looking down at the street, he thought he saw a figure standing at the furthest edge of a pool of streetlight on the opposite sidewalk, outside the collapsed house. It seemed to be looking right up toward him. Then, as if sensing his attention, it dissolved.

He stayed leaning out of his window in room 4A of Blixden Apartments, doing nothing but breathing in the city scents of dust and garbage and eucalyptus, nothing but listening to the everyday night sounds of cats yowling, dogs barking, the soft rise and fall of faraway traffic, then a siren's brief wail. Finally he racked the window back shut, pulled across the flimsy curtains, and dragged off the rest of his clothes.

Naked, he clicked off the light and lay down on the rucked mattress with no anticipation, tired though he was, of anything resembling sleep. He rolled over, turned back. In dark waves, the room pulsed and closed itself about him. Whispers of voices past, trust betrayed, and opportunities lost, came to him. Then he heard the sea, and bright edges of laughter, and saw all the lost faces of those he had once loved.

TWENTY SIX

Morning. Half in and out of sleep. All the old times, all the old faces. The big cars and the publicity shots and his name in *Variety* and boozing till dawn at the Marmont. Success not waiting around the corner, but right there in front or him, lying in his hands. Soft as a puppy. Warm and clean and bright as this Californian sunlight. And driving his lovely Pierce-Arrow in midnight blue.

Clark smiled. He turned over. A hot blaze spilled into his face. He grunted. Raised an arm to shield his eyes. Saw light surrounding a silhouette like the glittering aura of a saint.

"Who the hell *are* you?" A woman's voice demanded. "And what exactly are you doing here?"

"Me?" His bare back sticking to the wall, he eased himself up. His penis, aroused from all those dreams, chafed sorely against the sheets.

"You remember who I am?" she asked.

He nodded. He was remembering a lot of things now. "You're Barbara, uh, Usher."

"Eshel. It's Barbara Eshel."

"Right."

He watched as she leaned back on the chair which she'd drawn from the desk. Watched as she kept the snubnose Colt which he'd left there trained in the middle of his chest.

"And *you* are?"

"I told you yesterday. My name's Daniel Lamotte. I thought "

"You must think I'm really stupid. But I guess the only stupid thing I'm doing is sitting here and asking for explanations when I should just call the police."

"How did you get in?"

"That catch on your door. Either it won't budge at all, or you give it a shove and hey presto you're in. It's the same with half the locks in Blixden Apartments. But then you'd know that, wouldn't you? If you actually lived here."

"Look..." He was still having to shield his eyes from the brightness of the window and his head throbbed from the seemingly near-permanent hangover he'd acquired since April Lamotte had tried to gas him. He was also still conscious that he was in bed naked, for all that his prick was no longer tenting the sheets, and that his Daniel Lamotte glasses were tossed over on the desk. "... if you just stop pointing at me with that gun, then maybe we could talk."

"I'm very happy with this gun, thanks," she said.

"Look. Barbara. Miss Eshel. I just have this funny thing about having a lethal weapon aimed at me when I'm sitting in my own bed. Even more so by someone who probably doesn't know how to use it."

"It's not *your* own bed, though, is it? You're going to tell me next that the safety catch is on."

He nodded. "It probably is." Then, seeing as this wasn't the time and the place to worry too much about modesty, he began to lean forward. "If you just let me have that thing—"

A bright flare. A loud bang.

"See." She said through the feathering smoke. "The safety wasn't on. And I *do* know how to use a gun, thank you very much. Otherwise Mister whoever you are, we'd be sponging down your fucking brains."

He sank back. Plaster was flaking from a fresh indentation in the wall above his head. "You can't just... People will..."

"You've obviously forgotten that, unlike you, I actually live here. *I* know the Kitcheners always go out on Friday mornings, and that sweet Mrs Bruch on the other side's deafer than a post. I'm not some city kid. I shot coyotes and possums back in Fingerpost, Missouri the way folk here in this city stamp termites. So. Now that you know all about me, perhaps you might like to tell me a little about yourself?"

"Why are you suddenly so sure I'm not Daniel Lamotte? Yesterday—"

"I was sure you weren't him *yesterday* as well, you fathead! But I thought that it was none of my business. At the very least, I decided I'd wait and see. But that was before the cops came around here last evening saying they wanted to speak to Daniel Lamotte because his wife was probably dead. She is, isn't she? It's in the news this morning. I went out and got the early paper." She turned around, lifted a copy of the *Los Angeles Examiner* from the desk and tossed it to him. At no point did the Colt's barrel cease to aim at his naked chest. "It's folded at the right page."

SCREENWRITER'S WIFE FOUND DEAD IN OWN CADDY

The article was a half column in length. It said pretty much what he'd have expected. "You know what they say," he muttered as he put it aside. "It has to be true if it's in the LA press."

She snorted. "You've got a neat line in patter, haven't you, Mister whoever you are? For someone sitting bareass naked, that is, in someone else's bed."

"You're still convinced I'm not Daniel Lamotte?"

"Aren't you?"

This was getting ridiculous. He had to shrug.

"Who are you, then?"

"Will you put down that gun, or at least stop firing it at me, if I say?"

"Depends."

"I didn't kill April Lamotte, if that's what you think."

"Which is exactly what I'd expect you to say if you had killed her."

He nodded. She had a point. "I'm just this idiot guy. Believe me."

"Does the idiot guy have a name?"

If this girl was going to kill him, he decided, she'd probably have done so already. That, or she'd just tried to, and the shot had been a lucky miss. Either way, he was sick of pretence. "I'm Clark Gable."

She twitched her mouth. "Should that mean anything to me?"

"No."

"So why are you pretending to be someone you aren't? And what's happened to the real Daniel Lamotte?"

"That's too many questions. You'll have to be patient if you want me to explain . . . "

He had always liked to think himself a half-decent teller of tales, but this one came out as a confused mess. He muttered in broken sentences about being a private dick, about his lost acting career, and about the specialized kind of marital work he'd thought at first was all April Lamotte wanted. And Erewhon, and being shown the photo of a man scowling at the camera—a tall man who looked a bit like him if you discounted the beard and the glasses, and had gone so far off the rails in writing a feelie about the life of Lars Bechmeir that he'd supposedly been locked away in some fancy private clinic. Then the deal, signing the contract, and the swans on the moat and the meal at Chateau Bansar. And being in that car, the Delahaye which was like some dream turned into a nightmare, and the guy who was or wasn't some kind of security guard who might or might not have been following him... All of it was strange indeed, but somehow not as strange as the fact that he was sitting here in this flophouse on Blixden Avenue telling his story to a young woman who was still pointing a gun at him, and that April Lamotte was now dead.

Still, Barbara Eshel listened. The only question she asked was to find how much he'd been offered for the job. Toward the end, the Colt's barrel even drooped a little until it was aimed directly at his crotch.

"You expect me to believe all of that, Mr Gimble?"

"Not really. But it's all I know. It's Gable, by the way."

She hunched forward in the chair. "This Lamotte woman might want to hire someone to impersonate her husband for all sorts of reasons. Other, I mean, than just getting you to sign a contract on the pretence of his being temporarily mad. Hadn't that occurred to you?"

"It did."

"But you're saying you still went ahead?"

He shrugged. He was sitting here, wasn't he?

She chewed her lip. "Do you think Daniel Lamotte—I mean the real one—is still alive?"

"No idea. She said that she'd visited him a few days ago. Something about some clinic up in the hills. But she didn't say where... How well did you know him?"

She sighed and puffed at her fringe. "He was quiet, shy, nervous, kept himself to himself. He had that sort of aura about him—and I don't necessarily mean in the feelie sense—that didn't invite closeness. That stuff I was saying yesterday about hearing his typewriter going through these walls like a friendly ghost—that was true. But it was more about the typewriter being friendly than him."

"I think I get the picture."

"It must be weird. I mean, aren't I the first person you've met apart from his wife who actually knew him?"

"So you believe me?"

"Even someone as seemingly naïve as you could surely come up with something better than that ridiculous gumph if they wanted to lie."

The gun had drooped again. Now, it was pointing merely at the bed.

"Maybe I could get dressed?"

"Can't see why not."

"But you're not leaving?"

"I can wait."

"Don't tell me," he said, standing up and pulling the sheet with him in a vague attempt at modesty that failed when it snagged on a loose spur of raised floorboard, "You're a farm girl . . . You're used, I mean in Fingerpost, Missouri to seeing . . . ?"

"All sorts of stuff, yeah. But mainly cattle. A few hogs as well."

"Right."

Stupidly naked, he rummaged for clothes as quickly as he could whilst Barbara Eshel remained sitting on the chair with the gun still tracking roughly in his direction. He found a collarless shirt. Braces. He avoided bending in her direction when he opened drawers and pulled on fresh undershorts. In the feelies, he couldn't help thinking, this whole scene would have been done the other way around.

"Now . . . " He sat back on the edge of the bed. " . . . if you say you believe me, will you please put down that gun."

"Is there anything you haven't told me?"

"I'm sure there is." His hair was mussed and he needed a shave.

She studied the gun. "Is this yours?"

"It's Daniel Lamotte's. I found it right there in his desk drawer. I hate the things. They're always nothing but trouble."

"Doesn't look like it's been used much." She did something fancy, cocking and uncocking the hammer and spinning out the chamber, for all the world the female Jewish cowboy, then laid it down on the desk. "He must have been afraid of something to get it."

"That's what I thought."

"Unless he was planning on shooting himself."

"I've thought about that as well."

"How about you, Clark?"

"What the hell do you mean?"

"What do you plan to do?"

He glanced toward the blackened mirror. Heard again a hissing that could have been telephone wires or the sea. "I don't know... I'd run if I knew where I was supposed to run to. And what I was running from."

"And as you don't?"

He shrugged. Glitters of light from the edge of his dreams seemed to push by him.

"You know what kind of writer I am?"

"I rather assumed—"

"Assumed, yeah, the way everyone does in this city that the only kind of writing worth a rat's ass is for the feelies. But there are other things you can do with words, you know. Like telling the truth, for a start."

"That *would* be something."

"Would, wouldn't it? The fascists have tramped all over Europe and now they're here. Kisberg and his Liberty League cronies are busy turning all California into a white enclave—"

"That's a bit strong."

"*Is* it? Do you know how many Hispanics have been repatriated? Do you know what the penalty is now for what they call deviant activity? 'Cept they don't even call it a penalty—it's *treatment*." She took out her State identity card from her top blouse pocket. "You know what this is for?"

"Course I do. We've all got one. It's so cops can tell who you are. Or if you want a library ticket, or health treatment through State Aid."

"Come *on*—how many times have you been asked to show yours, even doing the sort of work you say you do? Never, I'll bet."

He shrugged. "Not that often." The cops hadn't even asked to see it before getting him to identify his wife.

"Funnily enough, I get asked to show mine all the time. You ask anyone else who's brown or yellow or looks Jewish or Hispanic. *That* is what this country is coming to, and California's in the lead."

"I guess I don't pay much notice to politics."

"Most people don't. Not until they can't live in their street no more, or some guy in uniform tells them they've broken some law they haven't even heard of. But I plan to do something about it."

"You mean..." He couldn't keep the incredulity out of his voice. "...by writing?"

She nodded. "We're printing a newssheet—it's an antidote to the Hearst conspiracy which controls most of the media here in California."

"What's it called?"

"*LA Truth*. I know that sounds like an oxymoron."

"Oxy...? Oh, yeah. Don't think I've heard of it."

"It's a tough gig getting it out. What with either paying the new State Stamp Tax, or running underground..."

She trailed off. He got the general impression that editions of *LA Truth* didn't hit the newsstands that regularly.

"There's a story in whatever's happened to Daniel Lamotte and his wife. And I can't believe it's just coincidence that he's written a script about Lars Bechmeir." She looked around her. "It's got to be *somewhere*. Maybe here—or wherever the real Daniel Lamotte is, or up in that fancy house in the canyons. Where do you think we should start?"

This room was filled with stuff—endless typed-up scripts and treatments and letters, and then even larger amounts of near-undecipherable handwritten notes—Daniel Lamotte wrote like a drunk doctor—all of which might contain potentially useful information. But from what Clark knew of April Lamotte, and from what he'd seen up at Erewhon, it seemed doubtful. Had she been up here and sorted through this mess? After a quick search showed no carbons of that burned blue screenplay, it seemed likely.

Barbara Eshel couldn't recall seeing or hearing anything untoward in Blixden Apartments, either, although she was often out trying to get the next edition of *LA Truth* to press, and comings, goings and strange noises at unlikely hours were hardly uncommon. Neither could she quite remember the exact last time that she'd heard the typewriter clacking in room 4A before Clark had dicked around with it yesterday. She was sure, though, that it was before last weekend. Maybe early last Friday.

Clients at a first interview would often tell Clark just how good it felt simply to *talk*. Now, he knew exactly what they meant. Barbara Eshel clearly had her own agenda, and might have shoved herself into his life by pointing a gun at him, but just running things through with her felt like some weight was lifting off his chest. As he finished dressing, they agreed that she'd wade through more of these papers, speak to Blixden Apartments' other residents, check up on places Daniel Lamotte was likely to have visited for research, try to find out a bit more about his and April's lives from the public records, and then maybe the addresses of some upmarket mental health clinics. All of which would keep her more than busy enough to stay out of his hair whilst he drove up toward the mountains to find the pine cabin—Larch Lodge—that Dan and April Lamotte supposedly owned.

"Let me see. This map looks almost new. You say it was found in her car?"

For all that she smelled nice, he wasn't so sure that he was happy about the possessive way she was leaning over his shoulder to try to help him work out where he should be heading.

"Have you looked to see if there are any marks? Or, you know, worn bits where people have been prodding at it?"

"Of course I have." He was doing it as she spoke.

"So the road up around *here* is where she's supposed to have killed herself. And this . . . Lookee here. See—Bark Rise! It's on the way to that lodge of theirs, Clark! It's *got* to be. Can you remember what she wrote in the suicide note? It doesn't say in the paper . . ."

She leaned back from him and pushed at her hair, which glowed auburn in the light streaming from the window, as he described what he could remember seeing on the notepad, which the police had kept.

"You mean different bits of phrases?" she said. "Sentences not complete? Doesn't that sound like a draft, instead of something finished?"

"You're trying to make sense of an act that never makes sense. Or rarely. Barbara, I've *known* suicides. I've done work that's—"

"So you think she really did kill herself?"

He stood up. Even in this bright and cluttered room everything briefly darkened, faded. "I don't know," he said. "I wish I did, but . . . " He felt in his suit coat pocket as if some devastatingly clear idea might be in it. Instead, he found the typed envelope he'd taken from April Lamotte's bedside drawer. Now, when he shook it out, barely a few grains of sand remained.

TWENTY SEVEN

He left the gun with Barbara in room 4A, although he got her to empty the cylinder and shove the thing back the drawer where he'd found it. Down in the hallway, the day's mail had arrived inside a rusted wire box hung on the back of the door. He sifted quickly through it. There wasn't much for anyone, and only one letter addressed to Daniel Lamotte. The envelope, smooth and heavy and slick, had yet to absorb the must and damp of Blixden Apartments.

Inside were two invitation cards and a compliments slip from the office of Mr. Timothy Townsend, Senior Production Executive at Senserama Studios. Scrawled in a big, eager hand, the slip read:

See you both tonight!

In gold swirls and curlicues, the embossed cards beneath informed him that Herbert Kisberg requested the pleasure of Daniel and April Lamotte's company that night at his Beverly Hills address. It seemed odd to see both those names written out like that. As if they were still real and alive.

He stood for a while on the sidewalk on Blixden Avenue, heard clock chimes through an open widow—it was ten already—and set and rewound his Longines watch. Then, fishing for change in his pockets, he headed for the phone booth. The air inside was fetidly hot. The heel of his shoe skidded on a used rubber on the concrete floor. Fishing for the newsprint advert for Nero Securities in his pocket, a strange chill came over him. What exactly *was* he doing? There was a steel mirror screwed in behind the phone set, but it was far too scarred with gum, grime and spittle to make out anything more than the vague and anonymous outline of a man's face.

He checked the number he had for Nero Securities against the telephone listing, just to see if it was current. It was, and the operator put him through without question. Once again, the line just rang and rang.

The sudden sound of the change rattling into the tray as he pulled down the cradle made him shudder. He told himself to forget. Concentrate. Stay in character. What would a writer who worked in this city do on the day after his wife had supposedly committed suicide? Go on a long walk? Have a shot at some In Memoriam poetry? Drink himself stupid? Most likely all of those things. But first, he'd call his agent. If, that was, she didn't happen to be his dead wife as well. He took a long breath and looked at his watch again. Then he checked the phone number on the compliments slip from the letter he'd just opened.

What sounded like the same glossy Senserama secretary who'd greeted them the day before put him straight through to Timmy Townsend's office.

"Dan? Jesus—*Dan*. Is that really you?"

"Yeah, Tim. Have you heard—"

"Fuck. Jesus. It's right here on my desk. How are you feeling ol' buddy? How the fuck could a thing like that happen?"

"I just don't know. It's . . . " For a moment, he felt genuinely blocked-up. " . . . The police came to find me at Blixden Avenue right after you'd seen me yesterday."

"Must have been awful. God, I'm sorry. Where are you now?"

"Still Downtown."

"And you got that invitation I sent you for tonight?"

"Yes . . . "

" . . . Guess it seems ridiculous, right now, eh, Dan?"

"Guess it does . . . "

The pauses down the line were growing longer.

"Look, Danny boy. I know this is the worst possible time to suggest such a thing . . . Well, you know, maybe not . . . Fact is, Dan, the big Indian chiefs here at Senserama have read today's report too. And here's me, I mean I'm just some fucking squaw. Terrible thing to say, I know, but my balls are just the teeniest bit on the line here. And, let's face it, you *have* been out of the loop for a while, credits-wise... Well, push come to shove, the smoke signals I'm getting are they want to know that you're still the guy who'll produce a working script with a shooting schedule this autumn."

"Writers write, Tim. It's what they do. Nothing's going to change about that."

"Great to hear you say that, Dan. And *I* believe you. But it might just be the teeniest bit helpful... Jesus, I feel such a shit for having to say this..."

"You want me to show my face at the party this evening? Show them that Daniel Lamotte's still up to it?"

"Sounds like crud, I know. But yeah."

He took a long breath. "Okay. Message received, Timmy. I'll see what I can do."

"Dan, you're an absolute—"

He put the earpiece back in the cradle, thought for a moment, then jotted down the number of the booth. The kid Roger and his mates were clustered around the post box up the street as he came out.

"Hi there," he called as the rest of them scattered and Roger shoved something into the back of his pants. "Thanks for that message last night on the windshield. It meant something. Never happened to actually see my wife, did you?"

"Never saw your wife, no." The kid spat. "Never will now, by the look of it."

So much for sympathy. Although the kid's mini-hardman act was a million times better than Timmy Townsend's balls-less squaw. "And thanks for keeping an eye on the car."

"Yeah."

"Another dime help?"

"Wouldn't do no harm. But a half buck would do even better." The kid took the two quarters, rubbed them as if they might be fake, palmed them into his pocket. "You in trouble? I mean, what with the police and your wife and that."

"Wish I knew."

"Well, if you don't, pal—"

"Yeah, I know. Nobody does. But I got another little job you could do for me..."

Wary as a bird, the kid cocked his head and stood one-footed.

"... It's no big deal. But assuming you're around here as often as you seem to be, you could maybe listen out for that phone?"

"And do what?"

"There's a girl up in those apartments I got doing some, ah, research for me that I might need to get a message to. You know her? Name's Barbara Eshel."

"You mean the kike?" The kid gave a grinning wink. "You got something sweet'n'sticky going on with her?"

"Where'd'you learn to talk like that?"

"Probably the same place you did."

"Sure." Clark gave up; the kid was still grinning, and sharp as a razor. "I'll see what I can do. Another fifty wouldn't hurt, though, buddy."

TWENTY EIGHT

Hungry, he drove in search of a local foodmarket or eatery. Downtown was a confusing jumble of dead ends and old shadows even on this bright morning. It was a district he'd never gotten the hang of. You could walk, drive or crawl here and some turreted building you thought you recognized could seem so close you were sure you were only a block off. Then you'd turn a corner and find some tunnel or ravine or whole run-down area you'd never seen before in your way. He drove on past the once-grand old rooming houses, then braked sharply and pulled in past a rundown lot when he saw a sun-faded sign for a place called Edna's Eats.

Not so much a trolley car diner as a lunch wagon—barely a distant relative of one of those sleek steel and chrome Fodero creations you saw drawn up along the new strips toward the coast. Inside, hung fly papers and the thick brown air stirred to the creak of a fan. The sign above the chalked board of specials—bean and barley soup, pineapple pie, home made lemon sponge cake—stated NO SERVICE UNDER 5 CENTS. He took a table by the windows at the far side, lit up a Lucky Strike from Daniel Lamotte's book of Edna's Eats matches, and squinted through his glasses at the menu, which was covered with food stains. Meat hissed. Smoke drifted. Two guys a few empty tables along were talking about some insurance deal. An old woman with small dog in her basket was nursing a coffee. The well-dressed couple in the furthest, darkest corner were talking with quiet animation.

"You want . . . ?" The remains of a bruise was fading around the thin, tall waitress' left eye. The name stitched on her lapel said MARY HAMILTON.

"How you doing Mary?"

"Oh, just fine." She sighed a thin, tall waitress' sigh.

"Mind if I ask a stupid question?"

"We don't do credit."

"Nothing like that."

"Didn't walk into no door, either." She wiped her fingers down her apron and touched her face. "And the guy who did this has got balls even sorer than my face. Okay?"

"Nothing like that either. I was just wondering if you can remember seeing a guy in here who looks a bit like me. Tall, same kinda suit, these sort of specs. Same hereabouts ears and teeth as well. But with a beard . . . " He watched her eyebrow raise. "Told you it was a stupid question."

"I heard stupider." She gave the matter some thought. Or maybe she was just staring at him. "An' I know who you mean. He was last in about five days ago. Maybe a tad less. Say about last Friday. Yeah. It was Friday for definite, and about this time. Don't look that much like you, though, with or without the beard.

"So people keep telling me. He a regular?"

"You might say. Ain't spoke as much to me as you in all the months I seen him, though. Don't tip worth pickin', either. Course, I only do mornings, so I quit at noon. And the guy's usually got this notebook he writes in."

"Alone?"

"Usually, yeah. But last time he was with this broad. Okay with the questions . . . ? You want to order or not? I don't get paid none to shoot the breeze."

"This woman he was with—was she red haired, well dressed?"

Mary Hamilton watched as he unpeeled a dollar from Daniel Lamotte's billfold and laid it on the table. Then she nodded. " . . . That'd be the one. Looker like her, you'd have thought she coulda done better."

"What do you mean?"

"Guy's obviously a boozer. Last time, f'instance, came in okay but could barely stand up came time to leave. Lolling like Raggedy Anne.

Woman had to help him—and, believe me, I know what a bastard *that* one is. Probably pissed his pants."

"He was that bad?"

"What do I care? Woman say she had a car outside, and that was the last I heard and I ain't talking to no police . . . "

He let all of that sink in. After all, April Lamotte had told him that she'd first met Dan at this diner on her way back from shifts at the Met, and that they'd come here since to discuss his work. And he knew that she was more than capable of doping someone. What it sounded like this waitress was describing was April Lamotte drugging and abducting her husband later on the very same Friday morning that Barbara Eshel last remembered hearing him typing in room 4A. What felt weird wasn't the oddness of this, but the fact that it made sense.

"When they were talking before that, how did they seem?"

"He was plain agitated. Like he had something big and exciting he needed to explain."

"Didn't happen to hear what he was saying, did you?" He put out his cigarette in the tin ashtray and unfolded another one buck note.

Mary Hamilton skewed her mouth as she stared at him, then at the note, and then back at him again. "No," she said eventually. "Like I said, he seemed agitated. And she was trying to calm things down at first. You know, being reasonable, the way us women are when men do what they're best at an' act pecker-stupid. At least, that was the drift. Spend too much time listening to what people say in this joint and you'd end up even more cracked than you are."

"Anything happened since? People in asking questions?"

She shook her head.

"Well thanks, Mary. I'll have the standard breakfast with an extra glass of squeezed orange and a large coffee."

"Well, hallelujah." Mary Hamilton scribbled his order. "Used to be there, didn't you?" she added as she bunched the notes from the table into her apron pocket.

"There what?"

She gazed up and away from him into the diner haze. Something softened the harsher edges of her face. "Up on that screen..." Her hand went to her hip. "Now, what *was* your name...?"

"I used—"

"No, no, no—don't tell me! I like things to stay the way they were. Meet someone. Talk to them. Find out they got bad breath and want to sell you dishcloths an' aint too careful about how they prune their nails. All it does is mess with a girl's head. I'll go get that coffee..." She turned to slump away.

"Uh, one last thing, Mary."

She swiveled.

"That man and the woman. Where exactly were they sitting?"

"Over there," she nodded to the furthest, darkest corner of Edna's Eats.

"You mean where that couple are?"

"What couple?"

"That couple who were arguing over in the back..." He trailed off. The booth was empty.

"There ain't been no couple there, Mister. Ain't served no one there all morning. Now, are you sure you want that extra juice...?"

TWENTY NINE

Up along Arroyo Seco past the neat, sweet Arts and Crafts houses and over the Colorado Street Bridge where Betty Bechmeir had hung herself, he paused to check April Lamotte's roadmap outside a sprawl of new real estate signs on the fringes of Pasadena, then found the scenic byway which led north and east through green foothills. Soon, there were winding switchbacks. Increasingly fantastic views. Buzzards. Flashing waterfalls. Eagles. He checked the rearview for the umpteenth time and pushed the button which made the Delahaye's top fold down.

A poker-burned rustic sign pointed to an overlook on the road's right. He pulled in and stopped the Delahaye's engine and climbed out. There was no one else around. There was no sound of any cars approaching on the road. This was some spot. The air was raucous with the wind, the trees, the sunlight, and with the tumbling rush of a creek which glimmered in the valley somewhere far beneath. The drop beyond the old wood and iron barrier was spectacular. Whether or not April Lamotte had chosen it, this was some place to die.

He pecked and peered at the loose gravel. Saw evidence of many recent cigarette butts, screwed-up Chesterfield packs, gritty lumps of discarded gum, half-eaten sandwiches, a few fluttering sheets of yesterday's *Van Nuys News*. Cops were such slobs. Amid the recent swirl of car treads, there were also the wider tracks of what he took to be the ambulance and tow truck. He peered more carefully over the flimsily-guarded drop where rocks gnashed and tumbled through scrub larch toward the flashing creek. Something long and black had been tossed that way and was lying curled, nasty as a snake, about thirty feet beneath. His heart hammered. The wind rushed in his ears. The length of hose which had ended April Lamotte's life had probably been thrown that way by the walkers who'd found her, or the guys from the tow truck. Evidence or not, no-one was going to risk climbing down there to get it. Neither was he.

He wandered about some more. Found a small rill and splashed his face and drank. Water had rarely tasted so good. Then he went to edge of the trees which raked up toward the mountains to take a piss. Just as he was finishing, he noticed a glassy glint amid the pine needles down by his feet. He picked it up. It was a glass and steel hypodermic. The plunger was fully depressed.

Driving on and up the road toward Bark Rise, he passed a small settlement of prefab bungalow houses and a gas station-cum-general store. He pulled in. A rangy, mangy dog was growling and yapping at the end of its chain. The old man who came hunching out from the dark of his hut was white-eye blind in the same eye as the dog, and had similarly bad teeth.

"Nice ride," the old man muttered as the meter clanked and he filled the Delahaye up with gas. "Shame about that busted window. City kids do that?"

"Yeah. You hear much about what happened down the road there yesterday? That woman who killed herself?"

"Not much. Other than that the cops came up this way an' bought me clean outa Chesterfields."

"Many people use that overlook to end it all?"

"Not soas I'd know of. Nice enough spot. More likely to make you want to start afresh than dump it all down the can."

"That was what I thought." He remembered those bleak little scraps April Lamotte had written. What had the last one been about? Something about being in *a dead and empty place* . . .

"You ain't some ree-porter, are you?"

"No. Just happened to know the woman."

The meter stopped clanking. "That'll be three fifty on the nose." The old man gave the nozzle a shake.

"Say, you didn't happen to see a guy around here who looks a tad like me? Tallish. Same pale suits. A beard, but these teeth and ears."

"What? You related?"

"You could say."

The old man shook his head, took the money, and hooked the nozzle back into the pump. "You *sure* you ain't some kinda press?"

"Yeah. I'm just—"

"Heard the broad was some looker, as well. Car almost as fancy as this here. Done dead like that, real waste. More as like, someone might take that bend wrong and go down the ravine. Them barriers ain't gonna stop nothin'. 'Bout time they got it sorted, just like I was telling that cop yesterday."

"The ones who came up after the suicide?"

"Nah. The cop who was here earlier. Saw him when I was coming that-away. Puttin' up some kinda roadblock on the same spot. Said it was for a survey."

"When was this?"

The old man gave him a wall-eyed version of the you-must-be-stupid look Clark was getting used to receiving. "Like I say, early yesterday."

"What time?"

"'Bout nine thirty, maybe ten. Mist hangs there sometimes 'til almost midday."

"What was this cop like?"

The old guy rubbed his stubble. "Tall, I'd say. Almost as tall as you. 'Bout middle age the same. But thinner. Had one of them longish faces that looks sad even when it ain't. Wore them newfangled glasses people put on against the sun. Didn't take his cap off either."

"Any kind of accent?"

"Cop had what I'd call a churchy kinda voice."

"You mean, sing-song?"

"Nothin' like that. Just mean ed-u-cated like he's come from no particular place at all and ain't we all supposed to be impressed by it."

"Happen to notice his car?"

"Like a zebra got stripes, it was a po-lice car, drawn right across the road with a stop sign put up beside it. Just one of them regular black jobs. Said through it was for some kinda safety survey before he left me."

"Any idea of the car's make?"

"The sort you don't notice. Like I say—"

"Just a regular black sedan, maybe a Mercury, with a badge stuck on the door and a light on the top?"

The old guy nodded.

"But you haven't seen him since?"

The old guy shook his head. "Not much you see the po-lice round here. Don't have no call for crime. Do get some am-bu-lances, though. People come up here from down there in winter, stay up in them cabins like they think they're Rebels. Do that thing on the snow." He worked his lips and gestured his scrawny arms.

"Skiing?"

"That's the one. Then they come back down again with their legs broke. Must be some way of passing the time."

"You visit LA much?"

"Just the once. Heard things have changed a lot since. Heard the picture houses these days got gadgets that'll pry up the inside of your head neat as a melon. Heard them ce-lebrities dance around in there like hobgoblins. Change the way a man thinks. Sure don't sound like the work of the good Lord to me."

"You're right," Clark agreed. "It isn't."

THIRTY

He followed the directions which the old man at the gas station had given him. Bark Rise was more an area than a single road, and everything along its forest drives was landscaped, screened, tucked away. This was moneyed LA transported up from the coastal bowl into the foothills of the San Bernardino Mountains without a single drop of its precious elixir being shed. A woman cycled by him from the other direction. She was blonde, tan, long-legged, extraordinarily beautiful. Everything up here looked like an advertisement.

There were polished oak signs, and he found his way to the turn which led to Larch Lodge easily enough. He parked the Delahaye under the trees just back from the junction, wondering why he hadn't brought the Colt, and how far he'd have to walk to reach the place. But it wasn't too far; just enough to foster the illusion that this log and shingle construction was the only habitation within fifty miles. The power cables buried. Nothing to hear but the sway of the pines. Larch Lodge was squat, trying hard to be pretty, and looked like it belonged in a clumsy fairy tale. There was a four car garage shaped like a barn around back, and a smaller lodge for servants or extra guests.

He checked the smaller place first, peering in at the windows. They were barred on the outside, and the place didn't look as if it had ever seen much habitation. He glanced at the wavering trees. Someone could be out there in the forest. Anywhere. Watching. Waiting. But it seemed more likely that the kind of creatures you got in cartoon feelies—chorusing bluebirds, sexily-voiced deer and dancing rabbits radiating playful bonhomie—would emerge into this rustic wonderland.

There were no windows in the garage, but he found a side door with a latch but no bolt. A car sat gleaming dully on the clean concrete. A mud-green Plymouth P9 Roadking coupe—nothing upscale like the Caddy or the Delahaye. He checked inside, sniffed the exhaust, touched the tires, felt the bonnet. It had rarely been used. A runaround for getting down to Pasadena for liquor? The garage was otherwise empty. There weren't even any tools.

He walked across to the main lodge. The windows here were barred as well. He saw unwashed bowls through in the kitchen. In the bedroom was a mussed-up double bed. He leaned back from the window against the logs, trying to get his brain into gear. Signs of recent habitation, but once again this place felt dead. He rooted in his pocket for Daniel Lamotte's keychain, flipped through it, and found the only key he hadn't yet used.

The nail-studded front door gave silently to the closed-in air. All the furniture seemed to have come with the house—heavy, raw wooden stuff trying to look like it had been knocked together by a backwoodsman instead of kids in a Mexico sweatshop. There was a moose head on the wall above the iron stove in the main sitting area. He checked inside the stove to see if anything had been burned, but it was factory clean. The kitchen was a mess. Despite the polished surfaces and gingham curtains, it had the same smell of booze and Campbell's tomato soup as 4A Blixden Apartments.

The bedroom was even more redolent of the real Daniel Lamotte. A cream suit coat much like the one Clark was wearing was still draped over the back of the dressing table chair. That gingery scent he'd noticed when he first opened the cardboard suitcase back in Venice was here. He rubbed the bedsheets between his thumb and finger the way an expert bookseller might touch a first edition. If April Lamotte had still been his client, he'd have told her that her husband had slept here recently. Not last night. But maybe the night before, and several nights before that.

The ashtray on the dressing table was heaped with Lucky Strike butts. Picking through them, he found four pastel stubs marked with burgundy lipstick. He looked again at the bed, but it was obvious to him that only one person had slept there, and restlessly. A glass tumbler sat on the table. As well as a toffeeish residue of what looked and smelled like dried bourbon, there was a chalky tidemark at the bottom. He checked the steel cabinet beside the shower in the bathroom. Next to the shampoos and toothpaste were almost as many boxes and bottles of downers as he'd found at Erewhon.

It felt like he was starting to get the picture. Of Daniel Lamotte being taken here by his wife—drugged, from Edna's Eats—last Friday. Her locking him up inside this quiet, solid place with its heavy door and barred windows. Maybe visiting him once or twice in the days since whilst she worked up her plans to fake his suicide. Telling him each time that it would be alright, she'd soon make the bad dreams go away, and meanwhile would he take another drink and down a few more tablets, just like always?

He tried many other drawers. Found nothing but a few broken pencils, worn right down to the nub, a dry pot of ink and a pen with a ruined nib. Most of the other storage spaces were empty; he got the impression the Lamottes had bought Larch Lodge a few years back and then not known what to do with it. Oh, for the troubles of the rich...

Only the drawer of a rustic-painted chest in the main sitting area resisted opening; it was a thin plywood thing put there to fill an otherwise empty space along the wall beneath two Remington prints. He went back to the kitchen, grabbed a knife, and pried the cheap lock open. He wasn't expecting much—if you'd wanted to hide anything, you'd surely have made a better effort—but inside was a checkbook, and a key. The key was straightforward; it was for a Plymouth, and would almost certainly fit the P7 in the garage. So, in an odd kind of way, was the checkbook. It was completely unused, and drawn on a Great Western Bank account in the name of a Mr Richard and a Mrs Elizabeth Tudor.

Elizabeth Tudor—wife of the writer of *The Virgin Queen*... And hadn't Richard been one of the queen's beaus? People could never resist doing something clever with their names when they tried to change identity. Not even the smart ones like April Lamotte. She'd even talked of heading off and starting afresh, how Argentina was a place where life could be made new again. For all the current Governor's efforts, Clark knew from his own work with quickie divorces that the Mexican border was porous as a sponge on the minor roads, and that the borders got even leakier the further south down the continent you went. Visas, passports, driving and marriage licenses simply didn't come into it. Not if you had the money, which she'd obviously been salting away in this new account under a false name. So what else would you need to start a new life with your supposedly dead husband, apart from a reliable but unobtrusive automobile and a book of checks?

Simple, really. Just left a few questions unanswered. Like what she'd been fleeing, and how and why she'd died, and what the hell had happened to her husband.

The guy had still have been writing up here in this lodge; that much was clear. He wandered some more. A built-in bookcase covered one wall of the living area. It was lined with yearbooks and directories which looked to have been chosen for no better reason than the nice leather spines they possessed. He shoved a few out from each row in case there was something tucked behind them, but no luck.

It might have puzzled some people that a writer should choose to live without proper books—either here at Larch Lodge, at Erewhon, or in apartment 4A—but Clark wasn't surprised. He'd met a few writers in his time. In most ways, they weren't a recognizable type, but if there was one thing they did have in common, it was that they didn't like other writers; not their physical presence, nor news of failures or successes, and especially not their work.

He was down to the last shelf, simply tossing aside the books by now— gold embossed yearly Almanacs for the *Los Angeles Examiner* from 1911 through 1938—and still nothing. But one fluttered oddly. He picked it back up and saw that many of the pages had had bits torn out of them. He checked the other almanacs more carefully—it was mainly the years 1928 through 1933 which had gotten this treatment—then sat down on a rustic chair with the volumes stacked beside him. Thing was, Daniel Lamotte could have torn out entire articles, or pages, but he'd mainly gone for just the pictures, and it was possible to make a pretty accurate guess at what was missing.

Not a single picture of Lars Bechmeir was left in any of the books. Howard Hughes was also missing—including all the many photos about his aviation adventures. Herbert Kisberg, too. Just an ingénue in those days; the kid from back east who was challenging the established giants with a twobit studio called Senserama. He supposed that fitted as well. But ripping out everything about the Metropolitan Mental Hospital? Escapees, inspections, changes on the board? Going through the rest of the almanacs, he found nothing. Or nothing his reeling mind could work out.

Focus, Clarkie. Think. Stay in character.

April Lamotte had almost certainly left Dan up here whilst she was in the city getting her plans sorted, coming back up again once or twice to keep him semi-calm, and probably take away and mostly destroy whatever he was writing. Except that last time, when she'd ended up dead a few miles down the road in her Cadillac. When someone else had perhaps come to get him instead. So many things to remember. The jigsaw sliding loose and somehow trying to fit in ways that made no sense.

But think—think like the guy you really are. It's just a matrimonial. Someone fucking someone else. Just a question of the wrong kind of stains, the right kind of evidence. So where else would you look?

He peered under the bed, felt between the base and mattress. Then, what the hell, tipped the whole thing over. Nothing but dustbunnies and a lost sock. He went back into the bathroom. He sat down on the toilet seat, looked sideways, behind and up. A small metal wastecan stood in the corner beside him. He'd seen them before in out-of-the-way places where the septic tanks couldn't cope with too much paper waste. But you're a matrimonial investigator, Clark, so where else would you look? Turning sideways again, using the toe of Daniel Lamotte's brogue, he flipped the lid up.

First thing he saw was enough to make him glad he'd done so. If glad was the word. A syringe exactly like the one he'd found at the overlook, or near as damn, lay on top of a balled mess of pink papers. Its plunger was down. He stood up and reopened the cabinet on the wall, just to confirm there was no sign that April Lamotte was using any of the kind of medicines you'd administer with a needle. He'd heard some dopers were starting using such things, but if that was what Dan had been up to, the signs would surely have been more obvious.

He sat back down on the toilet, lifted the lid of the wastecan again and prodded around in the toilet paper with some reluctance; there are some jobs even an unlicensed matrimonial private eye turns his nose up. Didn't look as if there was another syringe further down, but... but... Don't want to get too clinical here, Clarkie baby, but there's something pretty odd about some of the marks on those pink sheets.

He picked one out by its edge. It was marked alright, but not the way you'd expect. Scrawling bursts of letters and torn-through underlinings. Mostly in pencil, although some of the deeper clumps were written in splatters of blueblack ink. Some of the top stuff which he'd hesitated at first to touch was brown, but not in the way you'd expect. Jesus—the guy had actually written in *blood.*

As to what it said... The paper was flimsy in the first place, for all that it was expensive two-ply, and hardly designed for this purpose. And then there was Daniel Lamotte's handwriting, which had been bad enough in those sheets he'd tried to decipher in room 4A, but sometimes here barely looked to be English at all. Still, some words stood out. *Wake* and *Up* and *Dream*, for instance. And, repeatedly, *Lars Bechmeir*. Much of it, though, remained incomprehensible. The stuff was like some kind of code you could only understand when you already knew what it was about. Still, a scrawl that was recognizably *Howard Hughes* figured a great deal. The *Met* and the *Metropolitan Hospital* occurred frequently as well, which made just as little sense as it had in those missing torn out pictures, considering it was the place where the guy had ended up only after his sanity had collapsed. The seemingly made-up word *Thrasis* was in there as well, which sounded familiar. And many of the references were savagely underlined, or Daniel Lamotte had returned to the same sheet to re-mark them until the paper gave out. All very strange. But not the strangest thing of all.

Here was the first scene of the latest version—the *pink* version, it suddenly occurred to him—which came in the standard color sequence for script revisions right after blue. Something resembling the words *Scene One Wake Up and Dream* was written across the top. Picking through the sheets, some of which were still strung by their perforations and some of which had been torn into smaller scraps, he was even able to make some sense of them. The reason being not a sudden improvement in Daniel Lamotte's handwriting, but because he recognized the scene.

> A RUN-DOWN DINER. PAST MIDNIGHT.
> DAN
> DANIEL HOGG IS SIPPING A MUG OF COFFEE AND SCRIBBLING ON A NOTEPAD IN A DARK BOOTH AT BACK. HES TALL, BEARDED, NOT BAD LOOKING, BUT DOWN ON HIS LUCK. A WOMAN ENTERS. SHES DRESSED IN NURSES UNIFORM FROM THE METROPOLITAN HOSPITAL. NOTICES THE MAN AND
> SHE GOES UP.
> APRIL LAMOTTE. HI. SEEN YOU HERE A FEW TIMES. WHAT U WRITIN THERE...?
> DAN. ME? IM JUST TRY

Then the sequence gave out in a confetti of starbursts, scrawls, exclamations, pentagrams, weird symbols, and splatters of shit and blood.

THIRTY ONE

He took a wrong turn on his way back out of Bark Rise, and nearly got the Delahaye's wheels stuck in the ruts of a loggers' clearing. Peaks clawed into view above the treeline as he re-found a road and drove on. He glimpsed narrow ravines and cols of snow, then the landscape opened out. From here, the mountains fell away and the land opened north into high desert. He'd managed to find some kind of pass.

The wind whipped hard and cold. He got out, took a breath, had a smoke. The thought came to him that he could have left Daniel Lamotte somewhere back around that lodge. Buried in the ground, hanging from a tree, or burnt in another bonfire. The thing of it was, he felt sure that he'd have found the guy if he was there. Which, as thoughts go, hardly helped. For it meant that he was following a trail that had been laid down.

The high desert glowered beneath thunderhead clouds. Lightning flickered. Shadow chased shadow. Hard-driven sand abraded his face. He got back in the Delahaye, consulted April Lamotte's foldout map.

He stopped again at the gas station—with the wall-eyed man and dog—back on the Pasadena road, and used the payphone inside the dark little store. He again tried the number for Nero Securities. Once more, there was no answer. Then he got the operator to put him through to the phone booth on Blixden Avenue. It rang for about half a minute. Then came a clattering pick-up.

"Yeah?"

"That you, Roger?"

"Who else, my friend, do you expect it to be but I?" He was doing a cruddy English-baddie accent.

"Anything happening there?"

"Like what?"

"Haven't seen anyone around have you? Perhaps some tallish, thin guy—probably driving a black Mercury sedan with some kind of badge on the side, wearing aviator glasses and dressed in uniform. Police, or the utilities—"

"Uti....?"

"I mean gas, power, water. Possibly a security firm. You understand?"

"Yeah. But the only guy in uniform we sees around here apart from those cops you got sniffing everywhere last night is Schmidt the postie. And Schmidt's plain mad."

"Okay. But if you do see anyone else, just keep out of their way, will you Roger? You, and your mates. I'm serious. And can you tell my friend up in the apartments the same thing? She'll probably be in either room 4A or her own room next door."

"You mean the kike piece of ass?"

"Wish you'd stop talking like that. Her name's Barbara Eshel. And you can also tell her that I'm going to the Metropolitan Hospital?"

"The funny farm?" Roger laughed. "Sounds, my friend, like you're heading for the exact right place."

THIRTY TWO

He took lunch as he drove down from the mountains—a bottle of soda and a jerky-dry ham roll he'd bought at the general store—then back down Arroyo Seco, along Brooklyn, and past all the industries and warehousing around the Western Lithograph Building. He parked the Delahaye by a fence along the rail sidings beside Boyle Heights. He sat there for a while. Should have done this years ago, Clark, he told himself, when it was about something more than a will-o'-the-wisp. But, as it usually was for most things in his experience, it was way too late. Up the road, he bought a fifty cent return to Norwalk at the station booth, the same way you would if you were going anywhere. It was a few minutes gone one o'clock.

The Los Angeles Metropolitan Hospital, otherwise known as the Met or Metro, lay in farmland south and east of the city. Most of the people who worked there had to commute from the city as April Lamotte had said she'd once done. The Met ran a two shift day that went from early afternoon to early morning and back—that way, the busy times of *wake up* and *bed* were handled by separate teams—and most of the people waiting on the platform were recognizably hospital workers; females in faded caps and capes, bulky males in stained coveralls.

Pretending a deep interest in the posters on the corrugated walls—VOTE LIBERTY LEAGUE PROTECT AMERICAN PURITY; Uncle Sam pointing a finger to ask, ARE YOU LOYAL?—he wandered in the direction of a cluster of men in off-brown uniforms at the far end. When the train pulled in, he got in with them in a Whites Only carriage and sat down opposite a guy of about his height and age.

"How much you making at the Met today?"

The guy frowned and put his paper down. He had the sort of pencil-thin mustache Clark often thought of growing himself. "Waddya think, bud? It's fifty cents an hour, bring your own lunch."

"And that snazzy uniform . . . " Clark was already reaching for his billfold. "Bet you have to pay for that yourself as well?"

He kept with the main crowd outside Norwalk Junction, where a clocktower rose from the cluster of buildings amid a large expanse of grounds surrounded by a tall chainlink fence. Big iron gates set within an arched gateway bearing some Latin civic motto were already open to let the new shift in and the old shift out. Collar up and head down in his frayed uniform with its *Los Angeles County Department of Health Cleaning Division* badge on the breast pocket, and the only thing which might get him mistaken for Daniel Lamotte being the glasses—without which he was starting to feel oddly naked—he clicked through a turnstile and headed on along the cracked concrete path.

Security at the Met was even laxer than he'd expected and it didn't look as much like a hospital as he'd feared. There were fields, orchards, clusters of bungalows, and he could even see how the relatives of inmates could kid themselves that this was a rural haven, although the concrete bungalows looked like army blockhouses, and the bigger cluster of buildings ahead would have stood in for a scary feelie staged in Dracula's castle.

He aimed for the relative bustle of the main clocktower building. No sign of any inmates here, nor any of that obvious hospital smell, but business-suited admin staff, nurses and many lesser functionaries dressed in uniforms like his own were coming and going up the wide front steps. No one paid him any notice as he pushed through swing doors into a high-ceilinged hall, where someone had conveniently left a mop and trolley parked beneath an old portrait of some guy in a powdered wig.

"Say," he asked, blocking the passage of a portly nurse as he steered the trolley across the checkered floor, "someone told me there's a mess down in old staff records needs clearing up. Got any idea which way I should go?"

The nurse rolled her eyes as if his question was the final straw, but pointed toward an elevator and muttered something about *basement* before she waddled on. He clanked back the elevator gate, backed in the mop trolley, dragged the hooked brass lever down to B, then slid it shut. Just as he dropped from sight, he noticed that a big black guy was standing beneath the old portrait and staring right across at him.

The trolley wheels squeaked and the soles of his shoes made tick-ticking sounds as he followed subterranean tunnels. He clicked on lights and tried the door of every room he came to, and there were a lot. He found insect piles of ruined typewriters, massive drums of cleaning fluid, cockroaches dying and scurrying in the leaky pools which had formed around equally large drums of some unbranded soup . . . He even found heaped piles of stained, belted outfits which he took at first to be some weird kind of military uniform before he realized they were straightjackets.

The tunnels got lower and darker, although at least that ghastly ruined-soup smell became less prevalent. Then he reached a final door. Like all the rest, it was unlocked. He pulled the electric lever and the lights on the far side gave a reluctant flicker through shrouds of cobweb across tall avenues of file-racked shelves.

The prospect looked daunting. Thank the Almighty, though, for the predictabilities of bureaucracy. Each of the shelves was neatly labeled and dated. There was *Requisitions of 1936* and *Inventories of 1930*, both of which sounded like the kind of musical that no longer got made. Not to mention *Lobotomies of 1935* and *Sterilizations of 1938*. Easing out the tightly packed files from the grit of years to peer at them in the dim light, a curious muttering rose in his head. He stifled a sneeze, then glanced around, daring any of the shadows to move. But all he could sense was his own presence, and these long low passages lined with the lost history of the Met.

He ran his hands along sagging rows of *Staff Records* through coatings of dust and mouse droppings until he reached *Salaries*. If April Lamotte had worked here, it would have been—what?—before the turn of the last decade? He found January for 1928. The damp-warped volume crackled opened. Everything was still hand-written in those days, the inks color-coded in neat columns for payments and deductions.

He took the book over to the thin pool of light cast by the nearest bulb. The names were alphabeticized, with any new recruits for each month added at the end. NSE obviously meant nurse. LW would probably be laundry worker. CLNR would be cleaning guys like himself. *We decided he'd change his name to Lamotte, which is my name, rather than the other way around. It just sounded so much better than Daniel Hogg*... If she'd been telling the truth, Lamotte would also be her maiden name, but there was no sign of any Lamotte in all 1928... Then, there it was in red copperplate just above the bottom columns of March 1929's figures. *Lamotte, April, Nse.*

His breath quickening, he flicked on through the crackling pages. Add-ons for overtime and extra shifts. Deductions for uniform and laundry. Asterisks for small corrections. Approval stamps for some inspection by the IRS. She really had worked here. Then, in November of the same year, 1929, there were no entries for her. He flicked back. October. He tilted the page more carefully into the grainy light. There was writing at the bottom where the ink had gone spidery with damp. But there was a definite circle, and an arrow, pointing down. *Sec*—something... He struggled with the sense of it for a moment.

Seconded to

The final word was so thickly blacked out as to be impossible to read. He flicked on through the months, years, of the regular pay records, looking for more of April Lamotte. As far as he could tell, she'd never returned to the Met from wherever it was she'd been sent. He flicked back to the relevant few pages, tore them out, and stuffed them into his back pocket.

He spent some time longer picking his way along the dusty aisles, but there was no sign down here of the main patient records. Must be kept elsewhere, maybe up on the wards—but why look through old files when the guy Daniel Lamotte had been obsessing about was still here at the Met?

He wheeled the mop trolley back along the basement corridors to the elevator and set the lever to Up. He let the first floor—it seemed to be mostly offices—slide by. The second, though, presented a linoleum-floored corridor receding beneath rows of bright skylights to a steel door. He stopped the elevator, rolled back the gate. He looked in on empty nurses' offices and rooms filled with sour heaps of laundry as he pushed his trolley on. The puke-green gloss-painted door at the far end was thickly impressive. So was its lock. He glanced back the other way, still hoping for some nurse or functionary to emerge with a set of keys, or maybe for a reason not to be here at all. But there was no one about. For want of anything better, he tried the heavy brass handle. The door swung in.

The hospital smell which had been slowly creeping up on his subconscious was suddenly as obvious as day. Rankness undercut with disinfectant. Dust and sour flesh and piss and that halfclean odor you got when you first opened a medicine chest—all combined. Then there was the sound as well. He'd forgotten about that. A lingering echo which, even though it currently seemed to shiver along the polished linoleum with nothing more than the wheeze of the trolley and his own footsteps, still seemed to resonate with lost screams. This place was almost empty though, whilst the wheeled gurneys had been lined along the corridors like railcarriages waiting in some ghastly station when he'd last visited his stepmom Jenny, and there had been glimpses everywhere of things better left unseen. Flesh weeping around loosening gray bandages. Tubes entering unknowable orifices. People coughing and moaning as if to drown out that undertow of echoing screams.

"Hi there Billy..." It had been Jenny's voice, but somehow not her face. Flesh turned into grayed papier mache fallen loose and thin. A gumless smile and teeth red with what he thought for a moment was only poorly applied lipstick. But this wasn't how Jenny was or could ever be. She was always pristine. Always neat. She smelled of soap and laundry and cooking. There were blood flecks on the sheets also, which were otherwise as gray as her face. He felt his father's lumbering awkwardness as he stood beside him. Felt the hellbound heat of her fingers when she touched his face.

He forced himself back to the Met. Forced himself to walk on in what so obviously was nothing like the same place. That smell of soup, for instance, which he'd noticed down in the basement, seemed to fill this corridor, was now so strong that it almost cut out the undertow of bleach and unwashed flesh. There were no screams here, either. At least, not outside his own head. Carried instead on this green shining air were the calls of many voices which made him think of that bit in the Odyssey where Odysseus encounters the sirens. It was weird, but the sound really was that sweet. A large woman in a paisley shift breezed by in the hazed, metallic light. She gave a big smile and said *hi handsome* as she hummed her way past. He'd smiled and said *hi beautiful* back and pushed his trolley on before it occurred to him that he should have asked for directions.

Drawn on by the sound of voices singing, he passed through other unlocked doors. The Met was nothing like he'd expected. Where were the barred cells, the screams of tormented souls? Even the smell of this soup wasn't such a bad thing—fact was, he found that he was actually salivating. Thick pipes ran across the ceiling above him, and he could hear, *feel* them humming. As for the other smells, the sounds—the clanging doors, the muffled grunts of some kind of struggle he caught when he glanced through a half-closed door and saw three big guys in a tiled white space holding another much smaller guy down on a leather bench whilst a forth straightened out a rubber hose—they were as natural in here as birdsong . . .

The wheels of Clark's trolley whistled, and he whistled along with them, trying to find the right lilt for whatever song something inside his head was singing. He'd never have thought before that joy had any obvious color, but it hung here in a shimming pink mist above and around everything. It was a bit like seeing two places superimposed. On the one hand, he was pushing his way though a large, long room, with barred widows of wire mesh glass letting in gray light across a sprawl of metal-framed chairs and tables, a few orange boxes stuffed with jigsaws and magazines, and some heaped-up mattresses. On the other, there was a beauty to this scene which he might have associated with those fancy Italian paintings where centaurs and winged babies pranced to pipe music. Only this was better. This was for real.

The Met was all of a piece, and all just as it should be. It was just the way God Himself would have ordered it—if, that was, God had happened to be a doctor of psychiatry in a white coat and with a brown rubber hose draped around his neck instead of the usual stethoscope, and with maybe a couple of large crocodile clips attached to some kind of stand-alone generator dangling from his all-healing hands.

It was the people in here, he guessed, that made the difference. They were so happy they actually glowed like Chinese lanterns—and Clark, looking down at himself, realized that he was glowing as well. Greenish protrusions crackled out of him in flares of joy.

"Say, any of you folks know where I can find a guy called Howard Hughes . . . ?" Even as he asked the question, he knew that it was ridiculous. Already, he was laughing, and it was as if he'd told the funniest joke in history, for everyone else was cracking up as well.

Beyond the haze, outside the Met, he could see how some of these people might not be your first choice to share a streetcar bench with. Their mouths hung open, their bodies were lopsided, and they were wearing the kind of loose, white, ass-ventilating hospital shifts that didn't leave much to the imagination. One guy had a pair of galoshes on as if to compensate, whilst another, sporting a striped railworkers' cap, was holding his not inconsiderable dick out towards Clark as they drew closer to him.

Hands all over him now. Papery and meaty—*soupily*—scented, they swarmed across his face, sidewaysing his glasses and drawing him in and down. As he succumbed to their embrace, he looked up at the dimming ceiling, and saw once again those big pipes, and realized that what pulsed inside them wasn't soup at all. For surely they contained actual joy— they must make the stuff here in the Met, and then just pump it out like the LAWAP pumped out water. Joy wasn't soupy brown or any other single color, but a mingling of all the shades of this swarming, tingling glow. Joy was warm and it was prickly and it was smooth and it was cold; joy was all of those things—and so many others he couldn't even begin to express—as limbs and bright eager mouths joined with him in a single siren song . . .

"What ya'll doin'?" a voice rumbled somewhere. "Fella like this, he ain't like you, he *important*. He got the mop, he got the trolley. He got places to *go* . . ."

Broad arms took hold, drag-carrying him back out through swing doors into a corridor where the roseate light was so dimmed he could have cried for its loss as he slumped back against a wall.

"Why you gone stole my mop trolley?" The guy was black and bald and big. His smile was all gum, and his left eyebrow was stuck in a raised position which gave him a quizzical look.

"I'm sorry. I was just . . . " A sad, bitter residue washed over Clark. He straightened his glasses. His stomach looped. Then he tried to scratch at a weird itch in his skull. ". . . borrowing it to get something done."

"Covering up for someone?"

"Not exactly. What the hell was going on in there?"

"Don't know much about the Met, do you, if you ain't heard of the moodies."

"Moodies?"

"What you folk from the outside calls the feelies." The big black guy waved a stubby-fingered hand. "But that word for what goes on in here ain't anything like strong enough. Ain't what you *feel*. Puts you in a whole fresh *mood*."

Clark peered back into the room through a porthole. He could still sense a ringing backwash of the joy which had possessed him, but now it was it was like the cold echo of some ghastly bell. The feeling which had joined him to these sad extremes of humanity who wandered that big room with its vague, wan light was entirely lost to him now. One woman seemed to be thinking about eating another piece of jigsaw. Another was adding some extra knots to the ball of hair she was chewing. A third was hunched back in a corner and rocking back and forth. The guy with the railworkers' cap still had his dick in his hand. But they were all so *happy*. They were all still smiling, laughing, singing. He could clearly see the haze of plasm now hanging and drifting like colored sea mist, but somehow the last thing of all he noticed about the room were the two dusty-wired enclosures at opposite corners of the room, although he could hear their fizzing electric hum even from here.

"How the hell d'you manage to stay . . . " he trailed off.

"Sane? *That* what you gonna say? I'm Little Joe by the way. Hate to be impolite, but you still haven't told me who you are. Or whys you took off with my trolley."

Clark was still dazed. He scratched again at his head. "My name's Daniel Lamotte. I'm a screenwriter and I'm doing some research. You know, the way that writers do?"

Little Joe's permanently raised right eyebrow and absence of any teeth made his expressions hard to interpret, but, if he didn't smile, he didn't exactly frown.

"I'm working on a new script about the life of Lars Bechmeir, and there's an inmate here I'd like to talk to that the authorities won't let me see. So I thought if I borrowed a cleaning department uniform and wandered around a bit I'd be able to find him on my own. Very obviously, I was wrong."

"This is some big place. An' we don't bother overmuch with directions and signs."

"So I've discovered."

"Then there's the moodies."

"I've discovered about them as well."

"What's the name of this fella you interested in seeing?"

"Howard Hughes."

"How—" For a moment, the right eyebrow went up to rejoin the left. "Oh, you mean *Howie*, right? Howie's where Howie always is. Whole Met wouldn't work without him."

THIRTY THREE

Little Joe led Clark down ways he would never have discovered through the maze of the Met. He glimpsed and felt different communal areas; glee-filled havens of laughing and leaping, other places whose occupants lay drowsed by hissing purple waves in supine repose. The corridor they eventually reached was knotted and fronded with an even thicker mass of the same pipes and cables which ran everywhere in the Met. It became apparent as the humming and thrumming grew louder that they were heading towards its source.

Through impressive gothic doors lay a cathedral of an engine house. There were huge, kettle-like boilers of polished brass. Endless pipes and gantries threaded high above.

"You'd better go on," Little Joe shouted over the sudden roar. "Howie, he don't like crowd scenes."

High up amid the gantries, a single figure in oil-stained dungarees, an equally oil-stained shirt, brown flat cap and engineer's boots was at work. Clark climbed a ladder. Then another.

"Hey!"

The figure carried on working. Dials and regulators ticked and jumped.

"Excuse me . . . ?"

Howard Hughes continued to ignore his visitor as Clark crossed the last high walkway. He was still tall and regular-looking; still handsome enough to have starred in some of his own movies, even if the cap did sit slightly oddly on his head.

"Mr. Hughes? Howie . . . ?"

Only when he'd finished tightening the bolt he'd been working on and pocketed his torque wrench did Hughes straighten and turn.

"You want to speak to me?" He asked in that same slow Texan drawl Clark remembered from the newscasts. Remembered, as well, from that time he'd rejected him at an audition with a remark about how his ears made him look like a taxi cab with both doors open. But there was no trace of recognition in the soft brown gaze. Howard Hughes seemed incurious—more bored than surprised. And mildly impatient; you could tell that he'd like nothing better than to get back to tending his machines.

Ten years ago, every paper you opened had been filled with this guy. Howard Hughes at the premiere of one of his movies with a big-titted broad on his arms, or performing some new stunt in one of his planes. And the films, and the stunts, and the tits, had just gone on getting bigger and bigger until the feelies—which most people had taken as Hughes' crowning folly—arrived. With that first feelie-movie, a mess of a thing called *Broken Looking Glass*, Hughes had broken the mold. And the mold had stayed broken, for all that Hughes hadn't been the one to profit from it.

Borne in on a wave of new east coast money, new studios like Senserama had muscled in, and the old, mainly Jewish-run businesses had faded. So, apparently, as increasingly weird stories started to circulate, had Howard Hughes' sanity. Stories of walk-outs and arguments. Stories of ridiculously under-funded and over-budget projects which never made the screen. Stories of him refusing to eat anything other than one precise batch of one exact kind of food. Stories of him locking himself up for weeks inside packing cases. Stories of him keeping endless bottles of his own urine. All good reasons, Clark supposed, why a guy might end up here in the Met. But if Howard Hughes was a madman, he certainly wasn't looking or acting that way.

"Can I help you?" he was asking as he wiped his hands on an oil-stained rag.

"My name's Daniel Lamotte. I'm a screenwriter."

Hughes leaned forward and squinted as if peering through a gauze. "Sounds a bit familiar. Written anything I might have seen?"

"Maybe a feelie called *The Virgin Queen*."

"Of course!" Hughes' still easy-on-the eye face split into a smile. "Great feelie. Wish I'd made it myself, and can't say better that that." Then he looked puzzled. "But what are you doing *here*?"

"I'm working on another feelie project, and I'm looking for the kind of information I thought you might be able to help me out with."

"You got a contract?"

"With Senserama. Signed it only a couple of days back."

Hughes whistled. "That's a big name. Been a while since I've met any folks actually working in your profession. Though I do believe we've got one or two who are kinda between projects here at the Met..." He chuckled. He still had that easy swagger. And he was still wiping his hands with that rag. "So—what's it about? What's the main deal?"

"A biopic of Lars Bechmeir."

"I see." Hughes thought about putting down the rag, but then started wiping again. "Which is why you decided to try to talk to me?"

"Basically yes."

"Not sure that I can help you much. Have you spoken to Bechmeir himself?"

"Not yet, no."

Hughes nodded. "I guess not." He was still grinning, but it was getting harder to make sense of the smile. "Always was a real difficult guy to get a proper hold of once you got past the publicity. Even before he lost his wife."

"Still, you worked very closely with him early on. I mean, one of the key scenes—not just in my film, but in the whole history of the feelie industry—is that day when you let him come to your office in the Taft Building to demonstrate his prototype device."

"Sure. Came right in and sat down in front of me with that famous carpetbag with that weird gizmo in it. Well, it *seemed* weird at the time.."

"What was that like? Why *did* you agree to see him?"

Hughes gave an odd gesture. It was part shudder, part shrug. "Just thought, why the hell not, I guess. Look, Mister, ah, Dan, isn't it? *Dan—* I've given lots of interviews about this. It was all recorded in the press and the newsreels at the time. I appreciate you taking the trouble of coming here to see me an' all, but that part of my life is past, and most of the time I just think good riddance." Again, that odd movement. "I really ain't sure there's much I can add."

"I guess I was hoping for some kind of greater insight. I mean—what's Lars Bechmeir actually like?"

"Pretty regular sort of guy. Cares about the way things work, just like myself. You know—the German accent, the glasses, the beard, those double-button down suits. Not sure what else you want me to say. If I were you, I'd just keep it simple and write the story everyone knows and not start messing around with it. Sure sounds like an interesting project, though. Should have been done years ago, I guess, and I'd have liked to have had a piece of it, once upon a time..." Things slid and whirred and strained all around in a sourceless gleam as Hughes wiped his hands and maintained that fixed smile. "As you can see, I'm busy in other ways now. All of this..." He gestured with his rag. "...is what keeps the Met going. The heat, the water, the power. We got five big turbines."

"That's great, Howie. But, like I was saying, surely there's got to be somethi—"

"Two backups as well. Two hundred kilowatts. Plus we got all the steam and heat to drive the laundry house up top. Sweet set-up, don't you think?"

Clark nodded. He could appreciate a fine enginehouse as well as the next man. But where was this getting him? He decided to try a different tack.

"But I guess they were good times. You know, producing that very first feelie. The way everyone thought that it would all be some cockamamie freakshow. And then—"

"'Course, there's no field generators down here." Hughes' manner as he interrupted this time was more forceful, although he was still grinning like the regular, good-looking guy he seemed. "All you get here is the pure clean surge of power." He looked around his machine temple, a gleam lighting his eyes. "Couldn't get anything more clean and apple pie."

"I guess not."

"Reason I like it down here so much. No *interference*, you know? Nothing getting in your mind that shouldn't be there."

"Sure."

"You know how it works—I mean, those waves Lars Bechmeir discovered? They're processed the limbic node, then transmitted or received as low-wave electromagnetics by the lymphatic system, which is why you can sometimes get to see an aura with a roughly human shape when you run it out through a grid, or back along a cathode ray. Of course, there are blackouts, hotspots—all kinds of juju and interference. Sometimes it's just a kind of daze. Whole area's fascinating. Absolutely—the way thoughts and ideas, whole *concepts*, can be absorbed and given out again by the human brain.

"Take an example, you just wouldn't believe how many communists we get coming in the Met these days. Course, their disease is easily sorted. The surgeons can take the whole socialistic mess clean out of your head." He touched the side of his oddly flat cap. "Had it done myself. Piece of brain not much larger than an acorn. Not that I'm going communist, of course, but the thing can grow like a tumor, and you don't want to run the risk, right? I've seen some of them big as your fist lying all bloody right there on a silver dish."

Hughes was still talking in the same easy way, although his hands had got so busy with wiping and re-wiping that the rag had dissolved into threads. He tossed what was left into a nearby bucket, then took a clean rag out from his back pocket and began again. Clark realized that the brownish marks weren't machine oil, but blood.

"Brain's just like any other mechanism. Work out what the problem is, and there's nothing that can't be fixed. Pinkos, faggots, murderers—it's all down to some or other part not working the way it should. Same with hygiene, dirty thoughts or bits of grime. Get a piece of grit in a piston, stands to reason you have to ease it out. Exact same thing goes with the brain. It's like tweaking the best out of an engine by removing anything that's in the way of the power train. I mean, look at me, the stuff I've had done, and every single bit of it has been a step up in horsepower, a definite gain. You see . . . ?"

Hughes paused in wiping his stripped and bloodied palms to lift off his cap. The easy grin was still there in his mouth and eyes, but he was no longer the same man. Amid suppurating patches of stitching and scar, the top and sides of his head sprouted irregular bits of hair. But it wasn't so much the seared and clumped look of the skin that was bothering as the actual *shape* of his skull. Like a pie which hasn't risen properly in the oven, there were falls and indentations where the bone seemed to have given in.

He was still prodding this and that area of his ruined scalp with his long-nailed fingers, talking about craniotomies and lobotomies and psychographs—about how the skin needed to be peeled back and the bone cut right through and other bits pushed aside or taken out to get to the offending part—but Clark was horrified and lost.

"Yeah," Hughes muttered now, smiling once more and deftly replacing his cap, "best thing I ever did was get my brain properly sorted. Not that it's ever finished with, of course. It's like this here enginehouse. Soon as you turn your back for more than a moment, something is sure to start spinning loose or grinding too tight."

"Uh-huh."

"But the most important thing with any kind of machine is to keep it *clean*, right? Goes with a generator or pump, just the same way it does with the human mind. Any kind of grit of dirt, you got to root it out. Sand's the worst. Your oil's plain ruined no matter how much you filter it. Have to strip the whole machine down, wash it out—Yeah!" Hughes was grinning, nodding. His flat cap had slipped to the side of his head. "Bastard stuff bungs everything up. You can feel it grinding, hissing. Wish you could knock it out of your mind, but it gets everywhere. In your ears. Behind your eyes. Sand's the worst for sure. Matter of fact . . . " His hands moved over his face, leaving red streaks. " . . . I can feel it now."

Sand . . . ? Clark felt an odd drift to his own thoughts, like something outside of him was taking hold. It was as if he was watching some feelie from a seat too close to the screen, or was trapped upstairs again in one of those rooms in the Met. "But what does it feel like to you right now, Howie?" he asked. "What *is* going on?"

"It feels like—" Hughes hunched over the gantry rail, jaw spread wide as if he was trying to cough something out. "Feels like . . . Feels like . . . "

"Feels like what, Howie? What is it you want to say?"

Drool strung from Howard Hughes' mouth as the muscles of his face knotted and unknotted. Then his cap slipped from his head and floated in arcs though the churning machinery below.

"What is it, Howie?"

His whole body arched and convulsed. He was retching now like a cat with a hairball, or as if possessed by some kind of fit. He certainly looked to be beyond speech. Then he did manage to make a sound. It was a small harsh reflux, but nevertheless, as his tongue spasmed and his whole body jerked, it sounded remarkably like a T.

It came again. There was no mistaking it.

"T—"

"Can you spell it out, Howie? Can you say it?"

"Thr—"

It was like some ghastly process of birth. Then it all came at once, splitting his jaw so wide and pushing his tongue so far out that Clark feared that the guy's throat and guts would come out with it in slippery loops.

"Thrasis."

Howard Hughes subsided.

Howard Hughes slumped back from the gantry rail and crouched into a small, whimpering ball.

THIRTY FOUR

"Howie's like most of us here," Little Joe muttered as he pushed his trolley back toward the elevator. "Has his bad moments, but he'll get over it. Just needs a touch of the moodies, that's all . . . "

Clark's own thoughts were churning. He could still see that hunched and ruined figure at the far end of the gantry. It had seemed for a moment to be not one Howard Hughes but many, a thin blur of tremulous, agonized voices and scrabbling hands.

"How long have you been here, Joe?"

"Oh, I'm a newbie. Just the last five or six years is all. Only got to be a trustie these last couple."

"This may sound like an odd question, but does my name ring any kind of bell? I mean my last name, Lamotte? Or else a guy called Hogg?"

Little Joe thought for a moment, then pressed the elevator button with an oddly stubby finger before shaking his head. "Can't say it does."

"How about something called Thrasis?"

"Say what?"

"Thrasis."

Little Joe shook his head.

They ended up back in the Met's main entrance hall, with Little Joe parking his mop trolley in the same spot beneath the same severe portrait of one of the city fathers from which Clark had taken it.

"Come back any time you like," he said. "That is, if you fancy some more research. Now that you got the uniform an' all."

"Thanks. I'd be happy to see you again, Little Joe, but I'm not so sure about the rest. You shouldn't be in here either. Should ask to get yourself re-assessed..."

Little Joe's askew eyebrows rearranged themselves into something resembling a frown.

"Needn't worry about missing the moodies," Clark added. "You can spend all day and all night tucked up in the feelie houses in the city for all anyone'll care. And there's always plenty of work for a guy who can handle a mop."

"Wish it were that simple, Mr Lamotte." His gaze was sad and soft. "Truth is, the city air don't agree with me. I got this skin condition, see. Gets me all antsy so I can't move for scratching and a'nibbling. That's why I bit my nails so bad." He held out his big hands. All that was left of his nails were nubs of shiny scar tissue.

"That's why I had to pull out my teeth, an' all. My kids and my wife, they got the same problem. So I did them too." Little Joe balled up his hands and pulled his arms close around himself. "So I reckon I'm probably better in here 'til I stop getting the itches an' they get that city sorted."

THIRTY FIVE

Lights glowed out from poolhalls and poker parlors in the early gloom. The lowering sun across the intersections was angry and red. Roger and his pals cast lengthening shadows down Blixden Avenue as they chased their tin can. Clark got out of the Delahaye and squinted up at the sky. It was banking up with cloud. There was a smell of change in the air.

"That was *some* phone call." Roger ran over to him, ragged clothes flapping in the wind. "Mysterious geeks in uniform—and now you're wearing one yourself! Are you for *real*, Mr Lamotte, or is this all some feelie you think you're in?"

"Sometimes wonder. But you *did* tell Barbara Eshel?"

"I obey ze orders." The kid saluted, European style.

"And everything's okay? Nothing's happened?"

"Not much." The kid looked disappointed. Then his eyes traveled up the street toward the mailbox about halfway up. Clark followed his gaze. A thought came into his head.

"Why did you say the postie was mad, Roger?"

"'Cos he *is*. Hey, listen. The guy's . . . "

But Clark was already walking up the street.

" . . . it's just." Roger said as he tagged along beside him. "Well, something falls right into your hands, you take it, right . . . ?"

The mailbox was affixed to a lamppost beside a dusty willow tree. It was old, its drab paint peeling, U.S. MAIL embossed down the side. But this was probably the box which Daniel Lamotte had used to mail the blue draft of *Wake Up and Dream*—the one that Timmy Townsend said had never reached him. He crouched to look at it more closely as Roger continued to mouth excuses about whatever it was he and his friends had done. The only part of the mailbox that didn't look old was the lock, where a gleam of freshly drilled-out metal was showing. When he gave the front panel a push, it simply creaked open.

THIRTY SIX

Frying smoke and a smell of over-cooked eggplant hung inside Blixden Apartments as Clark climbed the stairs. Radios were playing. A fat lady in not much more than a towel pushed past him on her way to the bathroom. The door to room 4A was ajar.

"The wanderer returns." Barbara Eshel was sitting cross-legged in the middle of the floor, surrounded by papers. "Like the outfit, by the way. Did that really get you inside the Met?"

"You've seen the kid from the street?"

"The one called Roger? The one with all that guff about dark cars and guys in uniform?"

He put down the toilet wastecan he'd brought with him from Larch Lodge and sat on the chair beside the typewriter. He pushed at the letter T so that it was half-raised, then let it fall. He took off his glasses and pinched his nose. The room looked, smelled—*felt*—different. The papers were stacked now. Barbara Eshel had even thought to get rid of many of the old soup cans and bourbon bottles which he'd only looked at disgustedly. She'd even straightened the grayed sheets over the mattress.

"But *I* was okay." She picked up the Colt. Gave it an Annie Oakley spin. "Any baddies come to my hacienda, they get this. You okay Clark? What did you find...?"

He told her about the waitress at Edna's Eats who'd seen Daniel and April Lamotte there last Friday morning, and how he'd left the place apparently drunk, but more likely drugged. About driving into the mountains, and how April Lamotte supposedly killing herself only made sense when you put some guy dressed as a cop and some misleading signing also up there. Then there was what he'd found at Larch Lodge . . .

"April Lamotte even talked to me about starting a new life," he said. "It's the only thing that adds up. Something about the script that Dan was writing suddenly spooked her. Or maybe not so suddenly . . . Or maybe there was some kind of warning or somebody told her something. But whatever way it happened, she reckoned that if she used me to fake Dan's death, they could both run for it and start afresh with new identities. Somewhere they'd never be found. I mean, I may not look *that* much like the guy, but I'm close enough if all you have to go on is an ID, a diver's license, and a general description. And who else but April would the police have called on to identify the body?"

"And when morning came—after she'd left you for dead on Mulholland Drive—and she didn't get the phone call she was expecting from the police, she panicked and drove up to Larch Lodge?"

"Yeah."

"What I don't understand, Clark, is what she was going to do if her plan had worked. Okay, she's got her husband seemingly dead and the money sorted, but what about herself?"

He remembered again that new roadmap, and the gritty feel of sand he'd first got from it. And the notepad the police had shown him. The reason the phrases she'd written looked like tryouts, it suddenly occurred to him, was because that was what they *were* . . . "I think she was planning to stage her own death as well. Maybe not produce a body this time, and it's not what actually happened, but drive out over the mountains and leave her car parked somewhere in the high desert. Might not be found for months, and by then they'd hardly be looking for a body. Not with the note she was planning on leaving, and the vultures and coyotes. Makes perfect sense. Her husband's dead, after all. So why bother to live? Why not just drive off and walk into nowhere? Who wouldn't believe that?"

"But she didn't make it up to Larch Lodge yesterday morning, did she?"

"No."

"You think someone else got to her, made it look like the suicide she tried to fake for her husband, and then got to Dan after that and possibly doped him with a syringeful of something?"

"Yeah."

"So now Daniel Lamotte's been taken, without any obvious struggle, by person or persons unknown, but most likely driving a black Mercury sedan and wearing some kind of official-seeming uniform? And perhaps he's alive and perhaps he's dead? And all of this is because of something he's written in *Wake Up and Dream*?"

"You tell me why else. I don't think it's in the blue draft. Not in the script Dan first sent to Senserama, the one April Lamotte let me see, but the one he wrote after that, and she destroyed in a bonfire. But something *happened* to him. Like he'd found out something new and vital and big. Like he was gripped by a fever. And that discovery was what really scared April Lamotte."

She scooted over on her knees to the metal wastecan. Pulled a face. "And there's more of the screenplay in *here*? A pink draft?" She prodded it open. "Ow..."

"Watch the syringe."

"Jesus, Clark." She waved her finger. "Could have told me it was still in there. This is such a *mess*..." As she pulled out long, ragged bunches of toilet sheet he was reminded of the presence which had stirred itself out of the detritus in the City Hall mens' room. "Are you *sure* he hasn't...?"

"I'd be careful. Like they say on the signs, you should always wash your hands."

"Have you been able to *read* any of this...?"

"Enough to tell me that Dan had somehow decided that the real start of the story went back to him meeting April when he was still plain old Daniel Hogg and she worked at the Met—which, by the way, she really did. That, and that Howard Hughes was somehow at least as big a part of the story as anything to do with Lars Bechmeir."

"*Or* Dan was hearing voices, seeing ghosts—had gone plain mad... But did you actually get to see Howard Hughes? In that cleaner's uniform?"

"Yeah. I got there... The Met's a strange place. Even you or I would soon be acting pretty odd if we were patients. Howard Hughes works at keeping the furnaces and the generators going. Everyone calls him Howie, and I guess he seems happy enough. Almost sane, as well, until you start prodding him. He's had all sorts of operations done to his head. I tried asking him about what happened in the early days of the Bechmeir field, the way I suppose the real Daniel Lamotte had planned on doing, but, the way he answered the questions, it was like nothing was there."

"You mean he's forgotten?"

He shook his head. "It wasn't even that. He just talked like it had happened to someone else. And he said something about Lars Bechmeir being hard to get to beneath all the publicity. And this in a place where they actually *use* Bechmeir fields to keep the patients subdued. None of it seemed real . . . But I did get this . . . " He pulled the staff records from his pocket.

"Neat work." She smiled as she studied them. "You almost impress me, Clark. Might even make a half decent journalist if you weren't wasting your life sniffing other people's bedsheets. So she really did work at the Met, and for some reason Dan suddenly decides the place has got something vital to do with the script he's working on. All of which brings us right back to April Lamotte . . . And whatever caught up with her."

"And here's why that new script didn't get to Senserama—that mailbox down the street has had its lock drilled out. Dunno when, but the kids down there have been looking though the mail for money or whatever since early last week. Not that they ever saw anyone, and the postie's only just noticed, but it looks like it was done using the same kind of tool which did the padlock of the exchange up at Woodsville. April Lamotte was being watched, tracked, her phone listened in on. Dan was too—his mail was being intercepted and read. It all fits."

"And what about us, Clark?" She'd drawn knees up, her arms wrapped around them, and was looking at him with a sideways tilt to her head and an expression which was somehow both knowing and wary. "Where do we fit in with all of this?"

She boiled them up some coffee in her own room. It was the same kind of space Daniel Lamotte had occupied, but what struck Clark was its neatness and cleanliness. Proper drapes at the window, a patterned rug on the floor. Thrift shop stuff, maybe, but chosen by someone who cared about how she lived.

There were books everywhere—and papers—but they were all neatly stacked. Her typewriter had pencils laid tidily beside it like soldiers. This was nothing like the boarding house rooms of most women he'd encountered. No forests of slips and stays and stockings put out to dry. No dresser scattered with over-spilling ashtrays encrusted with residues of powder and lipstick.

"They definitely *were* married, by the way." He was sat down with his coffee on a threadbare easy chair. She was flicking through some of the stuff she'd moved here from next door. "*I've* been checking things, too. Down at County Records, for a start. Happened May 6, nineteen thirty three. Nothing fancy. Although, just like you said, April Lamotte kept her maiden name and Daniel must have already changed his from plain old Hogg. Now, *that's* something I can admire about this woman, whatever else she's done."

He nodded and sipped his coffee. He guessed she'd probably also checked on an unlicensed private investigator and once near-famous actor called Clark Gable. It was what he'd have done.

"That last sighting of Daniel Lamotte you were told about by the waitress down at Edna's Eats fits in with what I can remember. Now I've thought about it, I'm sure his typewriter was still clacking away earlier last week—say Monday and Tuesday. In fact, it was going so hard and fast that I remember sitting here next door and staring at my own machine and feeling envious. And then it went quiet. Maybe not Thursday, though. I'd say earlier than that. Wednesday at the latest. But it *does* figure—*if* last Friday he went down to that diner to speak to his wife about whatever he'd discovered." She sighed. "I wish I had a more exact memory."

"How about asking some of the other people who live here about what they've seen?"

"You think I haven't? One of the few joys of living in a place like this is that no one takes much notice of anyone else. Still, I'm pretty sure someone's been in there and sorted through his stuff. Not 'cos anything obvious is torn out or missing, but there's nothing *new*. There's nothing loose, or unfinished. It's all far too neat. But this I *did* think was odd." She handed him a pale blue sheet of typed paper.

```
Nuclear Power?
Space Travel?
Gold from the sea?
Mind Control?
Teleportation?
Jet power?
Television?
```

"He wrote *that*?"

"Unless you did."

"Maybe he was just riffing around for ideas for another project? Some futuristic kind of thing?"

"Who knows—but every other piece of paper and book and notebook next door is tediously and exclusively and repetitiously similar. I could carry on looking, I guess," she said, "but there's a limit to how many versions of the same sentence, written out with or without a comma, anyone can read and stay sane. We really need to find out where the guy is, and if he's still alive."

She then unrolled a list on a long sheet of paper. It was written in a neat hand which he now recognized as hers. "These are the names and sometimes the addresses of at least some of the private and generally unlisted clinics in and around Los Angeles."

Clark whistled. "That many?"

"It's far from complete. This is LA, don't forget. Seemed this morning like it might have been useful. All wasted effort now, by the look..." She sighed and pushed her fingers through her fringe. He got the impression from the gesture that not all her efforts had gone to waste. "But I *did* take the Redcar down to Willowbrook after I'd finished at County Records. You know, to visit the old theater were Lars Bechmeir worked on his invention that's now a museum. I asked the ladies at the souvenir desk if they remembered seeing a guy matching your—I mean Daniel Lamotte's—description. And they did. Could even show me his name in the visitor's book. He went there to look at the archives a couple of times about three months back, then once again three weeks ago. Although that isn't why they remembered him."

"Those earlier visits would have—"

"Hear me out, Clark. They said they remembered him from that last time because he'd been talking with the Director of the Charitable Board. A woman by the name of Doctor Penny Losovic. She works out of there. Didn't sound like he'd made an appointment to see her, more like they struck up a conversation in the reading room."

"Didn't you try to talk to this woman?"

"I couldn't—she isn't there. They haven't seen Doctor Losovic at her office in the museum since early last week. Normally, she comes and goes. It's not her job to run the place, or count all the money that the rights to the Bechmeir Field generate—what she does is oversee the donations that the Board gives out—so there's no one she really answers to. But they haven't seen hide nor hair. And they're just starting to think it's odd."

"Wasn't it her name on that letter that Daniel Lamotte got back from the Trust about the feelie, the one that said to speak to their lawyers?"

"Yeah, but it was p.p.—it wasn't signed by her. She'd already vanished on the day that letter went out."

"You mean, this woman had a conversation with Daniel Lamotte, and no one's seen her since?"

"Pretty much."

"Has anyone reported this?"

"Not that I know of. It wasn't something I wanted to get them thinking about doing, either. Once I got the picture, I kinda backed off."

"But Jesus—here's someone else who's disappeared!"

"That's just the start. Whole reason I went down to Willowbrook was to get a feel for the kind of stuff Dan was researching. To be honest, there's not that much to see. Just some bundles of press releases and the same old photographs we've all already seen in the magazines. That, and a couple of prototype versions of field generators in glass cases, a sensory room not much better than your average feelie theater, and framed versions of the early adverts when the whole industry was trying to promote the Next Big Thing. I'm surprised he went there as much as he did. But I did manage to smuggle out this . . . "

Looking pleased with herself, and with a theatrical rustle, she produced a sheet of yellowed paper densely typed with faded columns of names.

"It's dated May 12,1931, and it's the guestlist for the premiere of *Broken Looking Glass*, the first ever feelie. Hughes was there." She pointed. "'Course, it was his movie, I mean feelie, and then there's the production staff and the actors and some people I recognize as reviewers and the usual hangers-on from the press. Especially for something they thought was going to be a freakshow disaster. But there are quite a few others as well. See—Herbert Kisberg? Well, I guess he was showing an early interest in the technology that would make his fortune. Lars and Betty Bechmeir, of course—they would be there, wouldn't they? Then there's Cy Edgerton. He's ex-mayor, tons of directorships, and he's also on the Bechmeir Board of Trustees. Then Jerry Lock. He owns half the undeveloped real estate south of the Baldwin Hills. Famous and successful people, right? Or at least they are now. And we all know Peg Entwistle."

"Yeah." He nodded. "We all know Peg."

"It's like this is a list of the people who've made it big in this town since the thirties. But that's only half the story. Have you heard of William H. Frooney?"

"William H . . . ?"

"Don't read the papers much, do you?"

"Never did."

"Will Frooney ran a construction company. One of the biggest. Still going, far as I know. In fact, Frooneys might even be the firm that's at work on the site of what's now left of Grauman's Chinese Theater. Their signs are still all over the place. But Frooney hanged himself about four years ago. And Carel Srodzinski . . . I suppose you don't remember him?"

He shook his head.

"Srodzinski ran an electronics firm. People used to call him The Magician of the Wires, and that was before all the publicity he got from the way he died. *Fried By His Own Electricity*—don't you remember that? The LA press love an ironic suicide. There are quite a few other suicides on this list. Far more than you might reasonably expect. Of course, we all know about Betty Bechmeir. But there are even worse things happened to some of those people as well. Gabriel Halon, for example. Now, he was doing well out of airplanes and chemicals. Had a fine ranch-house up in Santa Monica. Place called Happenstance."

"You mean the Happenstance killings? God, that was *terrible*."

"Press *must* have had a field day if you've heard about it, Clark. All six of the family, and then even the dogs. Tortured for days. Like... who the hell knows what it was like? 'Course, the culprit or culprits were never found. And neither were they for the Theobold murders a year or two later. Ring any bells?"

"None that I'm hearing."

"Then you're the lucky one, and the Theobolds certainly weren't. He was a successful doctor—a pioneering brain surgeon. Basically, they were found starved to death in their own home in '38. Bad enough, right? But all their friends had thought they were in Europe and someone had kept them chained up in there for months. They hadn't just starved. They'd been forced to eat... Well, the coroner's report rather implied it was each other."

"That's sick."

"Is, isn't it? But there's a pattern. *All* of these people went to the premiere of *Broken Looking Glass*. And now they're dead successful. Or simply dead. And the ones that are dead either killed themselves, or had something far worse and nastier happen."

"Why hasn't anyone else ever seen this going on?"

"Because there *is* nothing going on unless you check against this guestlist. Far as I can tell, these people aren't particularly associated in any other way. Guys like Frooney and Srodzinski and Halon, they might have known each the way the rich always do, but as far as anyone knows, their deaths were just regular common-or-garden LA murders and suicides, and whoever takes any notice of those? And when it comes to those big showpiece murders, well, they do tend to happen in LA rather more than most places." She was looking at him with that sideways tilt to her head and an expression which was somehow both knowing and wary. "But there is one other name I want you to see..."

She held the guestlist out to him. It was badly crumpled. It must have been the actual typed sheet which had been used to check people in on the night.

"You see?"

Before he could say whether he saw or not, she was pointing toward the bottom of the list, where the name A. Lamotte (Miss) was just visible.

"This is *big*, Clark. This is *important*. This is a massive opportunity to put *LA Truth* on the publishing map..." Barbara Eshel was pacing the room now, flushed and excited. She'd already wrenched the two invites for Kisberg's party out of his hands.

"But—"

"We've *got* to go. It's an open secret Kisberg's going to announce himself as the Liberty League presidential candidate tomorrow, and here's our chance to get into his house. He's on the board of the Bechmeir Trust, for godsake, and he was on that guestlist of ten years ago before anyone even knew who the hell he was. Can't you see what a chance this is, Clark? Can't you see how it all adds up?"

"Look at us."

"Obviously, we can't go as we are—but didn't you say that Erewhon has walk-in wardrobes stuffed with expensive clothes?"

He put the cup with the remains of his cold coffee down on the table beside his chair. His eyes traveled back to the list. Barbara was right—there were some names he recognized, for all the little attention he paid to the news.

"We'll be seriously late," he muttered.

She flapped her arms and laughed. "Don't you know how *fashionable* that is?"

THIRTY SEVEN

"This is some place."

There were no obvious signs of forced entry at Erewhon, or of LAPD scene of crime notices or further violence or blood. Automatic lights flared on when they entered the hall.

"Just stand over there by the staircase. I want the reader to get a real sense of this place's scale. And put those glasses back on." Barbara Eshel screwed a new flashbulb into the Graflex camera which had taken up most of her handbag.

Pop. Flash.

"If you like, we can just say it's an old picture of Daniel Lamotte before everything went wrong. Depends how the story works out, but we'll certainly need something, a visual angle—especially if I can get a feature in one of the better magazines."

"I thought you said you were doing this for a piece in *LA Truth*?"

She lowered the Graflex to twist the winder around. "Yeah, but the more I think about this, and the more we find out—this story's got breakthrough written right through it like a stick of Long Island rock."

Flashbulbs hissed and flickered. She wandered off, cursing in surprise at the size and splendor of the rooms.

The same fine furniture, pale carpets and dark curtains swam into view beneath the recessed lights when they went upstairs to find clothes. The phone still sat on the glasstop table beside the bed in the room April and Daniel Lamotte had shared. So did the ashtray, still filled with all those ground-out pastel-colored butts. He could even see the dent on the bed where she'd sat and waited two nights ago for the call saying her husband was dead.

"You know," Barbara was saying, "this woman's not so very far from my clothes size. Might even be the same. But who the hell needs all of this stuff? Such a waste of money..." Nevertheless, she was lifting lots of it out; whole shifting, rustling piles of dresses and suits and skirts. "And by the way, Clark—do you really think they'd be able to afford this lifestyle on a feelie writer's money alone? Okay, he wrote some successful screenplays, but *this*? Thought you said you *knew* this industry?"

The guest suite he went to get changed in wasn't much of a come-down. Even though the boiler was off and the water was cold, the shower felt sweeter than anything he was used to. *And* not a cockroach in sight.

I could get used to this, part of him was saying as he sat on the edge of the bed and toweled himself. The walnut furnishings. The carpets. The mirrors. That car outside. The cost of a working man's monthly wages for a bottle of cologne. And that young woman in the room along the corridor—who was probably naked in the shower right now—I could get used to her, as well.

But nothing would settle. Not this weird new life he was living, nor the old one he seemed to have lost. Even now, it took an effort of will to look at himself in the long dressing table mirror, and the face he saw bought no particular relief.

He shook his head. Inspected the fine assortment of another man's clothes he'd gathered. Shirt collar pinned by solid gold. A suit of that deeper shade of black you never saw in any regular clothes shop, and only rarely in night skies. Shoes snug as a ballerina's pumps. A silk paisley necktie so beautifully painted it was a work of art. He already knew the look and fit all of it would be perfect.

He went downstairs after he'd gotten dressed and waited for a while in the hall for Barbara Eshel to come down. He smoked a Lucky Strike. He stared at the phone in the alcove. He wandered the long corridor after he'd finished his cigarette. The wraith was still turned off. He stopped and studied it. Then he felt around until he found a toggle switch around the back of the plinth.

Nothing at first but a soft swishing, like silk over flesh. He guessed that that was the looped recording wire passing and re-passing over the recording heads. Then came a humming, and a faintly cattish smell of warm valves and shellac as the amplifiers started to do their work. There was something floating now between the charged plates like a stream of sunlit dust, and the air seemed to have chilled as if a door somewhere had been opened. The plasm shimmer of the Bechmeir field was unmistakable now, a dance of light, and beautiful to behold.

The wraith floated before him, and it seemed that his mind was playing tricks, although he knew that what he was experiencing was, by definition, a trick of the mind. What had April Lamotte said about this feelie recording—that Daniel Lamotte had got some studio to mix in the auras of all his favorite actors, then put it on a loop? He could see what she meant. For wasn't that Peg Entwistle's queenly aura he was now feeling, and wasn't this one that guy with the ragged gait for whom things always went wrong? It really was like the distillation of some endless night at the feelies, and he could understand why Daniel Lamotte had got the thing made, and also why it had come to taunt him. But there was something else as well. An undertow that dragged oddly at the spirit—something bleak and powerful and strange...

He turned the thing off with a shudder, and watched it fade and drain away. Hearing something further down the corridor, he turned and saw that lights were on in the room where he'd talked with April Lamotte. A changed Barbara Eshel was standing beside the long couch.

"What kept you so long, Clark?" she asked.

Every time he thought he'd got some sort of handle on this woman, she went and did something like this. How, for example, could she have got herself dressed and downstairs so much more quickly than he had? And then, manage to look like she did?

"You don't brush up too bad," she said as she studied him. "For a failed actor, that is."

"Neither do you. For a twobit newshound."

"This . . . " she gestured—she'd chosen a long, dark dress which shimmered with turquoise blues—" . . . was about the only thing in April Lamotte's entire wardrobe that anyone move around in like a normal human being." It was loose and long from the hips down, low and tight at the bust. She hadn't done much to her hair, but whatever she'd done had transformed her. Or maybe it was the earrings or the silver choker. "I mean, what *is* the *point* of having some glossy fabric wrapped so tight around your thighs and ass that you can barely walk?"

"I think I can explain that."

"Don't bother! I already feel like some ridiculous society whore. And *I'm* someone who used to stand outside Liberty League rallies waving banners until the LAPD started beating us up."

THIRTY EIGHT

The sky roiled and flickered as they drove down from the canyons towards Beverly Hills. The Beverly Wiltshire, and the Electric Fountain. Billboards and billboards and billboards. JUDAS THE FEELIE WHO WANTS TO LOOK OLD WARM WINE ENEMAS DO YOU INHALE HOT DOGS BUY SELL DINE DIE THE LAST THE BEST THE LATEST NEW NEW NEW FRESH NEW YOUNG

The building beyond the raised chromium portcullis of Herbert Kisberg's gatehouse was so large and yet floated so delicately on floodlit tiers of lawn that it scarcely seemed to be made of stone at all.

"You're not going to tell people you're my dead wife, are you?"

"Of course not."

"But you're with me, Barbara. The way you look—anyone who heard about what's happened is going to think it's a bit quick to start a new romance."

"First of all, this is Hollywood and they wouldn't think that at all. Secondly, they'd care even less. But thirdly, Clark, I'll simply tell people I'm who I really am."

"You mean—"

"I'll say, *Hi, I'm a writer*. And they'll ask if I've had anything produced. And when I tell them I'm not *that* kind of writer, they'll walk away."

Some of the security goons wore dinner suits, and some wore Liberty League trooper uniforms, but they were all big and broad; nothing like the Gladmont guy, but the sort you'd get to play background heavies in a feelie. They didn't even ask to see Clark's invitation cards, let alone ask them about who they were, although Barbara looked like she wanted to talk to them anyway until Clark drew her on. They followed a grass pathway between flaming sconces and a vast slew of expensive cars toward marquees, piping music, flags and marching soldiers. The flashing cannon and falling horses of an entire battle scene which was being enacted in a wide auditorium beneath the terraced lakes before the house.

"Dan, Dan, Dan. You *did* make it after all..." Resplendent in tartan necktie, coat and trews, Timmy Townsend came bounding up. "So, so great to see you." Clark looked around for Barbara as Timmy pumped his hand, but she'd already vanished into the preening crowds.

"I thought I should make the effort."

"And *here* you are." Timmy took a snorting breath—half laughter, half disbelief. "And that news about your wife..." He looked jolly even when he made a serious effort to look sad. "So, *so* terrible. You *must* let my secretary know when and where the funeral is. Promise? Terrible business. And how about *you*, Dan? How are you feeling? Do you think you can face the next day and the next deadline and crack on?"

"Yeah." He nodded. "I think I can."

"That's..." The look of sorrowful concern had once again lost its battle with the bonhomie which dominated Timmy's broad face. "... good."

"Can I ask you something, Timmy— I mean about my wife. You must have dealt with her, to sort out the *Wake Up and Dream* contract?"

"Just a couple of phone calls, I think." The executive's lower lip bulged in the manner of someone who wasn't usually called on to reflect much upon the past. "After you'd sent the treatment in, and my secretary had shoved it across my desk, and of course I saw your name and I sat down and I read it and it was the most—"

"So *I* sent *Wake Up and Dream* in, and then April got in touch?"

"Well, Dan, I'd have to get my secretary to check. The way I remember, there was this brilliant treatment, and the next thing I know April's calling me to ask if I've got it, read it, and what did I think?"

"So *I* sent it in, not April, and from my Bunker Hill address? And then she chased it up, and brokered the deal?"

"That's the way I recollect it."

"Sorry to go on about this Tim. But I'm like you—I'm a big picture man, and my recollection's sometimes a little hazy when it comes to nuts and bolts. And of course I can't ask April now."

"A wonderful, wonderful woman." Drums rattled. Cannon flared.

"Sure. But what did you reckon to her as an agent? I mean, what was she like when she sorted the deal?"

From puzzlement, Timmy Townsend's expression was now shifting to alarm. "A deal's a deal, you know, old fella. Doesn't matter who's alive or dead. And this really isn't the time to be worrying about this sort of thing, Danny boy. You're bound to be shook up. I mean, I had no idea—"

"You're right. And neither did I. But I was just, I don't know, curious about the sort of approach she took..."

Timmy Townsend laid a hand on his shoulder. His smile had returned. "Your wife was a decent person, Dan. Not some money-grabbing, over-ambitious, super-bitch—feel like you have to put on armored gloves before you shake hands with them, their talons are that fucking sharp—which, *entre nous*, is a kind of agent I'm having to deal with more and more these days. April Lamotte was not just a loss to you, Dan, but a loss to the whole industry, and to us all. I can honestly say that dealing with her was like a breath of fresh air."

Understanding. Sensible. A breath of fresh air... In other words, good though it was, she'd just taken what was on offer at first base. That didn't sound like the work of any kind of agent, let alone April Lamotte.

"But you *must* let me show you some people..."

Even feelie executives had to be good at something, and this was surely Timmy Townsend's star turn. The hand across the shoulder, the warm smile, the friendly *hey*, the promise of a quick chat saved for later, the peck on the cheek, the fuck-off turn of the head, the avoiding or beckoning wave, the flirtatious pat on the ass.

He'd been to parties pretty close to this back in the old days, and not much seemed to have changed, apart from the hems rising higher and the cut of the necklines swooping lower. But the whole industry had moved on—if was the same industry at all. People like Thalberg, Goldwin, the Meyers, the Wallaces, and the studios they'd founded had all been gobbled up, and gone. Now, it was Senserama, and Arc-Plasm, and TLL, and even the Paramount part of Paramount-Shindo was just a name that the Japs had used so people wouldn't think they were Japs. Most of the big players back in Clark's day had been Jews, of course. Not that the Hebes were now being treated over here the way they were said to be back in Europe—not even in cutting edge California. No siree. Far from it. They could hold down jobs and open bank accounts and run businesses just like anyone else, as long as they were properly registered and didn't exceed the designated quota for their scientifically categorized ethnic group. Just like the Mexicans, Chinese and blacks, they could sometimes even use the same bus benches, schools, drinking fountains and public toilets as the white Caucasians; it was all just a question of sharing out limited resources in the fairest possible way. Get over it, get on with it, or leave our fucking country was the underlying message. This, after all, was the Land of the Free.

Just like at the studio, part of him was still waiting for someone to shake their head after he'd introduced himself and say—no *you're* not Daniel Lamotte, but, if you took off those science professor glasses, wouldn't you look a fair bit like that guy who nearly used to be famous called Clark Gable . . . ? He needn't have worried. These people weren't like Mary at Edna's Eats, or some of his sadder clients, or the people who still occasionally gazed at him oddly on the street. Here, everything which had or would ever happen was changed and refracted through the dazzling prism of the eternal now. As he was introduced and moved on, he soon realized that the vague *don't I know you?* expression with which he was most often greeted—and the warm nod which followed when Timmy explained who he was—was simply the standard way people at a party like this dealt with anyone they didn't recognize. Obviously, you wouldn't be here at all if you were nobody. Then Timmy, who could work this kind of thing the way Karajan had worked his orchestra in the recent Berlin Philharmonic tour, would come in with the terrible fact of his recent loss. Dan was fine, Dan was coping; Dan was the sort of writer who took this sort of thing and turned it into box-office gold—that was the message they all got from his warm tone. Women hugged him and murmured soft things into his ear. Men looked tearful and held on extra long as they shook his hand. He was given cards by lawyers, new agency proposals—*just give me a call soon as you're settled; better still, I'll call you*—someone even offered him the use of his yacht. He felt like he was the star of every crowd for the moments he was standing there with them, and knew that he'd be forgotten as anything more than some or other writer whose wife had taken a wrong turn into thin air the moment he was gone.

He remembered again that yellowed guestlist; the names, the people—dead successful, or simply dead. And here was the guy who now ran the Los Angeles and Salt Lake Railroad, and hadn't he been one of them? And hadn't this guy in the red frock just been Father Gerald of something, and now he was Bishop of Los Angeles? And this fat Liberty League apparatchik who was apparently the California Supreme Court judge who'd sentenced more prisoners to execution than any other—hadn't he been on the list as well?

Clark was drinking Champagne like everyone else, and it was all becoming a golden blur. Men who tossed back their heads and showed their perfect teeth to laugh. Women so invariably thin and blonde that they seemed likely to dissolve into pure aura. Under the chandeliers, within the mirrors and caught in all the silver trays and the melting iceberg sculptures and the shimmering crystal meadows of cut glass, everything was magnified and multiplied, and yet it all seemed so inescapably real that it was like a dream made of something more solid than mere flesh and effort and money, or even life itself.

"This is the place, eh?" Timmy Townsend was saying. "This is all that I've been telling you about! Herbert's just had this ruined castle moved over from Scotland and put up in the grounds stone by stone. Tonight at midnight, we all get to see it—I've heard there's even a genuine, verified, old-fashioned ghost. I've been nagging my secretary about getting this tartan suit made for weeks. I sure am glad I did—I mean, who wants to look an oaf?"

A bagpipe band was playing somewhere. A jazz band was playing somewhere else. If you stood mid-way between the two, you could hear them both. Timmy's main quest in hauling Clark through the swirls and intersections of the party was Herbert Kisberg himself, but the guy was elusive. Everyone had seen him. Everyone had spoken to him, or claimed to have spoken to someone who had. But he was never quite there.

Clark noticed that there really wasn't much talk of politics by these people for all the near-swooning that went on at the mention of Kisberg's name. FDR might be "that cripple" and they struggled to even remember who the new Republican candidate was, but the idea of that they were actually supporting the Liberty League's ideals by wearing these pins on their bosoms and lapels, or by casually tossing hundred dollar bills into the silver campaign support buckets which the servants were carrying around, seemed to be beyond them. After all, Herbert was a player, he was one of them. He'd made—financed, anyway—all those lovely feelies which everyone remembered so fondly, and he was in charge of California and his face was up on the billboards, and he was so, so good looking, and he'd invited them to this spectacular party and he knew them by name, or at least they wished he did. Above all, he was rich and he was famous, wasn't he? And that was as good as being good. Nah, it was better. Clark could foresee the time when even one of those muscle-building, grunt-syllabled goons out in the car lot could easily make it as far as State Governor when Kisberg stood down. Maybe further still.

Timmy finally reached a smaller room with little more than a few antique Persian carpets and Ming vases to decorate its walls. A few men sat smoking cigars and talking in large leather chairs. A few others stood. A similar number of women had arranged themselves as further ornaments between the vases.

Clark thought for a moment that they'd reached some outer edge of tonight's celebrations. But the way the men murmured to each other, and the measured way they turned to look at him, made him realize he was wrong.

One man in particular stood talking with a calm animation which seemed to hold the attention of the room. Even without that billboard outside the Senserama studios, Clark would have recognized the face. There was something about that kingly smile, those young-wise eyes, the almost boyish shock of dark blonde hair.

"Herbert, Herbert..." Timmy stammered in a flurry of gestures as Kisberg finished what he'd been saying and turned their way. "Here's someone I want you to meet."

"Of course." It was hard not to feel privileged when you were taken in by that gaze.

"This is Daniel Lamotte. We've just bought his script for a Lars Bechmeir biopic."

"Dan, how are you doing?" Kisberg shifted his tumbler of whisky and shook Clark's hand. "Without *The Virgin Queen*, the feelies wouldn't be what they are today."

"Thanks, Mr Kisberg. And thanks for buying my new script."

"You must call be Herbert. I wish I could be more involved in the creative process, but nowadays I have to let Tim here and his colleagues do all the hard work."

Timmy snickered. If he was a dog, he'd have rolled over to show his belly.

"I do truly thank you for coming tonight. Especially in light of your recent tragedy. But I believe it's better to get on with things, and I know that work can be a great comfort, especially in difficult times."

Clark nodded. He was trying hard to remember the vigilantes, the goons, the burly nurses with their rubber hoses back at the Met, and all the dark things which had happened to him and so many others in the sunlit blackness of this strange new world. April Lamotte's dead body on the Gurney. The names Barbara Eshel had shown him on that list.

"I've read *Wake Up and Dream*," Kisberg continued, "and I want to tell you it's the kind of work that makes me proud to be a part of this business. You've captured those times so well. I'm certain that the finished product will be a work of brilliance."

"Well, thanks again. Although I've been wondering, Mr Kisberg, why Senserama felt now was the right time to do a feelie about Lars Bechmeir. I mean, the subject's so obvious, there must have been other treatments and submissions over the years."

"But there are times when something simply seems right. You, as the writer, must have felt the same."

"Yeah. And there's some people I've been trying to speak to. A woman called Penny Losovic, for instance. I imagine you know her?"

"Of course. Penny does a great deal of largely unrewarded work for the Bechmeir Trust. Without her, it wouldn't be the organization it is, and a lot of people would be the poorer."

"Not around tonight, though, is she?"

"I don't believe so." With those steely eyes, it was hard to tell what Herbert Kisberg was thinking. "Penny's a private person. But if you're finding her hard to get hold of, I'll see what I can do . . ." He turned to Timmy, who was already nodding. ". . . or maybe you, Tim?"

"And there's Howard Hughes," Clark pushed on. "Truth is, that scene where Lars Bechmeir goes to the Hughes Corporation offices with his prototype device is one that I'm finding hard to sit right."

"Howard was a dear friend." Others were watching. Without raising his voice, Kisberg's smooth tone easily filled the room. "He still is, or at least a fond memory. We wouldn't be where we are without him. Not one of us."

"But the whole business of anyone believing in Lars Bechmeir's idea. The guy was a nobody, and the invention must have sounded like the work of a crank. Speaking personally, Mr Kisberg, what was it that made you go to the premiere of *Broken Looking Glass*?"

Kisberg took a slow sip of his whisky. "Maybe we were all a little younger and more foolish than we are now." He smiled a boyish smile. "A little foolishness—a preparedness to take a risk. Maybe that's something we should all try to keep in our lives?" There were solemn nods, and Clark supposed their conversation was at an end, but then Kisberg put down his whisky and leaned so close to him that Clark could smell the floral sweetness of the man's cologne. "I do understand your wanting to get to the heart of what happened, Dan," he murmured so close to Clark's ear that it felt like the breath of a Bechmeir field. "And I think I can help."

"How do you find my house, Dan? Over-large and over-ostentatious, I imagine. But one must put on a show. It's an obligation of power, just as it has always been. I imagine monarchs of the old days such as Queen Elizabeth in that marvelous feelie pic you wrote would have felt the same."

Clark Gable and Herbert Kisberg were walking red carpeted corridors lined with fine paintings and frail pieces of furniture, which Kisberg paused to explain with the vague air of someone who doesn't wish to disclose how much they really know.

"I don't fool myself into assuming that you're a Liberty League supporter," he muttered after pointing out the exquisite detail of a small dog in a painting by Vermeer.

"I don't usually vote, Mr Kisberg. Although you're right. I don't support your party and I never would."

"Is there a reason?" He glanced almost shyly up at Clark through blonde lashes.

"A few things. Timmy Townsend tells me that you're doing a deal with the Nazis to supply feelie tracks for Hitler's rallies, for example."

"Oh, *that*. Tim's an oaf, as you've doubtless noticed. But he means well, and he has a good eye for certain things—maybe even a successful feelie. Let's hope so, anyway. As soon as I heard that one of Senserama's executives had made that ill-advised approach to the Germans, I put a stop to it. The whole point of the Liberty League is that we don't—and I mean absolutely don't—support the Nazis. But we must leave Europe to deal with itself, and counteract the real threat which lies beyond."

"Which is?"

"World communism, of course. If we choose to fight the current German expansion, all we do is play into Soviet Russia's hands. Say we *did* go to war against the Germans, which is the way in which FDR's policies are inevitably leading. Say we did draft our young men into the army and waste our great nation's resources on building battleships and warplanes, all so that American blood could be spilled again in the fields of France—do you think that the Russians would simply stand by? And do you think the Japanese would either? I *know* about war, Dan. I fought as a captain in the trenches and I saw just how terrible it was. I don't believe in illusions or half-measures. We must understand where our interests lie. Which is here at home. I want a prosperous and peaceful nation where people understand what it means to be an American." He shrugged. "That's all my party has ever stood for."

"And what about the guys you see on the streets? The ones who dress up like blackshirts? The fools who want the Jews to wear badges and are calling for the blacks to be put in reservations like the Indians?"

"They *are* fools. But they're American fools, and they truly believe in their country and they feel a genuine sense of wrong. They've lost their jobs, their homes, their businesses, in these last difficult ten years. These are *real* Americans—they didn't arrive here ten minutes ago—and they want their lives and their self-respect back. Sure, they have their prejudices. But don't we all? It's only if we leave them out in the cold and ignore their voice, Dan, that they become dangerous. If we welcome them in and put a stop to foreign influence and immigration and embrace the truth of what this country really is about . . . "

In one direction lay the golden glint of some big, wall-consuming treasure—perhaps the altar of some Italian chapel; it was hard to tell. The other led toward a small and dimly-lit room.

Inside, there was a bed, and a radiogram, which was softly playing something probably classical and symphonic, although the sound was too low to be sure. There was also a portable lavatory concealed behind a railed curtain, and a trolley racked this high with expensive drugs. The purpose of the room was clearly medical but there were barely any of the usual signals to set Clark's teeth on edge. Apart, that was, from a dim aura of suppressed pain. There were several pictures on wall, but they were cheap reproductions. You could have got the painted plaster ornaments which were set above the unlit fireplace with a few lucky shots at the fair. After all he'd seen, it was the sheer blandness of this room which was shocking to him even before he'd fully taken in what was here.

There were two nurses, both wearing the sort of uniforms which showed off their figures so well you wondered about their other qualifications for the job. One of them was sitting reading a mail order fashion catalogue. The other was smoking as she peered out through a gap in the drawn curtains at whatever there was to see of the party outside. They both turned as Clark and Kisberg entered, touching their hairdos and adjusting the bored droop of their mouths into smiles.

"How is he?" Kisberg asked.

"Oh..." The nurse who'd been smoking popped her cigarette into a flip-top chrome ashtray, whilst the one who'd been sitting reading stood up and smoothed the rucks in her uniform across her thighs. "...he's fine..." They were so alike in makeup and hairdo that it was hard to tell which was speaking. "...been asleep..." "...for the last half hour or so..." They could have been twins.

The long bed which filled the middle of the room was of the gray metal-frame sort, with raised bars on either side to stop people falling out, which you also saw in hospitals, but it was empty and one of the sides had been put down. The man they were all now looking down at was seated in the wheelchair beside the bed, his small body hunched piles of plaid blankets, from which a single brown rubber pipe ran out toward some kind of jar beneath the bed. The toes of slippers protruded, along with a glimpse of bare and bony, blue-mottled ankle. Above the blankets, he was wearing a collar shirt and cardigan, both buttoned wrongly. His mouth had lolled and his chin had been down inside his skewed collar when Clark and Kisberg first entered the room. He'd stirred at the sound of voices, slowly stretching his stringy neck, blinking his eyes and opening and closing his mouth, for all the world like a tortoise peeping out of its shell at the end of a winter's hibernation.

One of the nurses leaned over to wipe a bead of drool from the corner of his mouth. The man responded with a sharp mash of his lips, and a spasm of irritation which had him raising his bird-like hands. He then made a series of wet clicking noises. The other nurse nodded; she seemed to understand these sounds as words. When she reached to a side counter, opened the wire arms of a pair of round-rim glasses, and hooked them around his ears and across his snub little nose, it was as if something had snapped sharply into focus within the room. Suddenly, there was no doubting who this frail old man gazed blinkingly up at them was. The beard might have grayed and thinned, and the double-breasted kaki jacket might be absent, but this was Lars Bechmeir. Propped up on the counter from where the nurse had picked up those famous glasses, Clark could even see the trademark Meerschaum pipe.

Much in the way a young relative might when visiting an elderly uncle, Herbert Kisberg bent down and smilingly took hold of one of the trembling hands. "Sorry to wake you, old chap. Must save your energies. But I've brought someone I'd like you to meet. He's a writer by the name of Daniel Lamotte..."

"...W...?" Thin lips strung spittle.

"That's right, Lars. He's a *writer*. And he's going to write the feelie that tells the story of your life."

Lars Bechmeir was looking more directly at Clark now. His mouth was still working, and he seemed to be trying to say something. Or maybe he was just gasping for air.

"Hi there, Mr Bechmeir." Clark heard himself mutter. "It's a real pleasure."

"Some other time, Lars old boy, when you're better rested, we'll set up an interview. Would that be alright...?"

"Al...right...?" It was the first definite word which Clark had heard Lars Bechmeir utter. And there was an increasing sense of sharpness, almost of agitation, to the gaze with which he found himself fixed. This guy, he thought, isn't quite all gone yet. There's still something in there, somewhere, that's alive and sharp... And there was something else, as well, about the way he was looking at him. The flurry of his hands was increasing—so much so that Herbert Kisberg had to stand back up and make room for the nurses. Instantly, all crooning lips and pressed linen asses, they were wiping the drool from his mouth, and steadying his flurrying hands.

"All..? *right*...?" But Lars Bechmeir still seemed agitated. As Clark and Kisberg left the room he was still staring in Clark's direction.

"All the sightings are false, of course," Kisberg sighed. "Those, anyway, that haven't been of him in the ranch down in Orange County where he lives a quiet life with a few select aides like Adeline and Marie-Louise.

I'm sure we'll be able to arrange a proper interview, but we don't want to tire him out. He's agreed to make his first public appearance in years tomorrow evening at the Liberty League ball at the Biltmore. Who knows, we may even get him to say a few words."

Lars Bechmeir backs the Liberty League! It would be the endorsement of the century—like God saying he supported the Nicks, or preferred Avis to Hertz. Assuming, that was, that the little man was still actually capable of expressing anything at all.

"So you really are going to run for president?"

Herbert Kisberg gave another of his bashful smiles. "We'll have to wait and see." He checked his watch. "But you must excuse me, Dan. I have work to do, I'm afraid. *Such* a bore. But it's near midnight, and I believe most of my guests will soon be heading outside . . . "

Music roared. Lights speared the sky. The rain was holding off, but a near-gale was blowing—spinning hats and toupees off into the darkness—although it was impossible to tell if it was due to the weather, or if the studio had brought in wind machines.

Clark had already heard several stories about the ghost which supposedly appeared at midnight on the battlements of the picturesque ruin of Castle Balaig, which had been brought stone by stone from the Scottish Highlands and cleverly re-erected in Herbert Kisberg's grounds. A woman wronged, a husband stabbed, a monk immolated, a nun buried alive or drowned . . . But, underlit by colored spotlights through a haze of dry ice, the castle seemed dwarfed by the spectacle which surrounded it; like the megalithic relic of some Indian tribe briefly unearthed in the excavations for a new shopping mall.

Velvet ropes formed a path through to the ruins, and there were tartan-dressed stewards to pour out tots of Scotch malt and usher people along the way. Some cynical souls were wondering aloud as they ascended the re-mortared steps if ghosts were aware of time differences, or perhaps stuck to the hour of the country of their birth, or death? And what about daylight saving time?

Midnight loomed, and with it came an eerie quiet as, for what seemed the first time that evening, or perhaps in all Hollywood history, the showbiz people crowded along the battlements ceased to bitch and crow. Then, just as the tower clock illuminated by a spotlight above Kisberg's house began to chime, the sky shattered in a veins of light. A roar of thunder followed. In another moment, it was sheeting rain.

Women screamed, clothing turned sheer and heels broke as people stumbled from the battlements as the storm took hold, but Clark remained standing there, looking down through the spotlights as the ragged crocodile of revelers slipped and skidded across the mud. The entire gardens quickly emptied. Soon, it was just him out here amid this crashing storm and with these misplaced old stones. The thought struck him as flickers of light froze the rain that, if anyone was ever likely to see a ghost up on these battlements, it was now. Then he yelped as a cold, wet hand clapped across his shoulder.

"What a night, eh?" Timmy Townsend spread his arms, tilting his head back into the rain. "What a fucking night, eh? Come on God, you bastard! Strike me down right now!" A thick layer of white mucus glistened across the executive's upper lip. "It just doesn't get any better than this. Have you ever felt this happy, Danny boy, in your entire fucking life? I know your wife's gone killed herself, and all of that. But you've *seen* him haven't you? Lars fucking Bechmeir is here tonight, and he's going to be at the Biltmore tomorrow!"

The sky flickered again. Thunder boomed, so loud this time that the castle seemed to tremble.

"But get this, Danny boy! I've got you on the *Star Talk* special live at the fucking Biltmore tomorrow to promote *Wake Up and Dream* in conversation with Wallis Beekins. We might even get a hi from Lars fucking Bechmeir, although I gather the guy ain't exactly up for running the Olympics. And we can certainly get a word from our other man of the hour Herbert Kisberg, who's our future fucking president. Who'd have believed it yesterday when we first met up? Who'd have believed it thirty fucking *minutes* ago—that this moment could be so fucking, fucking perfect?

"The feelie itself'll be a trainwreck. You do realize that, don't you, Dan? Now that we've got all the hype and the momentum going we'll take our eyes off the fucking ball and forget the dream—ha! *Wake Up and Dream*, right?—that got us started on this project. We'll produce some turgid piece of dross. And you know what? You know what the biggest fucking joke of all is? No one will notice..." Timmy Townsend was dancing now. Waving his hands. His feet skidding on wet stonework close to the edge of the thirty foot drop. "The crowds will come and the critics will cream themselves and dogs will bark at the sodding moon just as fucking always, and we'll clink our glasses and fuck our whores and send our girlfriends on shopping trips to Rome, Berlin and Madrid and swallow every jism spurt of the fucking hype, and *Wake Up and Dream*'ll be a travesty instead of the masterpiece it could have been. *That*, Danny boy..." He swung a hand—half punch, half finger jab—in Clark's direction. "Is the biggest joke of all. It's downhill here for the rest of our sodding lives and we won't even fucking care!"

Another wild swing, and he was falling back, arms flailing. Clark grabbed at him instinctively, and for a moment the two men teetered over the drop, then Clark got a better grip and pulled him straight.

"Nearly there, eh? Nearly the perfect fucking moment." Timmy was still laughing, although the usually buoyant coiffure was flattened into black wings from which dye seemed to be streaming. "You and Lars Bechmeir on *Star Talk* tomorrow fucking night at the Biltmore Liberty League rally. Just you see, Danny boy-o. Just you fucking wait..."

With a pratfall which poor, dead Harold Lloyd would have envied, Timmy slip-staggered his way down the castle steps.

Clark watched him go. The rain was lessening by now. Amazing, really, that no one had gotten seriously hurt in this storm. Although, with the things he'd seen recently, maybe he should give up on being amazed at anything.

He took the puddled walkway down. Then, glancing back up at the castle, he thought he caught sight of an indistinct shape close to the place on the black battlements where he'd been standing. Was there someone still up there that he hadn't noticed? Or was it just a flare of moonlight catching through the thinning clouds? But the thing was pale, half-solid, and it was moving, floating, and it seemed for a moment to be nearly alive. A chill passed over him, and with it came a sense of awe. He found that he was straining his eyes, holding his breath, somehow wishing for the moment to extend itself and become more real. But then came a fresh gust of wind, a new flurry of heavy raindrops. The darkness seemed to pulse and the shape extinguished itself like a black candleflame. In another moment, Clark was almost certain he'd seen nothing at all.

THIRTY NINE

A weird kind of democracy reigned at Herbert Kisberg's party in the aftermath of the storm. A few flecks of mud. A lost eyelash or cuffpin. The run colors of a silk shawl. These guests were unaccustomed to such discomforts, and, with their wet shoulders, hastily reapplied makeup and rearranged hair, they rejoiced in briefly becoming almost like everyone else.

Many were looking to find Herbert Kisberg so they could congratulate him for arranging such a dramatic storm. Others had heard rumors of a sighting of Lars Bechmeir, but at parties like this such things were par for the course. Factions were fragmenting, and there had even been talk of some people leaving, but that idea soon became ridiculous—for where else would you go, and what might you miss if you went? There was still that giddy sense that the next five minutes might spring that crucial role, screw or deal.

Whether to hang out with the drunkards, for example, or go with those who were just good at pretending to be drunk? Whether to slum it with the servants and maybe pick up a waiter or a maid? As was the custom, several feelies were now being played in Kisberg's suite of viewing rooms: showings from the rushes of new productions, or hilarious cuts of some big name having a strop. Other attractions were also being screened in more informal arrangements—legendary or rumored items which would never go on general release. The looped sound, film and feelie track of a famous leading lady's orgasm. Next door, the equally famous clip of a genuine starlet being strangled to death by a bathrobe belt. It would only be a matter of time before someone suggested running the two showings together.

Clark wandered. Meeting Kisberg, and then Lars Bechmeir, and getting that live slot on tomorrow's *Star Talk* . . . all in all, he didn't think he'd done a bad job tonight of doing whatever a real screenwriter would have done, whether he was Daniel Lamotte or not. But it had been a long day, and he was tired past caring, and he wanted to get back to Blixden Apartments, and to sleep for about twenty hours, and where the hell had Barbara Eshel gone?

"Clark?"

He was alone in a room where open French windows flapped and creaked. A smell of strawberries and caviar, and that feelie theater afterstorm tingle, changed and mingled in the air. He didn't instantly recognize his own name.

"Clark *Gable*? Is that *you*?"

Peg Entwistle's evening dress was wet and her blonde hair was plastered in a mid-parting across her head, but she still looked as regally beautiful as she had in *The Virgin Queen* and as he remembered her.

"Yeah. It's me."

"I thought I saw you earlier," she said, taking a few steps further, "but I couldn't be sure. You look *different*."

"It's these glasses. But you Peg . . . you look just the same."

"You wouldn't say that if you heard my idiot directors." She smiled. "But I've had a good innings. Near the top for almost ten years."

Innings. Idiot. Even that trace of a soft English accent, which Clark knew was really Welsh, remained. "I finally got around to seeing *The Virgin Queen* just a few days back," he said. "You were brilliant. It's everything everyone always says. Not that I actually follow the feelies much since . . . well, since. Although the screenwriter Daniel Lamotte's a kind of friend of mine."

"Really?" Peg smiled again. Was that a hint of recognition, or something else, or nothing at all? Whatever it was, she closed it off quickly. "So you're still in the business?"

"Not at all. I do investigative work."

"Oh." He was certain he now saw that famous gray-green gaze grow a fraction more wary. "What sort of things do you investigate?"

"Oh, I just serve subpoenas. Follow people. Find out where they really go when they're supposed to be playing poker on Saturday evenings. It's like the kind of roles I was expected to play on stage when I was still acting, but without most of the glamour. Or the money."

"But you're here."

"I live in Venice. I keep myself—well, pretty busy. Still occasionally run into a few of the old names. But less and less. You know how it is. But you're right. It's work of a sort that I'm on tonight, although it's nothing to do with you. So I'd rather you didn't mention you'd seen me."

She tipped her chin. "So that's how it is?" They both knew there was no point in him asking how things had gone with her. Just like her face, Peg's life was public property. The three marriages, the bust-ups with leading men. That car accident which had nearly gone to court when she'd crippled a kid. Even though Clark never read town gossip, all these things and more about Peg Entwistle had somehow seeped through to him.

"Do you think much about the old times?" he asked.

She gave a mock-actressy sigh. "What do you think?"

"Yeah." He waited. Looking at her. Then he pulled off the glasses, stuffed them clumsily away. "Look, Peg... I'm sorry about back then. What you went through. I mean, I know I let you down."

"Perhaps you did." She met his gaze. "But there were others who could have helped. Not least myself. And it wasn't as if you and I were in love."

"But we were close?"

Now they both had to smile, simply because it was true. He and Peg might not have been in love, but they'd certainly been lovers. And close. Yep, close probably *was* the best word. Things might have broken apart between them before she'd got in such a bad way that she'd ended up getting arrested for aggravated trespass and carted off to the funny farm, but not so broken and so bad that he couldn't have seen it coming. All that succeed or die shit. The crap she'd talked about trying to throw herself off that sign which had turned out not to be crap at all. Was his stupid dislike of any kind of hospitals even an excuse, and at that a feeble one, for not even bothering to visit her at the Met? He knew it wasn't. The real reason he'd ignored her pleas for help, he guessed, was that he'd been too busy being—or trying to be—Clark Gable. And look where it had got him. And her.

As if she'd been exactly following his thoughts, Peg gave a small tilt of her head in partial agreement. For all that they were talking about a catastrophic part of her life, she seemed less the actress now, and more relaxed. There were so few people who even knew about that time in her life, he realized, that it was probably rare that she ever got the chance to speak of it.

"I guess I was always desperate for fame," she said. "But I used to ask myself, isn't everyone desperate? And I looked around at all the other people I knew and convinced myself that I was nothing but normal." She smiled. "Which is always a bad thing to do in LA. So it wasn't your fault, Clark, that things got on top of me. And that Hollywoodland sign—it was a sort of promise I made." She took a breath. Her shoulders rose and fell. "And, like a bargain in a fairy tale, it assumed its own life. I don't know if I'd have actually done it that day, if those maintenance guys hadn't stopped me climbing and called for the police. But it was like I needed to find out."

"And now, nobody even knows it happened."

"The studios, both the old and the new ones, have always been good at hushing things up. But I doubt if anyone cares that much. I'm not really the Peg Entwistle you knew, Clark. I'm just a figure, a voice, a face. Always before the microphone, the iconoscope, the lens, and then down in print, and buried in the thoughts and dreams of people I'll never meet. It sometimes feels almost like the primitive tribes are supposed to feel—like something in you is constantly being sucked away. Everyone knows who you are, but . . . "

"The wrong kind of immortality?"

"Yeah. Maybe. But I always knew these things come at a price. And I wouldn't give it up. I *was* desperate back then. But I guess I did finally get what I was after . . . Even if it was . . . " Her gaze had drifted off. Those gray-green sparks had dulled. " . . . by a far longer and rockier road than I could ever have imagined." Then she chuckled, and Clark shivered, for it was an impossibly sad sound. Peg still had that maudlin side, even if it was now seemingly under better control. It was that same mixture of gaiety and sorrow which had first appealed to him. And, he guessed, to all the millions who sucked up her presence in the feelies. "But maybe that's what the price of fame is—that I can only feel real after the director in a studio calls action." She shrugged, smiled. "But it's not such a hard life, Clark. Of course it isn't."

"And what about tonight, Peg? Are you happy here, with these people, at the party of a guy like Kisberg?"

"He's a powerful player. It's part of my contract that I should be here—the most important bit that never gets put in writing. I really can't afford to think much further than that. The people back in Britain are already calling me a traitor and a whore for still working in Hollywood. They can't even show *The Virgin Queen* because I'm in it. Mina says—"

"Mina? You're with Mina Wallace?"

"Mina took over all Hilly's talent. What there was of it, anyway. She still does okay by me. Even though she's—"

"Jewish?"

"Yeah. Even though she's that."

"Not here tonight, is she?"

"You know what Mina's like. Won't come to anything unless there's a contract on the table. But you should look in and say hi to her."

Clark nodded. Mina Wallace had once been his own agent—back in those mythical times of what-might-have-been. But another piece of showbiz news he'd picked up on was that Peg's old agent Hilly Feinstein had blown his brains out in his office back in '35. Now that knowledge trickled through his head in a different way. It felt like cold mercury.

"Mina's still in that same old office and—" Peg stopped. Once again, she seemed to be tracking his thoughts. "Why exactly *are* you here, Clark? You're not doing anything stupid, are you?"

"I spend my whole life doing stupid things, Peg. But no. Not in the way that you think. But can I ask you a question?"

"I thought you said this was nothing to do with me."

"It's nothing special. I was just wondering if you remember going to go to the premiere of the first ever feelie."

"You mean *Broken Looking Glass*?" The drapes behind him flapped in a stronger gust of wind and Peg Entwistle's gaze flickered as if she was expecting someone to enter. Then she nodded her head. "Yes, I think so. I was just getting back on my feet. I *think* it was Hilly got me in . . . " She nodded again, a little too vigorously, like the poor actress she wasn't. "Yes. It was Hilly."

"And now he's dead and you're famous."

"Just what the hell are you saying, Clark?"

"I don't know, Peg. I really don't." The rain had dried from her skin but a sheen of sweat had replaced it. He was almost worried for her again. And almost ready to pull back. But not quite yet. "Can I just ask you one last question. Well, it's not even a question. You see, I was at the Met today, Peg—"

"—Clark, you're—"

He held up a hand to stop her. "And I spoke to Howard Hughes. Remember him? Although they've dug out half his head now and everyone calls him Howie. Anyway. There was this odd word he used, and I wondered if you've ever heard of it. It's . . . "

But he didn't even need to say it. Peg's face was white. She was mouthing that word. *Thrasis*. " . . . You want . . . " She took a breath. Swallowed. " . . . some advice?"

"Whatever I say, Peg, I get the feeling you're going to give it to me."

"Stay away. Keep well back. If you go around lifting up enough rocks in the way you seem to be doing you're going to . . . Going to . . . " Shakily, she waved an arm.

"Uncover a nest of rattlers?"

"That. Yes. That. Exactly."

"Look, Peg. I'm not after *you*. I'm just trying to make sense of a few things that have happened."

But she was looking around again as if sensing the arrival of some other presence, and didn't seem to be really hearing him. "I'd better go," she muttered. "You understand—there are still a few people here I haven't yet seen and I . . . "

Then she turned and was fleeing from him at a half run, damp skirt bunched in her hands.

FORTY

Once he started really looking for Barbara Eshel, she wasn't hard to find. *Flash. Pop.* Excited whoops. Starlets and has-beens and maybe even a few people who actually were someone were preening before the precious lens of her Graflex. He stood and watched for a while, amused but disappointed. She'd been wrong when she'd said people would ignore her once she'd told them she was a writer. For she'd somehow managed to convince them that she was that most precious and dangerous Hollywood commodity, the showbiz journalist.

"And who, pray, is this handsome man over here?" she announced when she finally noticed Clark. "Why, it's none other than genius writer Daniel Lamotte, who has just sold his latest feelie script for a rumored five figures."

He had to put his glasses back on and grin and pose like all the rest of the idiots before she finally agreed to be dragged away to the car.

"This stuff is brilliant, Dan. It's absolute dynamite. I've already got enough for fifteen editions of *LA Truth*!"

"My name's not Dan." The Delahaye's carpets were awash and fresh rain was coming in through the broken window as he drove. "And I didn't think your paper was that kind of trash sheet."

"Hell, Clark. Whatever you've been up to this evening hasn't done much for your mood."

"It hasn't. But it *is* some story."

"Well, I think I'm starting to get a proper handle on this whole thing..."

She instructed him to take a detour down Western Avenue toward Inglewood, then east along Manchester toward South Park. The only time he'd been around here lately was to listen to the nigger music at Topsy's Night Club, but apparently this was also where *LA Truth* had its base. He was still thinking of that conversation with Peg as the wipers thwacked and Barbara Eshel talked.

"... It makes every kind of sense when you think about it. Kisberg, right—he and his Wall Street backers are the ones who've made the real money out of the feelies. How *convenient* that was, to push the old LA studios into bankruptcy and take over with another new technology they couldn't afford just when the Depression was at its worst. And now they can fill people's heads with whatever they want. Sure, it's not all trash, but the bias is plain. That huge re-make of *Birth of a Nation* featuring as the guys in white the good ol' Klu Klux Clan. All those stirring tales of the good ol' South. Even the classic stuff. The way that when they do Dickens it's *Oliver Twist* with bad old Jewboy Fagin. And when it's Shakespeare it's *The Merchant of Venice*. And *White Legion*—my God, what a production that was! And now there's all these nice Germans. These people can convince anybody of anything they want just as long as they keep them entertained. They'll be telling us next that dinosaurs are Old Testament dragons."

"You obviously go to the feelies a lot more than I do."

"But can't you see what I'm saying? No wonder the Liberty League are successful. No wonder Herbert Kisberg's going for president. I mean, the Republicans are bad enough. It's left here, by the way. And watch that pothole."

"Sure." The Delahaye gave a splashing lurch.

"And now they've got your—I mean Daniel Lamotte's—feelie biopic nicely lined up as an extra bit of publicity."

"All it would take," he muttered, "is for Lars Bechmeir himself to put in an appearance tomorrow night at the Biltmore rally. Kisberg would pretty much have the whole country sewn up."

"Right! I mean, people are *relieved* it's going to be him that gets the ticket. Can you believe that? Instead of that creep in Chicago who looks too much like a gangster. And that oily twerp Pickens—no one's ever forgotten the way he lashed out at that woman. Or it could be—hold on, Clark, what were you just saying about Lars Bechmeir?"

"I saw him."

"Saw who?"

"Who do you think? Kisberg himself took me to see the guy. He was just in this room hidden away from the party with a couple of nurses. He's an invalid. Apparently he's been holed up somewhere quiet all these years, down in Orange County. But now they plan to wheel him out tomorrow night at the Biltmore and maybe get him to mouth a few words. And hey, it's the ultimate Liberty League endorsement."

"Shit."

"Yeah. Shit. The guy's barely there and I can't see him being around for much longer. I guess that's why they're planning on using him now... And why they were so keen on Dan's script. If Timmy Townsend's to be believed, they're even planning on squeezing an interview with Daniel Lamotte into the live coverage on *Star Talk*."

"But that's brilliant! You've got a chance to denounce the Liberty League in front of fifty million listeners. You know, great writer stands up for real liberty and—"

"For God's sake Barbara—you're sounding like Timmy Townsend in reverse. No. *Definitely* no. And who exactly am I supposed to denounce, and for doing what?"

"We've another whole day to find that out. And you'd better slow down. Here comes another pothole... *and* you've gone and missed the turn."

FORTY ONE

LA Truth was based along a strip of commercial holdings which, in typical LA mish-mash, lay between the high brick towers of the Firestone Rubber Company and the white frontage of Angels' Abbey, an up-and-coming mausoleum. He'd been expecting some kind of editorial offices, although he realized that was naïve. There were a few scattered typewriters, tables and chairs, but this was basically a dirt floor workshop filled with machinery most of which looked to be beyond working—apart from the one which *was*, and then only just. The man tending the thrashing, clacking device with a pair of oilcans held like sixshooters gave a comic start when he noticed them. He was dressed in overalls and was very young and very thin. The straggly beard which he affected only made him look younger and thinner.

"*Barbara*? Is that really you...?" They waited as he did the many things required to still the machine. "Almost didn't recognize you there." He glanced quizzically at Clark. "What are you up to?"

"I guess you could call it research. This is Clark Gable, by the way. And this is Dale. Dale's our printer, as you've probably gathered. Although he's got many other jobs here at world headquarters of *LA Truth*."

"Editor. Compositor. Delivery boy..."

They both chuckled. It was obviously a well-practiced routine.

Rain still pattered the roof, or dripped into overflowing buckets. They sat around a rickety table and Barbara gave Dale the eight reels of photographs she'd taken at Kisberg's party—seemed that another of his jobs was photo processor. She explained that Clark was a private detective who'd happened upon some odd events which seemed to have something to do with the invention of the Bechmeir Field. But she didn't say much else. Maybe, Clark thought, she was just protecting him from whatever was out there. Or more likely she was protecting her sources.

"There are some things we expect to happen tomorrow, and some stuff we hope to find out, which could turn this into the biggest story to hit this state since Julian Pete. What I'm saying, Dale, is I want you to hold working the next edition, and be ready to run with whatever I can get. And quick. Even if it's only one badly laid sheet."

Dale nodded. As they talked his eyes lingered for long periods on the vision that Barbara Eshel had become this evening, then drifted over to Clark, and then away from him and back to Barbara Eshel again. Dale was a good-looking kid if you discounted the beard, and he was probably about Barbara's age. You didn't have to be a matrimonial private detective to work out that she had him, as Peg Entwistle herself might have put it in her still classy lilt, on toast.

But he wasn't going to tell Barbara about Peg Entwistle. Not yet anyway. For all that had and hadn't gone on between him and Peg, he didn't think he wanted to be the one who put her back on the front pages for all the wrong reasons. Despite what the studios said, there was such a thing as bad publicity. And despite what Peg herself had said, feelie stars really were still people. Some of them were anyway.

Back outside and in the Delahaye, Clark thought for a moment that he saw a pair of headlights on the road behind them. Then they seemed to blink off. He started the motor, pulled slowly around the potholes. Then he took a quick right, turned sharply north along Central Avenue past Sears Roebuck, and took Ninth past the Cabrillo Club in a screech of tires. Then he stopped.

"What was all that about?"

"Nothing." He checked the rear-view. Either they weren't being followed, or whoever was following them was good. He pulled back out into the empty road. "So—you and Dale. Are you sweet on each other?"

"Why should we be?"

"No reason, I suppose. Or the same reason as always. Does he make a living, doing what he does back there?"

"Some, but not much. Tomorrow morning he'll be hauling trolleys in the fruit market."

"But how about you, Barbara?"

"How about what?"

"I mean, like Dale. What else do you do when you're not changing the world?"

"You really want to know?"

"Sure. I'm curious."

"Many a young lady," she began, putting on a cutglass accent, "suffers, without even knowing, from a terrible blight on the glorious blossoming of her early teenage years. As she stands at the gateway to womanhood, she finds that the strength of her happy childhood has ebbed away, and yet the poise and resolve of adult femininity still lies tantalizingly out of reach. Her back slumps. Her head droops. She is languid, uncommunicative, and often morose. What this delicate flower of early-blooming womanhood is suffering from, were she to know it, are all the symptoms of Feminine Weakness. And what she needs is *Tablon's Iron Purgative*... That, or a good kick up her oh-so-delicate ass."

"But you don't write the last bit?"

"You have no idea how much I wish I could. I guess *someone* has to produce this sort of rubbish—advertising copy pretending to be proper articles. You never think about who it is, though, do you? Not until it's you. *Tablon's Iron* whatsit. That was me. Or *The Woman Who Forgot Keep Clean Napkins*. Otherwise, the world'd stop turning, right? Actually, I rather enjoyed writing that last one. Pity they edited out the last paragraph. The way I told it, the woman ended up on the street turning tricks. And all because of a sauce stain on one of her napkins."

She was laughing now, and so was he. They were up on Bunker Hill. Past Edna's Eats, which was closed and unlit, then a final turn. They were still laughing as they climbed from the Delahaye, and he wondered as he took her arm if he'd drunk more of that endless free Champagne than he'd realized. Or maybe she had. They found the door and took the stairs together, arm in arm. He caught her as she tripped on a ruck in the rug, and turned her around in the process so she was leaning against the wall by her door. She was still chuckling. She smelled rain-wet and womanly, and of Champagne and laughter. She was so beautiful that, even in this dark little rooming house, she almost glowed. This wasn't the Barbara Eshel who'd aimed a gun at him—or even the one who'd been brandishing that heavy camera in a handbag which she now let drop to the floor. But he'd long known that women were capable of being many things, and often several of them at once. It was the same old mystery which he and a million other men had spent their lives trying to unravel. Never got there, of course. But it didn't stop you trying.

He could feel her body rising toward him. He could smell the sweet bitterness of her breath. Women were another race, a whole different species. He touched her cheek, traced lobe of her ear, and raised her mouth and covered it with his own. Then he stepped back.

"Goodnight," he muttered, and felt clumsily for his keys.

FORTY TWO

Sleep didn't so much come quickly to Clark as overwhelm him in a crashing wave. With it came a rush of memory as bright as the Californian sunlight which had first beckoned him west. For this town wasn't Akron, or Tulsa, or off-Broadway, or Portland, or even the Lurie Theater in Houston. This was LA and this was a different kind of acting to provide a different kind of entertainment to a changing world. He'd started off playing gangsters, wife-beaters and convicts and all the usual dross back at the turn of '30, and was all set by the middle of that same year to head back east for a new production of *A Farewell to Arms* when he received a phone call from his new agent Mina Wallis to tell him he'd been offered a year long contract with MGM, no fucking less.

He was suddenly being groomed for stardom, and *groomed* really was the word. He had his suits cut in the latest vee which emphasized his broad shoulders and svelte hips. Saxony wool, or Prince of Wales plaid, with silk accents. Double-breasted mostly. He went to the studio barber—who called himself a stylist—at least once a week. There was advice about where he should eat, and what sort of company he should keep. There was even a trip to the orthodontists in a mostly futile attempt to sort out his teeth, and some asinine debate about whether they should pin back his jug ears. But he was who he was—Clark Gable. Or he soon fucking would be. When he cut a ribbon at a new supermarket, the people cheered like he'd built and stocked the whole place himself. He took a ride in a monoplane wearing a plain navy blazer with cream linen slacks and an open-neck Lacoste polo shirt with dark willow tan brogues.

The whole business of banging out talkies the way Henry Ford was banging out cars struck Clark as a decent enough thing to be doing for a living. Okies were being driven west by starvation and duststorms to die in streetcars and sleep on railroad sidings, but hey, at least those who could afford to get into the movie houses were being properly entertained.

The previews and reviews for his first above-the-title role in *Susan Lennox* weren't so good. Garbo might be a bull dyke lesbian with a voice like a concrete mixer that would never have come out of the silents, but she was a genuine star. So it was Clark Gable who got the blame for the movie being a mess. The results for the pre-screenings for his next effort, *Possessed* were also pretty mixed, and Mina told him it was one of those talkies that could go either way. Clark Gable was a new face, and he gave the women in the audience—many of the men, for that matter—a certain tingle, but it wasn't a tingle they yet felt entirely comfortable with. So was he just some gangling lout with big ears and bad teeth too clumsy to handle a scenery board, let alone act? Or was he the box office savior MGM had been promising themselves when they'd given him that contract?

Clark gauged his arrival on the red carpet outside the Carthay Theater on the night of the premiere of *Possessed* perfectly, leaving just enough time to hang around with the crowds without it seeming like he was waiting for Joan Crawford. They might have had to move this whole showboat to the Carthay because Howard Hughes was putting on some carnie ride called *Broken Looking Glass,* which wasn't any proper kind of movie at all, up at Grauman's on this same night, but you sure as hell wouldn't have known it from here. Flashbulbs flashed. Floodlights hazed the sky. Then Crawford arrived, and the crowd went apeshit, and Clark gave the newshounds a knowing grin as he offered her his arm. Then she planted a kiss on him for just that teenie bit longer than expected. All in all, the two of them put on as good an act out on that red carpet as anything they'd done in the talkie.

"Savor the moment, Gable," she'd murmured. "You never know how long it'll last."

He got a call from the studio a week or two after to come in on a day between shootings. He was living in a serviced bungalow in the grounds of the Marmont by then. A low, adobe-walled structure, the roof a shrug of pantiles, windows a raised eyebrow of arches, it and a cluster of other similar peasant-style dwellings formed a corral amid the winding drives, hibiscus bushes and palms. Quiet Mexicans in white pajamas did the watering and clipping. Every time he stepped outside and climbed into whatever car he was currently driving, he decided that paradise, if you excluded the Mexicans, must look pretty much like this.

He drove south toward Culver City with no particular thoughts in his head. Some publicity thing, most likely. Maybe there was a new director or leading lady they wanted him to meet. Past the Beverly Wiltshire and past the Brown Derby and past the Cotton Club, he reached the fortress-like walls of MGM studios, and followed them around to the Grecian-pillared entranceway, where the security guard gave him a smile and a salute as he raised the barrier. Trying to remember the guy's name—was it Walter, *Willy*?—Clark Gable responded with a cheery wave.

MGM occupied several lots around Culver City in those days, but this, the largest and the headquarters, was a city in itself. Not just a congested jumble of the new enclosed soundstages which had replaced the open or glassed-in lots of the silent era, but also a school, a small hospital, several decent restaurants, and even a small railroad to carry things here and there.

He pulled in at his designated space in the main parking lot beside the offices. He smiled back at himself as he checked his parting in the car mirror. It went without saying that it was another beautiful day.

The receptionist didn't quite get up for him—that was reserved for *real* stars—but she did make a small bobbing movement, almost a curtsey, from behind her glass and chrome desk. Then another broad came from somewhere to find him, one of those near-edible gofers who bumped at you with their breasts, and fluttered their eyelashes so much you were sure you felt a breeze. She reminded Clark about a party up in Laurel Canyon she was *sure* they'd both been to as she led him along corridors to wherever it was they were heading, although he concentrated mostly on the sway of her ass.

He'd imagined the usual handshakes in an exec's office, but he was being taken down deeper, darker routes into one of the technical areas. A small *uh-oh* sounded in his head. If he was being required to revoice some of his lines, the request to do so should have come down the channels from the director, or at least his assistant. Anything less was a diminution of status. Maybe he should speak to Mina about this. Maybe he should have spoken to Mina already. Or maybe Mina already knew about this, and simply hadn't bothered to tell him. All that Californian sunlight which Clark had been carrying with him started dimming inside his head.

As if sensing his unease, the pretty gofer stopped and turned and nudged at him sweetly with her breasts. This was, she assured him in breathy pants, something that all the MGM roster of actors were doing. Just a small, quick, test. Nothing really, but rather exciting nevertheless.

He was put in a room where all the walls had been faced with what looked like chickenwire, except for a window into a bigger and better lit space. With the amount of electrical stuff in there, and but for the chickenwire and the absence of a microphone, he could have been in a sound booth. But he could tell that the creation of corkscrew glass and wire which dangled from the ceiling before him had nothing to do with receiving sound. Just looking at it made his teeth itch, and set off a weird, resonant buzzing inside his head.

The guys who were mooching and prodding in the space beyond weren't wearing white coats. This being Los Angeles, they wore paisley cravats and Palm Beach suits. One of them leaned to a microphone and spoke to Clark through a loudspeaker. He had on a scratched namebadge which said he was *Hiram P.* Something-*or*-Other *the Third*, but he had to squint at his clipboard before he called Clark Mr, ah, Gable. He peered at Clark a little more closely like he maybe even recognized him from some movie he'd seen. Then he smiled to reveal a most un-Hollywood set of buck teeth and told him, just like the breast-bumping girl had, that this was nothing more than a few quick tests. Best to think of it as simply a rehearsal, Mr Gable. Better still, a test shoot.

Dials twitched. Valves glowed. Things buzzed and hummed. Then the frail coil of glass and metal hovering before him started buzzing and humming as well. This, he was just about starting to realize, must have something to do with all that voodoo stuff about—what was the guy's name again?—Lars Bechmeir's new discovery that Howard Hughes had then gone and invested in so heavily.

"All we want you to do," Hiram P. Something-or-Other's voice crackled, "is exactly what we already know you're good at. We want you to try to act for us, Mr Gable. Is that alright?"

Could have done without the *try to*, and there was nothing worse than being dropped into a situation for which you'd had no chance to prepare, but Clark swallowed, nodded. Then, after the first one-two-three count-in, there was a sudden increase in the angry buzzing and a smell of rubber burning, and Hiram and his mates were flapping around for several minutes as they struggled to fix some fault.

These guys didn't have the look of MGM employees, although they were some of the oddest ever hired guns. Clark tried asking them a few questions as he waited. He even got some replies. No, this equipment wasn't even MGM property—this Bechmeir guy had already set up some kind of trust through which they were employed and all use of his patents had to be channeled. Neither was any of it owned by the Hughes Corporation, although Hughes had already shot and premiered that first feelie-movie to what you might call *mixed* reviews. The whole business sounded odd to Clark. It was probably just another flash in the pan like 3-D or Smellovision, although he understood that MGM had to try to keep track.

"I want you to feel happy, Mr Gable. Just straightforward common-or-garden happiness. Any time you're ready."

"Now?"

"No, *no*. Sorry, no. Not *now*. You've got to *tell* us you're ready. And then I'll get this spool here turning—you wouldn't believed how much magnetic wire costs by the foot—and then I'll count one, two, three, like it's the start of a song. And *then* you feel happiness. Right?"

"Right."

Clark thought of himself as generally a pretty breezy kind of guy, at least off-set, but he knew he was better at doing brooding, dark performances. Until recently when he did happy as an actor, it had generally been because he was being especially nasty. Like raping the leading lady, or torturing the guy who'd come to rescue her.

"What's the, uh, premise?"

Hiram and his colleagues exchanged glances. "It's just, well, *happiness*. There isn't a premise. Try using your imagination, is what we suggest."

No use doing what any actor would normally do, which was simply to *act* happy. Not with this icily humming twisting thing reaching down from the chickenwire ceiling to claw at the insides of his head like the underneath of the iceberg that did for the Titanic. No use changing the way he stood and moved, or using the smile and the eyes and the voice. For these were just effects, calculations. Sure, when you acted happy, you felt happy, but it was as different to regular happiness as kids playing baseball in a dusty backlot was to Walter P. Johnson winding up on the mound for the Nats. Poor Peg Entwistle had once explained Stanislavsky to him, but as far as he was concerned, acting was a craft, plain and simple, and he really didn't buy all that *acting-from-the-inside* shit. Far as he was concerned, if it was inside, it might as well stay there.

"You ready, Mr ah Gable?"

"Sure."

Sunsets, maybe. Or cars. Yeah, cars. Or better still, sex. No, no, no, no. Not sex. That was some other emotion entirely. But what about kittens? Weren't they supposed to make you feel happy? Yeah, kittens at Christmas. Or sex in a car filled with kittens at Christmas. Or how about . . .

But the damn thing had broken down again. He could tell that just from the renewed smell of burning and the bellyache which now seemed to start right down in his groin. Eventually, though, after much fiddling from Hiram P. Bucktooth and his minions, they managed to get the thing working. It still felt odd. But odd wasn't even the word. It was like he was being joined, stretched, swallowed. No. It wasn't even that. It was like, in some way which had nothing to do with those guys on the other side of the window, he wasn't *alone*. His fingertips tingled. His scrotum crawled. He looked left and right and glanced behind his back in case someone had somehow snuck in here without his noticing. He also felt, if he was totally honest, like he needed to take a shit.

"Seem to be having more than our usual teething troubles with the equipment today. If you'll just bear with us, Mister, ah . . . I'm sure we'll get there . . ."

Get there they did. Or somewhere. They made him do fear, which was all too fucking easy. And elation—although wasn't that just happiness with extra gravy?—and all he reckoned he'd come up with was more of this sick displaced feeling, which was how he actually felt. Then there was another glitch, and more smoke. No way of telling from the reaction of the guys beyond the window with their off-kilter teeth and fashion sense how he was doing, but it was already pretty obvious he wasn't doing that well. If Hiram P hadn't called an end to things when he did, Clark was seriously concerned that he was either going to have an embarrassing personal accident, or faint.

"Guess you'd like to see the results?"

He shrugged.

He was already fully convinced by now that nothing would ever come of this process. Too fiddly. Too messy. Too—well, just plain *wrong*. Nevertheless, he was mildly curious to see what they'd done as they took him into their temple of bakelite, glass and bad acne and wowed him with their talk of wavelengths, volts and amperes. Then they showed him a big glass bulb with a green ghost floating in it, and told him that was what he looked like to the receiver thing in there. They respooled the wire through the reading heads and reminded him again about how expensive this stuff was, and ran it back through crocodile clips out of some kind of amplifier into a dome-shaped grid that looked like a large, upturned sieve sat on rubber grommets right there before them on the desk. The sieve sparked and crackled. It gave off that thunderstorm and clean armpits smell with which the whole world would soon become familiar. And then it actually *glowed*, and to Clark it felt as if the devil himself had just shoved his coldest, biggest finger right up his ass.

"You okay, Mister ah . . . ? We've found that some performers have a particular sensitivity to their own emanations."

"Felt better." He guessed he was probably swaying a little in the chair in which they'd sat him. And they probably thought by now he'd come straight from the speakeasy.

"This, er, is, erm, happiness."

The field danced and glimmered. It wasn't happiness, but it sure as hell was *something*.

"Jeeze..."

And then he found that he was reaching toward this fizzing pit of nonsense without even thinking about what he was doing. The weirdest thing of all was that the bloody stuff seemed to be reaching back to him—shaping itself to clasp his hand with wraith-like fingers before Hiram P grabbed him and hit the off switch and muttered about how he could have damn well gone and electrocuted himself. When Clark was finally led back along the corridors, he realized that he did need to visit the restroom—and pretty badly at that. As Miss Don't-I-Know-You waited outside and preened her tits, he hunched over the studio porcelain and was copiously, copiously sick in spasming yelps.

All in all, it was a pretty bad introduction to new technology that had become *de rigeur* in almost all the big studios within a year, even though the results were most often a mess. Clark's contract was renewed and he did his best to soldier on through *Windy August* and *The Raging King*, but the technicians were confused, and the rentals and royalties which the canny Bechmeir Trust were demanding of MGM for the use of their equipment meant skyrocketing costs.

None of the actors professed to like the new turn that their business was taking, and the demand in those early days was for nothing but crude emoting—all the nuance which had started to appear in the better talkies had instantly disappeared—but Clark seemed to have an especial antipathy. That first feelie experience with Hiram bucktooth in that chicken shed seemed to have set a jinx which continued to follow him. He got used to sparks and hissings and directors' curses and the smell of things burning. But he almost preferred those times to the ones when the iconoscopes actually worked. He didn't like the way those cold glass eyes made him feel—which was ill, basically, but a with whole lot of other crap going on around the edges. It was as if he was being sucked away. No, it wasn't even that. It was as if the real guy he was almost sure he was somehow wasn't standing there any longer and had slipped away like the sliver of last night's soap down a plughole into—what? Some other place, time, dimension? These weren't the kind of thoughts that Clark was used to having, and he felt no more comfortable with them than he did with the iconoscope itself. When he tried to explain all of this to his fellow actors, quite a few of them went partway to agreeing with him, but then they'd shrug and tell him it was a knack like any other. That it took a bit of getting used to, for sure, but it was like booze, or getting your sealegs, or smoking locoweed, or any of the other fancy new pastimes which were then making their way into the industry, and it was really just a question of giving it your best.

He'd never been much of a one for why-the-hell-am-I-doing-this-crap tantrums which were a regular part of any kind of dramatic production. But these things got to a guy, and acting of any kind was always an emotional process, and he soon reached the point where he was doing most of his best acting, as the saying went, after the director had called that's a wrap. Things came to a head when he was asked to break down in tears fifteen whole separate fucking times until the technicians finally managed to get something resembling a signal down on wire. And even then they said they weren't happy with it. Something about amplitude, the way the machine was picking him up. He'd been feeling it as well. That was the thing. He'd been sobbing like a fucking baby as if he was really mourning for something he didn't even know he'd lost. By the fifteenth take the process of emotional collapse had gotten so absurdly easy that he could barely stop. And still it wasn't right.

But for him that was it. As far as he was concerned, this wasn't acting, this was some new bullshit freaktent claptrap crock he was involved in, and Louis B and all the rest of them could shove it all the way to midnight up their tight Jewish asses. He wiped his face and blew his nose and left the set and drove to his suite at the Ambassador in his current MGM rented limo. There, he ate some complimentary chocolates and waited for the pleading phone call from the director which didn't come. Mina, though, did plead with him—at least, when she heard about the incident a few hours later—but even she seemed to have sensed some kind of defeat. Clark hung around some more, which was something any actor had to be good at doing. He even tried calling the director himself the next day, only to be told that the plug had been pulled on the whole project and that it wasn't his fault and these things were understandable and he wasn't to fret. So he kicked his heels for a few days longer as he waited for a courier to bring his next script. But it was the hotel maître came to his door instead, to enquire in that gratingly polite way of all maîtres why his last two week's bills for this suite, not to mention room service and the bar, hadn't been paid. Quietly, but in that lingering way people do when they know they're leaving somewhere they will most likely never see again, Clark gathered up the few things from the suite that he could actually call his own, and then a few others that strictly speaking weren't. And he left. He thought for a while that this was the end of Clark Gable. He only realized later that what he'd really witnessed was the end of MGM.

Things happened fast in LA—that was something he should have made proper note of when he was on the way up in this business. There were all sorts of reasons he could have given as to why he'd fallen from grace so rapidly, but in his heart of hearts he knew that the real fall from grace had been somewhere inside him. And now he'd got so far down what had briefly seemed like a golden way that he couldn't bring himself to tread the boards again, and the directors and producers were already wary of anyone with a taint of the old talkies about them, especially a nearly-star whose few headlining appearances had all nosedived.

It was one of those things you could look at in a hundred different ways, and not one of them would make the slightest difference, as Clark had long ago discovered. Sure, he could blame Mina, or the studio. Sure, he could—and he did—blame himself. He could even blame that idiot director, or lousy luck with the choice of scripts, or some wooden performances by his leading ladies, or not enough kissing of the right kind of ass. Or maybe he should have tried harder and been more patient with technology which everyone agreed was a hard enough bullet to bite. But none of that mattered, and Clark took the view that most things in life really weren't that complex when you took them apart and wiped the grease off them and laid them out. When people asked Clark what had gone wrong, which had happened less and less over the years and barely at all now, he preferred the simplest answer because he reckoned it was also the truest. There had always been that way the camera seemed to like some actors more than others, and it was the same with iconoscopes.

He told people that he hadn't liked the feelies much, and that the feelies hadn't liked him.

FORTY THREE

It was coming on nine next morning by the time he'd fully woken up. Pipes were hissing, radios were playing and a singer was practicing her scales as he lumbered along the corridors in search of a washroom. The place he found was in much the sort of state he'd have expected. Hopeful damp-furred notices about tenants showing respect for others. The ledge of a dusty window lined with rusting tins of Drano and jars of Sal Hepatica Laxative. Someone's socks and underthings left to marinate in the corroded lion's claw bath. A day or so longer here, and he'd be doing the same. But he knew it couldn't last. He cleaned his teeth using his finger and someone else's tin of Pepsodent. He cleared a space on the mirror glass with a wet hand and thought how odd the guy on the other side of it now looked without his glasses.

Barbara had fixed him coffee and a bowl of Cream of Wheat by the time he'd dressed. He sat down in her room and lit a Lucky Strike and thought again of Peg's worried face—and the way she had fled from him last night—as this pretty Jewish broad, who was scarcely old enough to be a woman, went on and on about some huge Goddamn conspiracy. Not that he didn't doubt that she was right, but couldn't she see that they were an ant's squeak away from becoming its next casualties?

The room soon hazed with his cigarette smoke and Barbara went to the window and pulled back the sash. She stood there for a while as the sunlit haze drifted around her like an aura. Then she turned and picked up something strange and dark.

"And there was something else I found."

He almost cringed when it she flapped it toward him.

"Although you might need a mirror to look . . ."

It was that piece of carbon paper with that same word stamped through into it on about fifteen hundred times.

"Yes. I know. It says Thrasis. I saw it a while back."

"And you didn't think to mention it?"

"Jesus, Barbara! How much crap have we had flying around here?"

"That word is there repeatedly on that weird toilet sheet draft that you found stuffed in the wastecan at that pine lodge." She was looking at him more intently now. "Or did you know that as well?"

"Not exactly. But I can't say I'm totally surprised. You see, Howard Hughes said it to me. Like it was some kind of full stop on everything. Like he couldn't help saying it even though it was the last thing on earth he ever wanted to say."

"And you didn't think to tell me that either?"

"Take me out and shoot me, Barbara. It's a word written down backwards that someone has also said to me. What the hell else can I say?"

"Only it isn't a word." She nodded toward her bookshelves, which were lined with encyclopedias and dictionaries. "I've just looked it up. It isn't listed. But it's somehow important, isn't it?"

He shrugged. For a moment, he heard a weird hissing sound, and sensed a faint return of the presence he had glimpsed before. "I guess it probably is."

FORTY FOUR

But there were still so many questions.

Crowded in with Barbara in the phone booth on the street, he tried calling the Nero Agency again. Still no pick up. If Abe really was the guy April Lamotte had hired to find a lookalike for her husband, they'd have to find another way of working it out. He used the same dime to get put through to the communal hall in Doges Apartments, and the phone rang for almost as long as the Nero call before Glory picked it up.

"Hello?"

"Hi. It's Clark. Just thought I'd ring to check if anything's up."

"Up?"

"Any mail? Visitors? That kind of thing."

"The guy about repossessing your car no show again if that what you mean."

"Great. And, er, mail?"

"I look..." Footsteps. A long pause. Footsteps again. "Final demand for the IRS. Bill for the landlord. What look like a bill—"

"Just bills, then?" He could tell Barbara was laughing even though he could only see the back of her head. "Nothing else?"

"No, but you hiding or somesuch thing? Where you been?"

"Just busy on a case. Might take another day or so."

"I hope she worth it."

"I really do wish it was that kind of case, Glory."

"Oh, and that woman I tell you 'bout call again. She still no give her name but say how much she worry about the husband. I give number again?"

"I guess so," he muttered, knowing what Glory was like if you didn't humor her.

"Well, Clark," Barbara said, still chuckling as he put down the phone. "That was an interesting glimpse into your exciting life."

"I'm not the one who's living in that flea pit over there."

"Sounds like your apartment is the total height of luxury..."

The air back out in the street smelled fresher this morning after last night's rain, and there were puddles in the gutters, but Roger and his pals were busy as ever kicking their usual tin can.

"Say..." the kid drawled, chewing what was probably an entirely imaginary piece of gum. "It's Tim Cookson and Frederica West. That car of yours still needs looking after, you know. Get all sorts of savory types around here."

"It's unsavory." Clark handed him a quarter. "Anything much you noticed out here?"

"Not out *here*." Roger winked at him, then looked at Barbara, who was back to wearing her usual mannish slacks and a Fairisle sweater, up and down in a way which was far too knowing for someone his age.

Barbara sighed. "Shouldn't you be at school? Or in a reformatory?"

"Ain't nothing I can learn there, lady, that I can't pick up ten times neater on these here streets."

With another quarter stuffed in his pockets, Roger agreed to listen out again for the phone.

FORTY FIVE

The inside of the Delahaye smelled damper than ever. It was like something was beginning to rot, and there was a gouge down the driver's side which Clark presumed Roger and his mates had caused. The engine didn't sound quite right, either, as they drove past the fake palms and papier-mâché hula girls outside the new Clifton Cafeteria on the corner of Broadway and First.

Abe Penn's offices were in a three story building set between a lower sprawl of warehouses and lots. There was a failed oil pump site and few signs of life.

"Thought you said he was up the pecking order from you, Clark," Barbara muttered, looking up at the spackle-filled three story frontage as they climbed out.

Plates for all sorts, sizes and types of business clung to the wall outside. A chiropractor. A lonely hearts bureau. The registered offices of some oddly-named companies, amongst which was Abe Penn's Nero Detective Agency. None of the plates looked new. The glass pane in the swing door had once had a long piece of surgical tape stuck across it to try to hold together a long crack. Once the door had stopped screeching, it felt very quiet inside. The only sound was the stick of their feet on warm linoleum and the buzz of a few flies. There was a noticeboard beside the stairs, one of those things that you slide letters in like a feelie signboard or the hymn numbers in a church. It repeated some of the names from the business plates outside, and added a few others. Abe Penn's office was apparently up on the top floor.

There was no elevator, and the air grew even hotter as they climbed. More silent, as well—they were both almost holding their breath—apart from the continued bumble and buzz of those flies. Most of the business signs in the glass-windowed doors along the final corridor had been stuck over with brown paper or scratched out. The words NERO DETECTIVE AGENCY faced them from the far end, and Clark thought to himself as he swatted another fly and tried to peer through the glass frosting that this whole place was such a distillation of a certain kind of existence that they'd probably use it in the feelies—in the unlikely event that it ever became fashionable to work this city as a private dick, that was.

He couldn't make anything out, and fully expected the door to be locked. But the oval handle instantly gave, and something terrible hit his senses as the door swung. With it came a rush of flies.

"Jesus. Shut the door." He was fumbling for a handkerchief. "No—not on the *outside*, Barbara." He hissed. "You've got to come *in*..."

The remains of what could only be Abe Penn depended from a rope which had been looped around the rosette of an old metal fan on the ceiling, and a swivel chair had been kicked away from underneath. Flies were everywhere. On the walls. In the air. Darkening the metal-framed windows. Seeking their eyes and mouths. Keeping close as he could to the corners of the small room, Clark went around to the far side of Abe's desk. He used the handkerchief to work open the first window catch and a few thousand flies swarmed out, but most of the rest seemed happy enough to stay in with Abe. The other window was already half open.

"What the hell is this?" Barbara was covering her mouth with one hand, fumbling in her handbag with the other.

"What does it look like? Don't touch *anything*, right?"

"As if I would..."

The roar of the disturbed flies was so loud they were having to shout. Abe looked like a large bag that had burst. His head was so ballooned and distorted, and his neck had been stretched so far by the weight of his leaking body, that it seemed that it could only be moments before the two broke apart. Clark had encountered one or two suicides before—they came with the territory when you dealt with separation and divorce—but never anything this bad. Abe must have been dead for days. No—make that weeks...

An impressive double page a day desk diary was open on the blotter for Friday June 21st, which was seven days ago. The only entry was a doodle of several breasts and the single word *Haircut?* Somehow, Clark found that question mark especially touching. Keeping his fingers wrapped in the handkerchief, he flicked quickly through the previous pages of the diary. More poorly done doodles of impossibly endowed broads decorated the pages, but that was all until, in the looser kind of hand someone might use when they were jotting something down whilst talking on the phone, Abe had written *Lamotte. Erewhon—Stone Canyon—Lookalikes?!?* and a phone number on the page for Friday June 14th.

Barbara was standing beside him now. The only other thing on the desk apart from the flies was a solitary buff gray folder. He lifted it open. Instantly the flies began to crawl over old cuttings—curled and yellowed images of Clark's face from the middle pages of single column articles in *Variety* back in the days when he was just about famous—and a bigger glossy that he remembered having done at Mina's considerable expense and never feeling happy with. Abe had also gotten hold of one of Clark's business cards, and he looked, from the emphatic way he'd crossed out the disconnected number and the tiny breasts which decorated its edges, to have tried calling it. He'd then written another number on the back of the card which Clark recognized as belonging to a service office he'd briefly used to take messages until he decided the whole thing was a rip-off. Finally, in a fresher, crisper hand, was the number for the phone in the hall of the Doge's Apartments, and then the words *Glory Guzman?!!!* deeply scored with a kind of frustration Clark could understand.

"Looks like he did try to speak to you," Barbara muttered. "Is Glory always like she was this morning?"

"No. We got her on a good day."

"So he chose you, and the message about the whole business didn't get through, and then he... Do you think this is really a suicide?"

"No." Abe swung gently in the fresher breeze from the open window. Quite a lot him had already leaked onto the floor, and was forming a black, slow-spreading pool around the chair which the flies seemed especially to love. They'd have to hurry up here, or he'd need to find somewhere to vomit. "But that's what it's supposed to look like."

"You don't say."

No sign of a suicide note, fake or otherwise, but would this kind of guy really need an explanation as to why he'd killed himself? Clark doubted it. The cops, when someone finally got around to noticing the smell, would be happy to file a *Death By Own Hand* report and leave it at that. Wouldn't ever get as far as being looked at by homicide, any more than had the death of April Lamotte.

Picking out a fly which had crawled into the edge of his mouth, Clark closed the folder. Was it so surprising that Abe had chosen him when he was asked about finding a guy who was prepared to play at being someone else's husband for a few hours? He supposed not. After all, who else was Abe likely to think of when he was looking for a tall guy with big ears, not too many scruples, a background in matrimonial affairs, and some experience of proper acting? He checked the diary again. There was nothing else beyond that previous Friday. After that, he reckoned, Abe Penn was probably dead. Otherwise, and for all this frustrations at trying to speak to Glory, he'd have tried to get in touch again.

Clark riffled through the desk drawers. Nothing much more, beyond some copies of a business card for Nero Investigations. There was some dried-up orange peel in the bin, and a sandwich with a bite mark which the flies, with so much of Abe to go at, had chosen to ignore. Also a copy of the *LA Times* for that same last Friday as the diary. Abe had made a less than successful stab at the crossword.

A crackling flash detonated in the room. Every fly on what was left of Abe's body instantly took off, momentarily revealing an anatomy squirming with millions of fresh white maggots.

Barbara thumbed on the Graflex's winder. She paused, and looked over at Clark.

"What?"

They was no one about as they left the place. Outside, the combined city reek of horse dung, gasoline fumes, hot tar and tamarisk had rarely smelled so good. Clark stood out front of the block for a moment, looking up. Abe's office was on this side. You could see where the window had been left half open—and the lazy circle of a few flies as they went in and out. He walked over to the spot directly beneath. No proper paving here, just gravel and dog dirt. He pushed around at the gravel with his shoe, vaguely remembering how people said the sidewalks in this town were supposed to glitter in the sun like gold. Then he saw something flash. He stooped down and picked up the broken remains of a needle-tipped glass tube.

FORTY SIX

"We go to the police?"

"'Course we don't."

"Another suicide—but there's no Abraham Penn on here." They were sitting back in the Delahaye, and Barbara had unfolded that faded guestlist for the premiere of *Broken Looking Glass* once again.

"I think Abe was just . . . " He shook his head. "What would the military call it? A civilian casualty."

"The wrong person in the wrong place?"

"Exactly."

Poor old Abe Penn. Not that he'd known him well—not that he reckoned anyone had. Just another sleazy guy in a too-tight suit, and not particularly fragrant even when he was alive. He remembered him mostly from a case where they'd been hired by opposite sides in a divorce, which had been no problem at all. They'd gone and got drunk on the fees after the case was finished, which was when Clark had probably given him his card. Since then, he'd heard that Abe had been mostly doing freelance employee reference and insurance investigations. Basic trudgework. Abe might have had a license, but he couldn't do a *Don't you remember me from the talkies?* turn to persuade the lady clients to hire him for messy matrimonials the way Clark could.

Now the guy had gone and got sucked into this business and killed, probably for no better reason than that April Lamotte had seen one of his adverts in the cheaper rags promising secrecy and discretion. Not that Clark reckoned that Abe had ever got as far as going up to see April Lamotte. That had been someone else—whoever had listened in on her calls on a link from the automatic exchange, then staged Abe's suicide using whatever was in those syringes, and had driven up to Erewhon themselves pretending to be Abe, and then probably delivered that unpostmarked letter to the communal postbox at the Doge's Apartments, most likely driving a Mercury sedan.

Once again, Clark had that itchy feeling of being followed, hunted. What puzzled him most by now was how he and Barbara had managed to get this far along Dan and April Lamotte's tracks without being killed. That, and how all the others who'd been touched by this strange affair had also made it. Kisberg. That doctor woman—if she *was* still living. Lars Bechmeir, even. And, yes, Peg Entwistle. He remembered again the gaps he'd noticed in Erewhon's viewing library. Those missing feelie reels. *The Virgin Queen* amongst them.

"Barbara, what else have you got in that bag of yours."

"I told you, Clark. I'm just collecting stuff that's relevant. It isn't as if you've—"

"No. That isn't what I mean. Have you got that receipt—the big-bucks one for the feelie studio dated earlier this year?

FORTY SEVEN

The premises of Feel-o-Reel Inc. lay only a few blocks off and along Pacific Boulevard from Abe Penn's. But they belonged to a different world.

With its wide lots and dazzling aluminum and steel buildings, the Nueva Vision Business Park looked as if it should house the sort of technologies which Daniel Lamotte had once written about in those pulp "Scientifiction" novels. In a way, it did. If not death rays, rocket fins, instant cures for cancer and meals that came in a tablet, it did at least play host to the manufacturers of the Precious Poochie range of canine clothing, the T C Coolo automatic ice crusher (*You'll Never Choke on Another Cube*) and the SeaSlooosh! pool wave-machine. In this elevated company, the activities of the Feel-o-Reel Post Production studio seemed everyday.

Inside the rollback doors, men in white suits were pushing trolleys and tending machines that looked like hi-tech spinning wheels. One of the guys saw Clark and Barbara, and signaled emphatically, without removing his cotton mask, that they should wait right where they where. Another guy then emerged from a glass-walled office.

"Sorry, but we have to be very careful about contamination. Get the slightest bit of grit in the drawing or charging processes, and a whole reels gone to waste. Don't think I caught your names...?"

Pete Peters—his parents must have had some imaginations—was wearing an open-neck suit, expensively tailored to look casual in an oh-this-thing-I've-just-thrown-on sort of way. He had a relaxed manner and a dry, quick handshake.

"This is Barbara Eshel, and I'm, ah..." They'd agreed on a spiel outside, but Clark still had to think for a stupid moment before coming up with his own name. "... Clark Gable. We're working for someone called Lamotte. Reason we're here is, we're private investigators, and—"

"Of course, of course! My only surprise is it's taken you so long to get here. Are you working for their insurance company as well, or just for Mr Lamotte in a private capacity?" Peters beckoned them back toward his glass cubical. "Might as well come in..."

His office smelled of clean machine oil like the rest of the place. It was cramped, but expensively furnished in the modern way. Even though there was no outer window, the polished glare off everything made you want to put on sunglasses.

"Know much about what we do here?" Peters asked once he'd got them seated in hard little chairs.

"Well, er..." Barbara began.

"Thing is," Peters leaned forward across the glasstop desk, "the big feelie companies all have their own stock production facilities, but a lot of the kit they have is at least five years old. And the staff..." He chuckled. "They're a whole lot older. So what we offer is a faster turn-around and a better, more consistent finished product. A sharper field. A bigger kick for your feelie buck. Then we get used a lot by the independents. I can get our secretary to give you a leaflet. Then, of course, we do one-offs. But you know about that."

"You mean," Clark asked, "like the commission from Daniel Lamotte?"

"We do all kinds of stuff. It's still not that usual for us to do work for a private individual, but a lot of companies are getting more and more interested in feelie technology. All sorts of people you'd never even think."

"R H Macys? Howard Johnson's? The Liberty League? The Nazis?"

"Exactly!" Peters nodded as eagerly as Timmy Townsend had. "Although precisely who we do business for is commercially confidential..." He trailed off, and looked a trifle disappointed when Clark and Barbara didn't press him. "You really *aren't* the police, are you, by the way? I need to be entirely clear on that. Otherwise, my lawyer'll kill me."

"No." Clark said. "We're not."

"Absolutely," Barbara agreed.

"Okay. Because, well, some of the stuff we're asked to do gets at bit *edgy*, if you know what I mean . . . "

This Peters guy was interviewing himself, the way people sometimes did when they were confronted by a private dick. Again, they both nodded. Clark knew all about the sort of bad taste that went into modern stag feelies, and certainly didn't want to hear about anything that got more "edgy" than that.

"So I guess," Peters asked, "you want to know the details of the break in?"

Break in? "That sure would be helpful," Clark agreed, wishing he'd brought along a notepad to help things along, then seeing Barbara fish inside her handbag and produce one.

"Just in your own words, Mr Peterson," she said brightly, waving a pencil. "Might as well start at the very beginning."

"Not that much to say really. Your client Mr Lamotte came in, oh . . . It was in the spring. March, I think . . . " He reached to flick through a big Rolodex. "Here it is, the 26th. He brought in the recordings he wanted cut and mixed and transcribed with him. Said it was a surprise birthday present for his wife."

"Got a record of what the recordings were?" Barbara asked.

"We have to. Don't you know that everything to do with using feelie technology is licensed?"

"Of course. Silly me. So . . . ?"

"Well here is it." He unclipped a card from the Rolodex and handed it to her. "Although I guess your client could confirm as well . . . "

Clark and Barbara studied it. The neatly handwritten list on the card which contained an order number and Daniel Lamotte's contact details corresponded pretty much with the missing reels Clark remembered in Erewhon's viewing library. Basically, it was a list of all the feelies for which Daniel Lamotte had written the script. *The Magic of the Past* was there. So were *Sometime Never, Prospector, Sunday Means Tonight, Freedom City* and *This Point Backwards* as well. So, of course, was *The Virgin Queen*.

"It was quite an interesting challenge. Thing is, Mr Lamotte wanted us to edit and cut these feelies so that we could extract the aura of each of his favorite stars, then re-edit them into one single track." He shook his head. "Not sure if that sounds weird or not. But who am I to judge? I just do the work."

"What about this one at the bottom?" Barbara tapped the card with her pencil. "Where you've just put a number?"

"Yeah, that was an older reel. Mr Lamotte said it was from his private collection, or his wife's, or something like that. Rusty old thing. No label or anything. Hasn't *he* explained this to you? Jesus, it must have gone *wayback*, had to clean it up and run it at double speed, although it wasn't so bad once we'd worked out what it was supposed to represent."

"And that was?"

"Well, it was just this series of recordings of these different anonymous auras. Must have been some early demo or something, I guess. There were twenty separate sequences in all. It just ended in this glob of fused metal like it had been burnt out. That can happen sometimes—like if filmstock gets trapped in the shutter. Although you need to push the magnetic heads real hard to trigger a melt."

"Any idea where he got this recording?"

Peters shrugged. "Like I say, it was an ancient thing. Didn't have any of the usual identifiers. That was why we had to give it a fresh catalogue number. Otherwise, we'd have the Bechmeir Trust on our tail. Doing what we do, we don't want that. Like I say, everything we produce has to be licensed."

"How does that work?"

He shrugged. "Simple enough. Pat in our main office has to send off a chit for each recording we make and the Bechmeir Trust log it and send us back a bill."

"Where do you send it? It doesn't involve someone called Losovic by any chance, does it?"

Peters thought for a second, then shook his head. "You'll have to ask Pat. All I know is we send it to some office down in Compton and it gets processed there and it costs us a packet."

"*Compton*, not Willowbrook?"

"Isn't that just where the museum is?"

"You might be right. Now, about the break in . . . ?"

"Just happened one night. Of course, everything was locked up and secured, although we don't employ a nightwatchman—didn't then, anyway. We'd already edited and made Mr Lamotte's recording. I guess you know it's been delivered, so there's no issue there? The weird thing was, that those reels were the only things that got took in this whole facility, where we've got machinery worth tens of thousands of dollars, not to mention valuable reels of feelie wirestock."

"So the reels that Daniel Lamotte had brought to have transcribed were taken, and nothing else?"

"Exactly."

"Any other signs? Anything left, changed, disturbed?"

"Absolutely nothing at all. Like I keep saying, that was the weird thing."

"A neat, professional job?"

"You could say. Not that I'm any expert."

"And how easy would our client's stuff be to find, once you were in here?"

He shrugged. "Not that hard. I mean we keep things labeled. We're not Fort Knox. Weren't anyway . . . "

"You told the police?"

"Yeah. But . . . " Peters gave the sort of shrug which most Angelinos who'd dealt in recent years with the LAPD would have recognized.

"And how did Mr Lamotte seem about this when you told him?"

"He was . . . Well, he just about as puzzled as I was. His wife, though . . . Jesus . . . " Peters whistled and shook his head. "She was mad as hell when she rang up a few days later. Asking all sorts of stuff just the way you are even though it was supposed to be her surprise present . . . I mean, there was nothing *bad* on that reel. Nothing that any of us noticed, anyway. Are you *sure* you're not some kind of police? Or some kind of lawyers?"

Barbara managed to look gravely offended. "Mr Peters, we simply act for our client, but we also have a duty to his insurance company."

"Yeah. I'm sorry." Peters' enthusiasm for an interview with a private dick was fading, the way most people's did. "I'm just not used to—"

"So that was it? Mr Lamotte's reels got stolen, and nothing else? And you've seen or heard nothing since? Not from the police, not from the Lamottes, not from anyone?"

"Yeah." Peters began to stand up. "Maybe I could show you where the break-in took place. It's on the way out, anyway . . . Are you any closer to finding out who actually did this?"

Barbara smiled reassuringly. "It's something we're working on, Mr Peters, believe me."

They followed him back through the main processing area. Steel threads blurred on spinning tops. Reels unrolled into new reels. White flares thinned between copper stretchers. As well as the smell of machine oil, and despite the absence of air conditioning and the heat of the day, the place had the chilly air of a meatsafe.

"Here we are. It's the only way in and out. Course, we've reviewed security since. We now have a regular nightwatchman, and we've gotten ourselves a much stronger padlock. That's to replace the one that got drilled out."

Pete Peters slid the door back on a rumble of wheels. The sunlight outside was dizzying.

FORTY EIGHT

"So, Clark, how about this? Back at the turn of the thirties April Lamotte did something kind of hush-hush which was involved with developing the feelies. It saw her into a whole lot of money, but she keeps this old reel as a kind of insurance when she's finished. And what better place to hide it than where she did? It's like hiding books in a library— well, it *is* a kind of library... Then Dan comes along years later in all innocence with this idea of trapping his muse in this expensive wraith, which he wraps up as a surprise present for her even though it's really for himself, the way men do with lots of things. And he grabs all the obvious reels of his own, and then this weird old one as well which she's tucked at the back. Takes it all down to our friends at Feel-o-Reel to get the job done, and from there it vanishes. Which, when April Lamotte finally realizes what's happening, spooks her no end. It all adds up, doesn't it?"

No, he thought.

They were parked on 5th outside the County Library, and the tall figures representing water, light and power atop the Edison Building opposite seemed to be looking down at them.

"Best thing, Barbara, is you see if you can find any reference at all to that word..." *Thrasis*. He still didn't much like saying it. "And then there's this Doctor Losovic—the one who's supposed to be Charitable Director of the Bechmeir Trust and no one's seen for a while. If we can work out where *she* is..."

"If she's anywhere, that is. We should have looked up her home address in the phone book back on Blixden. You never know. It might be that simple."

"Yeah, but you can find that out in there as well." He nodded toward the County Library, which looked to him to be about as safe a place for Barbara to be as he could imagine at the moment. "Give me another look at that list."

"Just what are you—"

"Shush. Give me some quiet."

It was still strange to see all those names on the yellowed sheet of paper. Half the hugely rich in this city—and seemingly half the dead. That bishop he'd seen at Kisberg's party. The lawyer politician whom the papers called Judge Death. Not to mention Kisberg himself. Peg Entwistle's old agent Hilly Feinstein was there as well.

Peg, he supposed, had been what you might call a Bohemian back then. She'd taken the boat over from Wales with her Dad when she so young she could barely remember, was showbiz through and through, and smart in the way you didn't get from going to school. She'd read more poetry than he had, and knew about classical music. And she also had some weird friends, which was saying something in this city. There was that little guy with the hook nose and no prospects, for instance, who Clark remembered lived in the room next to hers, and used to bang his broom on what passed for the walls when she played her gramophone. Otto Frings, his name was. He'd liked to peek in on her as well. Clark had come up to Otto once, standing outside in the deep night and looking right up at her lit window. Clapped his hands and said *boo*. Little guy had jumped like a sandlouse.

Quite a lot of Peg's crowd, little Otto included, had worked or often didn't work for Hilly Feinstein. Hilly was a piece of work like most agents, and Clark recalled meeting him just the once, and that was with Peg on board a gambling boat. Gambling didn't much appeal to him, but he loved the theatricality and the booze and the cheap new paintwork which turned some old hulk out in the bay into something which glittered on the water for a few weeks until the cops raided it or it got sunk.

There was roulette, and craps, and blackjack, and slots. Clark enjoyed the spectacle for a while until Peg drew him down to where the more serious games were going on. Hilly Feinstein had been sitting at the poker table, big as a toad and just about as greenish. He beckoned Clark over, bid him sit down, shooed Peg off; this was the kind of game men played alone. The other players were vague shapes across the green baize table in the dense fog of smoke, and the boat now seemed to be rocking as a swell rose up. Looking at Hilly, the long slope of his enormous underchin, his near-invisible eyes and the gritty, milky stuff he was drinking instead of whisky, Clark felt almost as greasy and queasy as the guy looked.

Cards were dealt. Clark played. He bet low. He lost. Then the game seemed to draw back, and Hilly was like some freakish conjurer, shuffling a new pack so hard it wouldn't stop blurring, not even when he held it out to Clark and told him to take a card. Instead of clubs or aces or kings, Clark saw a sequence of weird pictures of skeletons and hanged men which ended with this picture of a naked woman pouring water into a pool beneath a glittering night sky. Hilly was telling him in his asthmatic wheeze that this was something called *The Star*—which proved to be a real joke, the way things ultimately worked out—but Hilly had taken the whole pack back and the next game was on before Clark could get a proper handle on what he'd been shown. He had to excuse himself, stagger back up the gangways and throw up. He hadn't liked the sound of Hilly Feinstein before, and he sure as hell didn't like him now.

That sour, displaced feeling he was left with after meeting Hilly Feinstein was one of the reasons he let things between Peg and him drift apart. Of so he told himself. That, and the fact that you could never expect these things to last. And when word got through that Peg had pulled that bizarre stunt and ended up in the Met, he never visited her and let things drift even more. And so it went. And then, a fair few years later, long after his career had vanished, he saw Peg's face again. It was on a billboard. Suddenly she'd become PEG ENTWISTLE. And he'd ceased to be CLARK GABLE—if that was who he'd ever really been. But that's how it goes in this city. You never look down or back. At least, not if you can help it. That's how you pretend to keep sane.

"Jesus!" Barbara flumped back in her seat. "How much quiet is this going to need?"

"Not much more. But..." He gave it another moment. The idea wouldn't go away. "There's someone I'd like to go look up."

"Who?"

"I'd rather not say."

"Why, then?"

"Probably for no better reason other than they're still alive. Last time I heard of, anyway. "

She frowned. "Will it take long?"

"Depends. I shouldn't think so."

"You're not going to do anything stupid?"

"You sound like my stepmom."

"And you'll come right back here?"

"Give it a couple of hours."

"Right." She nodded. "I really want to try to get an edition of *LA Truth* out tomorrow, and someone has to do the proper research. Maybe we should try the Trust's administrative offices in Compton. Just walk in there and say we think something odd's happening. Or, if I can't find out more that way, we could always try going back through all that toilet paper in a bit more detail . . . " She blew at her fringe. "Now *there's* a statement I wasn't expecting to make a few days ago."

He looked at her. She looked at him.

"Okay."

"Yeah."

He noticed as she tucked the list back inside her handbag and climbed out the car that she was carrying the snubnose Colt along with her Graflex.

FORTY NINE

It only took two phone calls from a public booth. He'd imagined he would probably need a drive to Sunset Pier or Hermosa along the coast, and be gone for far longer than he'd told Barbara. But he only had to go a few blocks. Even in a place like LA, he barely needed to get in the Delahaye.

There was so much activity going on outside the Biltmore that he had to turn off from the main frontage and park along Hill Street on the far side of Pershing Square, then cross over past the statues and the sleeping winos in the little park; no flustering studio flunkies or concierges or car valets to greet him now, but when he looked up at the giant hotel's three big towers he felt like he was tripping back into a world he'd briefly savored in his nearly-made-it days. But the world had moved on—California had anyway. Construction workers and lighting electricians were busy preparing the scene for tonight's big bash at the Biltmore Bowl when Herbert Kisberg would declare himself as a man fit to become the nation's first Liberty League president. Even as Clark watched, they were unrolling Stars and Stripes and Liberty League banners down the building's sides. A number of NBC radio trucks were also parked outside, readying everything for the live feed on *Star Talk*. There was absolutely no fucking way, Clark decided once again, that he was going to succumb to Barbara's suggestions that he reprise his performance as Daniel Lamotte with Wallis Beekins tonight.

The Clipper Bar was a basement affair, set around the side and down some steps. Although basement was hardly the word. The first thing which struck him was the place's smooth chill. That, and the odd taste he was getting in the back of his mouth. Just air conditioning, but to him it felt like stepping into a feelie theater when the Bechmeir field generators were turned full on. The place had the look of a feelie as well. All gloss mahogany and deep pile rugs and recessed lights. Some black guy was playing tasteful piano music in the background, and the theme of the Clipper Bar, now his skin had stopped crawling and his eyes had grown more used to the dimness, was supposedly maritime. There were fishnets which had never seen a trawler hooked across the ceiling. There was a whole chandlery store of unused shipping brasswork screwed gleaming to the walls. And there was barely anyone here.

The sole figure who sat at the bar turned to look at him with sad brown eyes. He returned his attention to his drink as Clark drew up a stool.

"How they biting, skipper?"

The man shook his head. "They ain't biting at all." There was a near-full ashtray before him and he spoke without shifting his cigarette from the corner of his mouth.

"Another?"

"Yeah. Why not? You paying?"

As Clark opened out his billfold, he saw his old friend's gaze focus through the smoke haze towards it. He wasn't sure whether there was enough light in here for anyone to make out that he was using another man's driver's license and State ID.

The barman did them two fresh mint bourbons in the quick, efficient way that barmen in swish places like this always had. The taste of the cool, exquisite drink in the heavy shot glass hit Clark like another lost memory. The piano played on. "How long's it been?" he asked.

The guy shrugged. "A couple of years. More... What made you find me now? I'm guessing from the way you're dressed you ain't looking for a pleasure cruise."

"Not exactly, no. And I'm guessing from the way you're dressed that you are?"

"Guess away." Humphrey Bogart was wearing a striped seaman's sweater. Beside him on the bar counter he'd placed a braided old captain's cap. Up on the wall in the far corner, there was even a poster of him, standing on a pier with a boat behind. The lettering above said *Bogey's Tours*.

"Aren't you a bit far inland?"

"Not if you want to get the prime work. I've got a deal with the Biltmore concierge. Anyone with enough money fancies a spot of fresh air and fishing, they don't expect to have to drive out to Playa del Rey to make a booking. They just ask him, and he sends them down here and I do the sea dog act and sell them a nice boat trip . . . Or they just come in for a drink, they get the same act." He shook his head. "Most are sorts have got no idea how far they are from the coast here, anyway. The only kind of breeze they're interested in is the one that comes out their own ass."

"Right. So you're the Ancient Mariner?"

Bogart looked at him as he ground out his cigarette. "And that makes you the visitor with the glittering eye. Although I've seen glitterier . . . "

Clark took out what was left of his pack of Lucky Strikes. When he offered one, Bogart shook his head. "I'll smoke my own. Thought you used to roll yours."

"I did. But I've—"

"Yeah. Changed. Like that suit, and that snazzy watch you're wearing. Business taking photos of yourself screwing other men's wives so they can sue the broads on grounds of adultery must be good."

That was unfair. He'd only ever done that a couple of times. And the wives had been more than willing. But Clark let it pass. They talked then of people they'd known—friends and rivals. Some who'd just been starting to get used to the limousines and the easy fucks and the rooms which always had flower displays, and others who were starving in soup kitchen queues, when the feelies intervened. Women like Garbo, who'd been so big in the silents that she could barely walk down the street, and whom he'd once heard had high-tailed it back to wherever it was in Europe that she'd come from. Guys like Spencer Tracy, who was still scraping a living with walk-on character roles in B-feelies the last time Clark had heard, although that had been near-on five years ago. Pals, really. Proper mates. But fame, or the loss of it, or the realization that it would never be there, did funny things to friendship, like it did funny things to your head.

"Another drink?"

"Why not?"

Just sitting here, two anonymous middle-aged guys that no one would now give a second glance, it was still so easy to fall back into the old ways.

"It's like," Bogart said, pulling a face that showed the scar on his lip, "the whole thing we thought we had was blown apart by a bomb."

"Yeah. A bomb... But can I ask you a question or two?"

"I've been waiting to find out why you're here." He held up his hands. "Whoever she is, Gable, I didn't screw her."

"Nothing like that. It's just... Well, it's about those times. Remember Hilly Feinstein?"

"Sure, I remember Hilly."

"Know much about how he killed himself?"

"Well..." Bogart was watching him more closely now. "Only what I read in the papers. Hadn't seen or heard of Hilly for a year or two by then. Guy was found in his office with his brains blown out. Simple as that."

"Suicide?"

"Why not? Gun in his hand. Brains all over those weird paintings he liked on the walls and the rest of him more than filling up his chair the way Hilly did. It wasn't like Hilly was your regular kind of guy, and that was a thing you could like about him or not. Only person sadder than an actor without any roles is a agent without any clients."

"And before that—say, round about '30, '29—didn't he have you on his books?"

"Are you gonna tell me what this is about?"

"Would if I knew. I'm sorry, Bogey, but this is something you're going to have to take on trust."

Bogart ground out his latest cigarette. The piano music was still playing. He took a slug of his drink. "Hilly did kinda represent me. Or he said he would. You remember what the guy was like. He'd talk the horn off a rhino, then grind it up and say it was fairy dust. All that kind of witch doctor stuff."

"Do you remember anything about the premiere of the first feelie, that thing Hughes did called *Broken Looking Glass*?"

Bogart thought for a moment. Then he felt in his pants' pocket. Clark was half hoping that he'd produce some vital new piece of evidence. All he came out with was another crumpled pack of Chesterfields, although the impossibly elegant way he lit one up and tossed the still-smoking match into the ashtray somehow reminded Clark of what a fine actor Humphrey Bogart was—or could have been if the world had turned out different.

"Not much, no. Although I do remember Hilly was pretty excited about it—so maybe that was another pie he had his fat little fingers in. Said how it would bury guys like Warner, Thalberg, D W Griffith..." Bogart chuckled. "But then, he also said he'd make me the next Lionel Barrymore. Well, he sure as fuck got *that* wrong didn't he? But Hilly was Hilly. He believed his own bullshit better than anyone else—weird stuff about tarot cards and God knows what else. And that in the end was probably what did for him. With Hilly, nothing was simple. There was all this Svengali shit about auras and the circle of the something he was giving me. How some people cast a special shadow across all possible worlds. All kinds of nonsense."

Clark, remembering that, took a while over his drink. "Can you tell me any more? I mean, what kind of work did Hilly get for you?"

"Way I remember it, barely any. I mean, kinda guy Hilly was, it was probably easier for him to find work for the ladies. You know, doing nude life classes, and those ridiculous tricks they used to pull at parties where they'd have a dozen girls jump out of a huge cake. That kinda stuff. And I'm guessing that's just the, uh, top layer."

"So nothing at all?"

"It's hard to remember. I was on a few agents' books back then—not that *they* knew that—and I was pretty desperate for work. If Hilly had asked me, there were probably days when *I'd* have jumped out of a frigging cake and shook my titties."

The both laughed.

"You know what this sounds like, Gable?"

"What?"

"Like you're angling for a bite from something big, deep and dangerous, and you don't even know what it is."

"You're not far off."

"Okay. And now you're about to go, and I'm supposed to say—Oh, there *is* one thing now you mention it..."

"That's about right, Bogey."

"There is."

"No kidding?"

"Christ knows what it has to do with anything, but yeah. Hilly was all the things you and I know about, and he had a finger in some pretty odd pies. That's the only way I can figure why he was trying to persuade his clients to do construction."

Clark nodded. Although he couldn't see where this was leading, the idea of getting actors into building work wasn't so odd. Many of them had come up the same way he had—through putting up sets. Give them a trowel or a hammer and they'd know what to do with it. And actors weren't unionized. And they almost always needed the money.

"Hilly got me in and gave me all the usual *this'll help tide you over* bullshit. But what it amounted to was hanging around on the corner of 3rd at five in the morning for a bus to take you to work your guts out in the desert. It was in, I'd say, oh, about the middle of '29."

"So...?" Clark tried to keep his voice calm and easy. "Did you do it?"

Taking his time, Bogart chain-lit another cigarette. "I was never quite *that* desperate—not even in '29. But I knew a few guys who were. Remember Wilfred Bird—big guy, but bent as a three dollar note? He did a couple-a weeks. Frankie Smott. Then that creepy guy with the lisp that went away as soon as he was reading lines. Him as well. A few others. I saw them around that time. You know how it was. And they were saying they were putting up buildings and pouring concrete in this nowhere place, and no one would tell them shit. Not so much that's unusual there, maybe. But they kept saying it didn't feel right. Frankie especially."

"Didn't Frankie...?"

"Yeah. Killed himself just a year or two after. Jumped right in front of an express train. Anyway, by the time they'd scraped up what was left of him, there wasn't else you could tell. Wilfred Bird didn't last much longer, either. Believe it was supposed to be a heart attack. A stroke. Some kind of embolism. Hard to say."

"You mean, he was just found dead?"

"That's the way it was told. Found dead in the gutter and gazing up at the stars just the way a whole bunch of others have been found in this city over the years, and no one was that surprised to hear that Wilfred of all people had gone that way. Guy got himself in a real bad state. Rang me up a couple times close to what turned out to be the end spouting all the dumbest kinds of Shinola. Stuff about how he knew something and he couldn't say what it was but he was scared as hell and if he did let it out there'd be people after him and he'd be dead." Bogart exhaled. "And then of course he *was* dead. But he'd been drinking. Maybe doing some other stuff as well. And we weren't exactly bosom pals—like you can imagine, Wilfred had his own set. And you can't start believing the things people tell you in LA. So I'm not saying there was a link with anything that Hilly had Wilfred doing. At least, I wasn't saying that 'til just now when I saw that look on your face."

"This thing—this construction project out in the desert? Any idea where it was?"

"None at all. I don't think the guys ever knew themselves. I remember Frankie saying the windows on the bus were so dirty they couldn't even see out."

"Did anyone ever mention a name?"

"What kind of a name?"

"Thrasis . . . Something like that."

Bogart frowned. "You should stick to dirty bedsheets, Gable. An' I'll stick to letting rich men play sailor on my boat."

"But that word . . . ?"

"It could have been . . . Like I say, the last time I heard from Wilfred he wasn't exactly . . . *Thrasis*? It's got a weird sound . . . It's like—I dunno."

Clark suppressed a shiver. He still hadn't got used to this air conditioning, and the pianist was playing too loose and loud, the way pianists did when they knew no one was listening.

Bogart shook his head. "Back in the times, eh, Gable?"

"Yeah." They clinked glasses. "Back in the times."

"Only person I ever heard did any good out of knowing Hilly was Peg Entwistle. And *look* how good she did. So maybe that counts for all the rest of us. I mean, in the bigger picture."

"Yeah. The bigger picture."

They laughed, and clinked glasses again.

"Remember, Gable, that little guy Otto? Used to live next door to Peg for a while, said he was a trained classical actor and had done all the big roles in Shakespeare yet never got a single sniff of work in this town about three years. All he ever got was someone punched him in the face so bad that the last time I saw him he was all bandaged up like the invisible man."

"Well." Clark knocked back the last of his drink. The cubes had melted and the bourbon was almost warm, but it felt like something chill and sleek as the shadows at the back of this bar had crept up behind him and was playing its fingers down his ribs. "Guess we're all invisible now."

"You fancy another?"

"Better be going."

"You're wrong, by the way."

"About what?"

"Whatever it is you're chasing, it'll never make any sense. Nothing ever does. You know that, don't you?"

"I guess I do." Clark smiled at his old friend. "And now I know where you are, Capt'n. You're either here or up on that poster."

"Sure. I'll take you out, bring some bottles, we can fish for bluefin. It'll be like the old days but without the women. Just you make sure the bluefin aren't fishing for you."

Clark stood up, and they clasped hands.

He heard Humphrey Bogart shout at the pianist, "Hey, Sam, will you clam up that racket?" as he left the Clipper Bar and climbed back out into the warm city.

FIFTY

He crossed Olive Street and headed back across Pershing Park toward his car. There were many things on his mind. Thrasis, for example, which still felt less like a real place than some expression of undefined dread. But then he guessed that that was exactly how you'd have it if you wanted to make sure that whatever had gone on there was kept quiet. Even—no, *especially*—by the people who'd been directly involved.

Jesus... That hissing sound. He spun around amid the noon-pooled trees at the edge of the hardscape in the center of the park. But it was only the sprinklers, come on to keep these geometric patches of grass Los Angeles-green. The raised sheets of water fanned rainbows. A scatter of sparrows chirruped and preened. Clark smiled. There was always a moment when these gizmos started swishing you felt like you were getting a glimpse into some lush underworld. Which he supposed was exactly what the gardeners and the engineers were trying to create in their endless efforts to push back the halfway desert of this coastal strip of California all the way into the sea.

The water flicked and scattered. The grass glittered, an emerald sea. The whole dusty little park turned briefly beautiful, although the down-and-outs and the deadbeats lying safely dry on their benches didn't even bother to raise yesterday's newspaper off their faces, or stir the hand which gripped today's bid for oblivion inside a brown paper bag. Only he and the sparrows seemed to care. But there *was* someone standing in the prismatic shade nearby under the billowing spread of some European tree. The wash of the sprinklers seemed to leave whoever it was unaffected. In fact, as they stood there and Clark stood watching them and realized with a slow, stupid dawning that they were watching *him*, the fleck of the sprinklers and the sunshot glitter which dripped through the tree's lower branches seemed to be all of which the watcher was made. For although the figure had a shape of sorts, there was no true sense of definition—of any face or mode of dress or of any single identity. It was more as if the wet spray had caught and darkened in a vortex of many identities. And then, as the sprinklers slowed their arcs and the sound of all the surrounding traffic returned and the sparrows settled back on their branches, there was no one at all left standing under that tree.

Clark wiped his glasses. Looked around him. This was getting ridiculous. He was chasing shadows, wraiths. Or, to be more exact—although exact didn't seem to be the kind of term that was in any way appropriate—the shadows and wraiths were chasing him. And all of it happening in the easy sunlight of this bright, busy city, which was depicted as paradise on the sides of thousands of orange boxes and had spread its glow across the globe in a million other different ways. He thought again of something that April Lamotte had said to him about the quality of LA's light and the quality of its darkness, although he guessed it stood to reason that shadows got blacker and deeper the brighter the sun blazed.

You're thinking plain old crap, Gable. Thinking the same kind of mumbo-jumbo that got that guy Wilfred Bird—whom Clark vaguely remembered as the kind of big, breezy, happy-go-lucky, up-for-anything character who gave fairies a good name—lying dead in some Sunset sidestreet on the wrong side of 4 am. All it took when you got far enough out was a nudge, a mere word or suggestion, to send you falling all the rest of the way. And there was Barbara with her neat lines of pencils back in the Los Angeles library, and her plans to turn everything into commonsense. Some hope, although he felt a surge of the same old bug-eyed protective instinct toward her that had seen him breeze most of his life away on the kind of lost causes for which he rarely ever ended up getting paid. Or, for that matter, laid.

But just over the Biltmore's turrets was the Hollywoodland sign, and it gleamed so much it looked like it was made of the breath of angels rather than being the tawdry thing of peeled paint and rusted metal he knew it really was. And as he stared at it, and then back at the space beneath the big old tree that was now filled with nothing but empty shade, a slow kind of dawning passed over him. Then it grew into a rush.

He slammed the Delahaye's clattering door and scrabbled with the ignition and headed along Wiltshire and then cut through Hollywood and past Glen Oak and veered up into the tight winds of Beachwood Drive and through the pretentious stone gates where the development which that stupid sign had once advertised began. Huge cacti flourished here in the hilly little gardens of the upscale houses, and there on the left was the sharp rise of scrubland which called itself Mount Lee. He parked by a chainlink gate where the expensive real estate finally gave out in a heap of discarded *For Sale* placards and old litter. The fencing around the gate wasn't much of anything. He was over it with only one tear snagged in the left elbow of his linen suit, and then climbing like some goddamn idiot up through the thorny brush. The Californian sunlight grew less benign and he was thinking of scorpions and blackwidow spiders and whatever else kind of nasties you were likely to encounter in what was still a dangerous wilderness for all the cookie cutter rooftops and blue pools below.

Breathless, and with more tears nicked in his suit, he finally made the top of the rise where those letters suddenly loomed close and grubby and fifty foot high. Now that he'd actually done the whole foolish thing and got here, he fully expected that he would be alone. But he wasn't. A woman was sat on the dry ground before the H. She was petite and pretty and strikingly blonde, and she had a kind of aura about her of the sort that only genuine stars have. It seemed like Peg Entwistle had been staring out across the city, but she glanced over at him as he struggled over the last straggle of dirt and rocks and loped toward her. Then she looked back toward the city. There was nothing about his appearance here that seemed to cause her any surprise.

"Is it going to be you, Clark?" she muttered into the breeze. "Of all people—are you the one who comes to kill me?"

"Peg..." He slumped down beside her and fought for breath. "... that's not what this is about."

She pulled a bitter smile and tossed a rock down toward the undergrowth below. "You really don't think so?"

"I barely know what the hell's happening. I just know..." He had to stop again. His throat hurt and his glasses were dusty and kept slipping down his nose. He wiped them clear and put them back on. That really did seem to be better. He was getting to the point where, in order to see something, he actually felt like he needed to put the damn things on. "...well, I guess that all I really know is that name I said to you last night...and that maybe it's a place—and that it's something to do with Hilly Feinstein and a whole lot of other people who all went to the premiere of the first feelie. And that most of them have either done pretty well for themselves like you have Peg. Or they're dead." He shrugged and rubbed some grit from his mouth. "Or both."

Peg nodded slowly. She was plainly dressed in midbrown slacks with a short knitted waistcoat over a mannish white blouse. The boots were low-heeled things—simple and sensible as well. Even though America was still resolutely at peace, this soldierly and utilitarian style of daywear had crept across from Europe.

"You're supposed to be Daniel Lamotte, right?"

"How did you get to that?"

"Fairly simple, really. After all, you did mention his name at Herbert Kisberg's last night. So I checked the guestlist after I saw you, and you weren't on it but the Lamottes both were. I've even met Dan once or twice, and I used to know his wife quite well. But April's dead, isn't she? Unless the news is all wrong."

"No, Peg. It's not wrong."

She blinked slowly, pursed her mouth. The Hollywood Reservoir glittered, off amid the brown and green scrub. Then the land swooped down toward the great amphitheater of the city. It was magnificent, yet it was paled and slightly blued by the day's smog, like a Kodachrome panorama left for too long in a store window's sun.

"What about Dan? Is he dead as well?"

"I wish I knew. That's one of the many things I'm still trying to find out."

She chuckled. "Right in at the deep end, Clark, as always. And you really haven't been sent up here to kill me?"

"The nearest my current work gets to violence is when some husband's broad comes at me with a pair of nail scissors. And she's normally wearing a peekaboo negligee."

"So you're that kind of private eye?"

"Well, I was. I got roped into this because April Lamotte hired some other dick to find a lookalike for her husband, and I guess I was tall enough and jug-eared enough to fit the bill. I think her plan was to make it look as if Dan had killed himself by dressing me up as him and gassing me in his car, then stage her own suicide and make a run for it. Instead, she ended up dead, and so did the other private eye."

Peg flung another rock. "She must have gotten really desperate."

They sat there for a while in silence. Clark glanced over at Peg. The wind stirred her loose blonde hair, which he guessed was probably styled in this feathery way after the fashion of whatever character she'd most recently been playing. The loose strands of it seemed to cause the details of her face to blur, and he thought again of how difficult it was for someone like her. Always putting on the next veil, the next disguise. Even amid the car crashes and the marriage breakups, you were always playing someone other than yourself.

"You as much as anyone know how things were with me, Clark," she said. "I could never see myself as anything other than an actress. I suppose it was down to my dad and the way I grew up. I only felt good about myself when I was onstage or in front of a camera . . . Or perhaps just before or after when I was in front of the dressing room mirror, putting on or taking off my makeup. Then Hilly comes along with all sorts of promises to lure me out to Los Angeles and tales about how this place was the future of everything. Which I suppose it probably was.

"So I took the train from New York and I went to all the parties and I attended all the auditions, and I met people like you, Clark. For a while I felt like I was floating, but then it seemed as if I was falling. I remember . . ." She gave a laugh. "The very day I arrived and came out of Union station I looked up at this sign. And even then it sort of passed through my head that if I failed I might as well throw myself off it. Hilly..." She shook her head. "Well Hilly somehow picked up on that without me ever consciously telling him. When he did those cards for me—the tarot, they're called, aren't they?—the symbol he kept coming up with was this figure falling from a high tower. And he said nonsense things about a circle of worlds, and how events can happen in several ways and send our lives off in different directions, but that certain places and people will always have some kind of magnetic draw. So when the work stopped coming... Well, to be honest, it hardly ever started, and this sign seemed to be forever gazing down at me, it eventually came to feel like only a matter of time before I..." She paused. "I don't quite mean to say *threw myself off*. It isn't that simple, and perhaps it never is. That evening when I walked along Beachwood and climbed over the fence and up here I was in part just curious. I felt as if watching myself scrambling up over these rocks. It was like some kind of experiment. To see how far you can take something, and if it really can be done. And then I guess I was lucky. If you can call it that. Anyway, the police came and I got arrested before I could work out how to climb my way up. And when they asked me what I was doing up here in the first place, I simply told them the truth. Which got me into the Met.

"It wasn't so terrible. I mean, there are no poolside parties, no meetings with producers who basically want you to take your clothes off. When somebody in the Met tells you something, they mostimes genuinely mean it—even if it's some story about little men from Mars. So I kind of got to like being in there. It was almost like throwing myself off this sign. Another form of letting go—or giving up. April Lamotte was a nurse there. And Penny Losovic—you're heard of her as well, haven't you?—she was a young intern. You form friendships in such places just like any others, and by some standards I was less mad than some of the other residents. I soon became a ward trustie.

"So when I'm asked if I'd be interested in helping in some research project, I really wasn't likely to say no. They said it was a new facility, and that it might lead to some great insights into the workings of the human mind. This was late in 1929 and I'd been in the Met for several months, and the thing I suppose I feared above anything was having to go back into the outside world. And of course there was still Hilly. He was egging me on as well. So there it was. We were taken to this place of low, new fenced-off buildings. We called it Thrasis after the old mining town that had once been there, but it was so far out in the Mojave that it really wasn't anywhere at all. I suppose we had to call it something, although I never liked the sound of that word.

"In some ways, Thrasis wasn't so very different from the Met. I was the bright spark, the helpful patient—good little Peg Entwistle who can be relied upon to be sensible and helpful and toe the line. There was a doctor there—I think he was pretty famous for his work on the human brain."

"Guy called Theobold?"

She nodded. "He's dead now, of course. But he and other experts said they were especially interested in me because I was an actress, and because I'd attempted suicide. It seemed weird back then—although I know that now it would seem far less so—when I was asked to sit in this electrically shielded room and try to work myself back into that state. Try to imagine, they told me, that you're climbing the back of that letter H, and then the moment of decision, and throwing yourself off, the act of plunging, falling... and how all of that might feel. It was sold to me like it was a kind of cleansing of the spirit, but in truth I think we all knew that this was about human minds pushed to their far extremes. I was mostly kept apart from the other residents. We lived I—I wouldn't exactly call them cells. We weren't allowed to mingle. But I knew enough. I heard enough. Sometimes, thick though the concrete walls were, you could hear screams. And I helped do the laundry, being good little Peg. And I tell you, Clark, there was far too much blood on the things that needed washing... So I'm not making excuses. I knew what was really going on in those shielded and soundproofed rooms at Thrasis, and in my own small way I was involved. I just chose somehow to close my eyes and heart and ears. I rather think that millions of people across in Europe are learning how to do the same..."

"So Thrasis really is a place out in the desert?"

"I think you could say that. But don't ask me where it is, Clark, because it was and is nowhere. You know how the wind sounds when its been coming at you for miles? It seemed to be saying this word. It was some other kind of presence. And then Thrasis was closed and we achieved what we achieved and that presence seemed to follow those of us who returned to what were supposed to be our ordinary lives. Of course, we were all pledged to secrecy. But the deal almost seemed to be worth it, and for our silence we were lavishly paid. There was money behind Thrasis, Clark, like you wouldn't believe, but there was influence as well. For me, it was about my career. For April, of course, it was getting Dan the breaks he needed to succeed as a writer of feelies. For Penny, it was a job where she could help others. It was . . . " She shrugged and wiped her eyes.

"A deal with the devil?"

"And we're all still paying the price. I mean, it was never *said*. It was never *explained*. But you started noticing it in the papers, and amongst people who'd worked in Thrasis that you'd known. The deaths, the suicides, the disappearances. The message was pretty clear. If you cracked, or came close to going public, you died. It was worse than that, though. It was Hilly who explained that. He'd been involved as some kind of supplier of whatever was needed—bodies, patients, muscle. I suppose, in a way, he'd supplied me. But he was losing it himself by then—I guess all that nonsense talk of spirits and other worlds had finally got to him—and he called me one night to say he'd had this letter filled with sand and he knows that there's nothing left to be done."

"A letter filled with *sand*?" Even though he knew it was empty, Clark felt his hand move toward his suit coat pocket.

She nodded. "It was a kind of signal—that was the cleverest thing about how it was all done. The deaths, you see, were mostly suicides. But if you didn't kill yourself and put an end to things neatly, it wasn't just you that died, but everything that was precious to you was destroyed as well. It happened to Doctor Theobold. He and his family died . . . in a terrible way. It's happened to many others. I used to keep up some contact with one or two others. April, for example. And Penny. But it's been years . . . I've been too afraid."

"So this is why you're up here? You thought that *I* . . . ? Last night . . . ?"

"When you turn up out of nowhere and mention Thrasis, what else was I to think? Look, Clark, I've honestly got no idea of how these people really got killed, or why they killed themselves. All I know is that they are dead."

Clark gazed out at the city. Everything about it seemed faint, distant. With or without these glasses, he wondered if Los Angeles would ever seem real to him again. "And all that guff about the Bechmeir field?"

"Just another way of covering up for Thrasis. That, and a marketing ploy. Lars Bechmeir is nothing more than a way of selling a product. He's the Quaker Oats man made flesh. Or was, anyway. And look at how he lost his wife... So there you are, Clark. *This* is what you've blundered into. And, if you didn't know enough before to get yourself killed, you do now."

"Peg—this old friend of yours. This Doctor Losovic. I'm sorry, but I think she's vanished as well. It might be nothing..."

She blinked slowly but said nothing. If this was a feelie, Clark thought, and Peg was any decent kind of actress, she'd be crying by now. But her eyes were as dry and glassy as the lens of an iconoscope.

"The thing is," he said, "that everything you've told me makes it clear that you can't let this go on. We have to blow the whole thing open. It's the only way." He thought of *Star Talk*. He thought of Barbara's busy little press. "I don't care what the hell happens. But from here on in I'm going to give it the good old college try."

"Then you haven't been listening to what I've told you at all." Her voice was a lost monotone. "You're going to do something stupid. I know you, Clark."

"Since when has that been news?"

Shade seemed to have fallen over them. Glancing back, he saw that the sign now lay between them and the sun.

"Look, Peg. What are you going to do? You're not going to—"

"No. I won't do *that*. Maybe I was never brave enough. I think I'll just sit up here a while longer. It's not such a bad spot. From here you can see that the city has an ending—that it doesn't just go on and on and on. Then I'll wander back down. Call a cab, check with Mina about any new scripts that are in, go back home and take an early night. You know what it's like. I've got a dawn call for a readthrough because the director and the writer can't agree about a comma. And if anything else happens, if anyone comes . . ." A dusty wind stirred around them. She gave a shivering shrug. "It's only what I deserve. Now, will you let me alone . . . ?"

He wanted to tell her no. Wanted to tell her how good things had once been and could be again. How the dream wasn't all lost and dead. Wanted to tell her a whole lot of things. But instead, he simply got up and headed off down the slope.

FIFTY ONE

He drove back into Los Angeles, parked the Delahaye, got out, dodged the 5th Avenue traffic and took the County Library steps at a run. It was coming up to two o-clock. He'd been in this library several times when he was checking up on cases. Dust made pillars of the sunlight. Huge friezes told the story of the city as if all of it—the Spaniards and the slaughtered Indians and the citrus farmers and the chanting monks—had all been leading up to some perfect moment. But there was a reek of incontinent bodies amid the tall avenues of shelves.

He looked quickly for Barbara. First in the main reading room. Then, in increasing alarm, he tried the smaller alcoves. Nothing but snoring hobos. He asked a passing woman to check the ladies' washroom, then went back along the way he'd come, telling himself to stay calm. But what had made him think that a place this public would be safe, even before everything that Peg had told him? He pushed through doors into private offices. He ran stairs. Then, bursting through swing doors marked Map Room, he found her sitting alone and calm-as-you-like at the big center table.

"Hey Clark, where have you been? You look as if . . . "

He drew up a chair and sat there panting. He could have used a cigarette. "Just saw some people. Like I said."

"Don't tell me you're protecting your sources?"

"It isn't like that, but . . . Well, I've got a pretty clear idea now about this thing called Thrasis. It's—"

"I know, Clark. It's a place. It's out in the desert."

All around her along the map room walls were wide, thin-drawed cabinets and racks of what might have been holes in a pigeon coop, only they were stuffed with rolls of paper.

"It was obvious, really," she said. "I remembered that Dan had a County Library ticket—stands to reason, he's a writer, and he'd need to do research. I work here quite a bit myself, so I just tried asking my old friend Max at the main counter. Not that he remembered Dan's name, but he recognized the description. And he took me in here. It's in the map room log that Daniel Lamotte was in here Tuesday and Wednesday last week. I was even able to find out what maps he'd been looking at . . . and here they are . . ."

A wrinkled sea of yellowed sheets covered the table. They gave off gritty crackles. Many had been rolled and folded so often that they had fallen apart. All were so aged it was hard to tell where the stains gave out and the real makings began.

"They show bits of the Mojave, the high desert, and were mostly done by prospectors and wildcatters last century. No one's ever got round to cataloguing them properly, and they don't make much sense. They weren't meant to. See, a map you'd marked out to show where the mineral seam or an oil seep that you'd discovered was—that was valuable information, and you sure as hell didn't want anyone else to work it out. So it stands to reason that these maps aren't coherent or accurate. They're in code, mirror-written, out of scale. They were *meant* to confuse—or possibly even lead competitors to their deaths. But it's right here—I mean Thrasis—on some of them anyway. Look . . ."

She dragged over a small square that looked to have flaked apart from a far larger map. The old paper had a gritty, glittery feel, and was discolored to dark brown in one corner with what might have been ancient blood. The writing was spidery and dense, and maybe his sight wasn't as good as hers, because Barbara had to show him where the word was. But, once you saw it blocked there in shaky print, there was no doubting. THRASIS. And there it was again, scrawled in a different hand on the corner of another map, which had been drawn on the back of a poster for some quack medical cure.

"Thrasis isn't on any of the more modern surveys or atlases. But the

State surveyors are only concerned with proper geological features. Some abandoned mining settlement would probably be ignored. There are dozens of places like that up in the high desert, or more likely hundreds, and these maps are scrappy things..."

"Like a jigsaw."

"Or several jigsaws with the pieces mixed. But Thrasis *is* somewhere real, Clark. It's a place that you can narrow down pretty accurately to a set of map coordinates and then get into a car and drive out to. Dan must have realized that as well. So what he did when he'd finished in this map room was pretty straightforward." She felt down in the bag beside her feet and produced the receipt for RTS Taxis. "I've been wondering about this since I first saw it. I couldn't understand why on earth anyone would pay a taxi firm more than fourteen dollars for one journey. But it's for Thursday June 20th, just over a week ago—the day after Dan finished looking at these maps. The Delahaye was up at Erewhon, and maybe he was getting wary of April by then, so he simply called a cab. That's probably the day he gets that gun, as well. And Friday's when he sees April at Edna's Eats to tell her what he's found. Although she knows most of it already because she was involved in it herself. And that's why she's afraid."

"And then he vanishes."

"Exactly. Just like everyone else who's ever got near the truth."

She took him to the main reading room and unfolded heavy volumes of bound newspapers.

There was a financier called Hilton Edwards, who'd been killed in a hit-and-run on Sunset in 1933. There was Sol Hayden, a civil engineer who'd won a Distinguished Service Medal in the Great War and worked for many years in LA, but had become a hermit and somehow contrived to starve himself to death in a fishing shack up on the Bay of Funday in Canada in 1935. And there was Ralph Kilbrack, whose body was found in a hotel room in Tijuana only last year. PART TIME ACTOR AND LIMO DRIVER FOUND SKINNED ALIVE IN MYSTERY MEXICO KILLING was the lurid headline in the *LA Times*. And the only thing these people had in common apart from being dead was that they'd attended the premiere of the first ever feelie.

"Of the people on the guestlist, it looks like at least eighteen are dead. And several others are missing." She tapped her fingers on the table and smiled at him. "But it's your turn now, Clark. You can tell me whatever you like about where you've been and who you've seen, but it's obvious that it has something to do with a name recognized on that guestlist. Used to be someone yourself, didn't you? Or nearly. Mr Clark Gable of the talking silver screen. Hollywood's a small enough village, and it was even smaller then. So the chances are you knew at least some of those people. And, being who you are, I also reckon that the ones you knew best would be young and pretty and female... And wasn't Peg Entwistle there last night at Herbert Kisberg's? And isn't she on that list?" She was still smiling. "Am I warm, Clark?" She tapped her fingers again. "Am I close?"

She was clever; there was no doubt about it. But what creeped him the most was how she was still treating all of this like some kind of parlor game.

He told her what he now knew about Thrasis. About the work that had gone on there. About the buildings, which had surely been out in that place in the desert which she had shown him, although they had most likely been razed. He even told her about Peg, and her story of Wilfred Bird and that sand-filled envelope, which was the exact same message which April Lamotte had received. Shut up or die. In fact, kill yourself anyway, seeing as you've blown things already. That, or be killed along with all that you hold precious in some worse and far more lingering way.

"So Peg Entwistle's pretty frail? This is a side to her that the press have never got wind of."

"Or if they have, they showed some compassion and kept it quiet."

"You really think *that*?"

He had to shake his head. "But I don't want her any more involved in this than she is already, Barbara. She's terribly spooked."

"Spooked seems to come with territory, doesn't it? I mean, no wonder April tried to fake Dan's suicide when she realized what he was on to with that script of his . . . " She snapped her fingers loud enough for some of the reading room's other occupants to look over. "Of *course*—and she was heading up toward that pine lodge where Dan was right before she stopped, or got stopped. From there and over the mountains, and you're right in the desert, aren't you? Leave a car out there with one of those suicide notes she'd been working on, and no-one would even expect to find a body. And those who needed to would understand that she'd chosen to walk off into the Mojave because of Thrasis. It's like a signal— I give up, I submit. After all, she had supposedly just lost her husband. And from there, they could both simply vanish and start a new life. It's not a bad plan is it, when you look at it that way?"

"Other than the part that would have left me dead."

"But when you *didn't* die, Clark—when you managed to get out of that car and she didn't get the message from the police that she'd been expecting, she panicked and headed up to the lodge anyway. She was probably just going to get Dan and run the hell for it. Only she got waylaid and died at that overlook. And that suicide, the way it was done, was also a kind of signal. And whoever did that probably also saw to Dan as well. It all makes perfect sense."

He could have laughed. Had it been funny. "It would hardly stand up in court."

"But it would look pretty good on the front page of a newspaper."

"The Bechmeir Trust'd sue the hell out of you."

"Let them. Once the cat's out of the bag and running around knocking over all the chinaware and spilling the milk and the horse is out of the stable, there's not much anyone can do to shove it all back in there."

"I guess."

"But you're right. There are holes everywhere and a lot of hearsay sources you don't want me to credit even if we could get them to speak out. We still need to do all we can to get more evidence before I go to print. Like, for example, if we could show exactly where Thrasis was, and then prove that Dan went out there. Then there's that doctor woman. You're saying she used to know both Peg and April. And she's got this job in the Bechmeir Trust, and now she's vanished, and none of this can be a coincidence. If we could find out what's happened to her. Maybe talk to her. Lay things out and tell her that she's a crucial witness."

"If she's alive."

"I suppose that's a tall order. She still isn't showing at her office, Clark. I rang again from the public phone in here. But I was right when I said we should have looked up her home address in the phone booth. She lives in Edendale."

"You've tried calling?"

"Guess what? There's no answer. So? What do we do?"

FIFTY TWO

They agreed that Barbara would contact RTS Taxis, which according to their telephone listing had a depot down in his old stamping ground of what had once been the MGM studios, whilst he went to try to find out what had really happened to Doctor Penny Losovic. This time, he took the gun.

He drove north. The queues were already lengthening outside the feelie houses for the matinee showings. Not just the stargazy types who never did anything else, but mothers with babies, and kids who should have been at school, and old ladies so withered and sour-faced they looked to be beyond such fantasies, and businessmen in button-downs, and secretaries in shiny black heels, and negro maids in starched caps, and pot-bellied shopkeepers still in their aprons.

Edendale was an area which had once been at the heart of the moving picture industry. Max Sennette and the Keystone Kops had tumbled down these hilly streets. Harold Lloyd could have hung from that post office clock. But that was back in the ancient times of the silents. The studios had moved west, and Edendale had been forgotten, just like MGM. Nothing in this city ever stayed still. Now, where the gods of a different era had once walked, there were only gas stations, parking lots and drive-in churches.

The roads off the main drag went steeply up into a slew of smart new whites-only housing developments. Clark followed one, and parked the Delahaye just before a turn.

Aurora Avenue was a wide crescent of well-spaced split-levels with white-painted wooden sidings. Birds sang. The air still smelled rainy up here from the lawn sprinklers. Everything was in its place, from the second car on the driveway to the wrought iron hummingbird feeders. It was like a front cover for *American Home*. But actual people seemed as rare here as they were in the more extravagant houses of Woodsville. There was nothing much to distinguish number 16 Aurora Avenue from any of the other properties, although there was no car, and the front lawn, which would have passed for pristine anywhere else, looked a touch ragged in comparison with the others. He paused and stooped down as if to tie up his shoelace, noticing as he glanced across that the windows were shut, the drapes were open, and that there had either been no mail or newspaper delivered this morning, or they had been taken in.

He walked on to the end of the crescent, then took an immediate right. They were still putting up new houses here, and the area was a cleared wasteland filled with foundation trenches, separated from the rear of Aurora Avenue's gardens by nothing more than a chainlink fence. Trying to look as if he had a reason to be here—maybe he was a realtor or prospective purchaser—he strode across the mud and dust, then studied the back of the houses until he was sure he'd got the right one. He quickly climbed the fence and dropped down into number 16's yard.

No yapping dogs or playing children. Just more birdsong. He could also hear the hiss of a sprinkler, but that came from a fair few houses up. All the drapes were open and all the windows were shut here, as at the front. Once again, there were neat borders, impressive blooms of fuchsia and bougainvillea and many other kinds of plant he didn't recognize, although the turf was a little wilder and thicker than he'd expected.

He peered in the windows. Everything inside looked orderly, but there was no sign of occupancy. He checked the garbage bin, which was empty, and smelled clean. He nudged open the screen door, tried the inside handle, then looked through the keyhole to see if a key was still in the mortise lock; it wasn't. Neither did this Doctor Losovic strike him as the sort who'd leave a key under the mat. Still, he felt in all the obvious places and found nothing. Then he searched the borders for a medium-sized stone, and gave the nearest of the windows a sharp rap. Using the tip of the Delahaye's key, he worked out the putty from around the crack he'd made—with a house as new as this one, it was an easy job—until he could loosen and pry out the triangle of glass. Then he reached through to twist the handle, pulled the window open, and dropped inside.

Dining room furniture regarded him with the same cold surprise which the furniture in people's houses always did when he broke in—no, if anything, it was far colder; everything here was so *clean*. There was an odd, moaning, flapping sound. It was followed by a loud hissing. Then the moaning and flapping started again. His skin chilled. Lifting the Colt from his pocket, he moved around the gleaming table and across the hall toward the sound's source. He laughed out loud when he shoved the door open with the Colt's barrel. A new Bendix washing machine squatted in the kitchen, suds and flaying arms of clothing sliding past its porthole. So *someone* had been here recently. Although what that told him, he wasn't sure.

Doctor Losovic had a liking for expensive new gadgets, and not much taste when it came to decoration. The gleam of a Presto pressure cooker and a streamline Electrolux fridge competed oddly with the gingham lamp shades and the pink rose wallpaper, at least as far as he was concerned. It was the same throughout the house. Wrought iron light sconces. Cellophane curtains. Chrome and jadeite electrical equipment and modern housewear set amid strews of cushions and floral rugs. The phonograph in the front lounge was especially ugly. A big "cathedral style" thing—more like a tombstone—of bakelite knobs, gleaming valves and zigzag marquetry. He checked the records stacked beside it. Churchy stuff, mostly. Masses and requiems. Those big German composers whose names generally began with B whom Peg had once told him were old hat. But at least some of the pictures on the walls—sepia reproductions of medieval religious paintings—made a kind of fit.

He moved upstairs as the Bendix began to rumble through another wash cycle, wondering as he did so what he'd been expecting to find. The links with Thrasis had seemed plain when he'd been talking to Barbara, but here...

Doctor Losovic favored straight, simple skirts and tops, and even simpler underwear. She used two different types of sanitary product, nothing fancier than Palmolive soap to wash herself, and her shoe size was on the large side at 8. The second bedroom was set out as a study, with pen and paper laid beneath the glass petals of a lily-shaped desklamp, and everything looking as if it had never been used. Facing the desk were a few framed newspaper cuttings. Yellowed photos of smiling kids, grinning pensioners. Even a bunch of dogs outside a new kennels. Headlines about how grateful everyone was. In each of the pictures, with her hands on the shoulders of the happy staff or holding the fluffiest puppy or kneeling with the kids, was the same tall woman with broad shoulders and shortish dark hair. The lace-topped bookcase behind the desk chair contained titles about the understanding of the mind, titles about the understanding of pain, titles about the understanding of dreams, and every one of them was pristine in its dustjacket. He eased one out, and flicked through pages filled with dizzying diagrams and Latin terms and cutaways of skulls. They should have seemed wildly out of place in this temple to modern America, but somehow they didn't.

No holiday seashells. No love letters. No cellar stuffed with boxes in need of sorting. No human stains on those oh-so-clean sheets. Everything fitted, but somehow Doctor Penny Losovic didn't seem to have much of a personal life, and it was hard not to feel sorry for the woman. Even her toothbrush looked barely used.

He found another picture of her on the telephone stand back down in the hall. She was looking up at the photographer from behind what he took to be her office desk. She had clear, Nordic eyes, a big jaw. They were features which might have been pretty on someone else, but she looked purposeful and severe. He set the picture back down beside the Ray-Ban aviator sunglasses which she'd left there with what by now seemed like uncharacteristic abandon, then slid open the small drawer beneath. Nothing but a slew of the usual business cards and we-called-when-you-were-out notes from meter readers for the utilities. He slid it shut, and stared once more at that photo—that almost smiling mouth—and then again at those Ray-Bans.

He worked the drawer open again. His fingers skidded through cards for telephone repairmen, cards for electricians, cards for plumbers, a card for RTS Taxis, and a card which said *Clark Gable, Private and Personal Research a Specialty* with a corner folded over and the phone number changed and crossed out. That infernal machine in the kitchen was still swooshing and groaning. He ran through to it and struggled with the porthole handle until it gave in a wet rush around his feet. Amid a spill of navy fabric, a badge proclaiming Gladmont Securities glittered through the suds.

FIFTY THREE

He backed the Delahaye around, slamming the rear fender against a tree. Gears skittered as he took the hills down from Edendale and through Silver Lake, dodging pedestrians, narrowly missing a farm truck at the junction with Alvarado. But there was one thing about where he was heading; he knew the way.

Palms flew overhead as he shot stoplights and overtook dallying drivers and raced south toward Culver City. There had been nightspots along these roads ten years ago—brazen as you like even at the height of Prohibition—with hat check girls and cigar girls and camera girls and girls who'd do pretty much whatever else you wanted. But the Green Mill and the Kings Tropical Inn and Fatty Arbuckle's Plantation had all gone the same way as poor Fatty himself, and the hot places to be seen were along West Sunset. Or so he'd heard. Instead, he passed blimp fields and golf practice ranges and all the many building sites which endlessly swallowed up this city's past and turned it into the all-consuming present. Then he hooked east toward the fringes of the Baldwin Hills, where a bent sign which no one had thought worth taking down or stealing still pointed in the direction of the old MGM Studios.

He parked the Delahaye off along a sidestreet of boarded-up shops which were seemingly awaiting redevelopment, like this whole area. The only billboard now beside the MGM lot was a realtor's sign, and the long external expanse of once gleaming white wall was a territory across which the city's many billposters, graffiti scrawlers and outdoor urinators had marked their identities.

That Grecian-pillared entrance remained, although the barrier had long gone, and rusted girders poked through where the plaster had fallen away. He looked around the familiar and yet desolate landscape beyond, trying to think what Barbara would have done. Most likely, she'd have phoned that number on the receipt for RTS Taxis from the library payphone, spoken to the guy in the office, then called for one of their cabs to take her here to ask the divers about what they remembered about their fares for last Wednesday. But her presence seemed as distant as that guy called Walter or Willy who'd once saluted him here. Taking the gun from his pocket, thumbing the safety off, he walked through the stretching shadows toward the giant rows of soundstages.

The gutters were falling. The concrete was weed-grown. Peering through gaps in boarded-up entrances, it was easy to imagine the residues of old get-rich-quick schemes, miracle cosmetics and pyramid-sale encyclopedias inside. Some of the buildings, victims of age and earthquake, had slumped into piles of rubble, asbestos and iron. A few bore business signs. *Fine Antiques.* Some business called *Adbel Acoustics.* Piles of teachests and rusted-out trucks.

Soundstage 1A was the biggest of them all, and looked to be more intact than most of the others, although its vast main doors were closed. The car parked out front—a black Mercury sedan—looked bizarrely out of place in this wasteland. It had a yellow *For Hire* light on its roof, and badged signs with a logo for RTS Taxis on its front doors. He gripped the Colt in both hands now with his finger hooked around the trigger. His heart was hammering.

He hunch-ran to the shadowed alley beside the soundstage in search of a side entrance. Which talkie had he shot here? Was it *A Free Soul* or *The Secret Six*? Which laughing starlet had he drawn into this very alley after the post-shoot party? He found a rusty sidedoor. There was no sign of a lock or bolt. It swung creakingly open when he gave it a shove.

Near darkness. If a setup called RTS Taxis really worked out of here, they did a good job of not showing it. He stood and waited. All he could hear was the thump of his heart. All he could see, as his swimming gaze slowly adjusted, was a stretch of deep woodland. Giant oaks canted their huge limbs. Some of them lay sideways. Others were fallen and torn. They gave off that once-familiar smell of dust and paint and canvas. He looked up and saw the dim gleam of chains, pulleys and lighting rigs overhead.

He moved on through changing landscapes. A stone dragon reared from Chinese hills. He passed Venetian gondolas, ornate gardens, primeval swamps. There were buildings within buildings. Signs for Makeup and Accounts. Long lines of beautiful frocks collapsed like cobwebs to the brush of his hands. The racks of uniforms were somewhat tougher, and gave off a smell of unlaundered sweat which he remembered from his own spear-carrier days. At their far end there was a mirror. Stacked against it were what he took for a moment to be shields. In fact, they were shields, but not of the kind which any cinematic soldier would carry into battle. Two bore the coat of arms of the Los Angeles Department of Water and Power. Others were for a company called Orkin Pest Control. There were shields for the US Postal Service, shields for a variety of County Police Departments, shields for the Bell Telephone Company and shields for Gladmont Securities. All matched in size, and had the same small screwholes which would allow them to be fixed and removed from the sides of a car. Down beside them was what looked to be the blue dome of a police light. There was also an open toolbox with a screwdriver and a good quality hand drill. He was bending to look at it when he heard a faint *phut* and the back of his neck suddenly stung. Reaching around, his fingers encountered something stiff and glassy. He was trying to pull the thing out as his sense of where and who he was slid rapidly away.

FIFTY FOUR

He was sitting at the edge of some kind of stage-set surrounded by constellations of lighting rigs and masses of film and sound and feelie equipment. High up ahead of him was a dusty backdrop of the view across what he took to be the city of LA. But the Klieg lights were strong and the individual features and buildings—the teeming streets, City Hall, Griffith Park, the Hollywoodland sign—were hard to make out in the glare from the flaking, fading paint.

He grunted, strained. The chair he was in sagged and creaked but wouldn't let him out. Yet the feel and shape of it was oddly familiar. He realized that he was in a fold-out directors' chair of the sort you found in their hundreds at any studio, and that he was tied to it by neatly knotted lanyards of rope at his ankles and wrists.

"Well bloody done, Clark."

His neck ached, but with an effort he managed to turn around to his left, and saw that Barbara was tied and seated a few yards off in pretty much the same way.

"Haven't you heard you're supposed to *rescue* me from this kind of situation, not get stuck in it yourself?" She hissed.

"That only happens in the feelies."

"What does it look like we're *in*?" She nodded forward. The front of the stage-set was crowded with looping wires and banks of equipment. He recognized microphones, the bulbous glass eyes of iconoscope lenses, and many wire recorders, and what he took to be the plates of Bechmeir field generators. *This whole set-up must be costing someone a fortune*, the ridiculous thought passed through his brain... Then, peering as one might through the boughs of a strange forest, he saw that another figure was tied and seated ahead of them amid all this equipment. The beard, the face, were unmistakable even without the glasses, but Daniel Lamotte's mouth was loose, and his eyes were closed, and, apart from something around his waist which looked to be an adult diaper, he was naked. Clark could tell from the quiver of his ribcage that the guy was alive, but he was either unconscious or deeply asleep.

He twisted toward Barbara again.

"What happened? How did you—"

A dart of her eyes silenced him. A figure had appeared from behind the backdrop and was moving through this electronic forest. There was a soft, atonal whistling as they quietly checked the tightness of ropes and the fit of connections in much the way that a regular gaffer or stagehand would. But the scene was so bright and confusing that it was hard to make them out as much more than a shadow. The buzzings and whinings and an accompanying discomforting feeling, which had always been there but which he'd somehow assumed were coming from inside him, increased. Then, when the shadow had finished whatever it was doing, it stepped closer to them, and its identity became plain.

If anything, Doctor Penny Losovic's eyes seemed kinder than Clark had seen in that photograph, and her jaw less square. There was a sorrowful curiosity—a sort of bland compassion—about her features as she studied them. It was exactly the kind of expression, he decided, that you'd hope to find on the face of a good doctor. She was dressed in an open-neck blue shirt with an RTS Taxis logo stitched across the breast pocket, a pair of light gray pressed trousers, and had on well-polished man's brogues. Her shortish light brown hair was tied back to a stub pony tail which would fit easily under a uniform cap. She was broad-shouldered for a woman, and he wondered if she wasn't wearing one of those chest flatteners which had been popular back in the twenties.

"I'm sorry you're here," she said. Her voice was lighter than the one she'd assumed when she'd first confronted him disguised as a security guard, although it had the same accent and timbre.

"If you're sorry . . . " He coughed to clear his throat. "If you were sorry, you'd . . . " Glancing again toward Barbara, he saw that she was gazing at Penny Losovic with an expression of undisguised loathing. It was clear she'd already tried the conversation he was now attempting about their being released, about no harm being done, about there being no need to involve the police... That, or simply pleading for mercy—he suspected she'd tried doing that as well... But at least Barbara showed no obvious sign of injury. At least, unlike Daniel Lamotte, they were both still conscious and fully clothed. But he couldn't help wondering how much longer any of these states would last. *We're going to die in here...* The thought passed through him like a cold wind, and he could see from a change in the glint of Penny Losovic's calm gaze that she saw it as well.

"You obviously know who I am," she said mildly. "I presume you finally got around to breaking into my house—is that what has finally brought you here? I suppose illegal entry is part of your stock in trade?"

Clark thought of saying nothing, but he guessed that it might help if they could keep this woman talking. He'd heard, at least, that that was what heroes did in the feelies, although his belly throbbed and his neck ached and he didn't feel particularly heroic. "So—are you going to tell us what Thrasis really means?"

"I suppose I could..." She tilted her head as if considering the idea. "Explanations are always helpful, even when they're not entirely necessary. Of course, everything that I've done *has* been governed by necessity, although I'll admit that necessity has taken me along some unfamiliar roads..."

As Penny Losovic talked on in this softly musing way, she continued to move around the stage-set, checking and straightening things. She even had a rag in her pocket which she used to wipe off coatings of dust. Bizarrely her whole manner was oddly familiar to Clark; he'd seen it from dozens of clients. Normally, it was about some stupid detail of their own or their partner's infidelity. Like—*I suppose you'd expect him to be naked, but why on earth was he wearing those dreadful socks?* Or—*I was finishing with her anyway, so why did my wife have to choose that of all evenings to turn up at work?* They'd ring a year later to put you back on the case, and when they talked it was like simply giving voice to a conversation which they never ceased to have in their heads. For whatever else she might or might not be and despite the things she was saying, the way Penny Losovic spoke now was much the same.

"I suppose you already know I was an intern at the Met . . . ? Although I'd already published original research by then on the psychology of pain, and I hoped that I was destined for better things. So I was interested when I received an approach about a well-paid research post in some unspecified new field.

"I took a train back east for the interview. It was in one of those giant brownstone castles overlooking Central Park which have now all been turned into hotels and apartments. The men who saw me didn't introduce themselves, and they were mostly age-spotted and tremulous, but I understood that they were the colossi who held up the pillars of Wall Street. And this—have I mentioned it?—was in the summer of 1929.

"The project they wanted me to work on was to be entirely secret—as far as I was concerned, that was never in question. They'd identified an old mining town back west in California as the site and building was already underway. As to exactly what this project would achieve, the brief was wide, but the basic premise was to prove or disprove the mind's so-called psychic abilities, and, if they existed, to see if they had any commercial application. You haven't been out to Thrasis, have you—either of you? Not that there's much left to see. The site was bulldozed when we finished, and the desert winds have probably done the rest . . . "

Penny Losovic was now working a winch, and its pulleys were bringing some object from up among the lighting gantries to hover above the soundstage. It swayed slightly, and creaked. It was a strange-looking thing. For a disconcerting moment Clark mistook it for a giant birdcage. But then he saw that the bars and the mesh had yet more wires looping into them, and he realized that the winged shape which flickered within was in fact the charged plasm of a Bechmeir field.

"Thrasis was never a large project as far as numbers were concerned," she continued, wiping her palms and securing the rope. "Most staff and subjects were either recruited from the Met, of through a certain theatrical agent. As for the rest, an influential group was established in California—I suppose you might call it a steering committee. They supervised the money side of things. I won't bore you with their names, but I suppose you've already worked out quite a few."

The thing in the feelie cage was stretching, humming. Clark swallowed back saliva and a sense that he might soon vomit. "You mean guys like Herbert Kisberg, Howard Hughes?"

"No—not Hughes. He was just a stepping stone who was used when the time came for the research to be marketed, someone who could be persuaded to produce some plausible real world backing. But Herbert, yes. I might say he was once a fellow visionary. He'd been in the trenches and seen too much needless slaughter, much as Lars Bechmeir was supposed to have done. He really did once share the dream that the world might be made a better place if people could genuinely share their feelings. This was vitally important work. It was understood from the start that all the usual restraints which hobble most medical and scientific research would have to be set aside. No one had ever trodden as far as we did to discover what the human mind is capable of. Except, perhaps, the servants of some Chinese Emperors and certain medieval kings..."

"So you tortured people to see if you could measure their pain?"

"You put it very bluntly. You have to understand that the signals at first were the faintest flicker of the dials—they were extraordinarily difficult to detect. But we succeeded, as is evident. By early 1931, little more than a year after the Thrasis project had started, we had prototypes of machines which could record and transmit what we then simply called a thought field. And the rest, I suppose, is what you might call history..." She paused to thread a wire out from its reel and across the head of a feelie recorder. "... Or history remade. If I'm honest, the over-emphasis on entertainment has been a disappointment to me. But then I've never sought the limelight. All of us involved—those who survived anyway—have been considerably rewarded and have no cause to complain.

"I took on the work of overseeing the distribution of the immense wealth which has been gathered by the Bechmeir Trust. The job is almost ideal. But there was always another side to what I had to do which was equally necessary. For all the reasons which I believe you now understand, the truth about Thrasis had to be kept from the public. At first, that simply involved monitoring gossip and the newspapers, and making sure that those who knew about Thrasis remembered that this was knowledge they could never disclose. But it was surprising how quickly people weakened. So threats sometimes necessary..." She paused again, clicking and re-clicking a switch until something engaged. All of the time now as she worked, there was a heightening sense of things increasing. "...and it's obvious that, once you make a threat, you have to be prepared to carry it out.

"At first, I tried using grubby little men much like yourself, Clark, when it became necessary to remove some weakening link, but I always found them unsatisfactory. Sadly, that old phrase about if a job needs doing it's best done by yourself is often true. Of course, few people knew that it was me who performed these necessary activities. A sense of fear and uncertainty was obviously an important element. Even Herbert and his business friends, the men in Wall Street or their successors who set this project going—they've long ceased to be interested. Nor have I ever received much thanks for what I do. All people care about, I sometimes think, is living their lives unhindered."

"Whilst you've been dressing up in men's uniforms and pretending to be the Power and Water guy?"

"As an ex-actor, I thought you'd recognize the challenge..." She altered her stance. "*Some fine morning isn't it, Mr Gable?*" Her voice had slipped down an octave and the effect of her becoming the Gladmont Securities guard was eerie. "But I've also taken some intellectual pleasure from doing this kind of work. Breaking in, following people, tracking down rumors, issuing threats—"

"And killing people?"

"The so-called Bechmeir field has been of huge economic, scientific and artistic benefit to America, and there are times when one cannot be squeamish. So, yes, I've killed people."

"Like April Lamotte?"

"April and I had known each other since before Thrasis. But, like everyone else who was involved, she knew that bad things happened to those who tried to disclose the truth, although she may have imagined that that early recording she stole when the project ended and that Dan found was providing some protection. Of course, there was no harm at all in her husband writing a feelie script about the supposed life of Lars Bechmeir. In fact, there was much to be gained. But when Dan started to have other ideas... Well, she called me as one of the few people she could genuinely confide in to explain her worries. She even described her plans for faking their deaths and making an escape..."

Penny Losovic had moved on from threading feelie wires to winding reels through projector gates. Now, as she pulled down a main power lever, several began to clatter at once. They were angled up toward the feelie cage and their beams fingered through its bars in changing shadows, although it was hard to tell how much of what Clark now saw was projected, and how much was already there. Legs and arms wavered in a Dervish dance. Bodies flickered like candleflames.

"I suppose we always sensed there was some kind of presence around Thrasis..." She was having to talk more loudly now. "...although we all might have expressed it in different ways. A ghost? A spirit? I don't know. For it often seemed that we were dealing in ghosts and spirits anyway. Then, when the world moved on and the project was disbanded, many of us felt that that presence remained. I think it may have been what sent so many to one or another kind of madness. But I think it's beautiful. Don't you agree?"

She was standing back now, admiring the thing which floated and twisted above them in the cage. It was brightening, and gave off a roaring sense of power. This was worse than any feelie Clark had even encountered but at the same time it was impossible not to look, and he was sure that he could see the most extraordinary things. Not vague shapes now, not the suggestion of auras, but actual limbs, real faces—as if something teeming and alive was trying to break out. But the one thing which endured as these figures spasmed was a sense of injury and pain. Many of these untwisting limbs were broken. Others were torn and bloodied. Bones were ruptured. Skin boiled and bled and suppurated. Skulls were laid bare. And the mouths, the eyes, the faces, were all differently distorted, but all equally agonized, as loudspeakers crackled an accompanying feedback howl of screams. This, Clark finally realized, was what Thrasis was. Not some empty place in the desert, but an existence, a thing.

"Resolving April's plans was never any particular challenge. The poor woman even stopped her car when she saw me standing by that overlook on the way up to her lodge because she imagined I was trying to warn her of something ahead. But Dan—he was of interest. I'm sure the process was largely subconscious, but I believe that the Thrasis presence was what led him to write about Lars Bechmeir in the first place, and then to find April's hidden feelie reel. I think he was even clumsily attempting to recreate what he was experiencing when he commissioned that peculiar wraith...

"I suppose one great discovery is more than any one person can expect to encounter in a lifetime. But this is something else again. I believe it has a kind of intelligence, a sort of consciousness. Yet clearly, for all that there are human elements in it, it is not human. Perhaps people in older times would have called it an angel. I really don't know. It's certainly drawn to Dan for some reason I don't pretend to understand, and most strongly when he is in a hallucinatory state. But, as you can see, I can only make the presence appear by using all this energy. Effectively, it's a whole series of feedback loops. And look what happens when I reduce the power..."

She crossed the stage-set, flicked a few switches. Like a guttering candle, the presence in the cage immediately dimmed. "You see—in these controlled conditions, it isn't self-sustaining." She shrugged, shook her head. "And that, at least for now, is about as far as I can currently get." She then walked slowly and carefully around the tripods and wires to the very far stage of the set. There was a small steel table there which Clark hadn't previously noticed. On it were a serious of bottles and small glass objects. She raised one bottle up, tapped it, and proceeded to fill first one and then a second syringe. Once again, a soft whistle crept from her lips.

"I've seen it," Clark said.

"Seen what?" She was still mostly absorbed in what she was doing.

"That presence—that bloody thing."

"You *have*..." She turned slowly, laid down the syringe, and walked over to him. Her manner, as she leaned forward to study him, hands on knees and a few strands of hair fallen loose across her clear brow, was still somehow curious and compassionate rather than threatening. "I do believe you have." She straightened. Considered. Then, in a characteristically neat gesture, she took out the tortoiseshell glasses which she herself must have placed in Clark's top pocket and hooked them over his ears and down across his nose. "I suppose it does make a kind of sense." Once more, head slightly cocked, she examined him. "After all, you have been pretending to be Dan. In which case..." She turned away to consider the stage-set, and raised her hand for a moment and twirled her fingers as if the thought which she was chasing might be grabbed from the passing air. "...perhaps we *could* try something before I'm finished with you. After all, faint heart never won fair maiden, did it?"

Clark wasn't sure what exactly he'd won for them here as Penny Losovic disconnected and rearranged equipment until the blind white eye of one of the several iconoscopes was turned and staring back at him. Except perhaps an hour's extra torment. He heard Barbara mutter, *This is fucking preposterous*, which, he thought with an odd, sad, twinge was as bad as he'd heard her swear. She had a sweet tongue on her, too. Was a nice piece of ass, as well. God alone knew why he hadn't done the obvious thing last night when he had her leaned up beside her door... Then, as Penny Losovic began to remake connections and pull switches, even the kind of stupid, jagged thoughts and regrets which any man might allow himself in his last few minutes on earth were blown away.

The dreadful sense of the Bechmeir field was overwhelming, yet he was being sucked in and back through what seemed to be tiers of his own memories. All those stupid arguments and the endless electrical breakdowns which had ruined his acting career, and then that first session with bucktooth Hiram and his friends in the depths of MGM. But from there he was back on board that gambling boat, and down in the scuppers with Hilly Feinstein. And the cards, the symbols, were flickering, and he was The Star and Peg was The Falling Tower, and then he was sitting up with Peg beside that Goddamn sign again, yet the city which was spread below them was peeling as if it was composed of nothing but cheap canvas and paint.

Then, back in something which was vaguely closer to the real world, he was looking up at the same view, before which hung the feelie cage, and the thing within was flowing, enormous. If such creatures had ever existed, it really could have been an angel. And still all the many machines were spinning, and the wraith seemed to be drawing in all the dust and the light—all the humming noise—which filled this stage-set. He remembered the thing he had glimpsed on the pier back at Venice, and again at the overlook, and in the restroom at City Hall, and under the tree shadows of Pershing Square—and how it had somehow always composed itself out of whatever lay around it. It seemed to be doing the same here. But the sense of presence and purpose was far stronger. The cage swayed. Then one of the wires which was attached to it flew off in dark zigzags, spewing sparks. It hit a book flat at the far end of the stage as it landed, which crashed over. Then another wire flew loose, and this time the flying sparks caught on a trailing rope, which had grown as dry as tinder in this hot and empty soundstage and instantly caught light.

We're all going to burn to death, Clark thought. But Penny Losovic, who surely could have pulled the plugs and cut down that rope and stamped the flames out before they took hold, was still just standing there. And her mouth was still moving in a continuation of that same quiet conversation in which she had long been engaged, although by now as other wires thrashed and hissed the noise was so great that it was hard to hear what she was saying. But she seemed happy. She seemed unconcerned. Her words, if anything, were things like *marvelous* and *wonderful* and *achievement* . . .

Another bookflat crashed over and flakes of paint, whole strips of rotting canvas, joined with the smoke and dust which were pouring toward the cage. Ribbon-like strips of torn set were flapped across the bars before they were sucked in like litter down a stormdrain. In another moment, the entire backdrop of Los Angeles was in flame. The next thing to catch were the ropes which were holding the cage. The thing yawed, then collapsed in a tornado of light and dust and fragmenting set props.

The entity stretched its arms then hollered a feedback roar. It was formed by now mostly of smoke and flame, but Clark could see the smog of this city inside, and its teeming lights and shadows as well. Loops of celluloid and wire writhed out as the projectors and recorders unspun. Just as with everything else, the entity sucked them in. It was far bigger than anything human now. Its head seemed to reach as high as the soundstage roof. There was an enormous shudder, and chunks of lighting rig rained down around him. He was knocked sideways, and as he went sprawling he felt something break in the chair to which he was bound. He kicked and pulled until it fell apart, then stumbled up, pulling trailing scraps of rope and canvas from his wrists.

He looked around. Barbara was still tied to her chair, but rocking back and forth as the flames licked closer. He tried to step toward her, and immediately fell across the rope which still bound his ankles.

"Jesus, Clark! Can't you just get me out of this..."

But he was. Or at least he was trying. Although his fingers were numb and he could scarcely breathe. Then the ropes gave and he was helping Barbara, fighting with her really, to get the fucking chair from off her arms and legs. Something huge—a crane perhaps—rushed by them in a gale of sparks. Although it was hard to imagine that the air could get any hotter, it was doing so by the moment. Retching and coughing, Barbara stumbled to her feet.

"This way!" he shouted, although he'd lost any sense of which way was out.

Barbara spat, shook her head, mouthed the word *Dan*.

They ploughed through a maze of thrashing wires and burning equipment. The air shimmered. Everything was dissolving into flame. But Daniel Lamotte was still seated on the stage-set, and still unconscious. With no time left to do much else, they hauled him across the floor, still attached to his director's chair. But wait, wait... There was another figure behind them. Penny Losovic's arms were outstretched, and somehow they could still hear her quiet exclamations as she walked, arms outstretched as if in welcome, toward a thing of living flame. Then, in a final cataclysmic shudder, some central strut of the building gave and they staggered away.

All the fake forests, plaster mountains and tinfoil lakes were ablaze as they dragged Dan off. They reached a wall and were beating their way along it—it was impossible to see through the smoke—when the whole soundstage fell up and away, and they were blasted out.

Later, Clark was to wonder about that moment; why, as the fire did what all fires did and sucked in more air, they should be flung away. But

297

at the time, as he and Barbara picked themselves up on the concrete and looked back to see the galvanized flanks of Soundstage 1A tumbling into the sky, all he could think of was taking another breath and crawling further from the flames.

For all the heat at their backs, the night felt blessedly cool as he and Barbara loosened Daniel's Lamotte's arms and legs. The man gave a drooling groan. His eyes flickered. Momentary puzzlement crossed his face. Bells and sirens were already growing loud. The first firetruck swung into view as they dragged him toward a grassy bank. A fleet of white ambulances and black police cars followed as they laid him down.

"Hey!" Barbara shouted as uniformed figures emerged. "We got someone injured over here!"

"We can't—"

"—what we *can't* do, Clark, is leave him here."

Clark and Barbara were already backing into the shadows as the ambulancemen turned their way. Soundstage 1A was beyond rescue—a roaring, groaning maelstrom—and the firemen were keeping well back from the flames. Ducking around to what had been the front of the building, Clark saw Penny Losovic's black Mercury sedan. Barbara was ahead of him and had already run to swing open its door and slide into the driver's seat before he could catch up.

"Can you drive?" he shouted.

"What the hell do you think I'm doing!"

Back through the rear window, the scene was amazing. Light from the soundstage pulsed against the sky. As Barbara swung the Mercury around a side alley toward the exit, Clark glimpsed the figure of a plump cop stood silhouetted against the flames. His cap was off, and he was staring their way.

"Where did you leave the Delahaye?"

They shot out into Overland Avenue past the first rush of arriving rubberneckers and journalists.

"East. Not that turn . . . The next . . ."

The car slewed. "There's still time, Clark. If I can get Dale started with the printing, and you can reach the Biltmore, there's no reason why you can't—"

"—This isn't some hold-the-front-page scoop, Barbara. This is—"

"Jesus, Clark! You've *got* to go to the Biltmore. You can't, simply *can't* just let this—"

"No, no. I'll do whatever I can. And you should try to get that paper of yours out—who knows, there might even finally get to be some genuine truth in LA. What I mean, Barbara, is I can't see how this can end for us in a good way."

FIFTY FIVE

The Delahaye's gears sounded like broken china, and this city had a steely, glossy look tonight—a mix of sea fog, smog and smoke from the fire at Soundstage 1A. It snagged in the palms and hazed the intersections and swirled around the streetlights, turning everyone and everything—the zigzag modern buildings, the women walking their diamond necklaced pooches, the shoeless bums trying to sell screenplays—into mist, plasm, dream.

The area around the Biltmore was almost as bright as the MGM lot had been. So many searchlights pillared the sky that it looked like one of those newsreels of London. All that was missing were the bombs and screaming planes. He parked at back of South Broadway and walked, weary and wary, toward the waiting bonfire of fame.

It was like the biggest kind of premier, with the three-tiered bleachers set up on either side of Olive and West 5th swept by sea-waves of excited commotion as each new limousine rolled in. All of Senserama's stars were there, and so were most of this city's other players. Harmensworth Fowley, with his trademark cravat and pipe. Mark Crave and Peyton Jones, still arm in arm despite the rumors about that dead Puerto Rican boy in their pool. Then came Monumenta Loolie, who made a far better performance out of squeezing herself out of the back of a Cadillac than any of her wooden efforts in the feelies. But tonight Herbert Kisberg was the biggest star. As he stepped from his limousine and pulled his cuffs and glanced around him with that *who me?* little boy smile he had, he seemed too real to be real, the way people did when they were on the verge of being great. No need for a Bechmeir field tonight—the crowd was already a rebounding collision of sweat and breath and need.

Beneath the reek of underarms and cheap cigarettes and even cheaper perfume, you could smell the natural plasm of all those thought waves like churned seawrack on a beach.

Clark remembered how there was a knack to facing the glare. The flick of the hair, the flash of a smile, the eternal challenge of dealing with the same shouted question like it was something new. Anacondas of electricity powered a forest of lights, camera lenses and microphones. KFI were there, and KJH, as well as the Pathe and Movietone cameras, and NBC had gone one better and would be broadcasting the entirety of their flagship show *Star Talk* across the entire country tonight on a live feed.

Despite how he must look, Clark found that Daniel Lamotte's name got him a tick on a clipboard and entry past the security goons. With his blackened clothes and face, they probably imagined that he was already in character for one of those nigger acts from which white performers made so much money. Not that he was allowed to walk up the red carpet itself, but, as the final rope was lifted and he was let into the Biltmore's lobby through a plateglass sidedoor, he got an echo of what the old days had been like.

But this was bigger. This wasn't just the movies or even the feelies, this was *politics* as well—assuming there was still any difference left. People talked with loud, breathless voices as they headed toward the Biltmore's famous Bowl, pausing only briefly to take a flute of Champagne and glance smilingly at the seating plan as if it didn't matter at all.

"Dan, Daniel..."

He was slow to react to Timmy Townsend's voice.

"Dan, where have you been? Well, thank God you're here—but what the *fuck* are you wearing? What happened...?"

"My car broke down."

"Take my advice, ol' Danny-o, and never have shit to do with anything that's mechanical and French. Your average Pierre might know about putting something tasty on a plate, but anything else...?" Beaming as ever, his eyes and cheeks aglow, the tip of his nose a drippy red, Timmy Townsend shook his head. "Just not in their blood. Like asking a coon to play chess. At least, that is, until the Germans get them good and sorted. *Then* things'll be different. Then, the frogs'll be like a whore who'll fuck you all night and clean the sheets up in the morning. Neat *and* funky at the same time if you get my meaning. Speaking of which, I think we need to get you sorted..."

The Biltmore accommodated for most things. In a long basement room, there were enough evening dresses, suits, shirts, ties and every other kind of apparel to kit out a largish department store. Timmy Townsend stayed around as Clark stripped and wiped himself down with steamed towels and then began to get changed. He was still talking about all the marvels the European nations would accomplish once the Germans had knocked the bastards into proper shape. Just like Barbara Eshel, although for different reasons, the sight of Clark's bare ass didn't even cause him to blink. It was strange to think how accustomed powerful men were to seeing each other naked: at the Turkish bath, in the shower after playing polo, or sharing a few broads for an afternoon in a hotel suite. It was like they always had an extra layer of gloss which nakedness alone couldn't remove.

"I sometimes wonder why Herbert even bothers with America," he was saying as he offered Clark a red-lined silk dinner jacket, "when California's more than powerful enough to be a country on its own. I mean, who needs fucking Iowa, or hillbilly dumps like Arkansas? We could fucking *invade* Mexico any time we wanted, just on our own..."

Clark finished dressing in his hundred dollar penguin suit, put back on his Daniel Lamotte glasses for what he was sure would be the last ever time, then followed Timmy into the Biltmore's main halls. He remembered that story in the Bible Jenny had once told him as they walked through long suites of differently-themed rooms. The one about the guy—Samson, wasn't it?—who'd had his hair cut and had been tied up to some pillars in a gilded palace much like this one, and had dragged the whole fucking thing down, low divans, leather Chesterfields and all.

"The way it's going to work is this, Dan baby. There's the first half of the show which is just good old entertainment, then comes the break, when you'll get to be live-interviewed by Wallis Beekins, and then after the re-start Herbert comes up on stage, and he'll get the spotlight to point at wherever it is that Lars Bechmeir's sitting. The crowd'll go apeshit, of course, and after that he'll announce—"

"What are you expecting me to say?"

"*Expecting?*" Timmy Townsend looked puzzled. "You just say whatever you want to say, Dan. About *Wake Up and Dream*. Why you wanted to write it, and what a journey of fucking discovery the whole thing's been. All that usual crap. You're okay with that, aren't you?"

"I guess."

"Hey." Timmy clapped an arm around Clark's shoulder. "There's no need to *worry*. Whatever you say, the listeners'll gobble it up. I mean, what the hell do they know that the likes of us don't know already?"

They'd reached the edge of the Biltmore Bowl's murmuring sea of glass, table linen and faces, and Timmy Townsend's attention was starting to drift. A quick check like everyone else at the seating plan, and they were working their way toward their separate tables just as the Fred Waring Orchestra struck up with *Devil Got My Woman* and the lights began to dim.

Things settled. Food was served. Clark noticed that his hands were shaking as he raised his first forkful of salmon mousse. Rope bruises were starting to show on his wrists. He shot his cuffs to cover them and smiled at the other people on his table. He wasn't with the big names here, and his announcement that he was merely a screenwriter had got disappointed looks. Here were guys who manufactured grape candy, room deodorizers and rods for shower curtains, who'd all come here tonight with their second wives to soak up a bit of vicarious glamour. After all the money they'd donated to the Liberty League, they'd obviously been hoping for someone who was proper Hollywood—a star, or at the very least a character player, instead of some friggin' guy who *wrote* the stuff—to share their table. Still, they brightened up once the entertainment started, and were happy to chat between turns about how the average working man wasn't worth jackshit, how it had now been scientifically proven that niggers didn't have proper souls (*I've seen the photos—believe, me your average Jimmy Crack Corn's got less aura than a bar of soap*), and how they were thinking of setting up a new factory in TJ because costs over the border were so much cheaper.

More of the Fred Waring Orchestra, then that woman who was famous for being able to sing and swim at the same time, and some beloved old comedian Clark had been certain was dead, and whole squadrons of dancers in not much more than sequins and smiles. Nothing that spectacular, really, although he knew it was an old enough trick. *If you want to make an impact in the second act, bore your audience 'til their asses ache in the first*... And now the lights were coming up, and the Biltmore Bowl was erupting into yet more applause, and an averagely drop-dead beautiful blonde in a lowcut black evening dress was tapping his shoulder and saying something about *Star Talk* in a fragrant murmur, and asking him if he'd mind coming this way...?

FIFTY SIX

So much muscle around. Guys so big inside their padded jackets that they looked like upmarket Michelin Men. Private security types with that gaze which went right through you even when they weren't wearing sunglasses. More obvious sorts in buzzcuts and khaki Liberty League uniforms. Career cops who'd never seen a sidewalk. Less obvious varieties he probably wasn't even spotting.

This, he thought, as he followed the hipswaying, averagely drop-dead beautiful woman along the fluorescent-lit corridor, is what the future is going to be like. Hotels like the Biltmore will spread, and they and all the shopping malls will link up, and these new Americans will spend their whole lives indoors and underground, lulled by hidden music and Bechmeir fields. It'll be like the Metropolitan Hospital already is, but with wall to wall carpets, endless opportunities for shopping and plastic palms. No enforced lobotomies, either; they wouldn't be necessary.

NBC were broadcasting from a suite of several rooms with their dividers concertinaed back. There were more beautiful women and guys, and more muscle, and geekier types fiddling with lots of expensive electrical equipment. All in all, the scene wasn't untypical of what Clark had gotten used to seeing lately. A set of big PA speakers were relaying the latest slew of adverts for Perquat Sheets. In the furthest of the rooms, which still had dividers drawn across to keep it separate from the rest, Wallis Beekins was spitting out orders and nursing a large whisky. He paid Clark no attention when he first came in. Beekins was wearing a tux like everyone else, although it barely covered the belly-bulge of a foodstained plaid waistcoat. He had on disastrous twotone wingtips as well, but Beekins was one of those rare creatures in showbiz whose looks didn't matter. It was that voice, which it was so odd to hear coming in real life from this plump little man with his greasy coxcomb of hair and his agitated pacing. Especially as he was swearing like a longshoreman.

Standing there, moments away from his chance to change history, Clark felt as focused as he had back in the old days just before he stepped onstage. There would be no need for the messy scene he'd imagined. He wouldn't have to blurt things out. He'd be clear. He'd be calm. He'd be fucking collected. Another beautiful woman—this one a brunette—was quietly explaining to him the questions that he would be asked, but Clark felt as if he knew them all, and his answers, already. Of course, and just like this broad was telling him over a Johnnie the Bellhop jingle for Philip Morris cigarettes, he'd be asked why he'd decided now was a good time to write a Lars Bechmeir biopic, and about the guy's lowly beginnings, and how the whole world—and not just entertainment—had been changed by his so-called discovery, and maybe even he could say something about the recent tragic death of April, his own wife? Yeah, he could do all that. Just give straight answers to the actual questions. The only trick he'd need to pull was to stay in character for just a few minutes longer as Daniel Lamotte.

"Okay, Mr Lamotte?" The beautiful woman was smiling. "You're ready?"

Wallis Beekins had put aside his whisky glass and was shaking hands with him now, weighing him up in that way all broadcasters did for ticks, nerves, signs of impending trouble. "So you're Daniel Lamotte." The voice had slowed; it was honey over warm chocolate. "And hey, I reckon I'm probably Wallis Beekins. Must be, 'cos every times I try to catch the guy's show on the radio, I'm always busy."

Everybody laughed. The guy was a real professional. Then shouts and signals were exchanged, onlookers and hangers-on were shooed out, and the door to the broadcasting room was closed. Just Wallis Beekins now, and Clark, and a guy with headphones sat down before a monitoring desk. The rest of the space was taken up by sound-deadening screens and a table, in the middle of which was set the fluted metal fist of a Shure microphone.

"Okay, fella. Been a bit of a delay. The newscast is taking up more time that scheduled 'cos of a fire at the lot of one of the old movie companies. All sorts of stuff going on down there, apparently. Still, that's the way it is, and we'll go live in one minute. I'll start off with a few words, then ask you some nice and easy questions. Then we're done. Simple as that. No need to lean forward or raise your voice. Just talk like you and me were having a chat at some bar round the corner over a beer. And if you fancy banging this table to make a point, don't, 'cos it'll sound like LA's finally been hit by the big one. We okay for levels, Eddie?"

"If Mr Lamotte could just say something, we'll be fine."

"Happy to be here."

Eddie gave a thumbs up.

Wallis Beekins smiled. "You're a natural, Mr Lamotte. Done this sort of thing before?"

"Just a little."

"That's great." Like all good pros, Wallis Beekins seemed to be growing more relaxed and at home as the moment of performance approached. In Clark's experience, it was the rest of their lives that guys like this had problems with. "Count us in soon as you're ready, Eddie..."

Eddie nodded, and everything went very quiet. Clark resisted the urge to clear his throat. He studied instead the map-like lines of broken capillaries on Wallis Beekins' nose, and thought of all the millions of families clustered at home around their radiograms, and Glory listening in her cubby hole back in Venice, and cleaners pushing mops in empty offices, and truck drivers following the black highway, and kids hidden under blankets with their cat's whisker radios, and forgotten old ladies in sixth floor apartments who never heard another living voice.

Then Eddie was holding up the spread fingers of both hands, closing them down from ten into a fist, and Wallis Beekins worked his face and smoothed his jaw, and Eddie was down to three when his hand went to his headphones and he shook his head and made a cutting motion across his throat.

Wallis Beekins sighed. He looked like he wanted to throw the microphone across the room, but he was too much of pro. "We're not live *yet*? How long is this newscast going to run for?"

"It's not that." Eddie frowned. "It's—"

The door burst open. Two of the muscles in dinner suits who'd been standing outside squeezed themselves in. Another three followed.

"Well..." Beekins sighed mildly as the guys hooked their hands under Clark's arms and hoisted him. "...looks like there's been a change of plan... Better go along with them, fella..." He was already turning to ask Eddie how they going to fill in the gap in the schedule as Clark was hauled out.

The muscles had big, well-manicured hands and they smelled like clean lockerrooms. They were dragging Clark out from the NBC recording rooms, and not one of the many drop-dead beautiful women or the other muscles or the technicians seemed to notice.

"If you'll come this way, Mr Lamotte..." They were murmuring it like it was a mantra.

He tried kicking and pulling against them, but their hands and arms were like leather upholstery. "My name's *not* Lamotte. Look—if you'll just put me down. If you'll just..." An expertly placed fist knocked out the rest of what he was going to say, then a doorframe slammed against his back. It was clear they weren't about to just do anything.

"If you'll come this way, Mr Lamotte..."

In one direction down this corridor, the Fred Waring Orchestra was playing *Don't You Mess With My Mister* with Irene Bosener on vocals, but he was being dragged somewhere else. Double doors swung open, cracking hard into his face and slewing his glasses sideways. All he could see now were lights blurring along a ceiling, but then the muscles paused and one of them muttered something. Clark, as he was dumped down, glasses askew, then shoved aside and trod on like a sack of potatoes, got the impression that something was coming the other way.

Something was. His vision swam with the sight of two nurses, although they were showing less uniform than they were thigh and cleavage, and an old guy in a wheelchair they were pushing between them. It was as strange a passing as the Biltmore's corridors had probably witnessed all evening, although Clark could see that Lars Bechmeir had been nicely spruced up. He had on a crisp new penguin suit, polished shoes, a starched wing-collar shirt and sleekly knotted tie, but the neck and the hands which emerged looked even more withered and reptilian than they had yesterday. But the eyes were bright within those owlish glasses. Even as the two nurses kept their gaze and pert breasts pointing resolutely forward, Lars Bechmeir looked down at the guy who was slumped against the wall as he was wheeled past until his big glasses bumped one of the nurses' rumps and slid sideways off the ridge of his nose. The guy looked so different stripped of those lenses, and the odd brightness of his gaze seemed increased rather than diminished by their absence. He was still twisting his head around as the distance between them extended, and Clark was now looking back at him with something like the same intensity. Recognition passed between them.

Otto! It was Otto Frings from the paper thin roominghouse wall next to Peg's. Otto, with his banging broom. Otto, who Clark had found that time staring up at Peg's lit window. Otto, who Bogey had told him he last remembered seeing with his face covered in bandages. Otto, who was another of Hilly Feinstein's clients. Otto, who for all his classical training, hadn't had work in years. Only he had. He'd got the plumiest of all plum roles. He'd got to play Lars Bechmeir.

"It's me, Otto! It's Clark Gable—remember? Remember Hilly, remember Peg? Remember..." But what the hell was there to remember? They'd never been close. "Thrasis. Remember fucking Thrasis, Otto. And all the people who've died—"

The muscles must have thought they'd got him decently subdued, for they were surprisingly slow in reacting. But now they did. Now another well-placed fist knocked out what was left of his breath, but Otto was still staring back at Clark as he was dragged from view. Clark's last glimpse was of naked eyes wide in surprise and a weak mouth—for all the things which had changed about him, that hadn't—shaping the word *Thrasis.*

Clark was hauled on. Through another set of doors and across grubbier, shiner halls filled with the nearby sounds of kitchens, then out down a tumble of steps and into the night where stars reeled and the air stank of garbage. He waited for the next hit to come, but it didn't, even though at least two of the muscles were still holding him. Meanwhile, another was rooting around amid the garbage cans and dumpsters as if he'd lost something. He drew out a yard length of iron reinforcing bar, thwacked it against his palm, then smashed it hard enough to put a big dent in the side of a garbage can. Everything went quieter than in the NBC studio. No one even seemed to be breathing. This, Clark realized, wasn't some standard beating up. These guys were going to kill him. He supposed it had to end somehow, and somewhere. But he'd hoped for better than this.

Hefting the bar like Babe Ruth, the muscle took a few steps forward, settled his stance and began to swing.

"Hey, hey, fellas..." A voice came out of the darkness. It was followed by a plumply uniformed shape. "I know you got jobs to do, but I got things here need doing as well. Like making sure, fer instance, that no one gets murdered on my beat. 'Til I clock off, leastways..." Officer Doyle hooked his thumbs into his gunbelt. "You get my drift?"

Clark was dropped on concrete. The iron bar was tossed with a clang. The muscles were already moving away.

FIFTY SEVEN

"I guess I could arrest you—if you really want me to, I will, right?—and I guess I could have left you to those thugs. But I've been getting this feeling that something ain't right in the time since we took you to City Hall to identify the body of the woman you said was your wife. An' I'm getting that same feeling even more tonight."

"What do you want me to say?"

"Say?" Officer Doyle chuckled. He was helping Clark along a corridor back inside the Biltmore. "Not sure I want you to say anything. In fact, make that a definite, 'cos I've got a pretty strong feeling that whatever you tell me ain't going to be what I want to hear. Few things I could tell *you*, though—watch that blood from your nose, pal, you're dripping, an' I'm sorry they trod on your glasses. Like we've just had a guy taken to hospital from that fire who swears his name's Daniel Lamotte, and he has no idea about his wife dying. Doesn't look much like you, either, and when I turn on NBC, they say this Daniel Lamotte's about to be interviewed live over here at the Biltmore by Wallis Beekins. Oh, and did I mention what *else* we found at that old studio lot? But you were *there*, weren't you? I'm sure I saw you and what looked like a broad from that cockroach academy scuttling off in a stolen taxi."

"It wasn't stolen. It was—"

"Just shut the fuck up, will you? There are times as a cop when you really don't want to know. Like when you shine a flashlight on some whore in a car and find it's your precinct major with this pants around his ankles, or there's a really bad smell in a private dick's office that someone's only just gotten around to noticing. Life's full of stones best left unturned, and I reckon this is one of them. Watch those steps. Real shame about the front of that nice shirt. There's more steps now. Upsadaisy..." They were climbing the Biltmore's service stairs. "So here I am as sole potential arresting officer, and the thought of all that paperwork just makes my head ache. There are at least a couple of people dead and several others in a bad way, and here we all are, right in the middle of vote-for-me-I'm-famous, and those thugs out there were fixing to do you something nasty, and the police RT's going mad, and I can't believe this is all coincidence."

Clark was feeling steadier on his feet now. People were clustered ahead of them beyond a half-parted curtain. They glanced back at Clark and Officer Doyle, then quickly returned their gaze down from the balcony on which they were standing. They were all hotel staff, and none of them were white, and Clark guessed they should all have been working. From here, though, there was a fine view right down across the Biltmore Bowl.

"So..." Officer Doyle murmured as they shuffled to find a space. "Why don't we just settle back and see what happens next?"

FIFTY EIGHT

One of those nights. One of those *Were You There?* moments. The commotion caused by the arrival of a figure in a wheelchair went beyond applause. He looked so frail captured in that spotlight, yet so unmistakably *here*. The shock would have been less if Christ had arrived, or the Lindberg baby, or Father Christmas. Then everyone down in the Biltmore Bowl—apart, obviously, from Lars Bechmeir—stood up and put a hand across their hearts as the band played *God Bless America*. It was a spine-tingling moment, and most of the servants up on the balcony with Clark and Officer Doyle joined in as well, even though Irving Berlin was a Hebe and now lived in Canada. Images were thrown on a silver screen of golden America prairies, snow-white American mountains and white American families. As the audience subsided, a fresh spotlight chased teasingly over them to settle on Herbert Kisberg.

He was seated at one of the regular tables just like everyone else, but now he stood up, and once again the audience erupted at the sight of that blonde hair and Rushmore jaw. Herbert Kisberg waved, smiled. Herbert Kisberg touched his bow-tie and parting as if either might need straightening. He was pulling back his seat now, crossing the floor toward that other spotlit figure as the rest of the great space fell murmurosly dark. Then the spotlights merged, and there were happy gasps, for here they were, together—the genius who had discovered the Bechmeir field, and the kingly man who would soon be president. Kisberg was even standing, Clark noticed, in such a way that all the shots and the newsreels would clearly show the Liberty League flag which had been unfurled across the wall behind them. Something Penny Losovic had said about the futility of what he and Barbara had tried to do came back to him. What could it ever have amounted to? A few garbled words? Some smudged print on cheap newspaper? Kisberg seemed to be made of bronze or gold. He already looked like the statue which would surely be put up to him at the Washington Mall by a grateful nation twenty years on.

If Herbert Kisberg seemed a solid presence, Lars Bechmeir, slumped in that wheelchair with owlish glasses reapplied, looked so frail that you feared some final extra surge of light, noise or attention might blow him away. It looked as if it had already been too much for him, and he'd have to retire soon. But then something happened. Lars Bechmeir began to move. First, to raise his own trembling hand to touch the princely one Kisberg had laid upon his shoulder, and then to mutter something which caused Kisberg to furrow his brow. Then, both Lars Bechmeir's hands settled on the arms of his wheelchair and made a series of straining motions which all the onlookers eventually understood to mean that he was attempting to stand.

A rush of puzzlement. But no, Lars Bechmeir was already half out of his seat and in danger of falling forward until one of the nurses who'd been hovering in the background like big-titted angels stepped up. A puzzled tableau followed amid gasps and shouts of encouragement, until Herbert Kisberg really had no option but to grab Lars Bechmeir firmly across the shoulders and help him the rest of the way to his feet.

The famous pair stood there, teetering, and the fate of the evening seemed to teeter with them. Was this just some antique spasm, or did the old man actually know what he was doing? Then, as Lars Bechmeir shuffled sideways and around, and it became apparent that, yes, the guy could move to some degree, the purpose of his efforts became clear. He wanted to get onstage.

Applause clattered like rain through the long moment that Herbert Kisberg helped Lars Bechmeir walk. Each rise in the steps to the stage was a struggle, and Bechmeir seemed to falter more when he reached the apron in front of the Fred Waring Orchestra beneath a Liberty League emblem. But there was a sense of determination as well. The will of the audience, and of everyone listening to Wallis Beekins' soon-to-be-famous, breathless commentary across the nation, and even the pull of the twinned spotlights, seemed to draw the old man on. The journey toward the central microphone was a drama in itself, and those who watched it on the newsreels after would often comment that you still wondered if he was going to make it.

He did. Lars Bechmeir stood, still half-supported by Herbert Kisberg, and with a microphone stand before him. He gripped hold of it with one hand, then gave a series of odd, shivery gestures with his free arm. Unmistakably, he was pushing his helper away, and Herbert Kisberg stepped back and the spotlight which was on him blinked out, leaving Lars Bechmeir standing alone.

The old man fumbled his glasses from his ears with what looked like impatience, or even anger. They clattered and bounced when he cast them across the boards. There was something sharper, and somehow redefined, about the gaze which now swept the crowd.

"I'm not..." He began. The microphone wobbled. He cleared his throat and gripped it tighter. "I'm not standing here to say the things you expect to hear. Nor am I the man you imagine me to be..."

FIFTY NINE

April Lamotte's funeral took place a week later after the coroners had finished their second autopsy looking for signs of intravenously administered relaxant. Even though he wasn't expecting a welcome Clark felt he should attend. He arrived early, and parked his rattly old Ford at the furthest end of Forest Lawns' main car lot.

He lit a roll-up and took in the view, still relishing the sense of being within his own clothes, his own skin. With its trim pines, lozenge lakes and winding paths, this place was more like an upscale golf course than a cemetery. He wandered past the gift store and the Hall of Resurrection and the Wee Kirk o' the Heather—a faithful reproduction of a village church in Glencain, Scotland, apparently. A scattering of confetti on the steps indicated how the Forest Lawns experience could also include weddings, along with a whole variety of other personal and corporate occasions.

More intriguing still was Forest Lawns' latest feature, the Chapel of Eternity. Appropriately enough amid the graves of so many lost or forgotten greats, this strange mausoleum was designed to look like a state-of-the art feelie palace from the outside. All curves and swerves; the prow of the future pushing into the present. Inside the soundlessly revolving doors, the light was watery green. Beyond the postcard stands and receptionist's desk and a rack of telephones that gave you a commentary, the air hissed and churned before a set of six huge Egyptian Baroque chapels enclosing six equally enormous wraiths.

You didn't need to lift one of the telephones or read the pamphlets about payment plans on easy terms and home-visit pre-passing consultations to understand that this was the ultimate memorial for the modern deceased. A recording of your beloved's aura would be played monthly, or weekly, or even by the hour, depending upon the kind of personalized portfolio which had been purchased. The atmosphere—at least, until you stepped within the transmission range of one of the field generators, was midways between a Buddhist temple and an ultra-modern rail station. Every ten of so minutes, a large gong, presumably specially coated with antique verdigris, would solemnly clang, and the flip displays beneath a stained glass oriel would whisper up a changed set of names. This, in turn, would cause a quiet commotion amongst the dozens of other people—what *were* they? onlookers? mourners? celebrants?—with whom Clark was sharing this colossal space. They would then shuffle off to stand in smaller groups, or bow, or kneel, or even prostrate themselves, before their chosen altar.

After hanging back for a while, Clark finally wandered toward the chapel which was currently commemorating a Robin James Calhoon, whose aura no one else currently seemed to be interested in bathing in. There was a heady smell of bouquets, and the plinth which housed the electrics would have made a mausoleum in its own right. The swanneck which emerged from it in frolics of gilded cherubs rose to something approaching the height of a house, and the wraith which floated between the two charged plates dwarfed the muse he'd stood before that first morning he'd gone to Erewhon. Even if he hadn't been a giant of a man, Mr Calhoon made a giant of an aura. Ill-tempered, as well. Vague flares of angry red and impatient orange shot through the coronal sheath. Clark was far more intimately touched by the guy's presence than if they'd been sat on nearby barstools, and he had to smile to think of some grumpy businessman in a hot tweed jacket standing in front of an iconoscope with the same lets-get-this-done-and-move-on attitude he'd have displayed at family gatherings, or in the boardroom. Clark was standing, he knew, before the most awesome technological achievement of his time, but once more the whole business seemed tawdry.

They were still repeating the guy who everyone now knew wasn't really Lars Bechmeir's speech on the radio like it was one of those new doo-wop songs. Only went for six minutes, and that was if you counted the many pauses and stumbles, but that was just fine, because it fitted nicely in between breaks for commercials.

Supported on the stage at the Biltmore Bowl, less, it seemed, by his pipecleaner legs or the microphone stand as by the breathless attention of all who were listening, the frail old man had spoken mainly not about himself, but about his lost wife. How it had started as just another kind of role which they had taken on as strangers because they were desperately short of work and money. How they'd shed what little there was of their past, had even submitted to have their faces changed, and had gone on those publicity tours and stood before the press and lived the kind of life which was expected of them. And, in their secrecy of knowing, had grown an alliance which had became genuine love. And all of this as a sales gimmick to promote some clever device. The rest—the darker lies, the threats and cover-ups and deaths, came later.

A falsehood which destroyed the truth... A conspiracy of suffering... It was hard not to imagine the old man hadn't been working over some of these phrases for many years—perhaps he was drawing on the Shakespearean performances he'd once delivered in touring theater—and they were spoken in a crackling whisper, only adding to their potency. Then came the moment when he unclasped his hand to point waveringly toward Herbert Kisberg, when the quiet storm of his rage had been palpable. And the way his eyes had pooled and flesh seemed to barely cling to his face as he described a place where terrible acts had been performed not in the name of science or knowledge, or even mere money, but out of a desire to control and deceive...

He'd been fading by then. Each sentence grew slower and weaker. Much of what he said—the repeated use of the word Thrasis, which many at that moment had assumed to be some spasm of the throat, and the mention of Doctor Penny Losovic's name alongside Herbert Kisberg's—only made proper sense afterwards. The thing which came out at the time was how the two lonely actors who'd been employed to become Lars and Betty Bechmeir had, as they cut supermarket ribbons and attended premiers of these new entertainments called feelies and unveiled plaques at the fake-filled museum which supposedly documented their past, grown increasingly afraid. They lived only because they acted out a lie, and that lie, and the terror which lay behind it, began to prey on Betty Bechmeir's mind. *I loved that woman more than anything...* He'd muttered with a falling sigh. *She killed herself because she could no longer bear the falsehood of what we were living. She knew that it would destroy her if she didn't destroy herself. And, look, see how it has destroyed me... As you see me here now... I am what I tell you I am. This, at least, is not a lie...*

At that point he'd collapsed to the stage. And the one crucial name which the man who'd once been called Otto Frings couldn't mention, but which Barbara Eshel, listening live to the broadcast in that printroom lock-up with Dale as they tried to compose their one-off edition of *LA Truth* had added, was that of a brave screenwriter, grieving husband, fearless investigator and all-round guy-in-a-white-hat called Daniel Lamotte.

Clark turned away from the colored swirl of Mr Calhoon's wraith and checked his wrist for a Longines watch he no longer possessed. But the gong was sounding again, the displays were flicking over and the wraiths were changing, and he knew that it was time to pay April Lamotte his last respects.

There had been spaces before in the main car lot, but now it was entirely full, and a couple of guys, one so small as to appear dwarfish and the other so tall that they could only have been put together as a joke, were directing further arrivals toward the overflow behind the Human Resources and Communication building. The service was due to take place in the Temple of Sighs, the largest and most expensive by the hour of Forest Lawns' mock-European chapels, but there were still going to be problems with getting everyone in. Erewhon's previously invisible neighbors had all decided to put in an appearance today. So, by the look of it, had half LA. In a rare show of cross-party unity, even the Republican and the Democratic candidates for the House of Representatives were there. But everyone, even the stars and starlets, were looking for the man of the hour, and his arrival didn't disappoint.

Daniel Lamotte arrived at the front of the colossal temple in a brand new, canary yellow Rolls Royce convertible. With him was a woman who looked somewhat like April Lamotte, although she was plumper, older and lacked her younger sister's dress sense. This was May Lamotte, who'd arrived from nowhere and right onto the front pages a few days back. She had the no-bullshit air of a successful radio pastor's wife, or the kind of secretary a rich man might employ to actually do secretarial work. She certainly looked to have knocked Daniel Lamotte back into shape. They were both suitably dressed in black, and looked suitably grave, and suitably famous, as they climbed from the Rolls to an explosion of cameras.

Standing well back as he watched Daniel Lamotte work the crowding mourners, Clark couldn't help noticing the guy's ticks and mannerisms—those long hands with bitten nails, that smile which didn't seem either sufficiently pained or believably happy, the dragging way he moved, that thing he did with his neck. At least the guy's beard was well-trimmed now, he didn't look particularly pale, and he'd put on some weight. He'd got himself a new pair of glasses, too, and in a different style. They were steel framed and rounded, more scholarly. After all, he was a serious writer and these were serious times. Truth was that, with or without the glasses, there was little you could say that he and Clark had in common apart from the ears and a shared tallness and less than perfect teeth. But Clark couldn't help feeling the way he'd used to in a theater when he saw someone else performing a role he'd done himself. Not that he generally thought the other guy was making a regular hash of it, but he couldn't help feeling he'd done a far better job himself.

"Dan, Dan..." Timmy Townsend's presence and voice were unmistakable as he barged through the crowd toward the man of the hour like an on-form quarterback. Famous writer and successful producer shook hands in a fresh flurry of photographs, and you could see how Timmy found it harder than ever to keep his face from cracking into a broad grin. The fact that Senserama were still prepared to go ahead with a radically revised version of *Wake Up and Dream* was seen, in the words of *Variety*, as *a rare and heartening act of corporate contrition*, and Timmy seemed unfazed to find himself clasping the hand of an entirely different

Daniel Lamotte from the one he'd first met a week before—so much so that Clark wondered for a moment if it was possible that he hadn't noticed. But the truth, like most things in this city, was simpler and grubbier: it simply suited Timmy and Dan, along with most of Los Angeles, for things to be exactly as they were.

Herbert Kisberg had already resigned from the Governorship and his position on the board of Senserama, just as he'd stepped away from the Liberty League's presidential candidacy and his many other offices, creating precious space for others to move in. As fresh witnesses of what was now known as The Thrasis Conspiracy emerged, the IRS, the Federal Grand Jury, California Secretary of State, the Attorney General's Register of Charitable Trusts and even the Patents Office were all waiting to hear from him. Others were also in line, including some of the biggest players in LA, and there had already been fresh suicides. Maybe Kisberg might find the courage to do the same, but on balance Clark could think of few better punishments than the slow death by orders of appropriation, attachment and continuance which the State and Federal legal systems were preparing to inflict on him.

The police were still unraveling the full extent of Doctor Penny Losovic's activities. The Bechmeir Trust, it now appeared, owned many out-of-the-way and semi-derelict premises across Los Angeles County. Bodies had been found in some. Evidence of torture in others. Weird combinations of technology in most. Photographs of Doctor Losovic smiling at the back of school groups at the museum, or shyly handing over checks to grateful good causes, kept cropping up in the papers. Parents were already using her instead of Lizzie Borden to scare their children into eating broccoli, and regular guys from the Los Angeles Department of Water and Power were reporting that many people were refusing to let them into their homes. Her mother had apparently died giving birth and her father, an impoverished art dealer, had struggled to give her the best upbringing he could. By all outward signs, he'd succeeded, and everyone who'd survived their encounter with Penny Losovic now testified how she'd been a skilled physician and dedicated charitable administrator, and what exactly did that tell you about the American Dream?

Now the mourners were filing in. Clark kept by the back, and in shadow. The place was a murmuring sea of hats and heads. Now that he was here, and like most other funerals he'd ever been to, and every single wedding, he found himself wondering why he'd bothered. The words, the hymns, all the expensively imported religious furniture, meant nothing to him. And here they were, celebrating the life, the compassion and neighborliness and *sheer healing generosity* (the pastor, who had a regular radio slot, made much of her having once been a nurse) of a woman who had cold-bloodedly tried to kill him. But all she'd been doing, when push came to shove, was to try to protect her and her husband's lives, and Clark realized, for all his long-ingrained cynicism, that this was something he could almost forgive her for. Compared with some of the other people he'd encountered, April Lamotte had been pretty straight with him. He remembered the smell of her hair, and the things she'd said as they sat in the Delahaye at that Mulholland overlook. *This city isn't good for any of us. People, when they first came here from back east to make movies, they said it was because of the quality of the light. But what they didn't talk about was the quality of the darkness. I mean whatever's lurking underneath . . .* All of it was true. Like so many others, she'd tried to flee Los Angeles, and had failed. And he was still alive, still here. So maybe there was something for him to mourn when you pushed aside all the bullshit.

Another hymn, then her coffin was processed back down the aisle on its flower-bedecked chromium trolley, out into the sunlight toward the waiting hole which some machine had trenched beside an encampment of awnings. A few final words, then, amid the small shivers of relief and reconnection which characterize the end of all funerals, the crowd began to disperse. The conversations, what he caught of them, mostly seemed to be about the best place to lunch. The actual internment, he noticed, happened with a dull electric buzzing now that everyone's back was turned. He walked back over and watched the flower-strewn coffin descend into its velvet-lined pit; the last red carpet of all. Then he bent down and dug with his fingers in search of some earth. But the turf here was too dense and well-watered. He felt instead in his pockets, and found a few grains of sand. He scooped them out and let them scatter down across April Lamotte's remains.

He'd finally gone to find Thrasis a few days earlier, and it had struck him that there was a new bustle as he headed out through the morning streets of LA. Seemed like there were more people on the sidewalks, and the queues outside the feelie houses were already lengthening, but the biggest crowds were around the street corner sellers who normally hawked star maps. He got a glimpse of one customer, a large lady in a pink two piece suit with matching handbag, dog and umbrella, detach herself from the melee and triumphantly uphold her precious scrap of poorly printed paper. It was *LA Truth's* latest edition.

Up past Cawston Ostrich Farm and the Hotel Raymond and the growing sprawl of Pasadena, then out through pines and on into the mountains. Here was the overlook where April Lamotte had died, where many sightseers had now placed bouquets, and here was the general store where the mangy one-eyed dog was barking at the limos, and this was the turn which led to the pine cabin. What was it called? His memory was getting as creaky as the rest of him. But it didn't matter—you could look it all up in the scandal rags, and a striped police evidence saw horse blocked the way.

He'd driven on as the Ford's engine strained, the air thinned and the landscape flattened until all that was left was space, and dust, and emptiness. Soon, even the road had faded with the mountains into the shimmering heat. Soon, he was wondering why he'd come. Then there it was: a sign scoured by the wind, the paint scrawled so faint you'd scarcely know it was there. He stopped the Ford by a low rise of mining slag and got out. Heat struck his face and burned up through his shoes.

A nothing place. Hard to tell which of these fallen ruins and jutting foundations came from the mining village Thrasis had once been, and what had been put up, and destroyed, more recently. Rusted chains creaked their pulleys. A bucket swayed over a dark hole which he had no desire to explore. Had there once been some presence here? Had the spilled blood of Indian sacrifices and the bodies of trapped miners and the terrors brought by Penny Losovic and her colleagues somehow empowered this landscape? Whatever it had been, it was gone.

He picked up a handful of sand, let it hiss through his fingers. Then he walked back to his car, climbed in, and turned the starter. Nothing happened. He tried again, then got out and lifted the hood. The radiator shimmered, dry and hot. He glanced around. He'd come here alone. There was no way he could reach anywhere before nightfall.

He sat down. His lips were already cracked, his mouth felt swollen and his clothes were stuck to him with wasted moisture. Then he saw something. A mirage, maybe. Or a dust devil. But it was too large, too *real*, and it was coming his way. He stood up, and felt his legs tremble, and wondered where you were supposed to run when you were already nowhere. But the shape remained, flashing and floating. And from it, unmistakably, now came the sound of an engine.

Clark stood and waited as the sightseeing bus rumbled toward him from across the desert. Then, he began to laugh.

Barbara Eshel and Dale fitted in so well amid all the handsome people loitering around their expensive cars at Forest Lawns that it took him a puzzled moment as they walked toward him before he realized who they were. Dale had invested in a decent new suit, had gone to the barbers, and had shaved off his ill-advised beard, whilst Barbara was a testament to the enduring fact that nothing became a good-looking woman better than the plain black outfits of mourning, just as long as they were nicely cut. Clark also detected a new intimacy between them from the way they walked, hands almost touching. The both looked happier, as well. He wished he could see their auras, for they truly would have glowed. Or, he thought, as Dale shook his hand and Barbara leaned forward to kiss him, or his private dick instincts were returning and he was simply detecting the signs of recent sex.

"You're looking great, Barbara."

"You're not so bad, yourself, Clark."

"I'm alive, anyway. Or someone who looks like me is."

She nodded, bit her lip. "Look, Clark, we'd already agreed, or I thought we had, that there was no way I could go into how April Lamotte had tried to fake her husband's death. It would have been too much..." She waved a hand, in search of a word.

"Truth?"

"If you want to put it that way. I saw how it would work when Dale and I were preparing the typeset and listening to the Broadcast from the Biltmore, and what they were saying about the fire at the old MGM. To have Daniel Lamotte right there in the middle of the picture, struggling to find out the truth about Thrasis and then why his wife had been killed... There couldn't be two of you, Clark. It was the only way."

Although, he wanted to say, *you still managed to leave in the intrepid reporter who just happened to live in the apartment next door.* "Well, it's got you some much-needed publicity for *LA Truth*. You both must be feeling pretty proud. The biggest story in years, and you're the ones who broke it. Only problem you have is, what you're going to do next...? But I'm sure you'll find something," he added, when Barbara began to look uncomfortable. "I mean, it's not as if–"

"Matter of fact, Clark," she interrupted. "We're negotiating with several buyers for the paper's sale. And no, I *don't* mean Hearst Newspapers. Contrary to all outward appearances, there are still some ethical corporations out there who'll agree to keep to *LA Truth's* core values and bring it to a much broader readership."

"Don't tell me—they've offered you and Dale here a consultancy on the board." He found it encouraging that she flushed at this. "When I'd always thought the whole point was–"

"The whole *point*, Clark—and *always*, by the way, hardly comes into it—we've only known each other a few days, remember...? The whole point was and is that I came here to LA to write a defining work of fiction."

"You mean a..." He struggled to correct his incredulous tone. "...novel?"

"A novel, yes. That's what I've always wanted, and now that Dale and I are planning to relinquish day to day control of *LA Truth*, I finally have the time and the money I need to write it."

Maybe Barbara Eshel and Daniel Lamotte made a better pair than he'd realized. There the guy was talking in loud and quavery voice to gurning members of the press about how much he missed his wife, and what a great support his sister in law May had become, and how he now saw Daniel Lamotte doing this and Daniel Lamotte doing that in the future. After all, he and Barbara were both writers, which was just another way of saying self-absorbed and arrogant.

"What I don't get," Clark said, turning back to her, "is how the hell you're going to beat what really happened in a work of fiction."

She nodded, and squinted out at the city, which shimmered like a mirage in the early afternoon heat. "I used to think before all this started that a good writer had to be realistic. But now I understand that reality's an illusion. If you can touch what people really think—or, better still, if you can reach into what they dream—then the truth no longer matters." She smiled and shrugged. "If there even *is* such a thing as truth, that is. I mean, look at us here. Who's to say this is the way things had to be? We could all so easily be dead, or living some other life . . . Look at you, Clark. You could have been the King of Hollywood—you so nearly were, and you deserve it far more than all these creeps . . . "

She'd meant it as compliment, but the words gave Clark a strange chill as he watched Dale and Barbara link arms and walk away. It was that feelie sensation again. Someone had just walked once more over his grave.

The cars were pulling away now. Doors were slamming. People were air-kissing, or shouting goodbyes. Amid the thinning groups, he saw one woman standing alone. She was blonde and exceptionally pretty, but no one went over to her, although many glanced her way. In real life, just as up on the screen of the feelies, Peg Entwistle managed to radiate a cool sense of independence and reserve.

She removed her sunglasses and took his hand. "I wasn't sure," she murmured, "whether you wanted me to say hello."

"Course I do." He smiled at that perfect face, those shining bluegray eyes. "But does the world know you knew April Lamotte?"

She shrugged. "Everyone knows everyone else in the city. Or hadn't you heard. Although our paths did legitimately cross when I was I working on *The Virgin Queen*."

"And that's it?"

"I wish it was. I'll always know it isn't."

"But you can still walk away from Thrasis."

This time, the shrug became a shudder. "I don't think I can ever do that. But Otto—well, he was never going to name me. And as for your pretty little friend—I know she's a journalist, but perhaps there are still some decent ones. And then there's him." They both looked over toward what was left of the crowd, which was still milling around Daniel Lamotte. "Although I did hear someone saying that it's amazing how quickly a man can grow back his beard. But I'm sick of secrets. And this whole place." Peg looked around. Her mouth tightened. "It's lost its way. That's why I'm leaving."

"Leaving LA? Isn't that what everyone says?"

"Not just LA—I'm leaving America. And don't look at me like that, Clark. I've already got the tickets, and the press release will be out from Mina in a couple of days. It came to me after you'd left me up by that sign up on Mount Lee. Even before . . . all that's since happened. It was as if I'd suddenly been released from something, or had woken up out of a bad dream. I just knew I had to leave. All I have to do now is hope the liner doesn't get torpedoed, and in three weeks time I'll be in England. And it isn't because I know my career in the feelies can only go one way from here, or that I've got a sudden inkling to play Shakespeare at the Adlephi before the Germans destroy it." She smiled. "Not *just* that, anyway. Apart from Mina, I don't think many people here will miss me. Not the real me, anyway. And they're welcome to keep or forget about what I've left up on the screen."

"You know what will happen, if you turn up in England?"

"That's the whole point. I *want* the English to use me as a propaganda tool. God knows, I've been used over the years to do far more terrible and worthless things. I *want* to be seen taking sides. The thing about most Americans isn't that they really support the Liberty League. It's just that the Liberty League is selling the illusion that no one has to decide and stand up for anything—just let them get on with it and everything will be alright. It's the same lie Hitler sold to the Germans, and look where it's got them. It's the same lie that was sold to me. What's happened these last few days is just a skirmish won, Clark. The war goes on—in every sense. But at least I now know what side I'm really on."

She was right. The Liberty League might have taken a setback with Herbert Kisberg's disgrace, but they were already recovering. Kisberg was now being portrayed as someone who'd deceived them just as successfully as he'd deceived everyone else, and there was still plenty of time to put forward another presidential candidate of the more down-to-earth kind that this changed climate suddenly seemed to demand. And as for those guys back east whom Penny Losovic had mentioned—the men in those big brownstone Wall Street buildings with their plans and schemes which went far beyond morality or simple politics—they remained as powerful as ever, and as nameless.

"Well . . . Good luck, Peg. Go break a leg."

"I probably will."

She leaned forward to give him a kiss which was as cool as ever, and he watched as she put on her sunglasses and walked across the car lot. Others were watching as well. Peg Entwistle had always had that aura about her—that thing which even the iconoscopes had yet failed to capture. She was like some high priestess. *A true star.*

Most of the cars had gone. A few more minutes and the guests for the next funeral would be arriving. Clark lit a roll-up and strode across the hot tarmac towards his dusty Ford.

"Mr Gable?"

He turned. Of all people, it was May Lamotte. She went a little heavier on the make-up than her sister had, and smears and sweat-droplets were starting to show through the powder. She stopped a few paces off and twitched her nose as if he gave off a nasty smell.

"I'm sure surprised you came." Her voice had a Midwest twang which her sister had shed.

"I think I surprised myself."

"And you must have been one of the last people to see my sister alive." It wasn't a question.

"Maybe that was why I came today. Felt like I owed somebody something. I'm still not sure who or how, though . . . "

Her nose twitched again. Her eyes narrowed. "If you're thinking about that there contract you purported to sign on my brother in law's behalf, Mr Gable, I really wouldn't bother. We've taken legal advice, and there are absolutely no issues just as long as both sides are prepared to accept the variations we've agreed."

"You mean, more money?"

"That's none of your concern. You were acting under April's authority and were effectively a sub-agent. And as for anything else . . . Well, I really wouldn't know *where* to start with all the many crimes, beginning with false declaration, that you've committed. So if you think–"

"No, no." Clark held up a hand. "Believe me, I've got absolutely no desire to get involved in your or Daniel Lamotte's affairs. As far as I'm concerned . . . " He drew on his cigarette, then tossed it aside. He couldn't even be bothered to say good riddance.

"Well, if that really *is* the situation . . . " May Lamotte made a stab at a winning smile. It didn't suit her. "And speaking of owed . . . I believe that my sister hired you for a fee, and that, apart from an advance, that fee was never paid." She'd already reached into her purse, and was holding out a scrap of paper. "I want you to take this here in full and final settlement. I believe it covers the agreed figure, plus a generous further amount to cover what I believe people of your profession call incidentals."

"Are you buying my silence?"

"As we've already made plain, Mr Gable, we have that already. And in consideration of that, we're also prepared to agree not to sue you for wrecking Daniel's beloved automobile. So I don't believe I'm buying *anything* from you right now. Unless, that is . . . " The smile was entirely gone now, and had been replaced by a far more convincing glower. " . . . You're an even bigger fool that I'm thinking you are."

She was still holding out the check. In the feelies he'd have simply walked away. But this was real life—or the closest he could get to it. And he needed the money, and—what the hell—he really did feel he owed himself a new car.

He snatched the check from May Lamotte's fingers, and walked away with as much dignity as he could muster.

The two guys in suits he'd seen earlier were still seeing off the last of the cars. As the smaller of the pair came heading up to him, Clark realized that his dwarfish stature was simply because he was a kid.

"*Roger*? What the hell are you doing here?"

"I could say the same to you, Mister no-name."

Roger looked him up and down with something close to distaste. Clark was back to wearing his best first-client-visit suit, but it wasn't anything like as flash as the outfit the kid was wearing. Roger offered Clark a hand instead of his usual act of spitting. His face looked clean and new and almost innocent now that it was no longer disguised by dirt. The shine of his Brylcreem-lacquered hair matched his suit.

"My name's actually Clark Gable. I'm a private eye."

"So?" The kid didn't have to make any effort to look unimpressed.

"So nothing, I guess. Just thought you might be interested. You can't start asking people here for money to look after their cars, by the way. You'll get yourself arrested."

"Couldn't be more wrong Mr Gooble. Places like this, *everyone* pays to get their car looked after. Only difference is, the cops don't call it extortion. But that's not why I'm here, although my mate Pablo over there thinks it is. See this..." He reached into the side of his suit coat. For one alarming moment, Clark was sure he was going to pull out a gun. But instead he produced a camera little larger than a cigarette case. "Beauty, ain't she? A Minolta, all the way from our cousins in the Reich."

"That thing really works?"

"Jesus, Gooble, you should go more often to the feelies! The Nazi spies use them all the time. Tucks into a garter belt if need be, and it that happens, I ain't complaining." He gave it a spinning toss. "Got it with my first advance as *LA Truth's* roving reporter. It's already paid for itself ten times over. Sold a shot just yesterday of Toni Bartoli coming out of

Company and Co with someone who didn't look much like a proper broad, let alone his so-called wife."

"*LA Truth* doesn't buy that sort of stuff."

"If they don't, there's always someone else that will. It's the easiest job in the world, and to think that a few weeks ago I was hanging round street corners and not getting paid a cent—or at least only the pittance the likes of you were giving me. Up in Beverly Hills, you can take a few snaps of them cl-leb-ri-ties out shopping . . . *Zap, zap* . . . " He mimed the action. "Best of all as far as the editors are concerned is when they look like they've just been dragged out of the wrong side of the haystack. Touch of belly-wobble, double chin or varicose vein showing—that works just dandy."

"There's a market for *that*?"

"You'd be amazed."

"Not sure I would. But if you're a budding journalist, Roger, you should be studying—learning how to write copy."

"Less of the budding, buddy." He gave his camera a final six-shooter flip, then tucked it back into his suit coat pocket. "The written word's no longer ze main method of communication for ze human species . . . " He was putting on his German college professor accent now. "Everything is about—how you say?—ze *image* . . . Still, maybe I might put in a few hours at the library. Gotta know how to read them contracts so's I don't get skinned. It's a bad old world out there, so I hear."

"Yeah. So I hear, as well. But something tells me you're going to do just fine in it." Clark smiled. He'd have ruffled the kid's hair, but he didn't want to get his hands mussed with grease.

SIXTY

As he drove back down through the city, he saw, along with news hoardings about Australia refusing entry to fleeing Dutch Jews and all the usual No Blacks signs and racist scrawlings, posters on the walls for the Liberty League guy who'd still be standing to replace Herbert Kisberg as Governor, and others for a new biopic of the Richard Wagner. Peg was right. They'd barely won a battle against whatever they'd been fighting—the guys in Europe with their uniforms and parades, or the ones over here who hid behind big business and Ivy League educations. Roosevelt had just lost another vote to support Churchill in Congress, and the Japanese were pushing out across the Pacific. Even if you could work out who the good guys actually were, they never actually won. That only happened in the feelies.

The usual crowds were outside Saint Vincent's Hospital. Their vigil had been going on night and day since the guy they still thought of as Lars Bechmeir had been rushed there after his onstage collapse at the Biltmore. If anything, their adulation for their hero had increased after his tale of deception and suffering. And as for his name—after all, why would the Bechmeir field be called after him if he hadn't played a crucial role in its invention? Whatever Daniel Lamotte was planning on writing in his latest version of *Wake Up and Dream*, it would have to be at least as clever a mixture of truth and myth as any of the previous versions if the world was to believe it.

Clark had to park a way off West 3rd, and then push his way through praying and weeping sightseers, souvenir hawkers, and various representatives of the media, to reach the hospital entrance.

The atmosphere inside was closer to normal. Life went on, after all. Death, as well. Nuns clustered in their white cassocks. He passed a civilian nurse pushing a mewling newborn baby in a wheeled crib whilst an aged couple sat weeping on a side bench. There were also a fair number of police about. He'd liked to have looked in on old Otto but the *LA Times* had an exclusive deal and security around what both the state and federal authorities regarded as a material witness was intense. It sounded like the poor guy was dying in any case.

He asked for other directions instead, and got a strange look from the orderly who sent him down a seemingly little-used corridor, then up a back flight of stairs. A nun bustled up to block his progress at the far end of an ill-lit corridor. She looked solemn even before her surprise registered at his request.

"Are you sure you want to see her?"

"Well, I guess..."

"No one else has been. Well, I mean no one from the real world. Just the police, although they seem more bothered with our famous friend down in east wing. Did you know her? You'd think she'd have some friends somewhere, wouldn't you—even if..."

"No, I'm not a friend. I guess you could say our paths just happened to cross."

"You're not from the press or anything, are you?"

"I'm not from anybody but me. I'm just this guy. My name's Clark Gable. Like I say, we barely met..."

She looked him in the eyes for a long moment before she nodded. "I don't think I've ever seen anyone who I'd thought was a hopeless case," she said as they walked along the corridor. "There's always *something* we can do. But the priests talk of possession. The technicians talk of plasmic disturbance. The doctors talk of self-sustaining wound trauma. And the psychiatrists talk of madness."

"What do you believe?"

She glanced back at him. The face of a pretty young woman framed beneath that black and white wimple was deeply troubled. "I'm a woman of faith, Mr Gable, and I believe in God. But I also believe in the Devil."

This was some part of the hospital which had been marked for improvement or demolition, and there was little else in all the rooms he glimpsed but dust and emptiness. Little light, as well. He glanced up at the lights along the corridor ceiling. Despite the blotchy gloom, they all blazed.

"She's here." The nun's hand trembled as she gestured. "I think I should come in with you—unless you want me to send for someone else?"

"No. I guess we'll be okay."

Clark had no idea what he'd find as he stepped through the doorway, but at first glance he was standing in a fairly ordinary, if rather ill-lit and old, hospital ward. The ceiling was high, and the windows were small and seemed to look out on nothing but another wall, and there was an intense smell of iodine. One metal-frame bed was set in the center of a linoleum space which could have housed a dozen, and on that bed, but somehow not quite *in* it, was the room's—this whole wing's—sole patient.

As he walked over, the stupid thought crossed his mind that he should have brought some grapes, maybe a couple of trashy magazines—all the crap he'd heard you normally gave to people you visited in hospital—but then, as he saw more clearly, he understood something of the nurse's quiet horror, and the pointlessness of his visit.

The reason Doctor Penny Losovic didn't quite seem to be in the bed was that, through the trussing of a steel spider's web of wire and frame, she was hanging over it. What he saw made him think at first of trapped flies, and then of a scarecrow he'd once seen in a field as a kid back in Ohio. The farmers burned the fields come fall, and for some reason a scarecrow had been left. The thing had come back to him in his dreams, standing amid the charcoal with its blackened arms smoking, yet still outstretched as if reaching to grasp another's invisible hand. It came back to him again now. From where he was standing, there wasn't one inch of Doctor Penny Losovic's body which the fire hadn't seared.

"The suspension system is to try to minimize contact and encourage healing," the nun murmured. "We try to leave the flesh to the air, and use a tincture of iodine. Normally, the doctors would try to put skin grafts on the very worst areas, only there's no undamaged skin left to graft with. I've never seen such extensive burns—not on anyone living. She shouldn't have got as far as this hospital... Let alone still be..."

Clark took a further step forward, and the dimensions of the room seemed to twist. As if he'd turned an invisible corner, he was suddenly conscious of a ticking and creaking as what remained of Penny Losovic stirred. The pulleys moved. The metal rods strained. Glimpses of caked and weeping flesh glittered and parted.

"She must be in the most intense pain." The nurse's voice now came from another world. "Of course, we give her doses of morphine. The strongest possible, and then more. Enough to... But she won't die..."

With the creaking sound came the most extraordinary stench. A mixture of things rotted and roasted borne on a sense of unendurable yet continuing pain, it blocked his mouth and coated his tongue. If Hell had an aroma, this was it.

"Can you hear me?" He was surprised he'd spoken—his voice seemed to come from someone else—but the thing in its cocoon of wires seemed to twist. A head, or something which had once been a head, turned toward him with a sound of unpeeling flesh. The mouth was a ruined gape, and one of the eyes was a weeping crater, but the other stared across at him. With it came the murmur of a thousand voices.

What are you?

He knew he didn't need to speak for the thing to understand. But he also knew, as he met that blood-threaded gaze, that there was no answer to his question—or not one that would allow him to leave this room sane.

He stepped back through the polluting layers of stench and pain, and found that he was standing once again in the odd dullness of a near-deserted ward.

Leaving the hospital, he drove out through Los Angeles. Soon, he was passing stretches of farmland between gray-blue glimpses of the Pacific, and the usual sense of relief came washing over him as he caught a last glimpse in the rearview of the grubby letters of that sign. The latest plan he'd heard about didn't involve getting rid of the thing, or even cleaning it up and removing the Land part so that it simply said Hollywood. Some entrepreneur with more money than sense was talking of replacing the long-dead lamps with a newer kind of illumination. Fresh fencing and a large construction project would see those famous letters spelling themselves out across the city in the shimmering, ever-changing veils of a Bechmeir field. Then, as he passed the Culver City Kennel Club and the King's Tropical Inn, he realized that something else had happened. For everything else he'd experienced by going into that hospital, the feel and smell of the actual place itself hadn't bothered him.

The terrors and flashbacks he'd been having were also fading. Something which had been binding him to the past had snapped on the night of Penny Losovic's weird experiment in Soundstage 1A, although he still didn't know exactly what. But if there was anything that still bothered Clark, it was why the Thrasis entity had chosen to follow him, and then why his presence had triggered such a huge response from the thing within the cage. For he was nobody—right—and always had been? Or nearly always. That was how things were, and—and this to him was perhaps the best and most important part—the thought no longer hurt as much as it once had. So maybe that was how life in this new decade went. You waved goodbye to one set of ghosts, and said hello to the next.

The air improved as he headed away from the smog and bustle. He caught cow dung and the sweet aroma of orange groves. Then he hit the seafront Speedway and was met by Venice Beach's sharper odors. Vanilla and candy and frying onions competed with ocean salt and all the sun-warmed bodies which crowded the main boardwalk. The Ferris wheel was turning and the gulls were screeching and boys were cruising in their cars and the girls were preening in their summer dresses. Then another, sourer smell hit him. He was just thinking that the reek of hydrogen sulphide from the oilfields was especially strong when he realized what had happened. He'd spent so much time away lately that his sense of smell was returning. Ice cream and dog mess. Sea wrack and sun cream. Oil burnoff and bar-room beer. To everyone who didn't live here, this was exactly how Venice always smelled on a warm afternoon.

He found a space for his Ford a few yards further up from the Doge's Apartments, and pushed through the swing doors out of the sun, and headed quickly for the stairs.

"Hey, hey..." It was already too late. Glory had spotted him, and was lumbering out of her cubbyhole with what was, for her, a fair impression of haste.

"Hi there, Glory." He had to smile to see her, for all the news of the latest visit from the repo men she was likely to be bearing. "You've done a great job holding the fort lately—have I told you that? You really have..."

"I just take the phone." She was frowning the way she always did as she held out her latest scrap of paper. "Like some bleedy fool when it *ring ring ring.*"

Her frown didn't change noticeably when he took the paper and read it. Just a phone number, although it did look vaguely familiar. "Thanks, Glory. Is there, er, any kind of message to go with this?"

She let out an impressive huff and looked imploringly up at the flies which circled the ceiling. "Same message I get always, and from this same poor lady. She keep say she no trust her husband—he do things she not like." Glory shrugged. "She just not know what them things be."

Clark nodded. Sure, he remembered. It sounded like pretty much every message she'd ever given him.

"Men...!" Glory was far too genteel to spit, but the way she said that word was close to it. "You ring her, or not?"

"Sure, sure, Glory. I'll ring her."

"Now?"

"Okay. Right now."

She stood and watched, arms folded across her impressive bosom and slippered foot tapping ominously, as he crossed the hallway.

He checked the number again, then lifted the communal phone's receiver and fed in what change he had in his pockets.

The operator put him straight through.

Ian R MacLeod has published five previous novels and four short story collections. Amongst many accolades, his work has won the Arthur C Clarke, John W Campbell, World Fantasy and Sidewise awards. He was born in the suburbs of Birmingham, England, and currently lives, works and dreams in the riverside town of Bewdley, Worcestershire. He maintains a website at www.ianrmacleod.com. He has no current plans to write any feelie biopics—at least, not until the right offer comes along . . .